Mirror of Malice

STOLEN CROWNS
BOOK ONE

TEE HARLOWE

Introduction

If you'd like access to a free fantasy romance novella, plus exclusive content like bonus scenes, behind-the-scenes looks, and early sneak peeks at character art and cover reveals, then click here to subscribe to my newsletter.

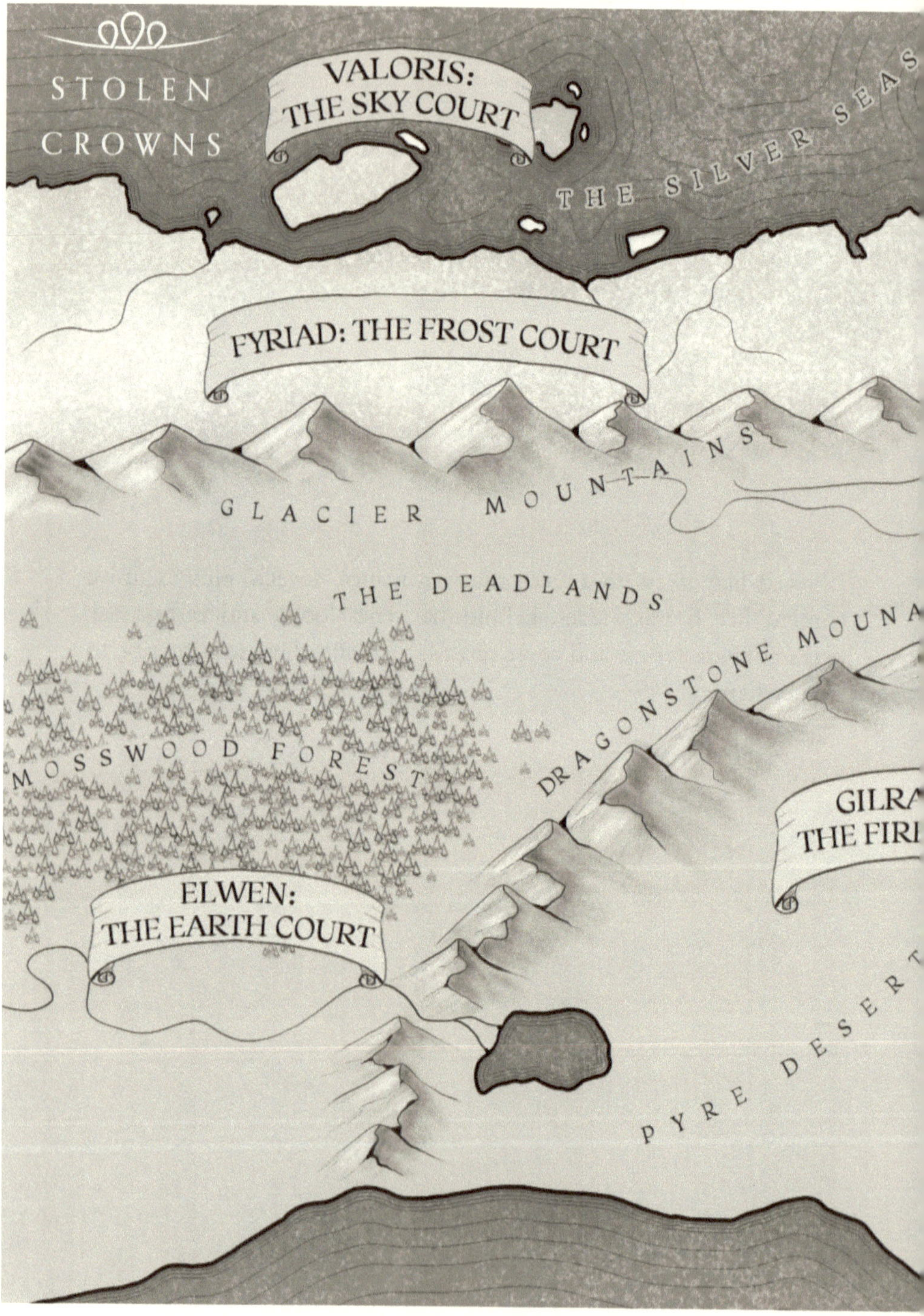

STOLEN CROWNS
VALORIS: THE SKY COURT
THE SILVER SEAS
FYRIAD: THE FROST COURT
GLACIER MOUNTAINS
THE DEADLANDS
DRAGONSTONE MOUNA
MOSSWOOD FOREST
ELWEN: THE EARTH COURT
GILRA
THE FIRI
PYRE DESERT

Arathia
THE DARK SEAS
SORRENGARD:
THE SHADOW COURT
APOLIS:
THE WATER COURT

Part One

"Mirror, mirror, on the wall. Who in this land is the fairest of all?"

Chapter One

There were three things in life I hated: my stepmother, apples, and the prison cells of my castle, where I currently resided. Oh, and my two best friends, who wouldn't let me sleep.

"Liliath, wakey, wakey," Driscoll said from the prison cell next to mine.

Okay, so, four things I hated.

Stone walls separated us, but I could hear his voice floating through the air. I peeked open an eye from where I lay on the cold, hard floor, then groaned and threw my arm over my head to block out the sound.

"Pretty please," Jillian said from the cell on the other side of mine.

I ignored them both, not moving from my position in the middle of the floor. A cold breeze whistled through the bars of my cell, which faced the outside of the castle, looking down upon the courtyard. I shivered and curled my body into itself. Why these miscreants were awake at this time of night, I had no idea. All I knew was that I wanted them to shut up and let me sleep.

"Well, if she won't wake up, this is going to be a huge waste of our time," Driscoll said. "And I hate wasting my time."

"Yes, because you have so little of it these days, trapped in a prison cell of Liliath's castle."

My former castle. This castle hadn't belonged to me in two years. Not since my stepmother stole it away.

"Liliath!" Driscoll's voice echoed through the silent night, and I heard a loud crack. "Oh. Ow. That hurt. Okay, note to self: do not punch stone walls."

"Stop badgering her, Dris," Jillian said in an annoyed tone. "She's clearly ignoring us, probably because of your driveling."

I smirked at that.

"Driveling?" Driscoll's voice rose three octaves.

"Oh, here we go," Jillian muttered.

"Driveling?" Driscoll said again. "Excuse you. I do not drivel."

"Why did you have to do that?" I asked Jillian, unable to help myself. "You know he thinks all the words that come from his mouth are of the utmost importance."

"Because they are," Driscoll said, which made me smile. "And the princess finally awakens!" Driscoll announced.

I could imagine the wicked smile lighting up his face, the way his dark brown skin glowed and his tight black curls bounced as he practically vibrated. Driscoll was always moving, could never stop. I missed that mischievous face more than I would ever admit to him—mainly because it would go to his head, and he did not need any reason to get a bigger head.

A scratching noise came from the wall between my cell and Jillian's. A rat, maybe? I slowly sat up, rubbing at my eyes. "You two better have a very good reason for waking me up at this hour." I gestured out the cell bars to the dark night sky, even though neither of them could see me. "It's the middle of the night."

"Trust me," Driscoll said, "I'm aware."

"Then why are we awake?" I gritted out.

"She's grumpy," Driscoll sang out. "I told you she'd be grumpy."

"She won't be grumpy once she sees what we're doing," Jillian said.

I perked up at that, suspicions rising. "What does that mean?" I looked at the wall separating me and Driscoll. "What does she mean? Please tell me you two aren't doing something stupid."

"We might be doing something stupid," Driscoll responded.

The scratching noise continued, followed by hammering.

"Are you almost done?" Driscoll called.

"I'm working on it. I didn't see you volunteering to do this."

"That's because I'm the brains in this operation."

"I guess that makes me the beauty," Jillian said.

Oh, good green earth. She really wanted to get on his nerves today.

"What?" Driscoll screeched. "You did not just go there."

"It's too easy," Jillian said, a smile in her voice.

And even though I was grumpy they had woken me up and still hadn't told me why, I couldn't help my rising amusement at their banter.

Driscoll huffed. "It's not enough that I'm trapped in a prison cell, forced to look over this depressing view of the castle grounds. Castle grounds that I used to enjoy immensely. Right down there, where the fountains used to be, was where I'd make out with the head of the king's personal guard. He got a little too invested, and I had to break it off with him, and then I caught the eye of the stable master—"

"Driscoll!" A crack formed in the stone wall where the hammering was coming from. "Shut up!" Jillian said.

"Um, Jil?" I asked. "Do you see that?"

"See what?" Jillian asked airily.

Maybe I was seeing things, hearing things. The crack spread, and I jumped back.

Outside, a crow cawed, landing on the branch of a spindly tree that sat below the bars of my cell, staring at me with its black eyes. The prisons were located on the top floor of the castle, all of them facing the castle grounds. The crow sat on what once was a magnificent tree, full of thick green leaves that turned golden brown and orange in the fall, that bloomed bright pink in the spring. Now it was black. Black as death. Everything surrounding this castle was. Rotten to the core.

Ever since she usurped my father and stole the crown. I swallowed, my attention falling back onto that crack.

"You really know how to draw things out, don't you?" This time, Driscoll's voice was dry as the desert land of Gilraeth.

"Draw what out?" I asked. "Jil, are you sure you don't see anything?"

"Nope," she said.

"Are you going to share why we're all awake right now?"

"Also nope," Jillian said, far too cheerful.

The crow flew off, no doubt to answer some call from its master. Maybe to tell her we were all awake in the middle of the night, causing trouble. It didn't matter. She wouldn't kill us. Death would be too easy after what I'd done to her. So instead, I sat here in this cell, watching as she destroyed the earth court bit by bit.

The crack now formed a square, and I gasped as a stone fell to the floor with a crash.

"Did you do it?" Driscoll asked. "Honestly, I'm surprised, Jil. I didn't know if you had it in you. You always did have a weak upper body."

Jillian's pale face, dotted by freckles, appeared in the empty square. I stared in shock, my gaze moving down to the stone block on the floor, then back up to Jillian's face. A face I hadn't seen in two years.

"What? How—" I could barely get the words out.

"Happy name day," Jillian and Driscoll said at the same time.

Oh. So that's what this was about. I swallowed back my tears.

"Does she look happy?" Driscoll asked. "Is she smiling, or does she look like she wants to kill you?"

"She looks sad," Jillian said, reaching her hand out through the opening.

"I knew it." I could just imagine Driscoll throwing his hands up in the air. "I told you she hates her name day, ever since . . ." he trailed off.

Ever since my name day became synonymous with the worst day of my life.

I reached out and grabbed Jillian's hand, reveling in the feel of it, the feel of a human touch.

"How did you guys do this?"

"It was Driscoll's idea," Jillian said, smiling. "When the guards were doing that construction on a new cell. You were sleeping, and Driscoll suggested that to celebrate your twenty-seventh name day, I should swipe some tools off them and try to cut a hole in the wall so you could see me. I've been working every night for weeks while you've been sleeping."

Twenty-seven. I was twenty-seven years old, and look what I had to show for it.

My mouth dropped open. "That's amazing. It's so good to see your face. I've missed you so much."

"Oh, your hair." Jillian pointed.

"What? What's wrong with her hair?" Driscoll asked.

My hair had been my pride and joy. Long, silky, and black, reaching down to my waist. I'd often donned elaborate hairstyles that always drew the attention of the earth court. Now, I didn't know what it looked like, but I could only imagine. I patted the knots and tangles self-consciously. "I can fix it when we get out of here."

Jillian's green eyes settled on my face. "We're not getting out of here, Liliath. How can you still think that's going to happen?"

"Because . . ." I huffed. "Because I just know it."

Jillian bit her lip. "We've been stuck here for so long." Her voice was quiet. "Everything we love has been taken from us. The only reason Driscoll and I are still alive is to punish you. We're just pawns in her game, and sooner or later, we're going to have to admit defeat."

My chest tightened. It was true. The queen spared them, put them in cells on either side of me, knowing it would kill me that my two best friends had been imprisoned because of me, that they'd been sentenced to the same fate as me.

"Jillian, we are celebrating Liliath's name day," Driscoll said, an edge to his voice. "Maybe stop talking about how we're going to be stuck in here forever and ever."

Jillian ignored Driscoll. "I don't have your eternal optimism, Lil. Jasper isn't coming for you. And he's definitely not coming for us."

Her words stabbed at my heart. "No, don't say that. He's going to find a way to rescue me."

"It's been two years," Jillian said. "When are you going to realize that he doesn't care? Tell her, Driscoll."

I paused, slowly turning to face the opposite wall. "What is she saying? Have you two talked about this?"

The silence from Driscoll was deafening. Well, there was the answer to that question.

"We might have had a few conversations when you were sleeping," he said. "Which I thought were private." Annoyance filled his voice.

I turned back and Jillian forced a smile. "Driscoll's right. It's your name day. Let's drop it."

I crossed my arms. "No. Let's not."

"Well, this is nice," Driscoll said.

What they were saying couldn't be true. I pressed my back into the stone wall and sank onto the straw-covered ground. A mouse skittered across my cell, sniffing, turning its beady little eyes on me, something like pity shining in them. Even the rodents felt sorry for me.

Jasper and I had been betrothed since I was three years old. He wouldn't abandon me. He loved me. I loved him. Yes, it had taken him time to come rescue me, but that's because breaking into these cells, this castle, was a huge undertaking.

The depressing castle grounds spread out below, a maze of dark hedges rising up, stretching all the way to the blackened iron gates that surrounded the grounds. The trees, the grass, the vines, everything reeked of death. Plump gray clouds littered the dark sky, the moon blotted out. It never shone anymore. I shivered as another cold wind rattled the bars.

Vines stretched out over statues, fountains, and stairs, writhing like snakes. Once upon a time, this had been my favorite view of the kingdom. I'd stand on my balcony and look over the bubbling fountains, the statues of former kings and queens, the beautiful sculptures and blooming trees and bushes.

Now, it was a reminder of my failures. I'd failed my people in so many ways, but I would do better, be better, and fix everything. If I ever broke out of here.

We'd seen what happened to those who tried to sneak onto the castle grounds, watched person after person get their necks snapped by vines, get their bodies broken by tree branches, get eaten and crushed by tree roots, get suffocated by bushes. My stepmother had turned her earth magic, the very earth we were supposed to protect and nurture, into a weapon.

That was why it was taking Jasper so long to come rescue me.

He had to plan everything very carefully to ensure he could survive the queen's deadly obstacle course. And then there was the fact that he'd have to breach the castle, find his way to me. That was no easy feat. Surely Driscoll and Jillian could understand that.

"I'm sorry." I felt a hand on my shoulder, and nearly jumped a foot in the air. I looked up, Jillian's hand poking through the little square she'd cut. "I shouldn't have said all that."

I sniffled. "No, it's understandable. And I'm so, so sorry I got you both into this." I stood. "But you have to keep faith. *We* have to."

Driscoll stayed silent.

Jillian's green eyes were empty of any emotion, but she nodded. "I think we should get some rest now. We can talk more tomorrow. And . . . happy name day, Liliath."

She lay down, her back to me. At least I could see her. That was enough for now. But her spirit was broken, and I wasn't sure anything other than us breaking out of here would fix it.

Soon her soft snores filled the silence.

"Well, that didn't go well," Driscoll said. His voice softened. "I know you hate your name day, but we wanted to make it special. I told Jillian you'd appreciate a bottle of wine more than seeing her face, but she insisted on this plan."

I snorted.

"You have to stop blaming yourself for all of this," Driscoll said. "I know you think you're responsible, but you're not. Night night, Lil."

He didn't understand. I'd done so many things I regretted that led to this, but it wasn't just my actions that plagued me. It was also the actions of my father. Of my stepmother. Neither of them had been the rulers my people deserved, and I was determined to be better. To be perfect. Nothing less would be acceptable.

I turned my gaze to the night sky. "Where are you, Jasper?" I whispered, wishing I could see the stars.

He was our only hope.

"Wait a minute, what is that?" Driscoll asked. "Down there."

My gaze automatically snapped to the castle grounds.

I stood, walking to the bars and pressing myself against them. "What is what?" I searched the area far below, the maze, the trees where the murder of crows sat, the destroyed fountains, but I didn't see anything.

"That figure on the gate!" Driscoll said, exasperated, and I could imagine the way he was currently rolling his eyes.

The gate. I searched the tall iron bars and finally saw it: someone was climbing the gates. Even from this distance, I could tell the figure was massive, a mountain of a man. They had to be a man based on those thick legs and powerful arms, though I couldn't be sure since the figure kept their face covered and their head hooded. Then I saw the wink of a red gem sparkling on his finger, and I gasped.

"Blood and earth," I said, my gaze fixed on that glittering red ring. It had to be. It couldn't belong to anyone else.

"What?" Driscoll asked. "Spit it out. What's happening?"

"Jasper." I could barely get the words out. "Jasper has finally come."

Chapter Two

My chest stretched so tight I thought it might snap apart. Jasper was here. I shot a triumphant look over at Driscoll before remembering he couldn't see me.

"Well, shit," Driscoll said. "I might have to actually admit I was wrong."

I snorted. "As if that would ever happen."

Jasper scaled the gate, reaching the top and then swinging himself over. He'd certainly filled out over these last few years. Maybe I just wasn't remembering him right. He'd always been slight, thinner and wiry, but now I watched as his huge form descended down the other side of the iron gate, hopping to the cobblestone ground, blackened by moss and mold.

It had to be him. I'd recognize that ring anywhere. It was his pride and joy, the ring that was handed from father to son in his family, signifying the heir to their estate and financial holdings. Jasper looked from side to side, then studied the maze that lay in front of him.

"You have to wake up Jil," Driscoll said.

I didn't want to tear my eyes away for a minute, but he was right. She needed to see this. Needed a spark of hope. Then again, maybe I should wait until Jasper made it through the death trap down below.

No, no, that would mean I didn't believe in him, and I did. He would rescue me, us.

I ran to the square in the wall. "Jillian, wake up!" I whisper-shouted. "Jil!"

She didn't stir, snores still escaping her mouth. I groaned.

"Throw something at her," Driscoll said. "Oh no!"

I whirled. "What? What happened?"

"He's okay! A tree branch almost grabbed him, but he dodged it. When did Jasper get so fast? I've seen him run, and it was not a pretty sight."

I ignored Driscoll and looked around for something to throw at Jillian. My gaze caught on my shoes. They probably couldn't even be called shoes anymore with how tattered and torn they were, a hole in the toe of both, the soles worn down to thin layers. Well, as soon as I woke her, she could give it back.

I wiggled the shoe off my foot, then stuck my arm through the square and launched it at her head. It hit her with a thud, and she sat straight up.

"What? What's going on?"

"Jasper is here," I whispered. "He's here to rescue us."

Her eyes widened, and she ran to the bars of her cell, clutching them tight and watching the scene that unfolded below. Jasper navigated the hedge maze, dancing over jabbing branches, ducking under darting thorns, whirling around razor-sharp leaves.

Huh. He was rather sprightly on those feet, definitely not the lumbering, clumsy Jasper I remembered. Lumbering and clumsy in a cute way, of course.

A vine snaked out from the wall of the maze, and I let out a shriek, which garnered a "shhh" from both Jillian and Driscoll, but Jasper dove ahead, curling into himself as he rolled across the ground, the vine punching over his head and missing him.

"Oh, he just dodged an impaling," Driscoll said cheerfully. "Good for him."

"This isn't a joke." My hands clutched the bars of my cell so tightly my knuckles had turned white. "He could die."

But no, he wouldn't. He'd make it. I had a feeling I was going to get out of this cell tonight. And then Jasper and I could take back the earth court together, and I could be the queen my people deserved.

The hedges shook like feathers ruffling.

"Oh no, it's the shuffle," Jillian said.

"That's what got the last guy," Driscoll added.

Black leaves flew from hedges as the shaking intensified, and the walls of the maze began to shift, entrances closing, walls opening, the entire route changing completely. Jasper stopped as a wall closed in front of him and transformed into a giant mouth, twigs and branches forming into teeth. The mouth snapped at him.

"Oh, here it comes. I can't look." I imagined Driscoll putting his hands over his eyes as he spoke. "He's about to get eaten."

I refused to look away. "Come on, Jasper. Come on."

He whirled, reaching for the sword strapped across his back and jamming it straight into the hedge monster's mouth. A shriek erupted from the hedge, and it shrank back as he leapt over it and continued on his way.

"*I* might have to marry him now," Jillian said. "That was impressive. Even for Jasper."

"Especially for Jasper," Driscoll muttered.

"Hey! That is my betrothed you both are talking about. Your future king. Have a little respect."

"Do you think he fixed his issue?" Driscoll said, voice suddenly curious.

"What issue?" Jillian asked, far too interested.

I glared at the wall that separated me from Driscoll, wishing I could reach through it and wring his neck.

"Nothing," I snapped. "Just something *private* I shared with Driscoll."

"He couldn't get it up," Driscoll said with glee.

Jillian gasped.

"One time," I said. "It was one time."

Okay, three times, but I wasn't going to admit that right now.

I saw Jillian's finger pointing through the bars of her cell. "That man right there has no problem getting it up. He's definitely fixed the issue."

My gaze trailed to Jasper's muscular form as he jumped atop the hedge. It shuffled again, and he walked across it with his arms out like he was balancing on a tight rope.

My friends had made no secret about their feelings for Jasper over the years. But they didn't know him like I did. Yes, he came off as arrogant and self-important, but it was because he had to maintain a certain persona in public, which was the only time they'd seen him. In private, he was different. They'd learn.

"Mother-fucking earth," Jillian said. "He made it."

Jasper now crouched on the other side of the maze like a deadly predator. The murder of crows began cawing, flying with a frenzy in the sky.

"They're going to warn her!" I looked around, wondering what I could do to distract the birds. "Hey!" I waved my arms. "Hey, idiots!"

"What are you doing?" Driscoll hissed. "Don't call them over here. Those things can fit through the bars, gouge out your eyes, eat your carcass. And I am not going down for Jasper. I haven't survived this long just to be crow food."

A few of the crows took notice of me, no doubt rankled over my insult. The beasts might have been loyal to my stepmother, but they also had humongous egos.

"Lil," Jillian warned.

"Hey, shit-birds," I yelled. My gaze flicked to Jasper, who was now scaling the castle walls. "Remember the time I tricked you into running into my cell bars?"

"Please stop talking," Driscoll said.

A few of the crows stopped their pursuit of Jasper and turned their bodies toward me.

"He has way too far to climb," Jillian said. "There's no way he'll make it."

I stared down at him as he ascended, surprisingly deft, clutching onto the black web of weeds and plants that spread across the castle walls like a virus. When had Jasper trained for this? Learned this kind of stealth and speed? Three of the six crows flew toward me with frightening speed.

"I swear to blood and earth, Liliath, if I die because of you, I will make sure my spirit comes back to haunt you for life," Driscoll yelled as the crows swooped toward the bars, pecking at my fingers.

I jumped back, the realization hitting me with the force of a mallet. "That's why it took Jasper so long to come for me! He's been training. For this very thing."

"That's what you're thinking about right now?" Driscoll yelled again as a crow cawed loudly, flapping its wings while it jabbed its beak at the bars of his cell.

I crossed my arms, staring at the birds. "Oh, relax. They've fattened up over these last few months, eating all the carcasses of those who have perished in the maze. They can't fit through the bars anymore."

That seemed to make the crows angrier, and they flapped their wings with force, snapping their sharp beaks. Hopefully this, at least, helped Jasper in his quest. A loud bang reverberated through the air, shaking the ground underneath our feet. The crows turned and flew toward the commotion, and I ran to the bars, an explosion of feather, blood, and bone down below.

"He killed the crows using some kind of explosive," Jillian said. "Oh, that's going to make the queen angry. No one messes with her crows. Maybe she'll send the Huntsman next."

I shuddered at the thought. I hoped not. The Huntsman was a fearsome creature.

The three remaining crows surrounded him as he climbed, higher, higher, higher. I didn't know how he'd managed to climb so high in such a short time. My heart fluttered at everything he'd gone through for me.

The birds swooped down, circling him.

"They're about to go in for the kill," Driscoll said.

A lump formed in my throat. I wouldn't be able to distract the crows again. Not after he'd killed their comrades.

"Be careful, Jasper," I whispered.

From out of nowhere, arrows sailed through the sky, piercing the crows. They fell one by one.

"Where are those arrows coming from?" Driscoll asked, and now it sounded like he was pacing back and forth.

"He must've brought reinforcements that are hiding in the trees." Risky, because the trees were under the queen's control. Everything in this godforsaken place was. But the trees stayed still in the dark night, and though I couldn't see anyone perched atop their branches, I knew there were others out there. The thought buoyed me. Jasper was close now. So close.

"Jasper," I yelled. "I'm here."

But he seemed to already know. He'd really done his research. Maybe he'd had spies watching me for months, reporting back to him. I couldn't believe he'd done all this. But of course he had. I was his betrothed.

I thought about shoving this in Jillian's and Driscoll's faces, but then Jasper swung himself up in front of me, standing at the bars, his feet balancing on the thin stone ledge that jutted out. I wanted to reach through the bars and pull down the cloth covering his face, to yank down the hood covering his dark hair.

"Jasper, you came for me." I choked back a sob. "I've missed you so much."

It was too dark to see his eyes, to see anything but the shadows all around. Something groaned, a loud sound that seemed to bellow from the depths of the earth.

"Nope, don't like that," Driscoll said.

"Jasper, do you have a plan for getting the princess out of here?" Jillian asked.

His head turned in my friend's direction, but he said nothing.

The ground shook again, and behind Jasper vines rose, twisting and turning, threading together.

"That looks like a monster," Driscoll said.

The vines formed a head, then a gaping mouth filled with thorns, then shoulders, two arms, and a torso that stretched down to the ground.

"Okay, yes, definitely a monster. Now is the time to break us free." Driscoll's voice grew frantic. "That is the plan, right? Jasper?"

I waited for him to say something, for me to hear his beautiful rich voice that I'd spent night after night dreaming of. But instead, he said nothing.

"Oh, fuck it all. He doesn't have a plan," Driscoll said.

"Well, that's more like the Jasper we know," Jillian said.

"Will you two shut up?" I snapped. "Jasper, tell them you have a plan."

The vine monster roared behind him, and the force of it shot out a gusty wind that pushed me a few steps back. The monster stretched back its thick, twisted arm, poised like a snake, ready to strike.

"You are so getting haunted," Driscoll said, presumably to me. But maybe also to Jasper.

"It's going to strike. Duck!" Jillian screeched as the monster's vine arm shot forward.

Jasper jumped up and disappeared from my view just as the vine broke the bars of my prison. Stone and iron exploded everywhere, and I heard the faint cries of my friends, but I had no time to think. Dust filled my prison cell, so thick I could barely see. Coughs sputtered out of my lungs, and a hand grabbed my arm, tugging me forward. Jasper. He'd finally rescued me. Just like I knew he would. His friends, the ones in the trees, would rescue Driscoll and Jillian. Jasper would never leave them behind, not when he knew how much they meant to me.

"Where are we going?" I shouted, but he didn't answer.

Instead, he continued to pull me toward the edge of my cell as another roar shook the ground below us. The queen hadn't appeared yet. But of course she hadn't. She never did the dirty work. She left that for her monsters. I had no doubt she was watching, though. Always watching.

"Jump."

The voice startled me from my thoughts. He spoke. It wasn't exactly the first words I'd expected to hear. Was it really that hard to say "I love you, Liliath!" or "You're stunning, even in rags and when you haven't combed your hair in two years!" But we had time for that, I supposed.

Then his words sank in. "Jump?" I repeated. "Jump where?"

No response. Okay, this was starting to get on my nerves.

"Jasper, where are we jumping to?"

"Count of three," he said, his voice deeper, gruffer than I remembered.

"Wait, you can't be serious—"

"One."

"No, Jasper—"

"Two."

"Will you just stop and—"

"Three!"

Suddenly I was falling, my legs and arms flailing in the air. A scream wrenched from my throat. I was going to kill him if I didn't die in this harebrained scheme of his. Well, I'd probably kiss him first. But then I would kill him. I yelled again, the strangled sound swallowed by roaring and other shouts and screams. Dust from the monster's attack on my prison cell still filled the air, and I couldn't see anything in the dark.

I braced myself for an impact that never came. My body hit a soft surface, something that wrapped around me, cushioning me, pulling me. A vine. But—how was that possible? My stepmother was the only one with the power to wield earth magic. Another thing she'd taken from me. Which meant I was going to die after all. She'd captured me and Jasper. It was over. At any moment, this vine would constrict around me, squeezing tighter and tighter until it wrung the last breath from my lungs while she watched and laughed.

Except none of that happened.

The dust cleared as I sailed through the air in the vine's grasp, but darkness veiled everything. Finally, my feet felt solid ground, and the vine released me just as two strong arms came around me. I turned and realized I was on the other side of the iron gates. Free. I caught the glint of Jasper's red ring in the night, but otherwise darkness cloaked everything.

"Jasper." I threw my arms around him, desperate to just feel him, his warmth. To feel anything at all. I grappled for the scarf over his face, yanked it down, and pressed my lips to his. He stiffened at first, but then his body relaxed and I melted into him, his mouth opening, the kiss deepening as he ran a thumb down my cheek. Heat exploded in my belly as his mouth moved against mine, lips soft and perfect.

Oh. My. Word.

So Jasper hadn't just learned how to navigate deadly mazes and scale castle walls, but the man had also learned how to kiss. Not that he was a terrible kisser before, but, well, this was on another level.

Warmth pooled between my legs, and suddenly I wanted all of him. Right here. Right now. It had been so long. He pushed me away, and my breaths came out ragged as I returned to myself. Our kiss seemed to have had the same effect on him, his breathing uneven, rattled.

I needed to get a grip on myself. I had been ready to maul the man right outside the castle that had just tried to kill us.

"Jasper, I've missed you so much."

He grabbed my hand, his skin rougher than I expected. Though I guess that made sense given he'd been training to rescue me. He yanked me further ahead into the darkness, dousing whatever flames still flickered from that earlier kiss.

"Jasper—"

"Shhh" was all I got in response.

Something about his silence felt distinctly off, so different from the talkative Jasper I remembered, but my mouth snapped shut. The queen had spies everywhere, and staying quiet was probably the smart thing to do. I desperately wanted to ask about Jillian and Driscoll, but they must have been somewhere behind us. As soon as I was able, I'd ask about them. For now, I followed him away from the iron gates and into the trees that surrounded the castle grounds.

We walked for what felt like hours, me staying silent the entire time for fear that a single word would summon the queen, Jasper not making any attempt to converse with me. He must have been tired after such a huge mission.

Darkness swallowed us. It was hard to see much of anything other than the faint outlines of trees and brush, vines hanging, red and yellow eyes peeking at us from the dark.

I was free. Finally free. The word repeated in my mind over and over, giving me the strength to keep going, until my legs couldn't move any more, my head nodding to my chest. I bumped into Jasper, and he abruptly stopped and turned.

I expected a hug. Maybe another one of those earth-shattering kisses. But instead, he just grunted and said, "Sleep," in that deep, gruff voice I didn't recognize. Had I really forgotten what Jasper sounded like? I'd dreamt of his voice for so long, yet it was so unfamiliar now.

I'd thought he would have horses waiting for us, but he simply laid down on the ground, back to me. I guessed that meant we were still expected to be silent. I had no idea how far we'd gone, but surely if the queen hadn't caught us by now, we were safe, for a little while, at least.

I swallowed, trying to hold back the tears. This wasn't how I'd imagined being rescued by Jasper. After that amazing kiss, I'd thought . . . Well, it didn't matter. I lay down on the hard forest floor, leaves crunching underneath my body. After two years of being imprisoned, I was safe. My love had come for me. It was finally time for my happily ever after.

Chapter Three

I was kissing Jasper again, wrapped in his arms, those warm, soft lips crushing mine, those strong arms cradling me, running up my back and through my hair. It was still dark, his face nothing but a shadow. But his lips, they tasted the same as earlier, like dew and earth.

Something shook my shoulder, and my eyes shot open as I jolted awake.

I blinked a few times at the man standing over me. A man who was definitely not Jasper.

"Who are you?" I flew to my feet and backed away, hands out. "What have you done with my betrothed?"

He rubbed his smooth jaw, looking far too calm given our current situation. My heart galloped in my chest.

"Jasper?" I called out, looking around us at the bleak forest. Blackened tree trunks surrounded us, their gray, lifeless leaves hanging limp. "Jasper!"

Alarm flashed across the man's face. "Okay, okay." He took a cautious step forward. "Just stop yelling, and I'll explain everything. I'm not your betrothed."

I stayed rooted to my spot, ready to run if he made a move toward me. "Yes, thank you for clearing that up."

"Your betrothed was never here. He's not the one who rescued you."

My mouth dropped open. But that was impossible. The ring. I saw the ring on his finger, the one that belonged to Jasper . . . My thoughts trailed off as I looked at the man's empty finger, no ring present. I shook my head.

"What have you done with him?"

"Look, Princess, I can assure you he's safe, but we are not. Word is, the queen's sent her Huntsman after you. He'll be looking for you, and we need to go."

"I'm not going anywhere with you until you explain. And—" I looked around. "Where are my friends? Jillian? Driscoll?"

"You're the only one who was rescued. There was no way to break out more than one person." He smiled gently, sympathy lining the curves of his mouth in a way that made me want to scream.

No. No, no, no, no, no. They got left behind?

I turned. "I'm going back for them."

His hand grabbed my arm, his grip tight. "Sorry, but I have orders, so you're coming with me."

"Orders from who, exactly?" I asked through gritted teeth, my mind muddled, thoughts tangled. This man had said he'd explain everything and so far he had done a fuck-all job.

He sighed heavily, his grip loosening. "We really don't have time for this. We've got to get out of Elwen and to safety." He gestured behind him, and I realized where we were.

A huge wall of branches, vines, and thorns rose up, so high I had to arch my neck. The border between Elwen and Mosswood Forest. No one crossed that border, not ever since the false king and queen had it erected. I'd only visited the border once, long ago. A day I'd forever regret. The day I made myself an enemy of my stepmother. I backed away, remembering what we were taught as children, how if you tried to cross the border, the wall would eat you up and spit your bones out. My gaze trailed to the ground, littered with bones and skulls.

The man in front of me grimaced. "I'm really sorry for what I'm about to do."

"What are you about to—"

He covered my face with a cloth, and once again, darkness overtook me.

21

Chapter Four

Voices filtered in and out of my mind, and light penetrated my eyelids, but darkness kept its firm hold on me, and every time I tried to open my eyes, they stayed firmly closed.

"Is she awake yet?" a female voice said, sounding distant and far away.

A man tsked. "I tried to flirt with her, but even my charms weren't enough to wake the sleeping princess."

"You tried to flirt with her? No wonder she's still sleeping. Probably pretending to be unconscious until you go away."

"Remind me again why she's here," a low voice growled. "What was Boss thinking? Need to send her straight back where she came from, if you ask me."

"I like her," yet another voice said, this one male, soothing, melodic. "I mean she wasn't particularly happy with me when I was putting a sleeping cloth over her face, but you know, I think I'm gonna grow on her."

"You like everyone," the female voice said.

"I think she just wiggled her fingers. My flirting must've worked after all."

I summoned all my strength to open my eyes, but I'd been in the dark for so long, it was hard to escape, and the voices faded away as I drifted back into unconsciousness.

MY EYES FLUTTERED OPEN to see a man standing over me, the same one who'd been with me outside the border. He raked a hand through his dark, curly hair as I shot up in bed.

"Take it easy," he said. "You're going to be a little groggy."

"What do you want with me?" I inched back toward the wall, as far away from him as I could get. "To sell me off? To ransom me? The queen doesn't care about me, so if you're hoping to get gold out of her, she's more likely to kill you than bargain with you."

"It's nothing like that," he said. "The name's Wayfinder. It's nice to officially meet you, Princess."

A flap in the tent opened, a few others stepping inside, and for the first time I blinked, noticing my surroundings.

I lay in a tent, dressed in a clean tunic and trousers that felt soft and warm against my skin, so unlike the scratchy rags we had to wear as prisoners. Sunlight filtered through the cracks. Sun. Actual sun on my face. I touched my cheeks where the rays hit, wanting to run out the tent and lather myself in it. My breath hitched as I caught a glance at the outside world through a little slit in the flap. Green. The leaves on the trees were green. Not black or gray or covered in tar. Not filled with holes or mottled by slugs.

"Oh, good," a man with blond hair said. He smiled, dimples appearing in his cheeks, and I marveled at his perfectly coiffed hair, gelled and styled with a part straight down the middle. "Tell me, do you recognize my voice? We had a few chats while you slept." He winked, and the woman next to him rolled her eyes.

"Blood and earth, Charming. She didn't hear you flirting with her while she slept."

"I've been known to charm women out of sleep," he said. "They'd much rather be doing other things when they're around me than sleeping."

The woman massaged her temples, walking across the room, her movements so smooth, reminding me of a cat.

She stuck out her hand. "I'm Shadow."

Wayfinder, Charming, Shadow. What was with these names?

"Who are you people?" I clutched my covers tight. "Where am I? What do you want with me?"

"Well, at least offer to buy me dinner before you start firing off all these questions," Charming said.

Shadow elbowed him, and Wayfinder let out a snort. She glared at him. "What? I think he's funny."

Charming crossed his arms. "Thank you."

Shadow sat on the end of the bed. "I'm sorry about these idiots. You're in Mosswood Forest."

My last memory flooded my mind. Standing outside the border. That had been why. Wayfinder had wanted to cross it with me, then he . . . he drugged me with something.

I gaped at him.

No one got into Mosswood Forest, no one except the mountain dwellers, who had built the border years ago, betrayed my father and Elwen. They were responsible for so many deaths, so much pain and suffering because of what they'd done. And he'd brought me here? Directly to the land of my enemies? Spirits below.

"Are you insane?" I hissed. "We can't be here. They'll kill us if they see us."

"Who?" Wayfinder asked, brows knitted.

"The mountain dwellers." I spoke the words slowly, like he might be an idiot who wouldn't understand them.

Wayfinder stepped forward. "Well, then, I guess it's a good thing I'm one of them."

My entire body tensed. "You—you're a mountain dweller?"

"We all are," Shadow said gently, still seated on my bed.

Charming shot me a smile. "I won't bite. Unless you want me to."

Unbelievable. So not only had I been kidnapped, but I'd been taken by a mountain dweller to a region that I didn't know, where danger lurked around every corner.

"Why am I here, then? What do you want from me?"

"Well, that's for Boss to explain." Wayfinder gave a shrug. "He should be by soon."

"Your boss?" I asked, the ominous tone behind his words sending a shiver down my spine.

This boss didn't sound like someone I wanted to meet.

Fuck.

I needed to find a way out of this place, needed to escape and get to Jasper as soon as possible. He'd help me rescue Jillian and Driscoll. He'd help me save the earth court.

My heart wrenched as I thought about my friends, still stuck in their prison cells, wondering what in the bloody earth happened to me. I tried to rise, but Shadow put a hand on my leg.

"You must be tired." She nodded to the bed. "You need to rest."

Wayfinder scratched the back of his head, those black curls bouncing with the movement. "Do you remember much of the night you were rescued?"

I thought back to it: that huge man that had bested my stepmother's twisted earth magic, the red ring on his finger. I studied the people in front of me. None of them met that profile. Had I imagined him? Who had my rescuer been if not any of these people standing in front of me?

Just then, the flap opened yet again.

One of the biggest men I'd ever seen stepped inside. He towered over me, frowning down, his shadow stretching to where I sat. His white-blond hair was tied back into a bun at his nape, a few strands of hair falling down the side of his face. He crossed his muscled arms against his wide chest, a green tunic stretched over his pecs, brown leather trousers hugging his thick thighs. A satchel was strapped diagonally across his chest, the pouch hanging at his side.

He wrinkled his nose. He had the audacity to stare at me like I was the disgrace. Me. Princess Liliath of Elwen.

"Princess Liliath, meet Penn Vanderbilt. The king of thieves," Wayfinder said from next to him.

That's when my gaze traveled to his hand, and I noticed the red jewel sparkling on his finger. The ring I saw the night I'd been kidnapped. My mouth nearly dropped to the ground. It wasn't any of them who had rescued me. It was him.

The king of thieves.

Chapter Five

I stood despite Shadow's protests, staring daggers at the ridiculously handsome giant of a man standing before me. How dare he be so loathsome and so attractive at the same time.

I'd heard of the king of thieves. Everyone had. He was the most notorious thief on the continent of Arathia, terrorizing all the courts, stealing valuable objects, and he'd never been caught. In fact, no one had gotten so much as a sketch of him, the descriptions from his victims always varying so much that it made profiling him impossible.

"I thought you said she bathed," Penn said to Wayfinder, studying me.

My mouth dropped open. He was absolutely vile.

Wayfinder stroked his chin. "Shadow cleaned her with a damp cloth while she slept. You should've seen her before. Trust me, this is a vast improvement."

"I'm sorry I don't look presentable enough for you after being kidnapped by criminals." They had to be if they were working with him. I glared.

Charming let out a low whistle. "I like her already."

Penn's gaze roved over my body. Those green eyes assessed me in a way that made me want to squirm. "She'll do," he finally said.

Oh, what an asshole.

"I'll do for what, exactly?" I jabbed a finger at him. "You owe me an explanation."

"I owe you nothing," Penn said in return, such a vast contrast to the others with his serious face that showed no emotion.

"You kidnapped me!"

"You're welcome for that, by the way."

"I didn't say thank you."

"I noticed." He tsked. "Not very polite for a princess."

I wanted to scream. I thought the others were bad, but after meeting Penn, I was starting to like them more and more. They were a fresh breeze compared to this arrogant man.

Penn looked at the others and nodded. "Good work. Get to the barracks."

Shadow raised a brow. "She needs rest, Boss."

"No time."

Shadow looked like she wanted to argue, but she just shook her head and brushed past him and toward the tent flap, opening it.

I sent a pleading look at her.

Wayfinder gave me a gentle smile before running a finger through his short curls. "He's not so bad, I promise. You'll be fine."

Penn crossed his arms again, muscles flexing under that green shirt. He just snorted and rolled his eyes. "I don't have all day."

Wayfinder strode outside with Shadow.

Charming stopped in the opening and turned, jabbing his thumb at Penn. "He can be a bit moody, and he doesn't have the best sense of humor, doesn't really like to smile. He tells it like it is, has been known to make people cry, and is generally very bossy." He shot me a cheeky grin before disappearing through the flap. "You two will get along great."

"Does he have any redeeming qualities?" I called out.

"Ah," Charming yelled back through the opening. "Well, you'll have to find that out for yourself."

I squeezed my eyes shut, reminding myself of my goal: escape and find Jasper. I wouldn't be stuck here, with this horrible man, for long. I'd find a way out.

Penn gestured to the tent flap. "Are you planning to stand there all day?"

Deep breath in. Deep breath out. I'd been stripped of my crown, imprisoned by my stepmother, made to watch my court fall apart, and yet this man, he might be my greatest obstacle yet.

I HAD to run to catch up with Penn. I was already missing the others and their banter and smiles. This man was like a storm cloud, ready to rain down and ruin a perfectly good day. Not that I was having a perfectly good day.

We walked along a sparkling river that glittered as it flowed through hills, homes built into the mounds with doors, windows, and little chimneys with smoke curling into the air. This must be where the mountain dwellers lived. Trees peppered the village, and a wooden bridge ran over the water. This was like nothing I'd ever imagined.

I ran to a tree, laying my palm against the brown bark, feeling a spark deep inside of me, too deep for me to reach.

Tears pricked my eyes as I lay my head against the trunk, just wanting to feel my earth magic.

I could feel Penn behind me. "Your magic is gone," he said, tone lacking any emotion. "It's not coming back."

I tugged at that spark anyway, hoping against all hope that I'd feel something more, that the power I'd been born with would flood my veins, that I'd be able to use it to move a branch, a leaf, to make a new plant sprout from the ground.

I pulled and pulled at the familiar thread, but nothing happened. So it hadn't just been the castle, the imprisonment. My powers hadn't just been dulled like I'd thought. Penn was right. My magic was truly gone.

I still didn't know how my stepmother had managed to overtake my father, to take away our earth magic, to inflict this damage on the land. She was born of the earth court, just like me, just like everyone who lived in Elwen and Mosswood Forest.

We all had the same magic: earth magic. We all had the power to control any living thing that grew from the earth, as well as the ability to create plants. We could all cast vines from our hands, make flowers and trees grow. Sure, some of us might be more adept at growing crops or controlling trees or creating new species of plants, but we all had the same powers at the core.

Penn stepped up beside me. "We don't have time for this—"

I shoved past him, just the sound of his voice making me want to punch something. Preferably him. "Then let's go."

He moved ahead of me, and I followed, blood boiling. They'd done nothing while my people suffered. The mountain dwellers lived here, in this beautiful village, going about their lives like my stepmother wasn't on the other side of that border destroying my entire court, stealing magic and twisting it into something dark, destroying our once beautiful lands.

It was unforgivable.

We walked across the grassy expanse, along the river and toward the wooden bridge. Mountain dwellers peeked out their windows as we passed. A few women walked past us, eyeing me. I tugged at my tunic, self-conscious for the first time over how I must look.

Good green earth, I'd give anything to have Jasper's arms wrapped around me right now while he nuzzled my neck, nibbled at my ear, pressed his lips to mine.

A memory flashed into my mind, unbidden and very unwanted. A kiss. A hard body. Probing lips. And they weren't Jasper's. The kiss after my rescue. Those soft, hungry lips that had made me melt. Those fingers that had stroked my cheek. I looked at Penn in horror as he walked a few steps ahead of me.

Oh, no. No, no, no, no, no. It hadn't been Jasper. It had been *him*. This horrid man. He couldn't have kissed me like that. Made all the bones in my body wilt, made me forget who I was and that I'd spent the last two years imprisoned. Him. I wanted to rip the memory out of my brain and hurl it as far away as I could.

"I know I'm handsome, but it's rude to stare," Penn said over his shoulder, drawing me from my thoughts.

My face flushed as I realized I was staring, though I didn't understand how he'd known that, given I was behind him. I raised my chin. "I've just never seen someone with such a large head."

Unfortunately, his large head fit his large body quite perfectly, but I wouldn't admit that to him.

He smirked. "Well, a large head means a large—"

"What do you want with me?" I cut him off, keeping my gaze level with his, using all my willpower to not let my eyes drop below the waistline of his trousers, which was no doubt exactly what he wanted.

I wouldn't give him the satisfaction.

He nodded toward a clearing in the distance. "We have a little further to go. If you could keep up, we'd already be there, and maybe you'd have your answers."

I. Hated. Him.

He turned and walked to the little clearing, where bright green grass filled the space. He stopped in the middle, waiting for me as I joined him. When I entered the area, my breath caught in my chest.

Planks criss-crossed overhead between the trees, and ropes dangled in the air, some with knots, some without. Huts were built into the treetops with little roofs and windows. I'd never seen anything like it. It was like a small village built into the trees. Tree stumps dotted the outside of the circular area. A sitting place, I assumed.

"What is this?" I asked, unable to keep the awe from my voice.

"This is the Academy of Thieves," Penn said.

The Academy of . . . I'd never heard of such a thing. It certainly didn't sound legal. A training school for thieves? That was detestable. People shouldn't be learning how to steal.

"Well, that sounds like something that needs to be shut down immediately," I said.

"Huh." Penn lifted the satchel over his head and lay it at his feet. "It's too bad you feel that way."

I rolled my eyes. "And why is that?"

"Because you're our newest member."

Chapter Six

The ground rocked under my feet. "Excuse me?" I sputtered.

"You wanted to know what I want with you." Penn spread his arms wide. "This is it. You're joining my academy." He raised two fingers to his lips and let out a loud whistle.

This was absurd. I was a princess. Surely he must understand how inappropriate this would be. I couldn't be queen, rule Elwen, if I'd stolen from people, trained with actual thieves—the king of thieves, arguably the most wanted man on the continent of Arathia. For the last two years, my people had seen nothing but evil and depravity from their queen. They needed a good leader, someone who wouldn't compromise their morals, but if they found out I'd been in league with these thieves, what might they think of me?

And why would he want me to be a thief, anyway? What could I possibly do for him?

People emerged from the little huts above, walking onto the planks, then hopping to the ropes and shimmying down. They each took a seat on one of the stumps, all of their eyes on me.

"Meet your classmates." Penn nodded to the others, four in total. Then Wayfinder, Shadow, and Charming emerged from the trees and sat. Seven, now. Seven thieves.

One of the men grunted, glaring at me under from his bushy red eyebrows and thick lashes, and I realized he was missing an arm, his right tunic sleeve hanging down empty. "She's from Elwen, a princess, and you brought her here, to our domain?" He spit on the ground.

"Lighten up, Hammer," Shadow said from next to him.

I turned to Penn. "Why do you want me?"

"That's what I want to know." Hammer's eyebrows drew together.

"He's right. I am a princess. I can't be a thief." I turned to the stocky man, surveying his long red beard that hung in a braid down his chest. "And what kind of name is Hammer? Shadow? Wayfinder?" Everyone stilled. "What?" I paused. "It's just a question."

Wayfinder scratched the back of his neck. "We all have nicknames in the academy." He pointed to himself. "Good with maps."

"So I'm actually supposed to call him Hammer?" I asked the group.

"If you know what's good for you," Hammer said, smiling to reveal a few missing teeth. "It took me a long time to earn that name."

Earn? As in, they were actually proud of these names?

Wayfinder pointed to another woman with red wavy hair and thick red lips. "And that's—"

"Enough," Penn said. "She'll meet everyone in due time. For now, she needs to start her training. The queen has no doubt sent her Huntsman after the princess. We can't afford to waste time, not with him looming ever closer."

A chill skittered down my arms, and I frisked them. The Huntsman. He was a terrifying creature. After what he'd done to my father . . . Penn was right. He would be coming after me. Just another reason I needed to escape to find Jasper as soon as possible.

"What is the point of this academy? Why would you recruit and train people to steal?" I looked at all of them. "And why on this good green earth would you all agree to this?"

"I get to meet a lot of women," Charming said. "You'd be surprised how many of them love the whole bad-boy thing I got going on."

Penn rolled his eyes. "How do you think I've been able to steal from the northern reaches of the frost court to the blazing bowels of the fire court, all the way to the isles of the sky court?" He stepped closer, his forest-green eyes searing. "How do you think I've been able to thwart authorities in every court on this continent? Keep their descriptions of me muddled?"

It all made sense. My eyes widened. "That was all of you? You're all the king of thieves?"

"They're all working for the king of thieves," Penn corrected. "They were trained by me, go on my missions, steal for me, and get a good cut." He gestured to the treetop houses. "Not to mention a nice home."

"And a chance to do some good," Wayfinder said.

"Good?" I wanted to scream. "You think stealing from the courts is good?"

The thieves shot each other looks that I couldn't decipher.

Penn sighed out an annoyed breath. I never even knew breathing could sound annoyed, but his did. Very distinctly. "I need you for a mission. To steal a weapon for me. Something only you have access to. In order to complete the mission, you have to train and learn a particular skillset, and you need to do it before the Huntsman arrives. Because he is coming."

"You want me to steal something for you?" Horror washed over me.

"Yes," Penn said through gritted teeth.

"So what is this weapon? Where is it?"

I didn't have access to anything powerful like what he was referencing. In fact, I had no clue what he could be talking about.

Wayfinder shook his head, those black curls of his bouncing. "He doesn't reveal our missions ahead of time. Too much of a chance that someone might be listening, spying, that the details could leak."

"You don't even trust your own academy members? That's not very inspiring."

My father had been the same. He hadn't trusted his advisors, hadn't trusted anyone, it seemed. I understood where the mistrust came from after the false king and queen had risen up and betrayed him, but my father had been stubborn whenever I'd brought up his lack of trust, whenever I'd told him that he needed to let people in. We'd had that same argument so many times over the years, and it never mattered. He wouldn't listen.

"You'll get the details when you need them," Penn said, his tone dismissive.

He turned to leave the circle.

"And what's your nickname?" I asked.

He stopped, his back still to me.

"Let me guess: Hardhead." I snapped my fingers. "No, maybe Unpleasant? Or, perhaps, Killjoy would best be attributed to you?"

Everyone in the circle stared at me with wide eyes, their gazes darting between me and Penn.

"Oh, I definitely like her," Charming murmured.

"We call him Boss," Wayfinder said.

"Never would have guessed," I replied. "So what's my nickname to be, then?"

"You'll get it when you start training, showing your strengths. You'll get one when you earn it," Penn responded, then continued on his way out of the circle.

I thought I might faint. He was serious. He was going to make me train to become a thief, to steal some stupid weapon. This had to be a dream. More like a nightmare.

Everyone else stood, some climbing the ropes back up to their huts, others disappearing into the forest. Wayfinder stopped on his way out, clapping my shoulder with his hand.

The only one left in the circle was Shadow. Her black hair sat like a cloud on top of her head, the afro perfectly coiffed, her light brown skin dewy with a beautiful glow.

"Where did everyone go?" I glanced around at the now-empty circle. "What's happening?"

"Today is day one of your training, and I'm going to be working with you."

"Am I the only student?"

Shadow smiled. "We don't admit students often. Penn is pretty picky about who comes into his academy."

I didn't like this, not any of it. But these people clearly had a skillset that I could use to my advantage. If I learned from them, allowed them to teach me, I would only be better equipped to escape and find Jasper, then take back the earth court. They'd think I was training so I could complete Penn's little mission, but in reality, I'd be training for my own mission. One the king of thieves would never see coming.

Chapter Seven

Shadow and I stood in front of what looked like an obstacle course. I didn't know what I feared more: the Huntsman or whatever this mission was that Penn wanted me to complete. Hopefully neither would be a threat once I escaped this place. I just had to find a map of some sort, figure out where I was.

I looked all around me.

Trees had been cut and turned into sharp points that could impale someone should they drop onto them. Thin planks stretched between the uncut trees, some with gaping holes, some with spikes jutting up, some tilted diagonally. Ropes hung from branches, some high up, some lower to the ground.

"This is where you train?" I asked, my stomach fluttering.

"This is it," Shadow said. "Hey, you're gonna be fine. No need to look so alarmed."

She jumped up on a rope and deftly climbed it to the top. That was definitely not happening for me.

She looked down. "What are you waiting for? Come on."

I gripped the rope and attempted to lift myself up but could barely get my feet off the ground.

"Use your core," she shouted down at me, still clutching the top of the rope, not a bead of sweat on her.

"I don't have a core." I huffed and tightened my stomach, lifting my feet, now twined around the rope.

"There you go," she said. "Now just focus on one hand above the other."

She made it sound so easy. I moved a hand up, gripping the rope again. Then the next hand. I also used both feet to push myself upward. My muscles shook with the effort, and after just a few minutes I dropped back to the ground. Penn had lost his mind if he thought I could do this. It wasn't even a confidence issue; it was that my body was not built like the rest of these thieves. I didn't have the training they did, the strength. My strengths lay in other areas, like being a smart-ass and looking pretty.

I glanced up and jumped to see Shadow in front of me in a crouching position. She really had earned her nickname. I hadn't even heard her drop to the ground.

"Listen, these kinds of skills don't happen overnight," she said. "It's all gonna take time to come together. So, right now, we're going to work on that strength and stamina, and once you build those two things up, I'll teach you how to be stealthy, quiet."

"Like a shadow," I said.

She nodded. "You're catching on." She pulled me to my feet and pointed to the rope. "Now try again."

My second attempt was even worse than my first now that my muscles were sore and tired.

"Again," she said after I fell.

So I tried it again. And again. And again. And again. The rope had rubbed my hands raw, my butt was numb from how many times I'd fallen onto it, and my muscles might as well have not even existed at that point.

"I can't do it anymore," I said from the ground, sweat dripping down my face, dirt coating my hair and clothes.

Shadow bent down, stretching her legs. "C'mon. Copy my movements."

I groaned, barely able to stand. I bent like she had and groaned again, my entire body protesting the movement. Blood and earth, this felt awful. Why did anyone subject themselves to this?

"Touch your toes," she commanded as she hinged over, her finger-tips grazing the ground.

"I . . . can't . . ." I gasped between the words, my hands only able to reach down to my knees.

"Go as far as you can right now," she said.

That wasn't very far. My legs felt tight, too tight, like they might snap if I bent any further.

"The more you practice, the easier it will be. You're going to want to stretch before and after every training session, and make sure you're bathing in the springs. The warm water will help your aching muscles."

Unable to stand the tension in my body any longer, I shot up just as Shadow straightened.

Her brown skin was just as dewy as it had been when we'd begun. Not a single drop of sweat on her, while I had no doubt my pale skin was blotchy and red. "Okay, are you ready?"

"I can't go on that rope again." I looked at my reddened palms, wincing at the forming blisters.

"I know." She jogged in place. "We're going for a run."

"A—"

Before I could finish, she'd already bounded off. Had this woman lost her mind? I could barely stand, let alone run.

"Let's go," she called over her shoulder. "Penn has been known to force those who quit their training sessions early to run laps around the village for everyone to see."

I snorted. Of course he did. The tyrant.

It was bad enough I had to run at all. I certainly didn't need an audience. I forced myself to move my legs, wincing at the aches and pains shooting through my body.

I ducked under branches and dodged trees. Leaves tickled my head as I focused all my attention on just putting one foot in front of the other. Blood and earth, I was barely an hour into my first training session, and I already wanted to quit. I had no idea how I was going to make it through this.

Jasper's face flashed in my mind, then Driscoll's, and finally, Jillian's. I gritted my teeth. I would do this. For them. I didn't have to be the best. I just had to survive and make everyone think I was willing to participate in their little plan.

A stitch formed in my side, sharp and jabbing. My lungs burned as I sucked in air, and still, we ran through the forest. Leaves and branches crunched underfoot, each sound like a splinter in my ear. I wanted to fall down and not move again for a very, very long time.

Shadow continued her steady pace while I fell further behind, finally dropping to my knees, wheezing while clutching my sides. My vision went blurry, and I fell to the ground.

A face appeared over me. "I might've pushed you too hard."

Water. I needed water. And air, though Shadow probably couldn't help with that part. I felt her hand gripping my shoulder, and she pulled me to a seated position. My stomach turned, all the contents rising up, burning through my throat, before I retched it out.

Shadow rubbed my back. "It will get easier. I promise."

I wiped my mouth, tears stinging my eyes. I just wanted to go home. I didn't want to put my body through this, didn't want to be surrounded by these criminals, these awful people who couldn't even manage to lift so much as a finger while my court suffered. And now they'd taken me away just so they could use me for some twisted scheme. I wanted no part of this.

"Here." Shadow helped me to my feet. "Let's get you back to the barracks."

I nodded, feeling numb, both inside and out. If this was how my first day went, I wasn't sure I was going to survive long enough to figure out an escape plan.

I walked into the clearing where the barracks were. The barracks up in the trees. Apparently now that I was apart of the academy, I had to sleep where the other thieves slept.

I groaned. Why did everything have to be difficult here?

Shadow gestured to the ropes. "We normally use those to climb, but we have notches in the trees that you can use today—"

"No," a gruff voice interrupted, and I would've whirled around, but my aching body only allowed me to turn very slowly.

Penn stood there, those piercing green eyes assessing me.

"No, what?" I said.

"No, she cannot use the notches." Penn grabbed a rope and swung it to me. I didn't even try to catch it, and I noticed the tick in his jaw. "She uses the rope or she sleeps on the forest floor."

Shadow's eyes widened. "Oh, Boss, c'mon—"

He held up his hand, a challenge in his eyes. I glared at him, once again imagining the day he would be on his knees in front of me, hands pressed together as he begged me not to throw him in the dungeons.

My nostrils flared. Without another word, Penn spun on his heel and strode away.

That arrogant asshole.

"I can get you a bedroll," Shadow offered, and I nodded, rubbing my sore arms. She studied me for a minute. "Come with me."

I stayed rooted to my spot. "I can't handle another training session today."

"That's not what this is. Just come on, you'll see."

Chapter Eight

The walk to our destination was short, thankfully, and I gasped when we reached the edge of a cliff. Spread out below us were hot springs on the forest terraces. The terraces looked like giant steps carved into the hillside of Mosswood Forest, and cerulean blue water filled the naturally made pools. Steam rose in the air, making the air shimmer like a mirage.

Charming and Hammer sat in one of the pools, and Charming tilted his head. "Like what you see, Princess?"

Shadow huffed and looked at me. "Charming would flirt with a tree if he could."

He raised a finger. "I've done that, actually. Wasn't very fun. Tree didn't flirt back."

Hammer let out a bark that I thought was supposed to be a laugh.

"Just close your eyes." Shadow made a motion with her finger to the men.

"Well that's no fun," Charming said but complied, along with Hammer.

Shadow and I stripped and scaled down the grassy hill to join them in the steaming pool. I lowered myself in, moaning. Oh, that felt good. I'd probably strip naked in front of my entire court just to get ten minutes in this water.

My muscles relaxed, the aches lulled away momentarily, the water now covering my chest.

I peered at Charming and Hammer, Charming's chest bare while thick red hair covered Hammer's. "You can open your eyes now."

"Sorry about Penn." Shadow stretched her arms overhead, twisting her head from side to side. "He's strict and tough, but he has his reasons."

"He's not very fun," Charming added. "But we make up for it."

Hammer grunted. "I think he's plenty of fun."

"That's because you're a sadist." Shadow snorted. "You love yelling and being yelled at."

"Nothing wrong with a good yelling from time to time."

Charming looked at me. "He and Boss get into yelling matches regularly, loud enough to scare all the birds from the trees."

A vicious grin spread across Hammer's face. "I was proud of that one."

These people were lunatics, acting so casual about their illegal academy.

Still, I couldn't help but like them. They were kind, funny, normal, except for the whole stealing thing.

"He's horrible." I shifted. "And I don't know how any of you stand him, let alone follow him. He breaks the law, steals from people. It's wrong."

"Not everything is so cut and dry," Shadow said. "You may not understand why Penn does what he does, but at least give him a chance. He may surprise you. We all might surprise you."

I huffed. "I doubt that. He's exactly who I think he is. Besides, I don't have to give him a chance. He kidnapped me. Forcibly took me from my home."

Shadow laughed. "He saved you."

"So he could use me! That's not saving someone. That's . . . something else."

"He has no finesse." Charming twirled his finger in the air. "He probably just threw you over his shoulder like a barbarian. I would've been much gentler."

I thought about the kiss we shared, how Penn had held me so

tenderly, and my jaw clenched. No, no, I would not be thinking about that anymore.

"Lucky he saved you at all," Hammer said. "Still don't think we need you for whatever mission Penn has planned."

"You're a real ray of sunshine," I said, and Shadow laughed, then sobered her expression when Hammer glared at her.

A bird soared above us, flying toward the bushy green treetops. Pink and purple smudged the blue sky as the sun sank lower, and I took in the view. After spending so long in the dark, moments like these struck me. No matter how horrible life may be right now, at least I could feel the sun on my face, see the green of trees, breathe in fresh air. It was more than I could say for Jillian or Driscoll.

"How did you get your nickname?" I asked Shadow after a beat of silence, curious.

She laughed. "In order to be officially initiated into the academy, your final task is to spar with Penn. I wasn't great with my sword work or my archery lessons, and I didn't have the strength of Hammer. So I had learned to be quick, to be silent, to be like a shadow. At night, when everyone slept, I'd practice creeping up trees, across branches, jumping to the ground as silently as I could. I got better and better at it, and soon, I didn't need to be great with a sword or be the strongest in the group. I had my own assets that Penn could use to his advantage. So after he'd beaten me three days in a row in the sparring ring, I decided to play a different kind of game. I jumped up into the trees and disappeared from sight. No one could see me, hear me, as I crept over the branches and dropped right down behind Penn, sword at his throat."

Oh, I wished I could've been there for that.

"Am I going to have to spar with Penn?" I asked, partly horrified and partly exhilarated by the thought.

Shadow nodded. "Everyone does before they're allowed to go on a mission. Penn has to make sure you're ready. Too many lives have been lost on these missions."

I straightened at that. "What?"

Hammer grunted. "We weren't always the seven thieves. There used to be eight of us, but Butcher lost his life a year ago. Since then, Penn has been stricter about who he lets in, stricter when it comes to training. Except for you, apparently."

My entire body grew weak, like at any moment I might just sink under the water, unable to emerge. I knew these missions must be dangerous, but one of the thieves, a skilled, trained thief, had died? Spirits below. The Huntsman was after me, and now there was the very distinct possibility I might die on this stupid mission of Penn's. If I lost my life, there went any hope for my people. For Jillian and Driscoll. I had to speed up my plans for escape, had to get to Jasper as soon as possible so he could help me fight all these looming threats.

I leaned my head back against the rocky ledge of the hot spring.

"I know things are different here than where you're from," Shadow said. "But Penn isn't one of the bad guys, trust me. He shoulders all of our burdens. Sometimes to a detriment."

"And how does he do that? Shoulder your burdens?"

Shadow bit her lip. "His isn't my story to tell."

That's what I thought. They must be under whatever spell the king of thieves had over them, and I wouldn't be able to break it.

"What do you learn about us in Elwen?" Shadow asked. "The mountain dwellers, as you call us?"

I heaved a sigh. "We learned about the war for independence between Elwen and Mosswood Forest. The false king and queen."

When I was just three years old, a man and woman rose up in Elwen, gained a following, and soon had convinced a group of people that they should separate from Elwen. We dubbed that man and woman the false king and queen. They claimed Mosswood Forest as their territory, and they started a war to gain their independence and make Mosswood Forest its own court. The war was bloody, cost so many lives. We managed to kill the false king and queen, which had only angered their followers. They ultimately ended the war when they created a magical border that spanned the length of Mosswood Forest, cutting everyone in Elwen off from valuable resources, herbs, minerals that we depended on the forest for.

Charming gave me an amused smirk. "The false king and queen? That's what you called Queen Jarusha and King Damur?"

"Well, what else would we call them? They conspired behind my mother's and father's backs. They spread rumors and lies about them, convinced people to follow them and forsake their Elwen heritage."

"How do you know they spread lies?" Hammer growled.

I sputtered. "Because they claimed my father was evil, was corrupt. He made mistakes, absolutely." I thought of the ways he'd refused to listen to others, the way he'd always been so sure he was right, even when it was clear he wasn't, the way he retreated into himself the older I got. "But he wasn't as bad as they made him out to be. The false king and queen were two people who threw temper tantrums because they didn't like the way my father ruled. And they ultimately caused so much pain with their actions when they could've just talked to him."

Shadow raised an eyebrow. "Would he have listened?"

I sighed. Probably not. Still, having issues with a ruler didn't merit starting a war, being the cause of so much death.

I thought of my mother, who I barely remembered because of the false king and queen, because of the mountain dwellers. She lost her life far too soon, and I'd never be able to forgive them for being the cause.

"Hmm" was all Shadow said in response to my silence. She stretched her arms out, running her fingers through the water, but didn't say anything else in response to my claims. None of them did.

I sank deeper into the water, until only my eyes skimmed over the top. I hated this. Hated being here. But I'd keep playing their little game, because eventually, I'd win.

Chapter Nine

I tossed and turned in the bedroll, unable to get comfortable. The forest was silent, the sky above bright with stars that peeked through the canopies.

After all that time spent in prison, I should've been used to this. I huffed and flipped over to my other side. Looked like I wasn't going to be sleeping tonight. If Penn wanted me to train and become the skilled thief he needed, this was certainly not the way to do it. I'd be no use to anyone with a sore back and heavy eyes. But that was his problem to worry over, not mine.

I had plenty of my own.

I let out a groan of frustration. This was no use. I might as well get up and explore instead of laying here, uncomfortable and miserable. I stood, dusting the dirt and foliage from my pants and shirt. I needed to get a good idea of where I was, start mapping out this forest so that when the time came to escape, I'd be ready. I grabbed one of the lanterns that hung on a post just outside the little clearing. A chill ran through me as I walked out of the clearing and into the forest, still and silent.

I wandered aimlessly, but it was too dark to see anything of significance.

Maybe this wasn't the best idea.

It wasn't practical to try and map out a forest at night, but what choice did I have? I couldn't exactly walk around with a paper and quill during the day, asking for landmarks. That wouldn't raise any suspicions.

A branch cracked nearby on the forest floor, and I jumped, my heart galloping in my chest. Okay, this was definitely a bad idea. I just needed to return to the clearing and close my eyes and try to sleep. I turned to go back when I heard voices in the distance.

Male voices.

Something scurried along the ground, and I lifted my lantern, the light shining on a little mouse. That must've been what made the noise. Not a monster, just a critter. I could handle that. Especially if it meant finding out what someone else was doing out here in the middle of the night.

I steeled myself and followed the sound of the voices, using my lantern to keep me from running into any trees or tripping over stumps. Mostly. I did run into one tree, but that was because I was looking behind me at a screeching owl that had been perched on a branch.

The voices grew louder, and I crouched behind a few bushes, dimming the lantern light. I peeked over the top to see Penn and Wayfinder standing outside a white tent pitched in the middle of the forest. The same tent I'd woken up in after being brought here. Oh no, was this . . . Penn's tent? Had I slept in his bed? Maybe not. Maybe this was just a tent they used for mission planning and bantering and . . .

"I don't have time to argue about this," Penn said. "So tell me what is bothering you and then get out of my tent so I can get some sleep."

Oh, spirits below.

"We need a better plan," Wayfinder said. "She's not ready for this."

Even from here, I could see the way Penn's fists curled tight, could see the irritation in his tensed muscles. "That's why we're training her."

His bed. I'd slept in his bed. My skin touched the same places his skin touched. Heat prickled over my skin, and I gritted my teeth. *Focus. Focus, Liliath.*

"She's not a warrior. She's definitely not a thief." Wayfinder shook his head.

Penn's jaw tensed, and he stomped into the tent, not bothering to hold open the flap for Wayfinder.

Wayfinder sighed and followed him inside as Penn lit a candle, and I heard their voices again, this time muffled. I needed to get closer. I slowly stood, leaving the lantern behind and creeping toward the tent.

Their shadows stretched over the tent's walls. I crept as close as I dared and pressed my back against a tree, peering at them as they continued their discussion.

"Do you really think this is worth it?" Wayfinder asked, holding up an object. "The Huntsman is getting closer. You know he'll be here for her soon, and he won't spare the lives of anyone who gets in his way." I squinted, trying to make out what was in his hand. It had a rounded head, and he held onto the handle, raising it up.

Penn grabbed it and set it down on a table. "Careful," he hissed. "Do you know how hard it was to steal this from the queen?"

The queen of what? I couldn't help myself. I stepped away from the tree and closer to the tent. Maybe I could find an opening and peek through.

"I do," Wayfinder said. "This is the entire reason I had to escort Liliath to Mosswood Forest after you rescued her."

"I didn't rescue her," Penn said, voice quiet.

Well, at least we agreed on one thing. I stopped outside a corner of the tent, as close as I dared, but still couldn't see anything but their shadows from my vantage point.

"How did you steal the mirror from the queen, anyway?" Wayfinder asked. "You never did tell me."

My breath caught in my throat.

Mirror.

He stole that from my stepmother? Everyone knew about her mirror, some piece of dark magic she'd acquired after she betrayed my father. Betrayed me. No one was sure what the mirror did, exactly. Just that she kept it in her chambers, talking to it at all hours of the day. Rumors had swirled about what she might be using it for.

Driscoll, Jillian, and I had theorized for hours.

Maybe she just really loves looking at herself, Driscoll had said.

Jillian and I had both groaned at that, and the memory made me smile, then want to cry. I missed them so, so much.

In truth, other than idle gossip and using it as a topic to wile away the hours, I'd never cared much about the mirror. It didn't affect me, didn't matter in the scheme of things.

But if Penn stole it from her, it must be important. I couldn't imagine what he'd want with her mirror. Maybe he thought he could sell it. My anger flared. It was one thing to steal jewels and sell them. But to steal a piece of dark magic for coin, to be willing to make profit off something that could cause harm, that was just vile.

Dark magic was illegal, not just in Elwen, but in all five courts of Arathia. It was also dangerous, and in the wrong hands could spell disaster. My stepmother was a perfect example of that. I didn't know what kind of dark magic she'd dabbled in, but it was clear she'd used something sinister to aid her in usurping my father.

"Do you really think this is what's going to bring you happiness? You've been obsessing over this for years now." Wayfinder's voice interrupted my thoughts. "Come on, Boss. I know you're not that naive. You need to let this go."

"Enough." Penn's voice held a finality to it.

Happiness? I wasn't sure how that mirror could bring Penn happiness, or what he had planned for it. He'd gone to so much trouble to steal it—and me. Which meant it had to be important, somehow connected to whatever he wanted with me—and I needed to find out what.

Chapter Ten

Unable to sleep after that revelation, I wandered through the forest, finding that I didn't even need my lantern with the moon so bright and big in the sky.

My thoughts raced after everything I'd heard in that tent. Penn needed the mirror for something, something that Wayfinder sounded like he was against. Perhaps not everyone in the academy was just a blind follower like I'd thought. It's not like Penn listened, though. Not surprising, from what I knew about him.

I wondered if he knew the true power behind the mirror, knew what magic it held. He must have, to have gone to such great lengths to steal it. It couldn't have been easy to take the mirror, especially after he'd just rescued me.

Then I remembered the other part of what Wayfinder had said: that's why Penn rescued me and then handed me off, because he had to go back and steal that mirror.

None of this made sense, more questions arising and not enough answers to satisfy them. Maybe Shadow would know more about all of this. Even if she did, she probably wouldn't tell me.

"Didn't anyone ever teach you that it's rude to eavesdrop?"

I yelped and jumped about three feet off the forest floor. Heart hammering, I turned to see Penn leaning against a tree, holding the lantern I'd left behind.

He strode forward, stopping right in front of me, and I had to arch my neck to look up at him. Moonlight sliced across his face, illuminating the line of his strong jaw, the sharp angles of his cheekbones.

"What do you want?" I asked, a bite to my voice.

"I think the better question is what do you want?"

I glared at him, keeping my mouth closed.

"You're the one sneaking through my forest in the middle of the night, lurking outside my tent."

I raised my nose. "Your forest? I didn't realize you owned it. And if I had a proper bed to sleep in, I wouldn't have had to get up and go for a walk."

He raised the lantern, and its warm light washed across my face. "If you knew how to climb a rope, you'd have a bed to sleep in."

My fists curled at my sides. This man was infuriating.

"So did you learn anything of interest?" he asked.

I looked away, not sure what I should reveal. Then again, he knew I'd been eavesdropping, so there didn't seem much point in trying to hide it.

"I know you stole my stepmother's mirror. What were you thinking?"

He cocked a thick blond eyebrow.

"That mirror is dangerous."

"And how would you know that?"

"Because it belonged to my stepmother. And even in the prison cells, we heard rumors about it, about the darkness that ebbed from it."

He shrugged. "Well, sounds like you just know everything, then."

"Do not patronize me," I snapped.

"I wouldn't dare."

I threw up my arms. "You are an insufferable thief."

"Better than an insufferable princess."

I let out a frustrated cry, and he just stood there, stoic as ever. Nothing rattled this man, which of course only made me want to rise to the challenge more.

Forget it. Talking to him was a waste of my time. I stalked away.

"You made a lot of mistakes, you know," he said quietly, stopping me.

I slowly turned. "What mistakes?"

"Well, your shoes are far too loud." He nodded at the boots I wore. "You brought a lantern, which might as well be a beacon in this forest. You didn't keep to the shadows outside my tent, of which there are many to melt into."

He was coaching me on my shortcomings when it came to eavesdropping. Unbelievable.

I gritted my teeth. "Yes, apologies that I'm not an expert criminal."

He continued, as if I hadn't even spoken. "You also breathe shockingly loud. Is that a medical condition of some sort? You should really have a healer check that out."

My mouth dropped open and I shoved him. He barked out a laugh.

"How dare you speak to me like that. I am a—"

He cut me off. "I don't answer to you. No one does. Not here or in Elwen."

The words twisted deep in my gut. He was right. I was a princess in the past, but without a crown, without a court to rule over, what did that make me now? Worse, what would my people think of me if they could see their future queen training to become a thief?

No. I wouldn't let him get inside my head like this. That's what he wanted. Make me doubt myself, weaken me so I could be another little puppet for him.

"What's to happen to me?" I asked. "After I complete your little mission."

"*If*"—he emphasized the word in a way that made me want to punch him—"you complete the mission, then you're free."

I eyed him warily. "That's it? You'll just let me go?"

"I don't have much use for you after that." He tilted his head. "Are you going to try and take back the earth court?"

"I'm going to find my betrothed," I said. "And together we will fight my stepmother, and I will take my rightful place as queen of Elwen."

A look of surprise flashed across his face, gone as quick as it had come. "Jasper Farrar, of the fire court? You're still betrothed?"

"Yes. And he will not be pleased to hear the king of thieves kidnapped his bride to be."

"Actually, he'll probably thank me for taking you," Penn said. "Saved him from having to do it. If he was going to, that is."

I hated him. So very much. The arrogance, the smugness, the way he acted like I was nothing more than a tool to be used.

"I think I'll be going back now. I need to get some sleep, since I assume I'll be training again tomorrow."

Penn held out the lantern, and I took it from him, the light bright in my eyes.

"If you could just—" I started, then looked up, but Penn had disappeared, melted into the shadows. King of thieves, indeed. I stalked back to the camp, darkness still enveloping the forest. I could get a few hours of sleep, if I was lucky. I hung the lantern back on its post, then lay on the hard, cold ground.

One thing was certain: before I escaped, I needed to get into that tent and find the mirror. It could be the key to eventually defeating my stepmother. And that meant I was going to have to steal from the king of thieves.

Chapter Eleven

A hand gripped my arm, and I shot up, eyes wild, heart beating hard in my chest. It took a minute for me to remember where I was and who I was with.

I shook my head, eyes heavy and crusty with sleep.

"Time to wake up, Princess," a gruff voice said.

I looked at the hand clamped tight around my arm, and my gaze trailed up to the face: Hammer.

His bright red hair was wild and curly, freckles stark on his pale skin. My heart sank. So Shadow wouldn't be training me today, then? As rough as our session was yesterday, I had a feeling I'd prefer it over whatever this man had planned for me.

Hammer stood shorter than me, but he was almost twice as wide, his chest broad, muscles thick, and even if he was missing an arm, I doubted it mattered. He looked fierce enough that nothing would hold him back.

"Let's go." Without another word, he dropped my arm and stomped away.

Great. This was going to be just delightful.

I stood and followed him. "Where are we going?"

He didn't answer as we wove through the trees of the forest, the early morning sun shining down and filtering through the leaves. I raised my face, letting the light wrap around me like a cocoon. I wasn't sure I'd ever get used to this again after spending so long in the dark. Squirrels ran across the forest floor, scurrying up trees and foraging for nuts nestled in the leaves. There was so much life here, so much vibrancy. I raised my hand to lower a branch for one of the squirrels to jump onto, and a pang struck my chest when I remembered I didn't have my magic anymore.

"This ain't a vacation, princess," Hammer said, snapping me from my wallowing.

He leaned against a tree, glaring at me, and I stomped toward him.

"Believe me, I know that." I shoved past him. "Let's get this torture session over with."

He continued on his way, and soon we came to a marsh, big round lily pads floating on the surface of the murky water. I swallowed, already not liking wherever this was going.

"It's not torture," Hammer said quietly from next to me.

I looked at him. "What?"

"This training is a gift. Yer learning skills to survive." He gestured to his missing arm. "Lost this on my first mission. I was up in the sky court, stealing valuable healing powders from some noble when a guard caught me. I wasn't prepared, hadn't listened well enough in these lessons, thought I already knew everything. She cut my arm clean off, and I'd have bled out in that tower if Penn hadn't come to rescue me, fought off the guard, and got me the bloody earth out of there. Didn't get the powders we needed, but Penn never scolded me, never reprimanded me. He allowed me time to heal, and then told me we needed to train, that I needed to re-learn how to fight. So I did. That's why we take this seriously. Because it's life and death."

I wanted to shout that I didn't need this training because I'd be escaping as soon as I figured a way out, but I knew this training would be valuable to me. Still, I felt stubborn and defiant, felt the need to point out that Hammer wouldn't have gotten injured if he hadn't been trying to steal something in the first place.

"I'm learning how to be a criminal," I retorted. "I've survived just fine without knowing how to sneak up on someone or disappear into the shadows."

He scoffed. "Yes, in your fancy tower, surrounded by guards."

I swallowed, anger rising. "Because I'm a princess. I've never needed to know how to do any of this. And it's not okay to use these skills to engage in illegal activity."

"These skills saved my life, everyone's lives in this place. We're not the bad guys. We help people."

Shadow had said something similar, yet no one seemed to elaborate on what exactly made them good. Because they couldn't justify their actions, no matter how much they wanted to.

It was my turn to scoff. "Right. Whatever you say." I gestured to the water. "So what am I doing today? Are you going to shove me under water and see how long I can hold my breath? Do I need to wrestle an alligator, perhaps? Oh"—I feigned excitement—"you know what would be really fun? If I could catch a poisonous snake and swallow its venom."

Hammer didn't look amused, and I realized goading him might not be smart given he had all the power in this situation. He just grunted and walked toward a tree.

"I'll be back. Don't move."

However much I hated this, I needed to pay attention, to put effort into these lessons. Especially now that I didn't just need to escape this place—I needed to escape with the mirror.

I'd thought about it late into the night. If I could get that mirror, maybe I could use it to bargain with my stepmother, to save the earth court. It was a shoddy plan, but at this moment, it was all I had.

"Oye, look out!"

My head snapped up, and Hammer sat in a branch high above, unwinding a thick vine from the tree. It swung like a pendulum into my head, and I rubbed at the spot it hit. "What am I supposed to do with this?"

"You're going to swing across this marsh, get to the other side, then you're going to come back by jumping on the lily pads."

I gaped up at him. "Do you all actually learn to do this? Why not just use your magic?"

He tugged at his beard. "Have you ever tried to use earth magic up in the frozen tundra of Fyriad, or deep in the fiery mountains of Gilraeth?"

I shook my head. I used magic in other courts but never to an extent where I'd have to be worried about it failing me. I used it for silly things, like growing a flower or sprouting a plant, not trying to get out of an illegal situation.

"Then you wouldn't know that our earth magic isn't reliable in other courts. We can use it, but not to its full extent. We all had to train and learn how to be the best thieves we can be without our magic. Everything we do during our training sessions has to be without magic."

I sighed, staring at the vine hanging in front of me. Well, at least I wasn't wrestling an alligator, but even so, this was not going to be pleasant. Hammer dropped down from the branch and landed lightly on his feet, which was surprising for how hefty he looked.

He handed the vine to me. "You need to get some upper body strength."

"Yes, so I've heard."

"So you're not going to do that without some practice," he gritted out.

I clasped my hands around the vine. "I don't know if I can climb it."

"You don't have to. Just hold onto it, and that'll be enough. Everyone has to start somewhere."

I blew out a breath. "Okay."

He crouched to the ground. "The key is to get good momentum. Use yer body weight to swing the vine forward."

I nodded and gripped the vine, then used my feet to launch it forward, lifting my legs and wrapping them around the bottom. A bug flew in my face, and I let out a squeak, my hands slipping as I fell into the marsh.

The water enveloped me, cold and suffocating. I sucked in a lungful, kicking wildly, unable to see what direction I needed to swim to get to the surface. Something slick slithered past me, and I let out a yell underwater before one hand gripped me and yanked me out.

I spluttered, falling to the ground and coughing up brown water. "Oh, yuck," I said, spitting out a wad of something that, quite frankly, I did not want to investigate further.

"Again," Hammer said, not even reacting to the fact that I'd almost drowned.

I glared at him and snatched the vine away, my hands now slippery, my clothes weighed down with water. "I need to dry these on something."

Hammer shook his head. "You need to be prepared for every situation."

"Right. When I'm thieving?" I asked, the word dripping off my tongue like poison.

"You could be wet, covered in slime, on fire." He ticked off his fingers.

Well, I didn't like any of those options, but I understood the point.

"Fine," I grumbled, once again launching myself from the ground and across the marsh.

And, once again, I fell. Hammer made me do it again and again and again, until I grew so fed up with the whole thing I yanked him into the water and used the opportunity to take a little break, sinking onto the ground and leaning against a tree while he flailed.

When he emerged, beard and hair sopping, I could practically see the fire in his eyes. "Yer going to pay for that."

"I don't even care. I just got a nice one-minute break." I studied my dirt-caked nails. "Worth it."

"Again," he said, voice hard as stone.

I tried to remind myself that this was important. If I was going to steal that mirror and escape from these people, I had to take this seriously. As much as I loathed all of this, I'd need every one of these skills to get out of here and defeat my stepmother.

Hammer stood over me, his eyes blazing as water dripped from the end of his beard. "This time, we're doing things a little different."

"What do you mean?" Sweat dotted my brow. Maybe throwing him in the marsh hadn't been such a good idea.

He pointed at the lily pads. "You're going to jump to the other side, then I'll swing the vine to you, and you'll have to use it to get back over here."

"But I can't swing!" I said. "I'll fall right away and have to swim the entire length of the marsh." I looked to the other side, which suddenly seemed very far away.

Hammer just stood there, satisfaction gleaming in his brown eyes. Yes, throwing him in had definitely been a mistake.

"Fine," I said and approached the marsh. "Any tips?"

"Oh, I think you can figure this one out by yerself," he growled.

Of course I could. I didn't know much about jumping long distances. Or jumping at all, really.

I had nothing to lose at this point. I'd already fallen in so many times, what did it matter? I bent my legs, reared my arms back, and launched myself forward. My feet hit the lily pad, and I stumbled down onto my knees, momentarily frozen. I stared at the green surface under me, hardly able to believe it. I'd done it. I'd jumped.

I let out a shriek and stood, turning to face Hammer, whose eyes were wide, like he couldn't believe it either.

"Did you see that?" I asked.

He gave me an unimpressed look. "Aye."

"I did it!" I pumped my fist in the air and jumped in excitement. "I did it. I did it. I did it—"

My feet slipped out from under me, the lily pad wobbling. I lost my balance and fell with a splat into the water. When I emerged, Hammer was doubled over, shoulders shaking, tears streaming down his face.

Tears of laughter. Unbelievable.

Something slithered by me in the water, and I shrieked and swam out as fast as possible—which wasn't very fast—hair dripping and full of moss, mud coating my arms and trousers.

He clutched his belly and laughed even harder upon seeing me emerge from the marsh.

"I'm glad this is so amusing to you." I swiped a finger across my face. A glop of sticky mud fell to the ground.

Hammer pointed at my forehead. "I think you missed a spot," he said through gasps of laughter.

I pursed my lips and crossed my arms, waiting for Hammer to finish. And waiting. And waiting. He finally straightened, wiping away the tears.

"Oh, I haven't had a good laugh like that in a while." He clapped a hand to my shoulder. "Well done."

He sounded . . . impressed.

"I'm not training to be a jester," I said with a bite to my voice. "So I don't know exactly what I did well."

"Ah, sometimes we need a good laugh to lighten the dark that surrounds us. Now let's go again."

I was afraid he was going to say that.

My arms, legs, and back ached. Sweat beaded my brow and dripped down over my nose. At this point, mud covered my entire body, random twigs and leaves stuck in my hair.

"Alright, Princess Liliath, you can do this," Hammer said from behind me.

We'd been at this for hours, and I had finally made it to the fifth lily pad. One more to go, and I would cross to the other side. I held my arms out to balance myself. The round green plant under my feet undulated in the water, making me stumble. I caught myself and straightened, hearing Hammer swear from behind me.

"Come on, Princess. Show me what you got," he said.

A snake slithered through the murky water beside me, its long body languid and fluid. I could appreciate the creature from afar, but I had no interest in joining it. I took a deep breath, shaking out my hands. Despite everything, I found myself wanting this, wanting to prove myself to Hammer. He'd been a surprisingly good teacher, warming up to me the more we worked together.

"Good," a male voice said. "She's made more progress than I expected."

My head twisted around, and there stood the king of thieves next to Hammer.

"What are you doing—" I started but got cut off when the lily pad dipped down, and I lost my footing, falling face first into the water with a hard splat.

The snake darted away. Not even the reptiles wanted to be near me. I surfaced for air, coming face-to-face with a toad perched on the edge of the lily pad.

"Well, maybe not as much progress as I'd hoped," Penn said.

I glowered at him as I waded through the water and stepped out. I wrung my shirt out. Right over Penn's shoes. The brown water sloshed over his leather boots, and he just smirked.

"That's okay." He kept hold of my gaze. "Unlike some of us, I'm not afraid to get a little dirty."

The way he said those words made me swallow, and warmth spread through my belly.

Penn looked from Hammer and back to me. "You know, I just thought of the perfect nickname for you."

"I am a princess. We don't have nicknames." I jabbed him in his chest and resisted the urge to wince when my finger bent back. Why was his chest like a freaking wall of stone? "You will address me by my title."

He wagged his finger at me. "I thought we talked about that. You're not technically a princess anymore." He stroked his stubbled chin. "What do you think about Lilypad?"

My mouth dropped open. "For my nickname? No, absolutely not. I hate it—"

He held up a hand. "I was talking to him."

Hammer shuffled, averting his eyes to avoid my glower. "Come on, Boss, she is technically a princess, and it wouldn't feel right to—"

"Perfect," Penn said. "Lilypad it is." With that, he stalked away.

Hammer turned to me. "You did good today, Princess."

I stared after Penn. "Is he seriously going to call me that?"

Hammer cocked a bushy red eyebrow. "It's not so bad."

"You're Hammer." I ticked off my fingers. "Then there's Shadow, Lightning, Arrow. And I get to be Lilypad?"

It was offensive, a reminder of my failures. The king of thieves was toying with me, laughing at me. My hands curled into fists. I would be the one laughing after I stole that mirror and escaped right out from under his nose.

Chapter Twelve

After two hours soaking in the warm baths, I still couldn't get all the grime out of my tangled hair. I let out a frustrated groan at the knotted mess.

"Need some help, Princess?"

I looked up to see Shadow standing at the edge of the bath.

"I can't get my hair untangled." I lifted a huge knot to show her.

She crouched down. "Get dressed. I have an idea."

My clothes lay on a rock, a clean pair that Wayfinder had gotten for me. After Shadow retreated back into the forest, I got out and dressed quickly, following into the trees after her. A cool breeze sifted through the air, and goosebumps rose up on my arms.

"That was quick."

My hand flew to my heart. "Blood and earth! You scared me!"

Shadow grinned, then started walking. "C'mon."

"Where are we going?" I trailed after her.

"Into town. I know someone who can help fix your hair."

"Really?" I patted at my knotted hair, grateful there were no mirrors anywhere, other than the one Penn stole, of course.

Soon enough, the thick foliage of leaves and branches parted, and my breath caught in my throat. In front of me was a hill with a dirt road lined by shops. Wooden buildings, some one story, others two, or even three. Wooden signs hung from the roof ledges, each one carved with different names. Apothecary, Tailor, Tavern, Blacksmith, Teller, and so many more. It reminded me of Elwen. Our streets were a little nicer, paved with stones, our shops painted bright colors. But still. This was . . . it looked like it was thriving. A pang shot through my chest at that. While the earth court was withering away to nothing, this place was booming with business and opportunity. It didn't seem fair.

"Is Elwen similar to this?" Shadow asked from beside me, as if she could read my mind. "I don't remember it very well since I was so young when I came to Mosswood Forest."

"Bigger," I said. "We have many villages, all of them with their own healers, weapon makers, dressmakers, restaurants. But in the center of the earth court, near my castle, we have a huge market, full of every kind of shop or store you could need. Tea, silk, ceramics, slippers—anything you want, you can find there."

"Sounds nice," she said as we walked up the hill.

"It is. Was," I corrected myself. "Now I don't know what life is like in Elwen for my people. I don't know if there's any kind of order or law. I doubt it."

She pointed. "It's right over there."

"What is?"

She tugged at one of her golden hoop earrings. "Where I'm taking you." She jogged across the street to a small one-story shop and led me inside. A few chairs sat in the little shop, wooden shelves on the wall lined with glass vials, tinctures I didn't recognize filling them.

"What have we here?" a woman said, standing next to one of the chairs.

My eyes widened. I recognized her. She was one of the thieves. Long red hair cascaded to her curvy waist. It reminded me of Jillian's hair, except this woman's was wavy instead of curly.

"Aren't you . . . ?"

"Arrow." She held a pair of scissors and snipped them in the air. "Never miss a shot."

"And you also cut hair?" I asked, shooting an unsure glance at Shadow. I didn't know if I trusted an archer with my hair. Though, at this point, I doubted it could get much worse.

Arrow patted a chair in front of her. "Yes, well, it turns out I don't just have a talent for thieving."

I sat in the chair, and she stuck her fingers in my knotted hair.

"This is a mess."

I twisted in my seat. "So what do you do when you have to go on a mission? Just shut down?"

She grabbed my head and wrenched it forward. "Look straight ahead. I have multiple apprentices who take over for me."

A cool mist of water sprayed across my hair, then I felt Arrow massaging some kind of paste into my strands.

"So people can just be whatever they want here?" I asked. "If you want to cut hair you just cut hair? Where do you get the money, the materials?"

Shadow and Arrow looked at each other.

"Believe it or not, we are civilized," Arrow said. "And we have our ways."

Shadow snorted. "You act like it's a bad thing we can choose what we want out of our lives."

I stared straight ahead, afraid that if I moved an inch, I'd get my neck twisted again. "Well, what if everyone wants to be a healer or a farmer?"

"People have different talents, different interests, and passions. We use that to our advantage. We don't force anyone to do anything they wouldn't want to," Arrow said, and I heard what she wasn't saying.

Not like you do in Elwen. No one was forced to do anything in Elwen, but most often, people followed in the footsteps of their parents. If their father was a farmer, they took over the farm. It was practical, ensured that everyone had a place in our society.

"When you turn fifteen, you start your apprenticeships," Shadow said. "Each month of your next year is focused on doing many different types of work. That way, you can figure out where your interests lie."

"And did you apprentice to be a thief?"

Arrow yanked on my hair.

"Ow." I brought a hand up to my head.

"Sorry," she said in a sickly sweet voice, her red-painted lips forming into a pout.

"We all came to the academy in different ways," Shadow said, not elaborating. "Penn found each of us, helped us in a time of need."

I doubted that. I couldn't imagine the king of thieves helping anyone but himself. He'd probably manipulated all of them, made them think he was some hero saving them, when really he was brainwashing them. It was like they were in a cult.

"And everyone is just okay with that here?" I gestured out the window to the town. "They're okay knowing that they have criminals, thieves, just walking among them?" I realized my words sounded harsh. "No offense," I added.

"We've earned our keep," Shadow said with a smirk. "We bring many items of interest to Mosswood Forest."

Well, I had no idea what the hell that meant, but I supposed after everything I'd heard of the mountain dwellers it didn't surprise me. My father had always said they cared little for the law, for any kind of justice system. Though this town surprised me. I'd always pictured the people here living in bushes or caves, nomads with no structure or organization to their lives. This all felt very organized, like they had actual systems in place.

"Who is in charge here?" I glanced around, like at any minute the person who ran this town might step out of the shadows. "After the false king and queen died, who took over?"

"We have a council who make decisions," Shadow said. "They're the ones who rule over us and enforce the law. And we often have town halls where the people can voice their opinions."

That sounded similar to how I'd always thought I would rule. I saw the stress placed on my father by him insisting on doing it all. I'd often told him it would be wise to have a council of people to help him, but he wouldn't listen, and it had frustrated me to no end. I saw all the ways he failed our people time and time again because of his stubbornness, and I resolved to learn from his mistakes.

"Okay, we're finished," Arrow said.

I realized I hadn't even been paying attention as she had snipped away at my hair, the conversation distracting me. Now my stomach twisted in anticipation. She grabbed a small mirror and held it up in front of my face, and I gasped in horror.

"My hair!"

I tugged at it, my black strands now hanging right above my shoulders. "Blood and earth, what did you do?"

"Do you not like it?" Arrow asked, green eyes wide and innocent.

I whirled in my chair. "No, I do not like it. I barely have any hair left. I look like . . ."

Someone else.

Shadow cocked her head. "I think it actually suits you quite well." She grabbed the mirror from me and held it up, and I tried not to flinch back from my reflection. I barely recognized myself, my face so gaunt, my skin so pale, and my hair now so much shorter than it had been before. I ran my fingers through it. At least it had regained some of its sheen, the hair thick and healthy again. It was just so much shorter than I'd ever worn it.

"I never knew what you looked like with your long hair." Shadow gestured. "You know, before it got all tangled and knotted. But I imagine it served as a good mask."

"A mask?" I had no idea what she was getting at.

"Something you could hide behind. Everyone would notice your beautiful hair and beautiful clothes and they never actually saw you."

That took me aback.

"But now, you have nothing to hide behind, Princess." Shadow smiled. "And I have a feeling you're going to shine."

She was trying to make me feel better, but it didn't work. This was a disaster.

"C'mon," Shadow said.

"Why," I asked warily, afraid she was going to surprise me with a training session. After the day I'd had with Hammer, I'd probably collapse if forced to do any kind of physical activity.

"You look like you need a drink," she responded. "And, lucky for you, I know just where we can go."

Chapter Thirteen

We entered the busy tavern, long wooden tables and chairs filling the space. A bar sat to the right of the entrance, a barmaid sliding tankards of ale to thirsty patrons.

"No," I said to Shadow. "I drink wine. If there's a feast. And only a few sips, at most."

"Princess," Shadow said, "trust me when I say you more than anyone in this room need some alcohol."

She strode toward the bar, and I had no choice but to follow, pushing past both men and women who stared at me. I patted my short hair as Shadow leaned on the bar top and ordered us two mugs of ale.

Maybe she was right. I was stuck somewhere in Mosswood Forest, kidnapped by the king of thieves, being forced to train to become a thief. At this point, drinking ale would be the least offensive thing I'd done.

I took the tankard. Foamy amber liquid sloshed over the side and splattered to the scuffed wooden floor, sticky with alcohol. Shadow led me to one of the tables, and I noticed many of the academy members were there, including Hammer, Arrow, and Wayfinder, who was currently cozied up to a man I assumed must be his boyfriend, neither of them paying any attention to the rest of us.

"Love the hair," Arrow said, blowing me a kiss.

I shot her a fake smile and plopped down, back straight and hands folded in my lap as I surveyed the room. Chandeliers that looked like they were made from antler horns hung from the ceilings, candles burning bright and lighting the space. Chatter filled the tavern, a few men at a nearby table roaring with laughter, others playing cards, and what looked like two lovers twined together in the corner. It made me miss Jasper.

"I think it suits you," Charming said, sending me a wink from across the table, his skin so smooth and pale, not a mark or blemish on him.

I leaned forward, taking another sip of my drink. "And how did you earn your nickname?"

I was starting to enjoy hearing these stories of how the thieves got their names. Hammer's had come from when he punched a wall of ice in the frost court and broke it clean in half, stunning the frost person he was fighting so much the poor guy actually fainted.

"Because every woman he meets falls in love with him," Hammer said, slapping Charming on the back. "He woos 'em and then disappears, leaving behind broken hearts and empty vaults."

The table roared with laughter at that.

"That's awful," I sputtered.

It also made a lot of sense. I'd always heard the king of thieves was dashing, that women often threw themselves at his feet. I couldn't imagine Penn wooing anyone, but Charming? I could absolutely see how he'd earned that reputation. Charming seemed to take no offense at what I'd said, now regaling the table of thieves with a story about a time he charmed a noble woman who found out his identity and didn't even care, giving him her jewels so that he didn't even have to steal them. I just rolled my eyes when he finished, everyone else laughing.

Shadow elbowed me. "Relax. You're so stiff. Do you need another trip to the hot springs?"

I cleared my throat, attempting to slouch, but I couldn't relax in this place, surrounded by these thieves.

"Good, you're all here," Penn said from behind me.

Everyone quieted, eyes wide as they took Penn in.

"Boss." Hammer nodded.

"Hi, Penn." Arrow wiggled her fingers.

Penn brought out a few scrolls and threw them on the table. "We have some things to discuss about the Huntsman. Word is he's scouring the entire court for her. It won't be long before he figures out we took her. We need to send decoys, something to throw off his scent."

I stilled at his words. Bloody earth, maybe I needed a drink after all.

But everyone just booed, and I looked around, confused at what was happening.

"Oh no," a woman with curly brown hair said. "We're not working right now. This is our time. We can talk about the Huntsman tomorrow morning. One night off isn't going to hurt anything."

Shadow pointed at the scrolls on the table. "Brains is right. You can take those right back to your tent, Boss."

Now this I could get behind. I wanted to know more about the Huntsman and his location, but it also delighted me far too much that no one was listening to Penn. His jaw locked as he stared at everyone, but no one touched the scrolls he'd thrown down. Finally, he gathered them up and dropped down next to me, grumbling about his disobedient thieves. Everyone erupted in cheers and clinked their mugs together, while Penn just shook his head.

"The Boss rarely comes out with us," Shadow whispered. "I wonder what could've brought him out tonight." She stared at me like she knew exactly what had beckoned him, and I looked away.

"It sounds like he came to force you all to work."

"Sure, work."

I opened my mouth to make a retort, but she was now engaged in a heated discussion with another member of the academy, her gestures wild as they argued about who would win in a game of darts. No one to rescue me from the man sitting next to me.

I was trapped next to the king of thieves. I took a deep gulp of my ale as he lifted his satchel over his head and placed it next to him on the bench.

"I'm glad you decided to cut your hair so that it no longer resembles a nest," Penn said. "You were far too noticeable."

"I did not cut my hair." I took a sip of my ale. "Arrow did."

Penn looked at Arrow, who gave a wave from across the table.

I glowered at my drink. "And it seems she's very pleased with herself."

She took a sip from her mug. "You look like a different person."

That was exactly the problem.

Penn reached over and brushed a lock of hair out of my eyes. "It suits you."

A shiver ran down my spine at the unexpected contact. He'd done the same thing the night I kissed him, and it burned a trail down my skin. He stared at me, his eyes dancing with amusement. He was laughing at me. Playing some sort of game that I wanted no part in.

"Luckily, hair grows back." I lifted the tankard, gulping the ale down. Shadow was right. If anyone needed to get drunk, it was me.

"Slow down, Lilypad," Penn warned.

"I told you not to call me that." I slammed down my mug, the table shaking underneath.

"But it's just so perfect." Penn took a sip of his own drink, his Adam's apple bobbing as he tipped his head back. Suddenly I wondered what his hair would look like down, framing his face, if it would bring out the green in his eyes, if it would brush against that strong jaw—

"There you go, staring again."

I straightened, looking away. "I'm not staring. And don't tell me what to do," I snapped. "I can drink however much I'd like."

He spread his hands out. "By all means, then."

However much it took to forget this miserable existence. I raised a finger in the air, and Penn's eyes traveled up the length of my arm.

"What are you doing?" he asked.

"Signaling for another drink."

His lips quirked. "There's no servants here, Lilypad. If you want a drink, you'll have to get it for yourself. At the bar."

"I'll get it." Hammer stood from across me, tugging at his long red beard. "You earned a drink after how hard you worked today."

"Well, while you're up . . ." Charming nodded his head toward the bar, and Hammer grumbled.

"Oh, one for me too," the woman with the brown curly hair said. Brains, I think, was her nickname.

Hammer's face turned red. "I was going to get one for the lady, not for the whole damn table."

"Thank you," Charming called as Hammer stomped away.

I turned on the bench, facing outward, studying a painting that hung on the wall. I knew what it was: the false king and queen leading their people from Elwen to Mosswood Forest, deciding to break away from the earth court and fracture it in half. I'd only been four years old and hardly remembered the war that followed as the mountain dwellers fought Elwen for their independence. In the painting, the false king and queen glowed with a light, both holding torches as they entered the forest, like heroes saving their people instead of the defectors they were.

"Do you know much about the Great War?"

I swallowed at the feel of Penn's breath tickling my ear, then shifted further away from him. He'd turned as well, now facing the painting with me.

"Yes," I said. "My tutors taught me everything, and whatever I didn't learn from them, I learned from our personal libraries, from scrolls that historians kept."

"Then why do you look so confused right now?" He crossed his muscled arms.

I quickly schooled my features. "I'm not confused." I refused to admit any kind of weakness to him, though he was right. In between the false king and queen was a little boy who held onto both their hands. I'd never heard they had a son, and I wondered if he died with them when they were killed toward the end of the war, and maybe that's why he'd never been mentioned in the history books or by my tutors.

"I'll never understand how the false king and queen could have broken away from Elwen like they did," I said. "They caused so much pain, so much destruction, with their decision."

"Sometimes, rulers have to make hard choices," Penn said. "But they did what they thought was best."

My jaw clenched at his words. "They did it because they wanted power, because they were selfish."

Penn snorted but stayed silent.

"I didn't know they had a son," I admitted. "That was never mentioned in any of the books I read or by any of my tutors."

"Maybe they didn't think he was worth mentioning," Penn said.

"Why?" I asked, my curiosity getting the better of me.

"Like his parents, he was flung into the forest by trees along the Elwen border, every bone in their bodies broken and mangled by the attack."

I stared at the little boy, my heart splintering.

"That's sad," I said. "He didn't deserve to die like that."

I felt Penn's stare and turned. "Yes?" I asked, feeling far too exposed.

"You're sad over the death of a mountain dweller?"

I bristled at that. "He was a child. I'm not a monster. I know there were many innocent people who died in that war. People who were misguided, lied to by the false king and queen. None of them deserved to lose their lives. None of them deserved to be cut off from Elwen after the border was closed."

After the mountain dwellers used their magic to erect the border, we lost so many wonderful medicines, foods, and other resources, but they suffered, too, their people trapped in Mosswood Forest, unable to come back to Elwen, unable to go anywhere since the forest was bordered by Elwen—and the Deadlands.

Once upon a time, the Deadlands had been called Shiraeth, the star court, its people powerful wielders of star, sun, and moon magic, but they'd been wiped from existence sixty years ago, and their court dissolved into chaos and ruin, a place for criminals, monsters, and darkness. The Deadlands was not a place anyone visited on purpose, only the most desperate using it as a shortcut from Mosswood Forest up to Fyriad, the frost court. And those that did try to cut through the Deadlands were usually never heard from again. I'd never understood why the mountain dwellers would close themselves off like that, how they could be so desperate to trap their people and separate from Elwen that they'd chosen to erect the wall of vines across the border like that. It was monstrous, and it hurt everyone involved.

I turned to say something snarky to Penn, only to find him studying me, a look I didn't recognize on his face. Memories of those lips pressed to mine flashed in my mind, and warmth flooded my belly as I thought about the way his arms had wound around me, the way I'd fit so snugly against his huge body.

I swallowed, unable to break whatever hold he had on me. My gaze traveled to his lips, the slightest quirk to them.

"Yer ale, princess."

The words snapped me from my thoughts, and Hammer stood before me, holding out a mug of ale. I nodded my head in thanks, accepting the glass and bringing it to my lips.

"Penn!" Arrow fell into his lap, roping her arms around his neck and pressing her breasts into his chest. Her red hair fell past her shoulders, hanging in perfect waves around her waist, and she made a pouty face at him. "We haven't gotten to spend nearly enough time together lately."

My face flushed, and I looked away. I couldn't believe I'd been so blatantly staring at his lips like that, thinking about our kiss. I needed to thank Arrow at some point for throwing herself at him and throwing me back into reality. And my reality did not involve kissing Penn Vanderbilt ever again.

<h1 style="text-align:center;">Chapter Fourteen</h1>

"Just a little farther," I said, stretching my hand up and gripping the vine tight.

"She is really drunk," Shadow said from behind me, and I ignored her.

"Are we placing bets on how long it takes her to make it to the top?" Charming asked.

"She's got grit," Hammer growled. "I'll bet she makes it."

"She's also drunk off her ass," Shadow said. "I'll take that bet."

I swayed on my feet, and my vision blurred as my fingers slipped from the vine, and I crashed to the ground, barely feeling the impact. In fact, I didn't feel anything at all. This was fantastic. Why hadn't I drank more often at the castle? I hiccupped. I supposed I didn't want my people to see me like that, to see their future queen unhinged in any way. My father often got drunk at our feasts and would end up a mess, blubbering over my mother, over the mountain dwellers, over anything and everything. I hated seeing him that way and vowed I would never let myself go like that. But I had to admit, letting myself go was nice. I felt less tethered, less rigid.

Tonight, I refused to sleep on the ground again. I was going to climb this vine and fall asleep in a real bed, and then watch Penn's shocked reaction. I could just imagine him standing on the forest floor, looking

up at me, those blonde eyebrows raised in surprise. Arrow would probably be draped around him. She'd practically given him a lap dance at
the tavern. Not that it was any of my concern. I couldn't care less. She
could have him.

I gritted my teeth and heaved myself up, hands closing tight around
the vine, legs lifting.

Soft, warm bed.

Soft, warm bed.

Soft, warm bed.

I repeated the words like a mantra in my head as my hands lifted one
over the other.

"Well, shit," Arrow drawled from below. "Shadow, you're about to
lose some of that shiny gold coin you got on your last job."

"Told you she could do it," Hammer said, his voice triumphant.

"It's the alcohol," Shadow said. "Listen, I believe in my girl. She's
got grit and determination and a lot of attitude. But she can't just magically learn to climb a vine in a day."

"A bet is a bet," Hammer said.

"What in the fuck is going on?" I looked down to see Penn striding
into the clearing. "What is she doing?" he demanded.

His voice sounded irritated. Good. Now he knew how I felt anytime
he was nearby.

"Trying to sleep in a bed tonight, if I had to make a guess," Shadow
said.

"And you are actually letting her climb?" Penn snapped. "She's
drunker than a sailor with a ship full of rum."

"And what does that have to do with anything?" I called down to
him. "Are you that much of an ass that you just don't want to see me
succeed?"

He squeezed his eyes shut and massaged his temples. "No, I don't
want to see you get—"

A gust of wind blew through the clearing, jarring me and causing
my hands to slip from the vine. I let out a scream as I fell toward the
ground, my hands grappling, reaching, for anything. I tugged at that line
of magic inside of me, flicking my hand to direct a branch to grab me,
before remembering I didn't have my powers. Likely would never have
them again.

I squeezed my eyes shut and braced for impact, but it never came. Instead of hitting the ground, I landed in strong, sure arms. I hated that I knew exactly whose arms I lay in, whose body I was cradled against, that I'd somehow memorized the contours of it.

"Told you," Shadow said gleefully, and I heard Hammer grunt. "Cough up the coin."

Charming let out a laugh.

"Everyone, bed. Now," Penn's commanding voice said, and I heard muttering and shuffling, then silence.

When I finally opened my eyes, everyone was gone, presumably up in their tree huts happily sleeping away. I glared at Penn and pushed myself out of his arms, falling to the ground, a cloud of dust rising up in front of me.

"Why did you do that?" I demanded.

He sighed. "Bloody earth. You're slurring. You must've drank more than I realized."

I stood on shaky legs and pointed a finger into his chest. "You distracted me."

He rolled his eyes. "Yes, I'm the reason you didn't make it up the vine."

"I was almost to the top!" I shouted.

Birds burst from the branches of a nearby tree, my words echoing around us.

"You were barely halfway up, Lilypad."

"Do not call me that," I said, shoving him, anger rushing through my words.

I wanted a bed. I wanted my friends. I wanted Jasper. I wanted my magic. I wanted so many things that I couldn't have, and this man was standing in my way of getting it all back.

He barely moved, so I shoved him again.

"You don't want to do this," he said, reaching up faster than I could register and grabbing my arm.

Tears sprang to my eyes. I wouldn't let him see me cry. He'd probably laugh at me, and then I would most definitely murder him, and then I'd get sent to the dungeons, or whatever their twisted version of dungeons was here. Probably some cage hanging from a tree.

"We do not have cages hanging from trees," Penn said.

I wrenched my hand from his. Had I just said all of that out loud? I hated this. I hated everything. I just shook my head and backed away, then turned and ran, stumbling through the dark forest. Clouds covered the moon tonight, but I didn't care. Maybe this forest would swallow me up and spit me out somewhere far from here, and then I'd find my way to Jasper on my own. Branches scratched at my face, and leaves crunched under my boots, and still I ran. Tears blurred my vision, and I swiped at them. I was sick of crying. I'd cried more here than I had in my entire life, mourning everything I'd lost. I didn't want to mourn anymore. I just wanted to live.

Yellow eyes peeked from the stretches of darkness between the trees, and I thought I heard the distant hoot of an owl, and possibly the growl of something more sinister. But still, I ran.

I ran until my legs wouldn't carry me any longer, and I could just make out the faint outline of a cave, right as lightning flashed in the sky above and rain began pattering down. No, it wasn't a cave. I walked closer. It was an enormous tree, bigger than any I'd seen before, hollowed out with a cozy shelter that looked to be the size of a small house. Rain splattered the ground. It was gentle at first, then pounded down harder. I ran into the shelter and sank down against the cold, hard ground, shivering.

My head pounded, and my stomach lurched. I leaned out of the shelter and vomited. My throat burned, and I wiped my mouth, the rain coming down even harder now.

I took a shuddering breath, then lay down and curled into myself, my eyes closing as I drifted off to sleep.

Chapter Fifteen

Warmth enveloped me. A glorious, all-consuming heat that made me want to snuggle in and never wake up. I guess technically I was awake, but my eyes were still closed, and I was going to keep it that way for as long as possible because this might as well have been paradise.

The lulling sound of a crackling fire drifted to my ears, and I tried to remember the last time I'd woken up feeling so good. What had happened last night? Flashes of the tavern, the ale, me running away swept through my mind. Wait a minute. I remembered stumbling into the shelter of a tree, a dark one with a cold, hard ground . . .

My eyes popped open, and my gaze traveled down to the large hand resting on my stomach, that red sparkling ring catching bits of light that filtered into the cave. Strong arms wrapped around me, thick with muscle and safety, and a hard wall of a chest pressed against my back, legs draped over my own. I scrambled to my feet, my head pounding and my stomach curdling. Penn lay there, eyes closed, blond hair tied back in a bun at the nape of his neck, wisps of hair falling over his face. Most days I wanted to grip those little hairs and rip them right out of his head. Actually, every day I wanted to. Especially in this moment.

How in the fuck had this happened? I fell asleep *alone*. So he must've chased me, built this fire to keep me warm? My eyes widened at the thought of him cuddling up beside me and falling asleep with me in his arms.

What a nightmare. I would never drink ale again. Now I understood why I stuck to wine, and very little of it. Obviously, I would never have slept next to Penn if my brain hadn't been addled by alcohol. And I certainly wouldn't have woken up enjoying being wrapped up in his arms. Those big arms that had no right to feel so good. It was the lasting effects of the alcohol. That was all.

I blew out a breath, still studying him, unable to tear my eyes away. When awake, his face was always so severe, as if the burdens of the world sat on his shoulders. But when he was asleep, those hard edges faded to soft lines, his shoulders relaxed, his hands splayed open instead of curled into tight fists. And those lips. I had a sudden urge to trace them, to know what they might feel like under my fingers after I'd already felt them with my mouth.

I quickly looked away, peering out of the tree where I'd fallen asleep.

I had absolutely no idea how to get back to Mosswood Village, so I either would have to wake Penn or wait for him to wake up. I weighed my options. He'd probably be in a better mood if I let him sleep. It had been late when I'd come upon this place last night, and I didn't know how long it had taken him to find me.

I blew out a breath, propping my hands on my hips. Something caught my eye on the tree wall behind Penn. Drawings of some sort, or etchings. I stepped over Penn's body and moved closer to the wall, studying the pictures. Once I stood in front of the drawings, I realized they stretched across the entire length of the wall, going deeper back into the little room. A torch lay by Penn, and I picked it up and held it to the fire, waiting for it to light. Then I moved back toward the drawings, studying them.

The first image portrayed a familiar scene: I'd seen these pictures in scrolls, in books from our libraries. It told of our history, how the original seven courts came to be. Seven people sat in a boat, rowing from the human lands to find a new home, a place where they could escape from the chaos, the depravity, the lawlessness of the human lands. They found Arathia, an undiscovered continent.

I continued moving, looking at the pictures that detailed how the seven people separated to explore the land, how they each decided to split up Arathia between them. The torch light flickered bright, illuminating a picture of the seven manifesting powers. One of them with a fireball in their hand, one with a flower, one with the sun floating over their palm, one holding an icicle, one with wings, one with swirls of water around their fingers, and the final one holding hands with a shadow. The seven elemental powers.

I loved learning about this in school, learning about how they left behind a world ripe with crime and injustice and decided to find something new where they could start over. I loved knowing that I was a product of this, that our line passed down from King Armond, the first king of the earth court.

The next picture showed more and more people arriving to Arathia, choosing a court to reside in, and as the people populated the land, their powers began manifesting based on where they chose to live. A new era had begun, a new life.

Tears pricked my eyes at the thought of what had become of Elwen now. We'd always prided ourselves in taking care of the land, and in return it took care of us. But my stepmother had ruined all of that. I didn't even know if we'd be able to rebuild the earth court, to get our magic back. We'd always learned that Spirit Earth gave us our magic, allowed us to wield the earth element as long as we treated it with respect, didn't use it for selfishness or greed. That knowledge kept everyone in check. Until my stepmother.

I swallowed back my tears. This was not the time to wallow, to doubt. I would get that mirror, then escape and find a way to save Elwen, to bring magic back to my people.

I turned to Penn, seeing that satchel he always carried laying on the ground next to him. A thought popped into my head. Maybe, just maybe, the mirror was in there. He kept it on him at all times. There had to be a reason for that. I crept toward it, stretching out my hand . . .

"I didn't realize you were so interested in history," he said, peeking open an eye and making me jump.

He stood, hair rumpled, tunic wrinkled in a way that made it look like we'd spent all night rolling together between the sheets. Heat prickled between my thighs and I clenched them together.

He gestured to the pictures behind me that I'd just been studying.

I cleared my throat. "I love history, actually. I think it's important to learn from the past, to not repeat history's mistakes."

"What mistakes?" Penn asked, and for once it didn't feel like he was mocking me, but rather like he was genuinely curious in what I had to say.

I sighed and sat back by the fire, and Penn followed, dropping down beside me. "I don't condone the false king and queen's actions," I said slowly. "But clearly there was some discontent among the people, even if the ones who chose to leave were misguided, them leaving signaled a break in communication, in trust, with my father."

Penn raised an eyebrow. "You're full of surprises, Lilypad."

"I've never claimed my father was perfect," I said quickly. "He wasn't. But that doesn't mean it was okay to rebel against him like that, in such a drastic way. Still, I want to foster the kind of community where my people feel like they can come to me with their problems. I want to listen to everyone, give everyone a voice."

"And how would you do that?"

I'd thought about it a lot over the years as I trained and prepared to become queen. "I'd have weekly citizen sessions, where anyone could come to my castle and speak with me directly about issues they may have. I'd appoint ambassadors to the villages who would be responsible for listening to concerns and working to solve them, and if they couldn't, they'd come to me as a representative of the people."

"Hm." Penn leaned his head against the wall, staring straight ahead. "That's not a bad idea."

"My father was spread too thin. Against my advice, he tried to do it all, and that responsibility weighed down on him." I swallowed. "Cost him his life, in the end."

He never saw the betrayal coming, not until it was too late. But maybe if he'd had less stress, less worry, less responsibility, he would've noticed the warning signs.

Penn folded his hands in his lap. "I know what it's like to lose your parents, what it's like to feel all alone."

I looked up at him, surprised at the vulnerability in his eyes, at the softened expression on his face. I hated it. I hated that he pitied me, but more so that he thought he could relate to me. We were nothing alike. He didn't have to see his father brutally murdered in front of him, didn't have to live with the knowledge that his mother could have lived if only the border hadn't been closed all those years ago during the Great War.

He pointed to a picture further down, one of the people of Elwen and the mountain dwellers fighting in what was obviously the Great War. Vines shot through the air. Trees lifted their roots, ready to stomp them down and crush the fighting soldiers. Blood soaked the ground. "So what lessons would you take from the war? How would you avoid something like this happening again?"

Yet another thing I'd thought about a lot over the years, had talked it over with Jasper, though he didn't show as much enthusiasm for my ideas as I'd hoped.

"I was only four when the Great War happened," I said. "I don't know the intricacies of the conflict. I'd been sheltered from most of it, and it's not widely talked about in Elwen, even today."

I suspected that was because it was so closely connected with my mother's death. She'd died right after the border closed, and I think it was too painful for my father, that when he thought of the war, of the border closing, he thought of my mother. Now, being here, I wondered if there was something else, another reason my father didn't like to speak of the Great War. But I couldn't fathom what that reason might be.

"I think I'd create a joint council." Penn arched a brow but didn't say anything, so I continued, "One made up of mountain dwellers and the people of Elwen."

"You know we have a name," Penn said. "We're not just mountain dwellers."

"That's what we've always called you," I said, "what our books refer to you as."

"That doesn't mean that's who we are."

Annoyance spiked in me. "Okay, then what, pray tell, do you call yourselves?"

"We're called the Jarushans."

My brows raised. I'd never heard that before. "After Jarusha? The false queen?"

He nodded. "Our queen. The one who gave us a new home."

He spoke of Jarusha with such reverence. She'd always been known in Elwen as more of a troublemaker, someone who spread rumors and misinformation about my father, turning others against him. It was odd to hear anything but contempt when it came to Jarusha.

"I like that, you know," Penn said, voice quiet and contemplative.

"You like what?" I asked.

"Your solution. A council made up of both sides. Though I'm surprised you'd even consider such a thing with us barbarians."

My mouth dropped open.

"Oh, come on. I know what's said about us in Elwen. What you all think of us."

It was true, and I couldn't deny it. But I also couldn't think of a better way to mend the tension between our two realms. "Well, I have to say that I have been . . . surprised during my time here."

He crossed his arms. "Oh?"

I looked at the pictures above us, avoiding his gaze and what I knew would likely be a smug smirk. "The people are nice. More civilized than I realized, and I suspect they're mostly innocent, people duped into leaving Elwen and then ultimately trapped here when the border was closed. It's been over twenty years since the war; so many of the people who are now adults were just children when it happened. I can't blame them for the actions of their parents." I paused. "I don't understand how anyone condones your thievery, and I don't understand how your society is structured, what kind of laws you have in place. But it's not what I imagined it would be."

"Well, that's something, Lilypad."

I lowered my gaze from the pictures to send a glare his way, but my annoyance fled when I found him staring at me, those green eyes so discerning. I swallowed but refused to look away, to be cowed by his intense gaze.

A bird cawed outside the cave, and both our heads snapped in the direction.

"Right." He rubbed his hands together. "We need to get going. You have training."

"Of course I do," I said drily. "Who am I training with today? Please tell me it's not Arrow."

An amused look danced across his face. "And what do you have against Arrow?"

The memory of her curled in his lap last night flashed through my mind. I tugged at my hair. "She butchered my hair, in case you don't remember."

"Really?" We began walking back toward the entrance of the cave. "I think it looks much better."

He really was such an ass, which reminded me, I was supposed to be angry with him.

I whirled on him. "And by the way, how did we end up . . ." I gestured to the fire, remembering that he'd been asleep when I woke up this morning, that he might not even know we had somehow found our way together while sleeping. "Uh . . ."

"End up . . .?" He twirled his finger in the air, beckoning for me to continue.

"Um." I cleared my throat. "How did you end up in this place with me?"

"I tracked you, and by the time I found you, you were passed out in the cold dark shelter as it stormed outside. Rather than wake you and have to make the miserable trek back to our camp in the middle of the night, I built a fire and let you sleep. Eventually, I fell asleep too."

"Oh." That sounded . . . not as assholish as I had expected.

"Couldn't exactly have you escaping before you complete your mission." With that he stalked off into the sun-bathed forest.

Nope, never mind. He was still an asshole.

Chapter Sixteen

Hammer watched as I slid under a tangle of vines, thorns scraping against my head. I hopped up on the other side, jumped to catch hold of a branch, and pulled myself up, arms shaking, sweat dripping into my eyes.

"C'mon, Princess, show me that muscle! The Huntsman gets closer every day, and you need to complete your training!"

"I'm . . . trying," I gritted out.

Lightning and Arrow had tracked down the Huntsman, their goal to throw off his scent, but just like Penn predicted, the Huntsman already knew who took me, had already been on his way—and now he was lurking outside the border of the forest. We didn't know how long it would take him to figure out how to cross it. The best-case scenario was that the border might take care of the Huntsman for us, but I had a feeling the Huntsman would not be so easily felled. Penn had made it clear we would be leaving for my mission soon, and I still hadn't figured out my escape plan.

Probably because these damn thieves kept me so busy training.

My teeth clenched together, and I grunted out as I attempted to lift myself all the way so that I could get up onto the branch and cross it.

My lungs squeezed the breath from my chest. Wood pressed into my hands, rough and opening already-raw blisters. I let out one more cry, then let go, and fell to the ground.

When I rolled over, Hammer stood above me, frowning and holding out a water skin. I took it and gulped.

"Yer going to puke again," he warned. "Take it easy. I don't need to see any more vomit than I already have."

I glared at him but listened to his sage advice and handed the skin back.

I sat up, roping my arms around my knees. We'd been training for weeks now, using every moment available, and I was getting stronger every day. I'd never enjoyed fighting, running—any kind of physical activity—but it felt good to know I was so strong, so capable. My father never encouraged me to train or do any kind of challenging physical activity. He said fighting was for the soldiers. But I could see now how wrong that was. This training made me feel like I had what it would take to fight my stepmother, to win back my court. I felt powerful.

"I almost got it," I said.

"'Almost' doesn't count," Hammer replied, tugging at his red beard, braided as always and hanging down to his chest. "'Almost' is going to get you killed. And anyone who's on the mission with you."

I peered at him. "Well, if I knew what the mission was, maybe I would have more motivation to train for it."

Penn still hadn't told me anything about what he wanted me to do. I'd barely even seen him since we'd fallen asleep together in that tree shelter. He'd appear at random training sessions, staring at me, reminding me I had a lot to learn in a small amount of time, and then he'd disappear.

I hadn't been back to his tent yet, afraid he'd see me and know I was up to something. But everyday I was learning more, how to make myself invisible, how to be silent as a shadow, how to fight back if I got into a sticky situation, how to pick a lock. I'd trained with almost all the thieves now, each one teaching me different skills, and I'd been surprised at how patient all of them were, how . . . nice they were. Except Arrow, who seemed to delight in every mistake I made. She'd been especially gleeful when I'd almost shot Penn with an arrow. He'd caught it before it impaled his throat and then lectured me for thirty minutes about the dangers of not using a bow properly while Arrow just smirked.

I almost felt ready to get that mirror and get the hell out of here.

Hammer dropped down next to me on the forest floor. "You sure your betrothed isn't going to mind all those pretty new muscles you have?"

I glanced down at my arm, noticing the defined edges that hadn't been there before. I'd filled out more with all the food everyone was shoving down my gullet, Penn an ever-constant reminder that I needed to eat enough to keep up my strength.

"Of course he's not going to mind. Jasper and I have been betrothed since we were three years old. We grew up together. He loves me for me."

It might be a shock for him to see me like this, with short hair, wearing a tunic and pants, but he'd be so happy I was alive and in his arms that he probably wouldn't even notice the changes.

"What do you like about him, anyway?" He reached up his hand, then slowly drew it back, beckoning a tree branch, which dipped down. Hammer pulled two apples off the branch before it snapped back up. He handed me one, and I couldn't help the pang of jealousy at seeing his magic. I didn't know if that ache would ever go away.

I sat the apple down next to me. "He's, well, he's . . ." I paused, fumbling for my words. No one had ever asked me what I loved about Jasper. We were betrothed, meant to be. It was my duty to marry him, to love him, to be his queen. Our marriage would strengthen my court.

"That's what I thought." Hammer finished eating his apple and threw the core.

"What is that supposed to mean?" I asked.

"Is he not good in bed?" He leaned in. "You can tell me."

I scoffed. "Hammer! That is your future—"

I stopped, realizing I was going to say king, but Jasper wouldn't be Hammer's future king.

Hammer just laughed.

"I . . . well, I don't really know how to tell if he was good or not. In bed. I mean . . ." Earth below.

In truth, sex with Jasper hadn't been mind-blowing, but it was good enough. I never had someone to talk to about it and compare notes. If I told Jillian and Driscoll too much, it would just give them added fuel for all the ways Jasper was wrong for me. But they didn't understand that their opinions didn't matter. He was my betrothed, the future king of Elwen, a valuable alliance—I couldn't forsake that.

Hammer just grinned. "That doesn't look like the face of a satisfied woman."

I shoved him. "What would you know about satisfied women?"

He waggled his eyebrows. "You'd be surprised."

Penn appeared from between the trees, and I prayed to Spirit Earth he hadn't just heard our conversation.

Hammer shot to his feet, scratching his head, ruddy skin redder than normal.

"This doesn't look like training to me." Penn frowned down at us.

I rolled my eyes. "It's called taking a break."

He cocked an eyebrow. "It's called gossiping."

Oh, good green earth. So he had heard.

Penn strode toward us, stopping in front of me and crouching down. "If you want to talk about your unsatisfactory love life, do it somewhere else."

My leg twitched, and I wanted to kick him right where I knew it would hurt most. "I don't have an unsatisfactory love life."

Penn looked me up and down. "Whatever you say, Lilypad."

Suddenly I felt self-conscious about my hair, the branches and twigs sticking out of it, the sweat covering my face, the dirt on my clothes. I didn't know why. I didn't care what Penn thought of me, but I did care what he thought of Jasper.

"For your information, Jasper is ten times the man you'll ever be."

Penn scoffed, and heat flooded my core as he leaned forward, our noses inches apart, his eyes boring into me. He was so close I could kiss him just like I had the night he kidnapped me, and the thought made me dizzy. "Just so you know, there will be no doubt in your mind when you've been satisfied." His voice was low, gravelly. "You'll know it when your body is aching in all the right places." He ran a finger along the side of my face, and I held back a shudder. "When your skin is damp with sweat. Your heart beating wildly. Lips swollen. You'll feel completely satiated but somehow hungry for more."

I could barely breathe, staring into his eyes, so full of a fire I didn't recognize.

Hammer cleared his throat, and I shot to my feet. "Training," I gasped out. "We need to train."

"Actually," Penn said, not ruffled in the slightest by our interaction, "we have a new mission, and you're going to help us plan it."

"Another one?" I took a step back. "That wasn't our deal."

"Well, I think this one will be of interest to you, Lilypad."

"And why is that?" I crossed my arms, ready to defy him, until the next few words left his mouth.

"Your stepmother's Huntsman is finally here, in Mosswood Forest, and you're going to help us figure out how to get rid of him."

Chapter Seventeen

The seven thieves, Penn, and I stood in his tent, all of us huddled around a table with a map spread out across it. I didn't see the mirror anywhere, but of course he wouldn't have such a powerful object just laying around. His bed sat in the corner, the same bed I'd slept in when I first arrived here.

My gaze traveled to a chest in the corner, and I wondered if perhaps the mirror was hidden in there. Though that might be too obvious for the king of thieves. Surely he had a hiding place for all his treasures. And I'd have to figure it out before I could escape this place. A few clothes hung out of a burlap sack in another corner—black pants, a gray tunic—and I imagined Penn in here at night, alone, laying in his bed—

"Princess," Hammer said, and my gaze snapped to him.

Everyone stared at me.

"Sorry?" I tucked a strand of hair behind my ear. "What was that?"

Arrow smirked like she'd known exactly what I was doing, what I was imagining. Oh, that's right. Penn probably wasn't alone at night. She'd be with him.

"Sorry if we're boring you, Lilypad," Penn drawled, "but if you'd like to keep your freedom, I suggest you pay attention."

I raised my chin. "Keeping my freedom would imply it's something I already possess."

"How did the Huntsman get into Mosswood Forest?" Charming asked. "Did he just punch his way through the border?"

Hammer pounded a fist on the table. "We cannot let that menace roam here, put our people in danger."

"He's very powerful," Shadow said. "Made from earth magic."

Penn looked at me. "What do you know about the Huntsman?"

I hesitated. "My father gifted him to my stepmother when they first married, a personal guard for the new queen. He'd been magnificent. My father used his magic to create the Huntsman, who was made of the strongest tree bark, vines, thorns." He was made to be indestructible and was ultimately my father's downfall. "If only he'd known his own creation would eventually turn on him."

Everyone stayed silent, staring at me, some with open mouths, others with looks of pity in their eyes. Penn's face was unreadable.

I cleared my throat and looked down at the table. "I assume he's only become more powerful, my stepmother using whatever dark magic she possesses to strengthen him. Maybe that's how he broke into the forest?"

"Or maybe our border didn't recognize it as an enemy threat because it's not human," Brains said, tugging at her brown curls. The only thief I hadn't trained with yet, but from her nickname, I gathered she was the intelligence behind these missions.

The flap to the tent opened and Lightning slipped in, bald with tattoos covering every inch of his head. I'd rarely seen him, and he didn't talk. Shadow said he'd always been like that, silent, brooding, and intense. During our session he simply started running, and I had to follow him for three torturous hours as we jogged, jumped, climbed. By the end of it, I'd fallen to my knees, vomiting everywhere, and when I'd looked up, Lightning was gone.

Penn nodded at him as he joined us at the table.

Wayfinder stared at the map, frowning. "Why wouldn't the queen have sent the Huntsman before this? Tried to penetrate our border and overtake us?"

"She wouldn't do that," I murmured, also staring at the map, at the little castle that represented my home. My former home.

"Why?" Penn asked.

"She just wouldn't," I said, voice sharp.

Shadow's eyes widened, and I nodded at her to let her know I was okay. I hadn't meant to display any kind of emotion over it, but answering that question would open up too many wounds that I wasn't ready to face. I wasn't sure I'd ever be ready.

Charming hunched over the map. "Well, I hate to break it to you all, but I don't think I'm going to be able to flirt the Huntsman out of here. I'm willing to try, though." He winked at the group.

Shadow rolled her eyes. "How do we know where he even is?"

"Is it a he?" Wayfinder asked, stroking his clean-shaven jaw. "I mean, it's made of tree, so—"

"Can we focus?" Arrow pursed her bright red lips, flipping her long, wavy hair over her shoulder.

Lightning grunted, which I took to mean he agreed with Arrow.

"The Huntsman was spotted here." Penn pointed to a circled area on the map. "By one of our villagers who was out foraging. He's getting closer to finding her." He tilted his head in my direction, and chills ran up my spine at the thought of that thing coming after me.

"Are you okay, Lilypad?" Penn asked, voice quiet.

"Yes," I said with a shaky voice. "I'm fine. It doesn't respond well to arrows or swords, or any weapons, really. You can fight the Huntsman with your earth magic, or at least contain him with it."

I remembered my father telling me that the Huntsman was strong but not invincible. *Never give your magic more power than you,* he'd said as I watched him create it. I'd begged him to make me my own guard, but he'd said I didn't need one because I had him, and he'd never let harm come to me.

If only I could've made him the same promise.

Brains drummed her fingers on the table. "So how about we come in, full powers blazing. We can recruit others from the village, and all of us can use our collective magic to kill him."

Penn stared at the map, no doubt mulling over the words.

"Yes." Hammer tugged at his braided beard. "I'll give that Huntsman a piece of my mind." He gave a jagged smile. "And a piece of my fist while I'm at it." He punched his fist in the air.

"No," I said. "Brute force isn't the way to go."

Penn peered up, gaze leaving the map to look at me. "Then what do you suggest?"

I surprised myself by knowing the answer to his question. "A specialized, small team. A surprise attack. The Huntsman is designed to be smart. He'll know an attack is coming if we just march to him. And he can take a lot of people at once, so strength isn't the way to defeat him."

"Cunning is," Brains said, eyes flashing.

"Yes," I confirmed.

"Okay." Penn tapped the map with a finger, and it took a minute for me to realize where the Huntsman had been spotted.

I'd been standing here for nearly an hour talking logistics with these people and hadn't even realized what I had before me: a way out. Mosswood Forest was huge, and I had no idea where we were—until now. The village was clearly labeled, as was the Huntsman's location: near the border of the forest—and then it was a short crossing across Elwen to Gilraeth.

The fire court. Jasper's home.

Excitement built, thrumming inside me. This could work. This could work well. I just had to convince Penn to let me come along.

Penn clapped his hands together. "Good work, everyone. Brains, Wayfinder, and I will work on the logistics of our plan. We leave early tomorrow morning."

That sent a shock through me. I'd have to find a way to steal the mirror tonight.

Everyone started shuffling out of the tent, Arrow pausing next to Penn and stroking his arm with her long, red nails. I looked at my own dirt-caked ones, missing my ladies' maids and all the pampering I got as a princess.

She left the tent, flap closing behind her, only two of us remaining.

Penn turned to see me still standing there. "Don't you have more training to do? Or gossiping about your love life with Hammer?"

"We were not"—I balled my fists—"you know what? Never mind. Think what you want. I don't care."

"Whatever you say, Lilypad." He turned toward his chest, clearly dismissing me.

A lump formed in my throat, and I willed my voice to stay steady. "I want to go on this mission. To find the Huntsman."

Penn stopped, those massive shoulders of his hunching. "No. Absolutely not. You're not ready. You can't even climb a vine, and without your magic—"

"I don't need my magic to be useful." I took a step forward. "You forget that I know the Huntsman, spent years watching him and learning how he dismantled his opponents. I watched my father make him from earth and tree and vine. I know his weaknesses. I can be helpful."

Penn studied me. "Why do you want to help so badly?"

"Because the Huntsman killed my father."

Penn's eyes widened, and he swore softly.

"I want vengeance. You have no idea how badly I want it."

Now that I'd said the words, I realized they were true. Yes, I wanted to escape, but I also wanted to see the Huntsman pay after how he'd so effortlessly taken away everything from me.

My heart lurched, and I had to swallow back the tears threatening to spill down my cheeks at the memories flooding me, the way my stepmother had described my father's death. I hadn't seen the Huntsman kill him, but she'd had no problem spilling every gruesome detail: the crunching bones, the squirting blood, the screaming.

"I do know." Penn walked to the table and studied the map. "My parents were killed when I was young. Everyone in the academy is an orphan. So you have more in common with these thieves than you thought."

I hadn't realized—in all our weeks of training together, no one had mentioned anything about their pasts. Though I hadn't exactly asked.

Penn placed his hand flat on the table. "None of us have gotten any kind of closure after we lost our parents."

"I'm sorry," I said quietly. "It's not easy, being all alone in the world."

"I'm not alone, and neither are you." He swallowed, his Adam's apple bobbing. "You have your friends, the ones who were locked in the tower with you?"

"Right." For one idiotic moment, I'd thought he was saying I had the academy, him and the seven thieves. That was silly. I clearly didn't belong here, didn't want to belong here. Yes, Shadow was kind and fun to talk to, and Wayfinder had this magical ability to make me smile, and

Hammer, for all his gruff posturing, was actually just a big softy. Charming was, well, very charming. But they were still criminals. So no, I'd never belong. Not with them.

"Okay," Penn said finally. "You can come. But I will leave you behind if necessary. I keep a grueling pace on our missions."

"Shocking," I mumbled.

We stood in silence for a minute.

I rocked on my heels. "Well, then—"

"What makes you think Jasper is still your betrothed?" Penn asked.

The question sent a shock through me. It was jarring, like the thought had just popped into his head and he'd blurted it out, which seemed so unlike the king of thieves, Mr. Cool and Collected, always so calm.

"Why wouldn't we be betrothed?" I crossed my arms. "We've been engaged since I was three years old, known each other our entire lives."

Penn stared at me like the answer was obvious. "You've been trapped in a prison cell for two years, and he never came for you."

"He couldn't come for me!" A defensiveness rose up in me. "It was dangerous and would take a lot of planning."

"Believe me, I know," Penn said. "But you have this unshakable faith in him. Why?"

This conversation was getting tiresome. "I already told you. Jasper and I are betrothed. He's cousin to the princess of Gilraeth. Our betrothal made an important alliance between the earth and fire court. And he was going to be king of the earth court. He wouldn't forsake that. More importantly, he wouldn't forsake me. Loyalty might be hard for a man like you to imagine, but I assure you, it does exist."

Penn looked at me with what seemed like pity, and I hated it.

"Is that all? I need to get to training."

He was already studying his map again. "Take the rest of the day off."

"Why?" I asked, suddenly suspicious.

"Find Shadow, go shopping. You're going to want to wear something other than your dirty trousers and tunic."

"Yes, but for what?" Blood and earth, getting information from this man was like pulling leeches.

"Have you been trapped that long that you've forgotten the earth court's biggest celebration of the year?" Penn leaned over, grabbing a quill and circling something on the map. "Tonight, we celebrate. It's the Festival of Earth."

Chapter Eighteen

The usually sleepy Mosswood Village roared to life around us. Shadow and Wayfinder flanked me as we passed a group of men and women playing a lively song with their wooden instruments: a fiddle, a banjo, and a flute. I missed these types of celebrations. In Elwen, we went all out for the Festival of Earth.

Servants would decorate our courtyard with garlands, flower petals, arches made of vines and leaves, and an altar depicting the earth spirit, with her hair made of ivy, her body made of branches, and long limbs made of flower stems. I'd spend the day wandering the courtyard with Driscoll and Jillian, snacking on candied plums and pear tarts, dancing, laughing. My heart ached to have it all back.

I was surprised Penn allowed us to even attend the festival, but Shadow told me everyone would've revolted if he hadn't let us come and celebrate. It was the most important holiday to the earth court, so even with the looming threat of the Huntsman, Penn gave everyone the night off to enjoy the festivities.

"Oh, here we go with the puppets," Shadow said.

"I love the puppets," Wayfinder replied.

"You love everything." Shadow rolled her eyes as we came to a stop behind a growing crowd of spectators.

"What do the puppets do?" I asked.

"Every year, a few villagers put together a puppet show of the Seven Spirits."

"That sounds . . ." I trailed off.

"Ridiculous," Shadow finished for me. "It's ridiculous."

Puppets popped up behind a wooden frame with a cloth, depicting Earth, Fire, Sky, Shadow, Water, Starlight, and Frost, each of them in human form but distinguishable by their elemental features.

Frost began speaking in a high-pitched, nasally voice, quickly getting into an argument with Fire. I laughed, unable to help myself.

Shadow groaned. "Not you too. Don't tell me you actually enjoy this? It's ridiculous. They make up trivial drama between the spirits for our enjoyment. The spirits are to be revered, worshipped, not put up like this as silly little props."

Wayfinder nudged her. "It's just some fun, Shadow. Something you could learn a little about."

Shadow worked hard, which I respected. But right now, I agreed with Wayfinder. I wanted to enjoy myself and not think about anything else, especially not the mission to find the Huntsman or how I needed to somehow steal that mirror before we left.

At least this festival was going to give me the perfect opportunity. Everyone would be here, drinking and having fun while I'd be sneaking into Penn's tent and finding that damn mirror.

But that would come later. For now, I could enjoy the puppets.

"Earth would never speak like that," Shadow was saying.

"It's a puppet!" Wayfinder shoved a hand through his dark, curly hair. "It's not supposed to be realistic. No one here actually thinks Earth speaks like that or . . ." He tilted his head as the puppet let out a loud burp. "Belches like that."

"This is offensive. I am actually offended by this." Shadow just shook her head and crossed her arms.

"You know," I started, "in Elwen, we create an altar for Earth, made of plants and flowers and wood."

"That sounds beautiful." Shadow shot a look at Wayfinder. "And appropriate."

Someone passed by with a tray of turkey legs, and Wayfinder grabbed one and flipped the man a coin. He started gnawing on it. "I don't know what you're talking about. This is pure art."

Frost lunged at Water, and Shadow muttered "blasphemy" under her breath.

As horrid as the show was, I couldn't tear my eyes from it. "To be fair to Wayfinder, they did a good job with the design of the puppets."

The Seven Spirits hadn't been seen or heard from since all those living in the Old World had perished, thousands of years ago. But we still worshipped them, celebrated them and the magic they bestowed upon us. Historians and scholars weren't sure what happened to the people of the Old World, why they'd vanished from this land without leaving a trace. But many had theories: that they'd become greedy and selfish with their magic, wanting more, taking more, so that the Seven Spirits waged a war on them and destroyed everyone. That war had broken out among them, and the Seven Spirits intervened, accidentally causing mass death. From all the historical evidence we'd found, it was clear the spirits appeared regularly to the people of the Old World. They talked to them, interacted with them, appeared at their festivals. It was all so fascinating to think about, and the drawings and depictions we'd found gave us a good idea of what the spirits looked like.

The puppets were now in an all-out brawl. "Oh, admit it." I elbowed Shadow. "This is kind of fun."

Shadow huffed.

I studied the Earth puppet, the way her hair looked like thick, ropey vines, her body stiff and thick like a tree trunk. Earth was the least-depicted of all the spirits, and the only drawings or etchings we had of her were torn, faded, or destroyed by time and other things. We had to guess more when it came to her appearance.

I gestured to her puppet, now dancing for the other spirits to distract them from their fight. "You know, I picture Earth so differently than that."

"How so?"

I whirled at the sound of that low voice that sent shivers down my spine. Penn stood there, staring at me and waiting for an answer.

Wayfinder choked on his turkey leg, and Shadow pounded him on the back. "Penn?" he finally asked. "What are you doing here?"

"I'm here to get some supplies," Penn said gruffly.

"Of course." Wayfinder tore off a chunk of the leg with his teeth.

"Because why wouldn't you come to a festival to work instead of, oh, I don't know, actually enjoy yourself?"

Shadow smirked.

Penn rolled his eyes. "Some of us don't have that luxury." He gestured to the puppet show. "So how do you imagine Earth, then?" he asked again.

I closed my eyes and felt the breeze that ruffled my hair, faint and gentle on my skin. "I imagine her in everything: not as a human form, but I imagine her face in the trees that give us shelter, her fingers in the flowers that show us beauty, her voice in the thorns that remind us of her power. She's everywhere, in every part of our world. And festivals like this remind me of how much she gives us, and how much she can take away if we're not careful."

My stepmother's face popped into my mind, and my eyes flew open at the intrusive image, finding Penn looking at me, his green eyes so intense I thought I'd somehow offended him with my answer.

"That was . . ." Shadow started.

"Wow," Wayfinder said. "Definitely more poetic than this." He gestured to the puppet show, which was coming to an end.

The band struck up another lively song, and Wayfinder stuck out his hand. "What do you say, Shadow? Mend our differences on the dance floor?"

"Don't you have a boyfriend for this type of thing?" she asked, quirking an eyebrow.

"He's not much of a dancer. C'mon." He grabbed her hand and led her away as others joined in the dancing. Women picked up their skirts, kicking up their feet, as onlookers clapped and tapped to the rhythm.

It seemed everyone had found a partner, except for me and the king of thieves. A man passed us by, carrying a tray of caramel-covered apples. I eyed it, mouth going dry.

Penn reached out. "Would you like one?" he asked.

"What?" My gaze snapped to him.

He waved the man with the tray down.

"No." I grabbed Penn's arm. "No, please. I don't want one."

Penn continued motioning for the man. "It's okay, Lilypad, I saw you eyeing it. Just let me get one for you—"

"No, Penn, I'm serious, I don't want it!" I said, my voice carrying over the crowd.

Everyone around us went silent, staring.

"That's a no on the apple," Penn said to the man with the tray, who'd finally come over to us.

After an uncomfortable minute of me staring at my feet, the chatter around us resumed.

"Wanna tell me what that was about?" Penn asked quietly.

I swallowed the growing lump in my throat. "Not really, but I suppose I owe you an explanation after that outburst."

A dancing couple bumped into us, then laughed and whirled away.

Penn crossed his arms. "You don't owe me anything."

I blew a breath out the side of my mouth. "It's not a big deal. My stepmother, her specialty was apples. She grew the most beautiful apple trees in Elwen, and everyone raved over them. She loved making apple-sauce, apple pies, apple tarts, spiced apples." I frisked my arms. "She and I never got along. I wasn't particularly nice to her, and I started disliking the fruit after we met. Every time I saw it, it reminded me of her. And now, after everything that's happened, I just can't stomach them."

"Right. Oddly enough, I get that," Penn said.

Silence fell between us.

"Did you like the puppet show?" I asked, grasping for something to say after that admission. He probably thought I was crazy now.

"I don't really care about the puppets or the shows . . . or any of this." He gestured around to the festival.

"Shocking," I mumbled.

"In case you hadn't noticed, I have a lot on my shoulders, Lilypad."

I crossed my arms. "Oh, yes, I forgot. You're too busy running your criminal enterprise to be able to enjoy anything else."

"Exactly." A stray strand of his blond hair fell over his face, and I had to curl my fist tight to keep from brushing it aside. "Glad you understand me."

"I don't understand you, and I have no desire to," I said.

"Well, that's too bad. I was just about to ask you to dance."

That stopped me. "W-what?"

He gestured to the crowd of people twirling and laughing. "I saw you eyeing the dance floor. You like this sort of thing."

It wasn't a question, but an observation. And, damn him, he was right.

"So you wanted to—" I flung a hand out. "Dance? With me?"

A small smirk lifted the corner of his lips. "If you think you can keep up."

He was enjoying this, enjoying watching me dangle like a little worm on a hook. Well, two could play at this game. I raised my nose in the air. Challenge accepted.

I placed my hand in his, and he led me out to the middle of the crowd. Our gazes locked, neither of us willing to look away. He pulled me into him, and a small breath escaped my mouth as we collided, his arm roping around my back as my hands slid up to his neck. Everything about this man felt so solid, like an impenetrable wall. I remembered watching him sneak onto the castle grounds, get through every trap my stepmother had laid, scale the castle walls with such efficiency. He was like a honed weapon.

"You know, the last time you were in my arms like this, I believe you were kissing me."

His words trickled over me, leaving trails of heat in their wake. I'd wondered when—if—he was going to bring that up.

"That's because I thought you were my betrothed."

He spun me around. "Ah, yes, easy mistake to make."

"It was dark," I said coolly. "And I was confused after just being rescued."

He once again was trying to fluster me. But I wouldn't let him.

"It was obviously a mistake that meant nothing."

"Whatever you say, Lilypad."

We stepped backward together, and he dipped me low, our faces inches apart. He paused, me hanging in his arms.

I swallowed, my throat growing thick. "It was just a kiss," I said, like I was trying to convince myself more than him.

He pulled me up in one smooth motion. "So you've said."

"And there won't be any more."

"If you say so." Those damn lips quirked.

Anger flared in me. It wasn't enough that he had to kidnap me and force me to do his bidding, but he also had to flirt and play games, games that felt dangerous.

Cheers erupted around us, and I cleared my throat. I'd forgotten there were even people nearby, music playing, an entire festival happening.

Shadow and Wayfinder stared at us, knowing looks in their eyes. I glared at them, and they both quickly looked elsewhere.

"I'm going on a walk," I said, spinning on my heel, all of this suddenly feeling like too much.

"Don't stay out too late, Lilypad," Penn called after me. "You've got a mission to go on tomorrow, and I don't tolerate tardiness."

Chapter Nineteen

I wandered the festival grounds, still stewing over Penn and his petty little games.

A woman stood by a nearby tree with a little girl.

"Just open your palm," she coached the girl, who followed her instructions. "It's going to be like pulling at an invisible thread inside of you. Tug at that thread and think about what you want."

The little girl squeezed her eyes shut, and I watched as a flower sprouted in her palm, growing, petals and leaves unfurling. She opened her eyes and gasped.

I hugged myself, remembering my father teaching me those same lessons on how to use my magic. Blood and earth, despite our differences, I missed him, missed my magic.

I glanced behind me, seeing Penn in the distance, drinking ale and surrounded by a group of people. And then it hit me: he didn't have that satchel with him.

Now was the time to steal away. I could find it and get that mirror, and then tomorrow, when everyone was busy fighting the Huntsman, I would escape to the fire court and find Jasper.

I was about to dart through the trees and head for Penn's tent when I noticed an elderly woman weaving together flower stems, petals, and leaves into beautiful necklaces. I could've sworn I'd seen them before, but I didn't know why they looked so familiar.

Penn would be here for a while. There was no harm in stopping and enjoying myself a little. She sat on the ground in front of her tent, her knotted hands shaking as they poked a thread through a flower petal that had been dehydrated.

"My mother would've loved this," I said, picking up a necklace.

She looked up, her eyes sharp, and nodded. "Aye, she would have."

My legs almost gave out from underneath me, and I dropped to a seat next to her, heart thudding. "Did you know her?"

She gave a sad smile. "She came by my stand at the market quite often, always wanting me to make her a new necklace or bracelet to give to her lady's maids or friends."

I stilled, not sure I could form words. So many questions flitted through my mind at the women's casual revelation.

The older woman laughed, and it sounded more like a bark. "I came here years ago, right when your mother got sick. Her illness felt like a sign."

"Her illness felt like a sign that you should leave Elwen?" My voice was sharp, but her gaze and fingers remained focused on their task of making the necklace.

She grabbed a small orange leaf and threaded it next to the flower petal.

"I loved your mother. Many in the earth court did. Without her, there'd be no one to balance your father." She shook her head. "I didn't want to be a part of it."

"A part of what?" I couldn't process what she was saying. Cold dread settled like a stone in my belly.

"His quest for power," she said, finishing the necklace and hanging it on a wooden board that sat propped up, displaying all her beautiful jewelry.

His quest for power.

Now that stone grew to a boulder, a specific memory sprouting in my mind. I'd turned twenty-one, ready to take the throne and rule, but my father had said I needed more time, needed to learn more, to grow more, before I was ready. It had been another argument between us. Another source of contention. And it had made me doubt myself, doubt that I was ready to be queen. As I grew older, I realized it was less about myself and more about my father. He had control issues, didn't like a lot of my ideas about how to connect with our people. He believed in ruling with an iron fist, and I'd disagreed. But I never thought of him as power hungry—just stubborn. Now I couldn't get the thought out of my mind.

I wanted to hear more about what the woman knew, but time wasn't on my side and my desire to hear more about my mother won out. She'd died when I was only five, and I had very few memories of her, but the ones I did have I held close to my heart.

"Can you tell me more about her?" I asked. "My mother?"

"She was kind," the woman said, and she looked at me with her sharp, brown eyes. "She wanted peace and happiness for her people. Always had an uplifting word." The woman winked. "Had a sweet tooth for candied plums."

I laughed. So that's where I got that from.

"Do you regret your decision?" I winced when I realized what a stupid question that must have been given Elwen's current state. "I mean, before my stepmother usurped my father. Did you ever regret leaving?"

She shook her head. "Mosswood Village is my home. You know, when I first came here, I wasn't sure if I would find my place. I'd lost all my materials when I moved here. My needles, my thread, my knives. I didn't think I'd be able to recreate my business. But he took the time to talk to me, get to know me, and after he left on one of his expeditions, he came back with all the supplies I needed to start my business anew. That was twenty years ago."

My brows furrowed. "Who? Who is he?" Though I had a feeling I already knew.

"The king," she said with a laugh.

That was an odd way of saying it. "Of thieves?" I finished for her, but she was already humming along.

My mind tried to work out her words, to process what she'd just told me, along with the things I'd heard from the other thieves, from Penn himself. A realization struck me. "Wait a minute. Is that what Penn does? He steals from other courts and brings the items back for you all?"

She grabbed a thread and snapped it off. "Yes, and he's brought back such wonderful things over the years. He's the reason we've been able to survive after the border closed, trapped us in this place, cut off all trade."

Penn helped these people to survive. I sat back, stunned for the second time while talking to this woman. I'd gotten it all wrong. I thought he was just a common thief, breaking the law so he could steal precious relics and jewels, but he had a purpose. A noble one.

Still, it was all wrong, the way he went about it. This didn't change anything.

The woman rocked back and forth, muttering something to herself now. She was clearly touched in the head, probably didn't even remember how she'd come to Mosswood Forest. I doubted what she'd said about my father was true, that she left because of him. She'd left because she'd been brainwashed by the false king and queen, like everyone else here.

She picked up a dehydrated rose petal and smiled lovingly at it, stroking it. It was good she still had this. I could commend Penn for giving her something that brought so much joy, even if I didn't agree with his methods.

I thanked the woman for her time and went on my way. The sun sank lower in the sky, its yellow glow cresting over the treetops above. It would be dark soon, and I needed to hurry if I was going to get that mirror.

Chapter Twenty

I hurried along through the forest, making sure no one saw me as I fled from the festival. By the time I reached Penn's tent, darkness blanketed the woods, everything still and quiet, only the faint sounds of the festival echoing far in the distance.

I stopped myself before darting out into the clearing, crouching behind a bush and assessing the situation like Shadow had taught me. It would be safer in the trees, up high and out of sight. I reached up, beckoning a branch to lean down, but when it didn't obey, I remembered all over again how I had no magic. A gaping hole sat where my power had once been. I pounded a fist into the ground in frustration but stopped myself from crying out. This was not the time to fall apart —another lesson I'd learned from Charming, of all people. He'd been teaching me about meditation and mindset, how to mentally prepare for a scary or hard situation. I took a few calming breaths like he taught me and focused my mind on my goal. Get that mirror. I envisioned myself finding it, holding it in my hands, and walking out of that tent with it secure in my possession.

A tree branch hung high over me, a thick one, perfect for climbing. I still didn't have the strength to pull myself up onto a branch, but Hammer had taught me other ways to climb a tree. I crept over to the thick trunk and dug my foot into a groove, then slowly worked my way up. I wasn't fast, not like Shadow or Lightning might be, but this was an improvement over my tree-climbing skills when I'd first arrived, which could be described as non-existent. I reached the branch and climbed onto it, losing my balance but catching myself before I fell to the ground. From up here, I could see the empty clearing. No one in sight, no one to see what I was about to do.

I wanted to be worthy of my people, a better ruler than my father, than my stepmother, had been. I wanted to foster trust and respect, and this felt like the wrong way to go about that, but I didn't see any other options.

Technically, I was returning the mirror to its owner. As long as she'd be willing to bargain with me, that was. I took a deep breath and launched myself to another branch, jumping from tree to tree until I was directly over the tent. I took a minute to catch my breath, heart hammering at the exertion. I almost wished Hammer were here to see me. He'd be hooting and hollering at what I'd just done, what we'd spent weeks practicing. He'd never admit it, but I knew I was growing on the grump. He was growing on me too. They all were. I peered down at the tent, which glowed in the moonlight.

It didn't matter.

We lived in two different worlds, and I was going to be leaving their world behind very soon.

I dropped to the ground, landing in a crouch, and crept toward the tent. Slivers of moonlight sliced through the inside, granting just enough light that I could see the dim outline of the table, the map of Mosswood Forest, the chest tucked into the corner. Here went nothing.

I tiptoed across the space and lowered myself in front of the chest. It opened with a creak. Shirts, trousers, belts filled the inside, each one as plain as Penn. No, that wasn't true. I could describe Penn in many ways, but plain wouldn't be one of them.

But blood and earth, this man's wardrobe was so boring. I couldn't imagine him in the earth court, dressed in the silk and finery that many of the men wore. An image penetrated my thoughts: Penn stripping off his shirt, his trousers, standing in this tent naked as moonlight illuminated his pale skin, his hard muscles. I snapped the chest closed and banished that picture from my mind.

The mirror. I needed to find the mirror.

I spent the next thirty minutes turning over every inch of the tent: the rug, the bedroll, a small chest of drawers, a few sacks. Nothing. Neither the satchel nor the mirror were here.

Disappointment welled in me. Of course it wasn't here. He was the king of thieves. He wasn't going to keep his most valued possessions unguarded in this tent. I should've guessed he'd hide it better than this. Now it was too late. Tomorrow morning we'd leave, and that would be my best chance at escape, possibly my only chance. I couldn't waste more time here than I already had.

Voices rang out in the clearing, and my pulse spiked hard. I needed to get out of here. I quickly put everything back in its place and fled through the back flap of the tent, escaping right as two shadows appeared in the entryway. I steadied my breathing and flattened myself against a tree, hoping I'd hid myself better this time than I had previously.

"Penn, are you sure this is worth it?" Wayfinder asked from inside the tent. "The Huntsman is dangerous."

"Exactly." Penn lit a candle, illuminating their outlines through the tent walls. "His presence puts our people at risk."

"Her presence puts our people at risk. Release her, let her go to her betrothed like she wants, and let's focus on the bigger goal."

"No." Penn's voice was rough, like the sharp snap of a twig.

"Think what we could do with that mirror," Wayfinder said. "We could finally defeat the queen and open the border that King Thamos closed—"

"I will never use that mirror."

The depth of emotion in Penn's voice took me aback. He was normally so stoic and unruffled, but something about using that mirror made him angry.

Then Wayfinder's words sank in: *The border that King Thamos closed.*

That couldn't be right. The mountain dwellers were the ones who closed the border between Mosswood Forest and Elwen. Not my father. Wayfinder was lying, confused, something. Anything.

But in my heart, I knew that didn't make sense, not along with everything else I'd heard since I arrived here. Wayfinder was alone with Penn right now—no reason to lie about something like that.

I could hear Wayfinder's sigh of disappointment.

"I'm working to free us all," Penn said.

"But you're doing it for the wrong reasons, in the wrong way."

"Because of her?" Bitterness tinged Penn's voice.

"That's one part of it." Wayfinder's voice was cautious, as if he were treading into dangerous territory. "You don't need to involve Princess Liliath. At the very least, tell her what you're getting her into."

"You know the rules," Penn said. "I won't disclose the details of the mission, not until it's necessary."

"That's not what I'm talking about," Wayfinder said, "and you know it."

"The mirror's true power is too dangerous to disclose to anyone. Think about what her stepmother has been able to accomplish with that mirror. She has decimated an entire court. In the wrong hands, that mirror could bring down the continent of Arathia."

His words floored me. I knew the mirror was powerful, knew my stepmother had used it to help her destroy Elwen, but I hadn't realized just how much power it held.

All the more reason why I needed to flee, with or without the mirror. Whatever Penn wanted me to do had even given Wayfinder pause. I couldn't risk my life for the mirror. I'd be no good to my people if I was dead.

"We need to sleep," Penn finally said after a beat. "We have a long day ahead of us tomorrow."

I heard Wayfinder's footsteps as he left the tent, and I slumped down against the tree, staring at Penn's shadow as he blew out the candle in his tent and lay down. I stayed there, sitting against the tree, staring into the darkness as I tried to make sense of everything I'd heard. One thing was certain: tomorrow I would finally be free and on my way to my betrothed.

Chapter Twenty-One

We left before the sun rose, sky still dark, splashed with lilac. Penn refused to give me a horse, despite Hammer, Shadow, and Wayfinder pleading my case.

So here I sat, on Penn's horse, which Penn had insisted on. Because of course he had. It was as if he didn't trust anyone else with me, that he thought if he took his eyes off me for a second, I would do something stupid.

Technically, I was planning to do something stupid, but it didn't make me any less grumpy about it.

His arms wrapped around me as he held onto the reins, his chest a hard wall against my back. I sat straight, refusing to let myself sink into him and get too comfortable. What I'd heard last night was just another reminder that he was using me to get something he wanted. He saw me as nothing more than a disposable tool, and he didn't even have the decency to tell me what he was using me for.

Our route had been mapped out based on where the Huntsman had been seen in Mosswood Forest, and Penn had said it would be a few hours' ride to the east, right by the border. From there I could sneak off, and it would only be a few hours' trek across Elwen and to the fire court. Once I was in Jasper's territory, I'd be safe.

I was disappointed I hadn't gotten the mirror last night, but Jasper would help me. Once I told him how powerful it was, surely the fire court would want to help retrieve it. They definitely wouldn't want to see it in the king of thieves's hands. No one on the continent would.

I'd spent hours last night thinking about what Penn and Wayfinder had said about my father creating the border.

Everyone in Elwen believed the mountain dwellers had closed our border to end the Great War after their false king and queen died—because that's what my father had told us. I couldn't understand why he'd lie about something like that, but he must have had his reasons, must've known something dangerous that the rest of us didn't. The mountain dwellers had been a threat to us, so he'd had to make a difficult choice, one he knew people might not understand. Mosswood Forest had been a valuable resource to Elwen. It was another reason I wished he'd been willing to hear other voices, other points of view. He might've realized there were other options than erecting that awful border. Just another reason why I had to learn from the mistakes of my father.

I couldn't imagine the amount of power he'd had to use to make something so huge, so monstrous. I'd always imagined hundreds of mountains dwellers working together, using their collective magic to create it, but it had just been my father. He'd spent weeks sleeping after the border had been made, and I thought it was because of my mother's death, that he'd been so grief-stricken. But now it all made sense—he'd drained his power, all his energy, by using that much magic at once. We didn't have magic in endless reserves, and my father had used a massive amount, which had left him bedridden for four weeks. Magic always demanded a price.

He'd also been grieving, of course.

My thoughts turned to my mother, how sick she'd gotten shortly before the border was created. The ragnose leaves needed to save her sat just beyond our reach, in the forest. We tried everything, but even with our earth magic, we couldn't get ragnose to grow in our territory. So we watched my mother fade away to nothing. It wasn't my father's fault. He couldn't have known she would get so sick with fever, that the best fever-reducing plant would be stuck in Mosswood Forest, unreachable.

I wiped away the tears forming at the memory. I needed to focus, to keep it together. I couldn't fall apart now.

Instead, my mind wandered to the other things I'd heard last night. Questions rolled through my mind like endless waves. More questions than answers. I didn't want Penn to know I'd listened in on his conversation with Wayfinder, but that didn't mean I couldn't still get answers. I just needed to ask the right questions.

I cleared my throat. "You know, my stepmother probably isn't just coming after me. She's going to have her Huntsman find that mirror."

"After today, the Huntsman won't be a problem," Penn said, shifting behind me.

We passed a tree with a low-hanging branch, and both of us ducked as the horse clopped underneath it.

"Someone is feeling cocky," I said.

"I'm not cocky. I'm prepared." Penn's voice was terse.

"Someone is also grumpy," I grumbled.

If anyone should be grumpy, it should be the princess being forced to ride with the brute who'd kidnapped her.

"Well, if you're not careful," I said, keeping my voice light, "the mirror might find its owner."

Penn stiffened behind me, his body tensing for just a second, before he relaxed. "You don't know what that mirror does, do you?"

Busted.

"The mirror has the power to show you anything you desire," Penn said.

Last night, he'd told Wayfinder that information was too dangerous to share with anyone, so I wondered why he was divulging this information with me now. Maybe he trusted me with it, knew I wouldn't use the mirror after seeing how it had destroyed my court. Or maybe he thought by sharing it I'd be more invested in whatever mission he had for me.

Up ahead, the forest began to clear, opening up to grassy fields, the sun slowly rising and painting the world with its golden hue. The other thieves rode on their horses behind us, and I twisted to look at Penn.

"Anything you desire? Meaning what?"

Penn sighed. "If she wanted to know where you were right now, for example, and she had the mirror in her possession, she could simply ask it. She could ask the mirror what the best day to plan an attack would be. She could ask the mirror how to strengthen her power. The mirror knows all."

My mouth dropped open. "This explains so much," I muttered to myself. "How she knows . . ."

"How she knows what?"

My gaze lifted to meet Penn's, and I realized our faces were far too close for comfort. I twisted forward.

"How she knows what, Lilypad?"

I was too tired to yell at him for calling me that. "Babies are brought to the castle, almost daily. They come in with the powers they're born with, and we watch them leave without their magic. We didn't know that was what was happening at first. But we'd heard rumors and never were able to confirm them. Now I know how she locates all these babies, how she knows when a new one is born. We still don't know how she steals their powers, though."

A slight breeze rustled the grassy plain around us, the long weeds swaying.

"Yes," Penn said. "That is exactly how she does it."

"You knew?" I couldn't help the betrayal in my voice. "You knew and you let her do something so vile?"

"Why do you think I stole the mirror?" he asked. "Do you know how long it took to plan that mission? It's not easy to steal from a queen who has that kind of power."

"I hate her," I said. "I hate that she's taken so much from me. She even planned her attack on what was supposed to be the best day of my life."

"And when was that?"

Tears pricked my eyes. "My wedding day."

Penn swore softly behind me.

I still remembered how I'd woken up that day, so full of hope and excitement for my impending nuptials.

"The best day of my life quickly turned into the worst."

"I'm sorry," Penn said.

I shook my head as an eagle soared overhead, so majestic and beautiful. "I always thought she chose that day to hurt me because she knew how much I was looking forward to my wedding. It was on my twenty-fifth birthday. She knew where all the guards were stationed, exactly how to attack to kill them. She knew we'd have our guard down, everyone celebrating the future king and queen of Elwen."

I still remembered how I'd been searching for my father. He was never late to anything, and yet, he hadn't been on time to my own wedding. Of course I hadn't known it was because the Huntsman had been squeezing the life from him in his own private chambers.

"That was the day she took our powers, no one able to fight against her." I shook my head, remembering the way the fire court had run away, none of them able to fight back against her, the way I'd lost sight of Jasper in the chaos of the blood and screams.

"Lilypad, that's . . . terrible." Penn's voice was genuine, none of his usual snark or amusement or sternness present.

"None of us could fight back because our magic was suddenly gone, and that's how she overtook everyone so quickly. If we knew how she was stealing our powers, maybe we'd be better equipped to stop her."

"We know as much as you do, that she uses that mirror to track all the new babies born in the earth court, to take their earth magic from them so that she's the only one with power."

Disappointment welled in me. Part of me had hoped he'd have more answers than I did. "So you don't know if there's any way to get our magic back? To restore it?"

"I don't, I'm sorry." Penn paused. "I do often wonder, though, why she hasn't attacked Mosswood Forest. Why she hasn't destroyed the border and descended her reign of terror down upon us. We've waited, prepared, but she's never come."

"She's been too busy destroying Elwen," I said flippantly, hoping he wouldn't push me on the topic.

Penn stayed silent behind me.

"What do you want with that mirror?" I asked.

Penn had told Wayfinder he wouldn't use the mirror's power, and now that I knew what the mirror did, I respected him for it. It would be hard to resist a power like that.

We approached the end of the grassy plain, a line of trees in front of us.

"I suppose it's time to tell you," Penn said. "I want to destroy it, and hopefully, weaken your stepmother in the process. And you're going to help me do it."

My heart stopped beating in my chest, and I struggled for words, but before I could ask any questions, a scream cut through the air. Both Penn and I whirled on our horse to see Brains hanging in the air, a tree branch wrapped around her throat. The Huntsman had found us.

HE STEPPED out of the surrounding forest and into the clearing. Dread curled around my body, its icy fingers freezing me to the spot as Penn jumped off his horse and flung out a hand. A tree bent down over the Huntsman, wrapping its branches around him, but the Huntsman shrugged it off, cracking the branches in two. He was strong, even stronger than I'd remembered.

He towered over everyone, easily twice the height of Penn, his long torso and legs made of tree trunks, his arms of branches, his mouth opening to reveal pointy black thorns. Leaves covered his head, fluttering as he whipped around to lash a branch out at Charming, who attempted to attack with his sword.

Arrows flew through the air, embedding into his chest. He looked down and simply plucked them out. Arrow jumped up onto a tree branch, continuing to shoot at him to no avail. It was complete chaos, and our plan of sneaking up on him was clearly ruined. He'd found us first. It was an all-out brawl, everyone using their magic, their skills, to bring down the Huntsman.

Penn barreled into him, and the Huntsman finally dropped Brains, who scrambled backward as Hammer helped her to her feet. Penn flipped the Huntsman onto his back while reaching out his hand and uprooting a tree, its roots roping around the Huntsman. But before the roots could tie him down, the Huntsman kicked a powerful leg out, making Penn fly through the air. Hammer ran toward the Huntsman, axe in hand, but the Huntsman simply flicked him away.

I hung back, watching everything unfold with horror. I should help, I should do something, but . . . my plan. Now would be the perfect moment to escape. I thought about my and Penn's conversation. Did his revelation change anything? He wanted to destroy my stepmother's mirror, destroy her. That's what I wanted as well. But . . . the question was why? Penn didn't do anything out of the kindness of his heart. He wasn't the evil thief I thought him to be, but he also wasn't innocent. He had to have his own motivations, and I didn't know that I could trust him.

Plus, he wasn't giving me a choice in this. His plan didn't change the fact that he'd kidnapped me and was forcing me to do what he wanted.

I swallowed, watching as the Huntsman punched Wayfinder, sending him to the ground. Arrow continued to shoot at him to no avail. Shadow had slipped away, and I wasn't sure where she was. Lightning ran at the Huntsman, sticking out his hand, blades of grass shooting like daggers. But the Huntsman easily swiped them away.

Guilt crept over me at the thought of leaving them like this, fighting for their lives. I'd told Penn I wanted vengeance on the Huntsman, and that was true, but the sooner I left this place, the sooner I could rescue my people. I had to find Jasper. I had no idea when Penn planned to go on this mission to destroy the mirror, how long it would take. Every day that passed was another day Driscoll and Jillian were trapped, another day my people were suffering. I couldn't afford to wait. I needed to get to Jasper and come up with a plan to take back my court.

I slowly backed away, no one even noticing as they tried to free Hammer, now clutched in the Huntsman's grasp. Hammer elbowed the Huntsman in his nose, and the creature roared, dropping him and stepping back just as Penn used his magic to bring branches down that wrapped around the Huntsman's neck. At the same time, Charming held out both hands, bringing roots up from the earth that wrapped around the Huntsman's feet and caused his body to crash to the earth. They might actually defeat him soon, and that meant I needed to go. Now.

I shot them one last look as I turned and fled into the forest, running as fast as my legs would carry me, screams echoing behind me.

Part Two

*"The envy and pride grew ever greater like a weed in the queen's heart,
until she had no peace day and night."*

Chapter Twenty-Two

I t took the rest of the day, but I reached the border of the fire court by the time the sun was sinking in the sky above. My legs, back, and arms ached. My throat felt like it was on fire, and my entire body was covered in dirt and muck.

I'd made it.

My stepmother hadn't found me, and my trek through Elwen had been surprisingly easy. Mainly because everything had been destroyed and abandoned, no signs of life anywhere, just the blackened, ashy land. The hardest part had been the border. I'd heard enough stories about the border from the seven thieves over the last few weeks and employed every trick and tactic they taught me—none of which helped, mainly because by sheer dumb luck I fell from a tree while trying to leap, and the border's jabbing vines missed me as I landed on the other side. Bruises peppered my body from the fall, but I was otherwise unscathed. I could imagine Penn's commentary at my attempt to get to the other side.

Well, that's one way to get across, Lilypad.

I didn't have time to dwell on him or on the state of my court: the sadness, the cruelty, of what had happened. I focused all my energy on making it to Gilraeth. Now I limped toward Dragonstone Mountains, which rose high into the sky, knowing that on the other side of those mountains was the desert land of the fire court. I'd been here enough times that I knew the way through. But I needed to rest. My body was tired, and there was no way I'd be able to reach Jasper today. It would take a few days to cut through the mountains and then journey on to Jasper's home, in the eastern part of Gilraeth.

Excitement bubbled in me.

I couldn't believe I'd actually made it here. My plan had worked. I'd escaped the king of thieves, and soon, I'd be reunited with Jasper.

I leaned against the bottom of the mountain, hard rock jutting into my back and poking me. I couldn't find it in myself to care at this point.

Caves dotted the base, an extensive network of tunnels behind them that I could trek through to get to the other side. Jasper had shown me map after map of the fire court, and we'd explored the tunnels together many times throughout the years. But his warnings rang in my ears: *don't ever come into the tunnels without me or someone else from the fire court.*

Komodo dragons, fire-breathing lizards, and snakes with three heads were just some of the creatures that lurked in the depths of the mountain, and I didn't have any kind of earth magic to defend myself. It would take longer, but it would be safer to go over the mountains. They stretched above me, dusty and orange, such a contrast to the vibrancy of the earth court.

Whereas the earth court was characterized by its lush beauty, greens and blues and yellows, the fire court was characterized by its rock formations and desert: orange, brown, gray, and yellow, the colors of fire and smoke. It had its own beauty, even if I preferred Elwen. I stood, searching for a path, and my eyes quickly landed on one. Steep stairs cut into the side of the mountain, winding up, up, up, until I could no longer see them.

I'd better start now. I could find a place to rest once I was deeper into Gilraeth territory. I began to climb the stairs, my joints creaking and protesting with each movement. I had to stop several times to catch my breath, slowing my journey even more.

My stomach let out a loud grumble, and I hoped I'd be able to find something to eat: berries, cactus, any kind of desert plant, really. Jasper had shown me the ones I could safely eat, as well as the ones to stay away from. I wouldn't be able to catch any animals. First, I had no weapons. Second, I had no skill.

Charming was supposed to have taught me how to hunt prey at some point, but things had gone awry with the sudden arrival of the Huntsman. With any luck, I'd be able to make it with the water skin I had and whatever I came across on my way to find Jasper.

My thoughts flitted to Penn and the other thieves, and I wondered where they were now, if they'd killed the Huntsman or had been able to detain him so they could escape, what they'd think when they realized I wasn't there with them. That familiar guilt bubbled up, but I pushed it down.

I'd done what I needed to in order to survive. Besides, the Huntsman never would've been a problem if Penn hadn't kidnapped me in the first place. They'd brought the Huntsman on themselves, and I could no longer worry about them or Mosswood Forest. That concern was something I'd focus on once I'd taken back the earth court. One problem at a time.

My feet slipped on the uneven steps, and I fell forward, hands catching the full impact of the sharp stone. I cried out, looking at the blood that now coated my palms. Great. I'd only gotten a hundred steps up the mountain, and I'd already managed to hurt myself. I could just imagine Penn's voice in my head.

Did no one ever teach you how to walk?

I kept going, annoyed that I'd left him behind yet still couldn't be free of him. Once I found Jasper, Penn would be out of my mind forever.

Soon the steps became so steep I had to use my hands to pull myself up, but they were too slick with blood, and every time I grappled with the stone stairs, I cried out in pain, the cuts deepening. I had no bandages, nothing with me other than the water skin hanging off my belt. I clearly hadn't come prepared, hadn't listened to Wayfinder during his lessons, which focused on the journey to and from your mission.

He'd warned me to always make sure I had essential items, and I admit, my mind might have wandered a bit during our sessions together, but now I wished I'd taken heed of his advice.

There was nothing to do but continue on, hands throbbing. Blood and earth, I hoped I didn't get an infection from this. I tried as much as possible to not use my hands going forward. The sun quickly sank lower, the sky darkening, and I had to find some kind of shelter soon. The stairs wound tightly around a bend in the mountain, and it was getting so dark I could no longer see in front of me. I felt my way up, and my boots hit a flattened spot that veered off the stairs. This would have to do for now. I had no way of making a fire, no way of seeing exactly where I was in the mountains. I just needed a safe space to sleep, and with the morning light I'd be able to continue on. I nestled against the mountain wall, closed my eyes, and let myself drift off.

A LOW GROWL woke me from a deep sleep. When I opened my eyes, the first thing I noticed was the bright sun, glaring over the mountaintop, everything bathed in its warm hue. The next thing I noticed was the dragon hanging overhead, wings pumping furiously, and I realized in that moment the mistake I'd made.

I looked down at my hands. Blood. Dragons smelled blood, used it to scent out their prey. I was either going to get burned alive or be this dragon's breakfast. Or possibly both.

Jasper had warned me about the dragons time and time again, of how dangerous they were. The people of Gilraeth had been fighting dragons for centuries, and every time we'd traveled to the fire court from Elwen, we had guards assigned to escort us and protect us should we come across the mighty beasts.

I'd been so excited about my escape and finding Jasper that I'd forgotten about all the danger that lurked in every corner of the fire court.

I stood on shaky legs as the dragon landed on the mesa where I'd fallen asleep. Green and orange scales covered its massive body, and it let out a snort of smoke that muddied the air. Its talons were as long as my arm, and one of them could easily impale me. I looked back to the stairs, which continued to wind up the mountain. I wasn't far from the top. But now I'd never make it. My fists curled, and I winced at the pain that lanced through my hands.

I had to fight. Maybe I wasn't as skilled as the other thieves, but I'd just spent weeks training every day with them. I wouldn't run from this, wouldn't give up, not when the earth court was at stake.

The only problem was that I didn't know anything about fighting dragons. I did know how to be quick on my feet, how to defend myself. I didn't have to kill the creature. I just needed to escape from it.

The dragon rose up before me and sucked in a sharp breath. I was already on the ground, rolling as fire scorched past me. The heat from it blasted the entire mesa. I tumbled to my feet, bracing my legs like Lightning had taught me, ready to jump in either direction based on what the dragon did. I needed to get to those stairs. They were too narrow for the dragon, winding and naturally enclosed by the mountain walls. I would be protected if I could reach them.

The dragon let out a roar that shook the ground beneath me. Its yellow eyes landed on me, and it sniffed the air. I looked down at all the dried blood on my hands, wishing I'd had the sense to wash them off with my water. I hadn't wanted to waste valuable drinking water at the time. I had so much to learn about survival.

"Of course you're being attacked by a dragon. Because you can never make things easy, can you, Lilypad?"

I whirled in the direction of the sound, and there stood Penn and Shadow. They'd come after me. I didn't know whether to be relieved or disappointed.

Penn nodded his head at Shadow, who ran to me, while he faced the dragon, summoning long vines that slithered along the ground toward the dragon's legs.

Shadow grabbed my arm and pulled me toward the stairs as the dragon's attention turned to Penn.

"What's he doing?" I asked as Shadow dragged me away. "He's going to get hurt!"

"He's faced a dragon or two in his lifetime. He'll be okay," Shadow said.

I didn't even know why I cared. If the dragon killed Penn, that would actually work out in my favor. But I couldn't tear my eyes away.

"Come on," Shadow urged. "We have to go. We don't want to get caught in fire court territory."

Actually, that was exactly what I wanted, but it wasn't why I resisted. I elbowed Shadow, who grunted, and I ran back to the mesa, where Penn was currently jumping back as the dragon blew out a stream of fire, incinerating his vines.

"Princess," Shadow hissed. "Oh, Penn's going to kill me."

Penn grabbed the sword strapped to his back and rolled with it across the ground. He popped up onto his feet, stabbing the dragon in the leg. The creature roared, rearing back, then swiped a clawed foot at Penn. Its talon sliced at Penn's stomach, just missing the thief as he jumped in the air and sent a flurry of leaves slicing at the dragon's face like sharp discs.

I'd never seen someone fight with so much skill. His movements were so smooth, so refined. For every move the dragon made, Penn had a countermove ready to go. I'd seen countless Elwen soldiers fight and train with their earth magic, but Penn could've beaten them all. And he was doing it in the fire court, where earth magic was weaker, not as strong as it was in our home land. Still, Penn couldn't defeat a dragon on his own. Jasper told me it took at least ten warriors to bring one down.

"We have to do something," I said to Shadow.

"That's not the plan," Shadow said. "I need to get you out of here, and Penn will join us later."

Not if he's dead.

I pushed away Shadow's hand. She groaned. "I told him you weren't going to come quietly."

Penn rolled underneath the dragon's belly, shoving the sword up at the creature, but the sharp metal just glanced off its hard scales. Dragons were not easy to defeat, and you needed special weapons to injure them, weapons forged in the fire court. We had to create a distraction and then run for it.

A pile of boulders sat up on a ledge hanging over the mesa. I scrambled to them, ignoring the pain in my hands and the ache in my body as I climbed.

"Get down here right now," Shadow whisper-yelled, but I ignored her, continuing to climb until I sat atop the boulders.

"Hey!" I yelled at the dragon and waved my hands.

Its head snapped to me, those yellow eyes blazing.

Penn got up from the ground, glaring at me. "You're not even supposed to be here!" He looked at Shadow, who just shrugged.

"You're welcome," I shouted as the dragon stomped toward me, nostrils flaring.

Spirits below, this thing was intimidating.

"What is she doing?" Penn asked, and once again, Shadow just shrugged.

"No idea, but she is determined."

"Fucking blood and earth," Penn muttered.

The dragon came to a stop in front of me, then let out a blaze of fire. I jumped from the boulders, the fire missing me by a hair. The dragon let out an annoyed grunt and swung its tail at the mountain wall. Here went nothing. I leapt down from the wall, and the dragon's tail smashed into it.

I ran toward Penn, grabbing his hand and pulling him. "We need to get out of here," I shouted.

The dragon turned, sucking in another big breath, ready to burn us alive, but just then the mountain rumbled. Rocks began to rain down over the mesa from the wall the dragon had just hit. Penn, Shadow, and I ran for the stairs, and the dragon tried to follow, but heavy boulders fell onto its shoulders, its tail. Rocks fell onto the stairs, blocking our way down the mountain. There was only one direction to go: up.

The dragon thrashed its head, roaring out in frustration as we dashed up the stairs, none of us daring to look back.

Chapter Twenty-Three

We didn't stop until we'd reached the top of the mountain, which was covered in spindly trees with bare branches and had very little life. Gilraeth spread out below, and from up here I could see the rolling dunes, the rock formations, and cacti dotting the ground and the bright oranges and yellows of the desert flowers.

I collapsed onto the ground, Shadow falling down next to me, Penn standing over us, a frown on his face.

"Why would you do that?" he asked, irritation lacing his voice.

"Rescue you, you mean?"

He crossed his arms. "If memory serves me right, I believe we were rescuing you."

"I didn't ask you to do that!" I shot back.

"No, you forced us to. You lied to me about the Huntsman, about wanting revenge. Your plan the entire time had been to run. And now, thanks to you, we don't have a clear path down the mountain."

Even though my legs shook with fatigue, I still managed to stand, facing Penn. "I didn't ask you to come after me. I didn't ask you to fight a dragon. I didn't ask you to kidnap me in the first place. So if you're going to be mad at anyone, maybe it should be yourself."

Shadow coughed out a snort, but Penn shot her a glare, and she sobered her expression.

He stepped forward, fists curled. "If I'm so horrible, then why didn't you run with Shadow? Why did you step in to save me?"

I swallowed at how close he now stood to me, at the hard planes of his face, the burning in his eyes. That passion. So much passion.

"I wasn't saving you," I gritted out. "I was trying to block the stairway path so you couldn't kidnap me yet again and take me back to Mosswood Forest." I spread my arms out. "Welcome to Gilraeth. I'm sure you're going to love meeting my betrothed."

Penn's eyes flashed with warning. "We're not meeting your betrothed. We are getting out of here, Lilypad. One way or another."

"No. I didn't come this far just for you to haul me back to your forest."

"You're—" He stopped suddenly, letting out a groan. For once he didn't have a comeback. Then I saw his hand over his side, the dark stain on his shirt, the red slipping through his fingers.

"Boss!" Shadow jumped to her feet and ran to him, and I stumbled back, staring at the blood seeping from the wound in his side. Shadow lowered him to the ground and looked back at me. "Get my rucksack. Now, Princess!"

I ran to it, fumbling with it as I handed it to Shadow. She shook her head, pressing her hand to Penn's wound. His face was pale, his eyes fluttering closed.

"Stay with us, Boss," Shadow said. "Mother fucking earth, that dragon must've sliced him open with one of its talons." She nodded toward the bag. "Get out the bandages and the salve."

I nodded, digging through it. "He didn't say anything." My voice shook.

"Does that really surprise you?"

"No," I said quietly, handing her the materials. "It doesn't."

"Okay." Shadow looked at me. "You need to press your hand down on his wound to staunch the flow of blood. I'm going to rip off his tunic and apply the salve, then get him bandaged. Hopefully the wound isn't too deep."

Penn lay unconscious now, and I knelt beside him, pressing my hands down just like Shadow instructed. He still looked so formidable, even when suffering from a deadly injury. His chest rose with shallow breaths, and sweat dotted his forehead.

Shadow lifted his satchel over his head and set it on the ground, then ripped his tunic, exposing his muscled chest and abs, covered in scars.

"What are those from?" I breathed out.

"That's his story to tell," Shadow said, applying a thick, clear salve to the edges of his wound. She grabbed the bandage and unrolled it.

"I'm going to need your help with this part. We need to roll him over and get the bandage around his waist."

I nodded. "Whatever you need."

I grunted as I pushed Penn's body, rolling him to his side while Shadow worked the bandage around him. His body was so hard and firm, no soft edges anywhere.

"Okay," Shadow said, and I gently lowered Penn to his back.

"Now what?" I asked, eyeing him.

"We need to watch his wound, get water to make sure he's drinking. Other than that, we wait. Can you stay with him while I go scout out the area?"

I nodded, not taking my eyes off him. When I finally did look up, Shadow was already gone. I scooted closer to Penn. The sun rose higher in the sky, but up here we had no shelter from its harsh rays. It was still early, and though we were at a higher elevation, it would only get hotter as the day progressed. We needed to make some sort of shelter.

His satchel lay by his head, the mirror most likely inside. I could snatch it and steal away. Now was my chance.

Penn took shallow breaths, and blood seeped through the bandage. I couldn't leave him. Fuck. I couldn't, and I didn't know why. I just knew it wouldn't be right.

A long scar ran from his chest down to his navel, raised and jagged, like a lightning bolt. Other smaller scars cut across his ribs, his abs, his pecs. Light blond hair covered his chest, and I wanted to reach out and touch it, run my fingers across it.

Instead, my fingers found their way to that long scar running the length of his torso. They danced over it lightly, and I wondered what could have caused such an injury.

"The trees," he whispered, and I snatched my hand back, cheeks burning. "When I was a boy. They almost killed me."

He was awake and talking. I looked around for Shadow, to call for her, but I saw no signs of her and didn't want to yell too loudly given we were technically in unfamiliar territory—and I was traveling with a well-known criminal. He might not be recognizable on sight, but the people of the fire court wouldn't just let strangers from the earth court wander freely without asking questions, getting personal. I couldn't risk that kind of attention, especially not with Penn injured.

I grabbed water and he lifted his head to drink.

"Tell me about the tree," I said, hoping I could keep him awake and talking until Shadow returned.

"I was supposed to be home," he rasped. "Hiding in our cellar. Instead, I followed my parents to the warfront."

"This happened during the Great War?" I asked.

He nodded and closed his eyes for a moment, breaths still shallow. "I hid, watching as my parents fought, using their magic to upend trees, send grass flying like daggers, to bring up barriers. But they weren't watching closely enough. A tree-like monster came out of nowhere, towering over them."

I didn't make a sound, listening to his story, the slow way he spoke each word.

"It swiped at them, knocking them back. That's when I ran out, using my magic to try and stop the tree. But I was young, my magic not yet strong. I could only pause the tree in its pursuit of my parents, but it wasn't enough. The tree picked me up, sliced me with its thorns, beat me with branches and threw me, knocking me unconscious. When I awoke, my parents were dead, and the border had been closed."

It felt so natural to hate the people of Mosswood Forest from afar, but I'd spent a few weeks with them, and for the most part, many of them reminded me of my own people in Elwen. Damn the false king and queen. Damn my father for letting the conflict between them get so bad.

Then I paused, a realization hitting me.

"Penn," I said slowly. That story he'd just told. It sounded so familiar, and suddenly I remembered the painting, the false king and queen holding the hand of the little boy. The story Penn told about how they died. Except . . . he never said the boy died. I'd just assumed.

"Were the false king and queen your parents?"

His eyes fluttered. "They were good parents."

"You're the false prince," I whispered. Which meant he was the king of Mosswood Forest. It made sense. Of course it did. That's why Penn was so determined to take care of his people, to go to the lengths he did to protect them.

My brows furrowed. "But if you're alive and well, why is a council ruling?"

He coughed, the sound raspy and throttled. I immediately gave him a drink of water.

"They rule while I'm away . . . which is a lot of the time. My people need stability. I can't . . . give that to them right now."

Once upon a time, this information would have made me even angrier, knowing that Penn was a product of the people who betrayed my father and the rest of Elwen, but now I couldn't find it in me to be upset. Penn hadn't done anything wrong. He was just a boy, this role forced upon him. He was doing the best he could with a shitty situation. I knew how that felt, all too well.

"I'm sorry I got you into this mess," I said when Penn had gone silent, his eyes closed again. They fluttered when I spoke, and I wondered if he heard me or if he'd fallen back asleep. "I know I blamed you, and to be fair, I do think this is partly your fault for kidnapping me in the first place, but I shouldn't have run away like that, left you to fight my battle. Sometimes, I don't think I'm cut out to be a queen at all." I looked out over the horizon, to the beige and tawny sand that stretched for miles in all directions. "I trained at your academy for weeks, and I might as well have learned nothing. I couldn't even defend myself against a dragon, didn't properly plan for my escape. I heard your voice, you know. Constantly in my ear, telling me everything I was doing wrong. Lilypad, indeed."

"You know why I gave you the nickname Lilypad?" Penn asked, and I jumped.

Oh, blood and earth. He had been listening, and I'd been far more vulnerable than I'd meant to be.

"Yes, I know why. Because I showed how weak, how inadequate, how entirely unprepared I am to be a thief when I trained with Hammer on those lily pads."

He shook his head, whispering, "No." A grimace overtook his features as he opened his eyes. "Did you know that lily pads strengthen their environment?" He winced, his hand going to his wound. "They help everything around them to thrive."

The words took me aback. "N-no, I didn't know that."

"That's why I nicknamed you Lilypad," he said. "Because from everything you've shown me, told me, it seems like that's the kind of queen you want to be . . . for Elwen."

"Oh." My voice was small. "Okay."

He turned his head slowly, looking at me, the green of his eyes bright and vibrant under the warm sun. I leaned in closer, heart beating hard in my chest.

"Penn, I—"

"Stop right there," a voice said. "In the name of Princess Seraphina of the fire court, state your business."

I stilled, rooted to the spot. I didn't even have to turn to know who was speaking. I'd recognize that voice anywhere. Had heard it in my dreams so many times over the last few years.

Jasper. Jasper had finally found me.

Chapter Twenty-Four

I turned to see a sword of flames pointed at me, another at Penn.

I opened my mouth to speak, but Jasper cut me off. "Don't say a word."

Well, that was confusing since he'd just demanded we state our business. I was a little miffed he didn't recognize me. My hair was shorter and I was covered in grime and dressed in these ridiculous clothes, but still. We'd been betrothed for over twenty years. You'd think the man would know his own fiancé. His dark hair was longer, curling around his ears and beneath his chin, and his golden skin was tanned by the desert sun. He wore loose pants and a long-sleeved shirt, common here in Gilraeth, to protect everyone from the unrelenting sun and heat. I wanted to step closer, but I was afraid any movement or word might earn me a fiery sword in my gut.

"Fiery hells," Jasper said, his gaze locking on Penn's hand. "That's my ring!" He stilled for a minute, looking back at the man who was with him, his guard. "The king of thieves."

Oh. Oh, no.

Jasper marched over to Penn and yanked the ring off his finger, not taking any care to be gentle. Penn let out a groan, and I reached for him, then thought better of it. His eyes were closed again, and I wasn't even sure he was conscious. If he was, the idiot would no doubt be trying to fight his way out of this, so maybe it was better he wasn't awake right now.

"Jasper!" I said.

He glared at me. "Excuse me, you will address me as 'my lord.' And how do you know my name? Have we met?" He frowned at me.

"Jasper, it's me. Liliath."

His eyes widened, sword still pointed at me, then he barked out a laugh. "Liliath. Princess of the earth court? Who's currently imprisoned by her stepmother?" He snorted. "You look nothing like her."

I rolled my eyes. "That's because I've been locked up in a prison cell for two years. I had to cut my hair, okay?"

He looked at the guard, and they laughed together. "Yes, you're Liliath. You with that raggedy hair and dirt-smudged face and tunic and trousers? Princess Liliath wouldn't dare be caught dead wearing whatever that"—he gestured to my tunic—"little getup is."

Well, this was not going well. "I promise you, I am Princess Liliath of Elwen."

Jasper smirked. "Okay, then, I'll entertain your little story. How did you escape, exactly?"

I closed my eyes. "I didn't. I was kidnapped by the king of thieves." I gestured to Penn. "He's taken me for his own purposes, and I managed to escape him and come here, but he found me before I could get to you. Does my voice not sound familiar at all?"

"Say something only Jasper would know," the guard said.

I huffed, racking my brain for something, but nothing came to mind, except . . . I couldn't say *that* out loud. I bit my lip. Then again, my life very well might depend on this. Good green earth, I really couldn't think of anything else?

Jasper stepped closer, the pointy end of his fire sword dangerously near my neck, the heat already burning my skin.

"Fine," I burst out. "There was a name you insisted I call you whenever we . . . made love."

Jasper tapped his shiny boot on the ground, not looking impressed.

He was really going to make me say it out loud. "Sir Stallion," I whispered.

The guard laughed, and Jasper sent him a glare, the laugh quickly turning into a cough.

"Liliath?" Jasper's eyes widened, and his sword dropped from his hand, the fire disappearing.

I rushed into his arms, relief flooding me. "Jasper, I've missed you so much."

He pressed a kiss to my head. "I can't believe you're here . . . and with him. Arrest him at once!"

I stiffened and pushed myself out of his arms. "No. Wait." I stood between the guard and Penn, holding out my hands. "He's hurt. He needs medicine."

Jasper scratched his head. "He's the king of thieves, and he kidnapped you. He's lucky I'm just calling for his arrest and not his execution." He gestured for the guard, who tried to step forward, but I blocked him.

"No, Jasper, please. I know he's done some bad things, but he's had his reasons."

I thought of Mosswood Forest, of all the people living there who depended on Penn. I couldn't believe these words were actually coming out of my mouth, but I didn't want to see Penn get carted off and thrown in prison. I'd fantasized about this exact situation so many times in the last few weeks, but all I knew in this moment was that I had to protect him.

"Reasons?" Jasper shook his head. "Oh, Liliath. Captivity has addled your brain." He put an arm around me and led me from Penn. "It's okay. I'm here now, and everything is going to be all right."

"No, Jasper, please listen to me."

Just then, the branch of the tree thwacked Jasper across the back. He whirled. "Who did that?"

I looked at Penn, still unconscious. Shadow. It had to be her.

"The other . . ." I was about to say thieves, but for some reason, I felt protective of Penn's secret, that the king of thieves was actually different people, all under his tutelage. "Um . . . he brought others with him, and we got separated. They must be back now."

Jasper gasped and looked at his guard. "We need to go."

"Yes," I said, "they're very dangerous. We don't want to get into a battle, not when there's only two of you against . . . ten of them!"

"Ten?" Jasper shrieked. "Let's go," he yelled to the guard as a tree bent down and whipped the guard's butt. He let out a yelp.

I hoped Shadow would get Penn the help he needed, hoped I was buying them time. Jasper hurried me away from Penn, and I couldn't help but look back, just so I could catch a final glimpse of the king of thieves.

<h1 style="text-align:center">Chapter Twenty-Five</h1>

I spent a glorious two days sleeping in the guest quarters of Jasper's home. I'd bathed, my hands had mostly healed, I'd eaten, read, played the piano and harp, even tried crocheting, all things I'd enjoyed in my past life.

I was also bored out of my mind.

In Mosswood Forest, I'd gotten used to always being busy, to training and moving and thinking nonstop. I was absent of that stimulation here. It hadn't helped that Jasper had dropped me off and then immediately left to go see his father. He was supposed to be back in a few hours, and I'd been summoned to have dinner in his private quarters. I'd use this opportunity to finally talk to Jasper about my plan—and about the mirror.

We couldn't waste any more time. I was not going to sit here and be pampered while my people were suffering. I appreciated that Jasper wanted me to rest and recover after my harrowing journey, but now wasn't the time. We needed to create a plan and strike out before my stepmother could get any more powerful than she already was.

I paced back and forth in Jasper's room, wearing a gown that felt luxurious. It was bright red, the bodice tight, the skirt flowing out to the ground. Delicate gold slippers had replaced my boots. It wasn't practical for fighting, but I had missed my dresses, and luckily, Jasper had kept a few for me. Red drapes covered his windows with gold tassels hanging from them. Delicate red silk sheets spread across his bed. All the red reminded me of blood, though I knew red and gold were the colors of the fire court. Just like green and yellow were the colors of the earth court.

I wrung my hands together, wondering when Jasper would finally arrive. I was eager to hear why he'd had to leave so suddenly after we'd been reunited. I wanted to talk to him, to kiss him, to feel his arms around me.

My thoughts drifted to Penn and Shadow. I hoped Penn had healed, that he and Shadow had found shelter and were headed back to their home. Penn would have to cut his losses now that I was with Jasper. Which was good. Because I didn't have time to play thief, not when the earth court was at stake.

The big mahogany doors swung open and Jasper strode in. I rushed into his arms.

"Jasper! I've missed you!"

He stepped back and gestured to the small table sitting in the middle of the room, covered with a gold tablecloth, adorned with napkins, silverware, and two goblets of wine. "Please, let's sit."

That red ring sparkled on Jasper's finger, and he motioned to it. "I'm so glad I got this back from that horrid thief. Your father gifted it to us after the Great War."

My brows pinched together. "What?"

He pulled out a chair for me, and I sat just as two servants swept in with silver trays that they sat in front of us. "Yes, after the Great War, your father felt guilty over all the trouble he'd caused. You know how the courts are. None of us like conflict, not after what the Seven Spirits did to the people of the Old World when they started fighting too much."

"So what does that have to do with my father?" I gestured to Jasper. "With the ring?"

My stomach growled at the sight of stew with rabbit meat, prickly pear, carrots, potatoes, and onion.

Jasper sat down across from me and smiled. "He wanted to appease the other courts, who were displeased that he'd allowed such a rift to happen, everyone worried that the Seven Spirits might appear and punish us for such conflict."

"But I thought you'd told me that ring had been passed down to you?"

Jasper took a bite of his stew. "Yes, he gave the ring to my father, and my father gave it to me when I took over our manor. Apparently, the gifts were spoils of war, taken from those mountain dwellers before the border was closed."

I'd never known any of this. Hadn't known my father had to appease the other courts because of the Great War. Maybe that's why my father closed the border, to end the war because he was afraid the Seven Spirits would smite us all if we fought any longer.

Maybe that was why none of the courts had helped us, why they'd left Elwen to rot under my stepmother's rule. They were afraid of entering into any kind of conflict, afraid of what the Seven Spirits might do should the fighting get too bad.

"You look lovely in that gown," Jasper said, interrupting my thoughts. "Thank the dragon lords that you're out of those horrid clothes. I can't believe the king of thieves dressed you like that."

"Well, it wasn't like he had gowns lying around," I said, feeling a defensiveness that I didn't understand. "And the tunics and trousers were practical. Much easier to fight and travel in than gowns."

"Fight?" Jasper's brows furrowed, and he reached a hand across the table. "You had to fight?"

"I was training," I said. "For a mission that Penn wanted me for."

"What a bastard," Jasper said.

Though I'd thought the exact same thing many times over, I didn't like hearing the word come out of Jasper's mouth. I shoved another spoonful of stew in my mouth, chewing on the rabbit meat.

"I'm so sorry for what you've been through, Liliath." Jasper swallowed. "We've had our own problems, here in Gilraeth."

"What's happened?" I dotted my mouth with my napkin and took a drink of wine.

"Princess Seraphina has been cursed, her parents both killed."

"Cursed?" I asked. "What kind of magic could curse someone?"

"Magic from Sorrengard." Jasper took a deep gulp from his goblet.

I gasped. The shadow court.

"But . . . but we haven't heard from the shadow court in sixty years."

Not since the little island had waged war on the rest of the continent. They'd managed to destroy the star court, but the rest of Arathia banded together and banished them back to their island, using our collective magic to defeat them and severely deplete their forces. We hadn't heard from them since that war so long ago, and most of us assumed their society was in shambles and they hadn't been able to rebuild.

"A sorceress came here from Sorrengard," Jasper said. "We didn't know of her true origins until it was too late. She overtook the throne, cursed my poor cousin, and now she uses her dark shadow magic to rule over us. No one has been able to overthrow her."

My heart pounded. The earth court was in shambles, and now this? The fire court was also in danger?

I stood, no longer hungry. "Jasper, this is why now, more than ever, we have to band together to save our courts. Have you spoken with the leaders of Fyriad, Apolis, Valoris?"

Jasper stood as well. He shook his head. "No one wants to help, to get involved when the shadow court is at play."

"But if one court is in danger, then we're all in danger." My voice shook. This shouldn't surprise me. After all, no one had come to save me.

Except Penn. But he'd done it for his own selfish purposes.

"We're doing the best we can," Jasper said. "But right now, everyone is scared, fearful of what this sorceress, what Sorrengard, wants. If they've sent her to destroy us, then I don't want to know what plans they have for the other courts."

"I'm so sorry," I said. "Poor Seraphina. Does anyone know how to break her curse?"

He shook his head. "Many have tried, to no avail."

I raised my chin. "We're going to help her. We're going to fix all of this." I stepped forward and grabbed his hands. "Together."

He chewed at his bottom lip, something he only did when nervous.

"What's wrong?" I asked.

"Nothing. Let's sit and enjoy our dinner."

We both sat again. "You've been dealing with so much here."

Jasper nodded. "Yes, I've been very busy."

I pushed my stew aside while Jasper continued to spoon his into his mouth. "Listen, we need to create a plan to overthrow my stepmother. Once we take back the earth court, we can rebuild Elwen's army and then defeat the sorceress and save Seraphina. Elwen will not turn its back on Gilraeth."

Jasper coughed, and I moved to stand and help him, but he thrust out a hand, keeping me back. "No, I'm okay," he rasped. "Just a little caught off-guard."

"About what?" I asked.

"The whole defeating your stepmother thing?"

I sat back in my chair. "I don't understand."

"Liliath, the earth court has been destroyed. It's Shiraeth all over again."

My body grew cold. "No, it's not. The star court was completely annihilated by Sorrengard. Elwen is still full of people, my people. The magic can be restored once my stepmother is gone. It's not a lost cause."

The look in Jasper's eyes told me he didn't believe a word I said.

"Jasper, that's my court, my home. I can't just give up on it."

He reached across the table and patted my hand. "You can have a life here, Liliath. No, you won't be queen or rule over a court, but maybe you can help me fight this sorceress. I'm next in line for the throne, you know. All I have to do is kill the sorceress, and then I can rule over Gilraeth myself."

"What?" I shot to my feet, my chair tumbling back. "How can you even say that? Your cousin is stuck in some curse. You can't just forget about her."

"She's already been forgotten about," Jasper said. "We've lost hope she'll recover. My betrothed thinks—"

He stopped himself, but the words had already been spoken.

"Your what?" Ice frosted my words.

"Uh." He ran a hand over his hair. "Well, Liliath, I had to move on at some point."

I crossed my arms. "When did you get betrothed, Jasper?"

"Just a few months ago." His eyes darted to the side. He was lying.

The realization hit me then. "You were never coming for me, were you?"

"Liliath, don't be silly." Jasper waved his hand in the air. "We can find you a new husband here. A nice man who will take care of you and—"

"I don't want a husband! I want to save my court!"

He threw down his napkin. "Stop being a brat. Your court cannot be saved, and you are not a queen or a princess of anything. You're now in Gilraeth and under our jurisdiction."

I stepped back, his words like a punch to the gut. "How can you be so cruel?"

He stood, straightening his beige tunic. "I was supposed to be king. Then you went and let your court go to ruin, so now I have to find another way to become king."

"That's what you care about?" I asked. "What about all the people suffering? What about Princess Seraphina? She's your cousin!"

This wasn't the Jasper I knew. I thought about Driscoll and Jillian, all their comments over the years about Jasper, how much they disliked him. Maybe this had been who he was the whole time, and I'd just refused to see it, refused to see anything other than my duty to marry him.

"Well, then I guess I'm leaving," I said.

"And where are you going to go?" Jasper took a step toward me. "Back to the earth court? By yourself? Back to the king of thieves? Admit it, Liliath, you have nowhere else to go. Besides, it's dangerous here. Wouldn't want to risk you getting caught by the sorceress."

"Why would you care what happens to me?"

Jasper's gaze softened. "Now, come on. We once loved each other. I still want what's best for you, and I just happen to know better. If I let you run off to the earth court and get yourself killed, I'd never forgive myself."

I clenched my teeth. "That's not your decision to make."

He strode forward and placed a hand on my shoulder. "You know what? I think you need some sleep. After a night of rest, you'll wake up refreshed, and you'll see that life here won't be so bad. You can meet my betrothed. I'm sure you two will have a lot to talk about." He started pushing me toward the door.

"No, Jasper—"

"I'll even let you pick your husband. You will have to choose someone. I can't keep feeding you, clothing you, housing you. It would be inappropriate, given the circumstances."

We stopped in front of the doors, and I whirled around.

"Anything else before you go?" Jasper said.

"Yes." I smiled, then brought back my fist just like Hammer taught me and punched him square in the face. "Goodnight." I turned and slammed the door behind me, hearing his cries as I walked down the hallway and toward my room.

Chapter Twenty-Six

W ell, that certainly hadn't gone as planned. I paced in front of
my windows, which overlooked the swelling hills of the desert,
stars blanketing the dark skies above. A fire roared in the hearth, but all I
could feel was the chill of Jasper's words. He was right. I was alone. I
didn't have anybody. My entire plan had hinged on Jasper, on him
helping me. I hadn't even thought there might be a chance he'd have
moved on.

A tear rolled down my cheek. It had been stupid to think he would
wait for me. Stupid to think he actually loved me. He loved my status.
Well, former status. Now that I had no court to rule over, I was useless
to him. Our entire history together had meant nothing to him. All those
times we'd taken strolls around my courtyard, kissed under the stars,
spent hours talking about our future together—it had all been a means
to an end. I felt sick over how he'd used me.

I chewed at the inside of my cheek, not sure where to go from here.
I couldn't just stroll back into the earth court and take on my stepmother by myself, especially not without any magic. I'd be thrown
back into prison, and this time, there'd be no king of thieves rescuing
me.

I couldn't go back to Mosswood Forest, not after I'd left Penn like
that. I doubted the king of thieves would be so forgiving. But then,

what were my choices? To stay here and be married off to someone while my court withered away?

No. No. I would go into hiding and come up with a plan. I just needed a little bit of time to think, and then I could act. I would save the earth court, and I would save Princess Seraphina. Jasper would never become king. He didn't deserve the title, not when he only cared about himself.

Blood and earth, I wished Jillian and Driscoll were here. Driscoll would offer to cut off his balls, and Jillian would say something about how he wasn't worthy of me. They'd make me laugh and they'd dry my tears. They'd remind me I wasn't as alone as I felt. I hoped they were okay, that my stepmother hadn't hurt them in my absence, or worse, killed them.

I stared out my window again, frisking my arms. It would make sense to try and escape tonight, with the cover of darkness. I knew Gilraeth's layout well enough that I could probably find some shelter, a cave to hide in or rock formation to sleep under. But the desert got so cold at night, and I wouldn't have any food. I needed more time to get supplies. A cloak, my boots, bread, dried meats from the kitchen. Surely Jasper wouldn't marry me off tomorrow. I could spend a day collecting what I needed and then steal away tomorrow night. If I could escape the king of thieves, then this wouldn't be that hard.

Jasper didn't know of the skills I'd learned, wouldn't be expecting me to run away. He'd think me stupid for even trying. And he'd be right —but I didn't care. I wouldn't just sit here and let yet another person decide my fate.

Some commotion outside caught my attention. Two people ran across the sand that dusted the courtyard of Jasper's home. Sand flew up behind them, the silver moon sending slivers of light across the ground. For a moment, my stomach dropped. Was the sorceress who'd cursed Seraphina here? Maybe she was working with my stepmother somehow, and now that she knew of my presence, she was going to return me to Elwen.

My eyes widened when I recognized one of the figures. Even under the cover of that cloak, I'd recognize those muscled shoulders, that broad chest, that peek of blond hair anywhere.

Penn was here.

Then my gaze caught on the second figure. Shadow was attempting to grab Penn's arm and yank him away. He wasn't supposed to be here. He clutched at his stomach, and she grabbed him, but he shook her off. I pressed my hands against the window, wishing I could shout down to them and warn them away.

Had Penn lost his mind?

If Jasper knew he were here, he'd be arrested. Executed, possibly. And I was no longer in Jasper's good graces. I wouldn't be able to save Penn's life, not again. I swallowed just as Penn's head lifted, and even though a hood cloaked his face, I knew he was looking straight at me. I shook my head, but he didn't heed my warning, continuing to sneak in the shadows. All of a sudden, shouts rang out, guards running toward the courtyard.

Oh, no.

Penn was injured, not thinking clearly. That would be the only reason he'd do something so foolish. The king of thieves had never been caught, and I couldn't believe he'd risked himself like this for me. My chest tightened as the guards grabbed Penn and yanked him from Shadow. He pressed his hands to his side, and I let out a small gasp. Shadow kicked the guard trying to apprehend her, but he held out his hand and a ball of fire appeared, ready to be hurled at her. She held out her hand, vines spiraling from her palms. But new guards appeared, and a wall of fire sprang up around Shadow and Penn. I stood there, help-less, watching as the guards let the wall of fire die down and led Penn and Shadow away, melting into the darkness.

My decision was an easy one: I had to rescue them.

And then . . . well, I'd figure out my next steps after that. Right now, all I knew was that Penn was injured and would likely die in that prison, and he might very well be the only one who knew how to destroy that mirror and destroy my stepmother once and for all. I needed him. And he needed me.

It was time to put my skills as a thief to the test. I was going to steal the keys to the dungeon. I was going to save the king of thieves.

<h1 style="text-align:center">Chapter Twenty-Seven</h1>

A loud banging jolted me awake from where I sat under the window. I must've fallen asleep here last night. After I saw Penn and Shadow being captured, I'd sank down to the floor, immediately forming a plan as to how I was going to rescue them, right out from under Jasper's nose.

The knock sounded again. "Princess Liliath?" a female voice said, one I didn't recognize. "Lord Jasper is requesting your presence."

"Come in," I said, and the maid entered, her dark hair plaited in a braid, her golden skin luminous in the sunlight that streamed through the big windows.

"I'll just draw you a bath and lay out a nice gown for you," she said.

Great. Just what I wanted. To play dress-up for Jasper. He was probably already plotting who he was going to marry me off to so he could get me out of his home as soon as possible.

The maid bustled into the attached bathing chamber, and my gaze strayed to the bed, molded out of clay and attached to the ground, with a feather-stuffed mattress and a heavy quilt. I'd had a bed right here, in front of me, and I'd chosen to fall asleep on the hard stone floor. I stretched out my neck, the ache in it throbbing. I wanted to crawl into that bed and spend three days there. Maybe a whole week. But I didn't have that kind of time. Knowing Jasper, he wouldn't waste any time in his plans to punish Penn, possibly execute him, and I couldn't let that happen.

Not when the thief had the mirror, not when he was now the only one who could help me defeat my stepmother.

The maid bustled back out and tsked when she looked at me. I must've been a poor sight. Hair askew, dress crumpled and wrinkled. At least my hair wasn't knotted now that it was so short. I'd never admit this out loud, but it had grown on me. It was so much easier to care for now that it was short. Blood and earth, if only Driscoll and Jillian could see me now.

They'd probably find this situation far too amusing—if they were still alive, that was.

The maid led me into the bathing chamber, the metal tub full of steaming water. She helped me undress, and I sank into the warm bath, dunking my head underwater, then emerging over and over and over. I scrubbed myself clean, knowing this might be the last time I had a bath like this for quite a while. I had to get Penn out today, and if—when—we escaped, who knew how long we'd be traveling. Jasper would have his people searching for us, scouring every part of Gilraeth, so it wouldn't be as straightforward a journey home.

Home. The word seized my heart. Mosswood Forest wasn't my home. I didn't know when I'd see my home again. That all depended on Penn and his plans for me.

"Princess Liliath?" The maid stood in the doorway, holding up a golden dress that sparkled and glimmered in the sunlight. This was going to be so impractical, and I could hear Penn's voice in my head.

I guess I should've included a training session on what to wear when going on a mission.

The dress was lovely, though. It was a shame that I was likely going to ruin it.

I stepped out the tub and wrapped a fluffy, warm towel around my body, steeling myself for what I was about to do.

I stood before Jasper in his lavish room, the adobe walls painted a navy blue and decorated with gold leaves and vines that stretched around the room.

He sat at the same table where we'd eaten dinner last night, this morning a spread of what looked like lizard eggs, curried emu, and roasted prickly pear sitting out. He gestured to the silver tray that sat across from him.

"Ah, Liliath, have a seat."

I stayed at my spot by the door. He sported a swollen nose from the night before, which gave me immense satisfaction. He'd deserved it. I wondered if Penn would be proud, then I threw that thought from my mind. I didn't want Penn to be proud of me. That would be a new low that even I didn't want to experience.

"Liliath, really, can we be civil?" Jasper dotted his mouth with his cloth napkin. "Just because we're no longer betrothed doesn't mean we can't be friends."

"Friends?" My nails dug into the palms of my hands. "Friends don't let each other rot away in prison. Friends don't force each other into marriage. Friends don't imprison each other. Friends don't—"

Jasper held up his hand. "Enough. I can see you're not going to be reasonable about this. What do you expect me to do, Liliath? I can't just have an exiled princess living in my manor. My father wouldn't allow it. Even if I wanted to keep you here, he'd insist I use you as leverage to gain allies, money, a sword for the army I'm going to need to defeat this sorceress and take the crown."

"I'm glad I'm so disposable," I said. "I thought I knew you better."

He slammed his hand on the table. "I'm doing what I need to survive."

"You're doing what you need to gain power. This has nothing to do with survival."

He threw up his hands. "Well, I was going to let you choose who you wanted to marry, but now I'm not feeling so charitable. Especially after what you did to me last night." He pointed to his nose, and I couldn't help the smile that came to my face.

"That's what makes you smile?" He shook his head. "I don't even recognize you. That horrid haircut, the way you're speaking to me. It doesn't suit you."

"I could say the same about that nose. Wonder what your betrothed will think of that? Will you tell her you got hit by a princess?"

His upper lip curled into a snarl.

"Anyway." I walked toward the table, thoroughly famished now that I'd gotten under Jasper's skin. I tucked the napkin laying on the table onto my lap and used my fork to take a bite of the curried emu. Delicacies like this were only served in the fire court. The last time I'd eaten this dish had been at Princess Seraphina's castle, her mother and father still alive, all of us feasting, dancing, drinking wine. All the royals had been present, from every court in Arathia, though I wasn't as close with the princesses from the frost or sky court. I mainly had spent my time with Seraphina and Gabrielle, the princess of the water court. We'd laugh and gossip about our love lives and talk about what it might be like when we would rule one day. Gabrielle wanted nothing to do with her throne, but I'd often be jealous of Seraphina, of the way her parents took the time to listen to her ideas in a way my father would never listen to mine.

Sometimes, doubt would creep in, a small voice that said maybe my father didn't listen because my ideas weren't good enough, because I wasn't good enough.

I realized Jasper was still talking, prattling on now about Seraphina and how foolish she'd been.

I couldn't believe she'd gotten cursed, that the shadow court was behind it all. But I had to focus on one problem at a time. I raised my gaze to Jasper as he took a sip of water from his goblet.

"I'm surprised you don't throw me in prison," I said. "It would be so satisfying for you to toss me into those sand pits that lay underneath your home."

"Don't test me," Jasper said. "I'd love to do just that, but your future husband likely wouldn't appreciate knowing I'd imprisoned you. I have to treat you as a guest."

So the sand pits were still where they locked their prisoners. Jasper had always reveled in showing me their pits, dug deep into the ground, covered with spiked metal grates. I'd found it all very disturbing, but Jasper had been so proud showing off the starving, scared prisoners that I'd always just nodded along, smiling. Now Penn and Shadow were among those prisoners, and the thought made my bones shrivel.

I hoped they hadn't thrown the sand vipers in there with them, a common torture tactic in the fire court, one that I'd never had the stomach for. It was one of the few things my father and I could agree on. He didn't like these pits either. Didn't like to pointlessly torture others.

I couldn't believe I'd ever wanted to marry Jasper. I'd been so blinded by my commitment to him, by the need to do what was best for my people, that I'd ignored everything about him that I hated. A list that was growing longer by the minute.

I cleared my throat, thinking about my training session with Hammer where he'd taught me how to prepare for a mission. "You know, I don't recognize any of your guards. Are they new?"

Jasper looked out the window, at the desert landscape that spread before us. "Many of my guards have died either fighting dragons or fighting the sorceress. I have to replace them often these days."

His tone was annoyed, like them dying was such an inconvenience to him.

"What a shame." I took a bite of the boiled egg. "It must be hard for the new guards to learn their rotations, placements, routines."

Jasper glanced at me, his brown eyes hard. "If you're trying to learn about my guards so you can escape, it won't work."

I rolled my eyes and set down my fork. "Where am I going to escape to? You said it yourself. I have nowhere to go, no one to rely on."

He sniffed. "Yes, well, we have an excellent training system in place here. So the guards man their posts just fine."

Well, that hadn't gone well. At least I knew where Penn and Shadow were located, but that wouldn't be enough. I needed to know the guards' schedules, the fastest escape route, and how I was going to get Penn and Shadow out of there. The sand pits were deep, and the barbed grates were heavy.

"You know, my father was always really impressed with those sand pits of yours."

Jasper snorted. "Your father hated them, talked about how over the top they were."

Damn. He knew my father better than I'd counted on.

"You'd be surprised. One day I came upon a few guards digging holes in a field near our castle. My father wanted to experiment with pits similar to yours." I forced a laugh. "One of the guards fell in and didn't know how to get out."

Jasper took a bite of egg. "That's because there is no way out. That's the whole point."

My stomach sank. I had no clue how I was going to accomplish this.

"Unless someone helps you out. We keep our sand pits deep enough that prisoners cannot climb out but shallow enough that the guards can reach down and pull them up if necessary. You know for executions and things like that."

"Of course."

My heart pounded in my chest. Would I be strong enough to pull out Penn and Shadow? Would I even have that kind of time?

"That must be hard, with those spiked grates." I tried to keep my voice even despite my uneven pulse.

Jasper studied his nails. "Yes, well, good thing our guards have special protective gloves to pull the grates up. It's not something you need to worry about, Liliath. You're well protected here."

I resisted the urge to roll my eyes. Of course he thought I was afraid. Weak Princess Liliath who needed protecting. He had no idea what I was planning. Probably didn't even know that I knew Penn and Shadow had been apprehended by his guards. I couldn't pry any further, not without raising suspicion.

"Good to know," I said, placing my napkin over my plate, stomach now churning.

I was going to have to somehow steal a pair of these gloves, find Penn's and Shadows's sand pits, ensure no guards saw me, lift the heavy grates, and pull them both out. Oh, and then somehow escape from this whole mess without being detected and find a safe hiding place. Not to mention, Penn was still injured.

This was going to be a mess, but it was the only way. I couldn't give up on the earth court, couldn't let Jasper dictate my life like this. I stood, the table rattling as I bumped it.

"What are you doing?" Jasper asked. "I have a list of suitors coming to meet you today. All very interested in the Princess Liliath."

I'd love to tell him exactly where those suitors could shove their interest.

"Oh." I put a hand to my chest. "Jasper, I can't wear this to meet suitors. And my face—I'll need makeup." I ticked off my fingers. "Ribbons for my hair. Perfume. Nice slippers. And are we having tea? It's the only proper way to meet a potential husband."

Jasper sighed heavily. "I didn't think about any of that." He drummed his fingers on the table, and I held my breath in anticipation of his answer. "No," he said decisively. "We don't have time for all that. You're presentable as is. A guard will escort you to your rooms, and you can wait there for one of the serving maids to collect you."

He waved me off, which I took as a dismissal. Damn, I'd been hoping to stall, but there'd be none of that now.

"Okay, then." I stuck out my hand.

Jasper stared at it warily. "What are you doing?"

"A truce," I said.

He accepted it and we shook. I held his hand a little longer than necessary and turned, a smile on my face as I slipped that ruby-red ring into a small pocket I'd cut into my dress earlier. Just a little token that Jasper would sorely miss, one that didn't belong to him in the first place.

I opened the door where a guard stood outside, wearing those baggy brown pants and tan tunics characteristic of the guards here, a sword hanging from his belt, scythes strapped to his back. My gaze dropped to his thighs. And there, attached to a belt loop, was a pair of black leather gloves.

Chapter Twenty-Eight

The guard hummed as we walked down the open-air corridor and toward my room, his boots clicking against the blue and white ceramic-tiled floors. We passed open archways that gave view of an inner courtyard, ground covered in sand, palm trees, cacti, and other plants native to Gilraeth filling the space. Jasper and I used to sit on the benches in this very courtyard, dreaming and talking about our future together as king and queen of Elwen. We were going to create an important alliance between our two courts, forge a new path forward. Now, I couldn't rely on Jasper. I had to forge my own path.

"Oh, my." I stopped, fanning myself with my hand.

The guard stopped and turned, his brows furrowed. "Are you okay, Princess?"

"I think I need to sit for a minute."

He gestured to the bench in the middle of the courtyard, and we walked through the archways and toward it. I sank down, thinking about my next steps. Charming said you always had to be ten steps ahead.

The guard sat down next to me. I'd gotten him on the bench, those gloves within reach. That was currently my only step.

I looked at him, then up to the sun shining above. "It's really hot here."

He just nodded.

Oh, good green earth. We were talking about the weather.

That's the best you can do, Lilypad?

Not now, Penn.

I worried at my bottom lip, eyeing the gloves. They'd be easy enough to lift off that little silver hook on his belt. I just needed the right distraction. For the hundredth time since escaping from my castle, I wished I had my magic. I could make a cactus explode or something. Though that might be a little obvious. Shadow told me Penn preferred we not use magic as much as possible when doing missions because magic tended to be less subtle.

Arrow had taught me distraction techniques, as well as how to pocket valuables off a person. I had to harness those lessons right now. I stood, stretching my arms high over my head as the guard stood as well.

Here went nothing. I stumbled into him, shrieking out as his arms came around me. My hands fumbled at his belt, and I grabbed the gloves. He grasped my shoulders and straightened me, just as I tossed the gloves behind the bench.

"Oh, I'm so embarrassed," I said with a giggle. "Falling into a big, strong man like yourself."

His face remained stony. Okay, switching tactics.

"Water," I rasped. "I need water. I think I'm going to pass out."

"Oh, dragon balls," he muttered. "Lord Jasper is going to kill me if you faint. He needs you presentable."

How touching.

He sat me down on the bench. "I'll be right back with some water."

I nodded as he ran from the courtyard to the corridors of Jasper's home, disappearing around a corner. I hopped up from the bench and snatched the gloves, then stuffed them down in between my cleavage and hurried from the courtyard. The sand pits were down below, the doorway leading to them in the next corridor over. I'd completed phase one of my plan. Here's hoping everything else went smoothly from this point on.

THE DOOR WOULDN'T OPEN. I gripped the handle, tugging at it, but no luck. It was locked.

Damn. Damn. Damn.

So much for being prepared, Lilypad.

I didn't know I needed a key to get down to the sand pits. I also had no idea where I'd get a key. Did every guard have one? Just certain guards? I couldn't very well wander around asking everyone in sight if they could let me in. The guard was going to be back soon with the water and realize I wasn't there. I didn't have time for this.

Sweat dotted my upper lip, my palms growing clammy. This would be the only chance I had at escaping. If they caught me, they'd lock me away until Jasper found me a husband. A few guards rounded the corner, and I flattened against the door, smiling and nodding as they passed.

"Just taking a little stroll," I said. "Good day to you."

They both nodded and continued walking. Okay, so no one knew I was missing yet. I spun back around, thinking about one of my lessons with Wayfinder. He'd shown me how to pick a lock, and I'd spent the entire lesson telling him I had absolutely no use for a skill like that. I would love to have a stern talk with Past Me right about now.

I swallowed and felt in my hair for one of the silver pins the serving maid had used this morning. I felt the cool hard metal and slowly drew it out of my hair. Once I opened this door there would be no going back. I would seal my fate, one way or another. I hesitated just a moment, the pin hovering right outside the lock. If someone in my court broke into our prison cells, broke out prisoners, I'd have them arrested. Now, I would be the criminal.

I jammed the pin into the lock. I might be a criminal, but at least I was fighting for my people, doing everything I could to make my way back to them.

The hallway was empty, but I heard shouts in the distance, calls for my name.

They knew I'd run away. But they didn't know where. Didn't know my plan. I thought back to all the questions I'd asked Jasper about the sand pits this morning and prayed to blood and earth he was as dumb as Driscoll always claimed he was.

I crouched down and stuck the pin in the keyhole, thinking through the steps Wayfinder had laid out. I squeezed my eyes, racking my brain. He'd said something about pushing it in straight and then to the left. Then I'd made a snarky comment along the lines of, "Have you tried knocking first? Oh, right, you can't because you're a criminal." I think at some point during that commentary he'd told me what to do next, and now I was blanking. I wiggled the pin back and forth, the voices echoing down the corridor, growing louder. Footsteps pounded on the ground, and my hands started to shake.

"I just went to get the bitch some water," the guard said.

"You idiot," another guard yelled.

"Do you think she's escaped? Lord Jasper is going to throw us in the sand pits for this."

I lifted my elbow, jamming my pin harder into the lock, moving it around. This definitely was not what Wayfinder had taught me, but since I tuned out 90 percent of his lesson, I was going to have to wing it.

"C'mon," I whispered. "C'mon, lock."

"Hey!" a voice shouted.

I turned my head to see two guards standing at the end of the corridor, one of them holding the water skin that was no doubt for me. I grunted and turned my focus back on the lock as the guards raced toward me.

I pushed with all of my might, and something clicked. The guards were almost on me. The door swung open, and I dashed inside, slamming the door shut and hoping they didn't have a key.

Fists pounded on the other side of the door.

"She's jammed the lock," one of the guards yelled.

I definitely had not meant to do that, but it actually worked out in my favor. Except now I wasn't sure how to get Shadow and Penn out of here. Not that we could just waltz through Jasper's home anyway. Maybe Penn would have a plan.

Always having to save you, Lilypad, aren't I?

I bit my lip. I should have had a plan. This was my rescue mission. I couldn't depend on others anymore. I took a step forward, the stench of urine and waste hitting me.

I'd forgotten how ghastly this place smelled. Stairs led down into complete darkness, and moans rose up from the belly of the prison. I swallowed, feeling for each step with my foot before I descended. The guards still banged on the door behind me, jiggling the handle, but it didn't burst open like I kept expecting it to.

Thank the bloody earth for those annoying pins the serving maid had insisted on jamming in my hair this morning. I got to the bottom of the stairs and my slippers hit gritty sand, everything still cloaked in darkness. I'd forgotten to bring a torch. I bit my cheek, mind working fast. I supposed I would have to wander aimlessly and hope I didn't fall into any of these pits, since there was a very real chance I'd never make it back out.

You don't go into a mission unprepared, Lilypad.

I hated that Penn's voice had penetrated my thoughts like this. I figured once I escaped from the thief, he'd be out of my mind, but it was like running away from him made him even more present.

I took a step forward just as a loud bang reverberated from the top of the stairs. They were going to break that door down any second now.

"Penn?" I whisper-shouted. "Shadow?"

"Here," a hoarse voice called out, and my heart galloped.

I tiptoed toward the sound, feeling my way in the dark until my slipper felt the edge of a pit. I crouched down, putting the gloves on. A hand shot up through the grate and gripped my throat.

"Well, hello pretty," a nasally voice said.

Not Shadow. Definitely not Penn.

"You're choking me," I gasped out, face pressed against the metal bars.

Another loud bang echoed through the cavern, which no longer mattered, because I was about to be strangled to death.

The hand stayed clenched around my throat. "You're going to lift up the grate like a good little girl, and in return, I won't bash your head into it."

That sounded like a reasonable trade.

"Yes," I rasped.

The hand loosened its hold on my throat, which was when I remembered that I had training in this exact situation. Shadow and I had sparred, and she'd taught me how to break several types of holds, including a chokehold. I wasn't some helpless princess. I could get myself out of this situation.

His hand stayed tight around my throat.

I jammed my fist down into the grate, right in his nose. He let out a yelp, and his hand fell from my throat.

I stood, out of breath and shaky from the encounter. Calling out their names hadn't worked, but I couldn't see anything and had no idea how I was going to free them from this place.

This had been a terrible plan. Well, it would've been terrible if I'd actually had a plan. Which I clearly didn't. How many times had Hammer told me you never go into a mission unprepared? And here I was, wandering around the sand pits like an idiot.

I had no magic, no way out, and no idea where Penn or Shadow might be. I should've pressed Jasper or the guard for more information, shouldn't have acted so rashly.

I continued through the dark, walking slow and careful. Then I remembered something that Jasper had told me a long time ago.

He'd said they put the most wanted criminals near the back. He'd taken me there, shown me a few of them huddled in the pits. Those were the deepest ones, the hardest to escape from, and they didn't want to take any chances. Surely Penn would fall into that category. Everyone on the continent of Arathia wanted to see him imprisoned. He was infamous for his heists. Feeling more confident, I marched forward, and that's when I heard a splitting sound that cracked through the air.

They'd broken the door.

Chapter Twenty-Nine

I hurried my pace, remembering that the pits were all in rows, so as long as I stayed my course and didn't veer from it, I shouldn't have to worry about breaking an ankle on one of the grates.

If I remembered correctly, it had taken Jasper and me about ten minutes to walk all the way to the back, so I had to be close.

"Penn!" I whispered. "Penn, where are you?"

"Please tell me this isn't your plan," a voice said in my head.

"Dammit," I replied, "not now."

Then I stopped. Wait a minute. That voice hadn't been in my head. It was out loud.

"Penn!" I made my way toward him.

"What are you doing here, Lilypad?"

"Rescuing you, you idiot."

"Fucking blood and earth," he muttered. "I needed you to stay put. Now you've brought the guards upon us."

Their shouts were getting closer. We had to hurry.

I glared down at him. "You know, a simple thank you would suffice."

"I'm still stuck in a pit, in case you haven't noticed."

"Will you two stop your arguing?" Shadow said from somewhere nearby.

She was right. We didn't have time for this. I grabbed the heavy grate with my gloved hands and used every bit of muscle I possessed to shift it over. I didn't need to move it far. I just needed to move it enough to make space for Penn to wriggle out. I grunted, my muscles straining with the effort.

"She must be here to rescue him," one of the guards yelled, his fire magic appearing, a ball of light now bobbing closer.

"Oh, shit," Penn said. "Hurry."

"I'm going as fast as I can," I grunted as I heaved the grate, arms and legs now shaking.

I dropped to my stomach and lowered my hand down. "Grab my hand," I said, hoping I'd be able to pull him up. "I don't know if I'm strong enough, Penn."

He gripped my hand. "Lower your other one."

I did as he said, and he grabbed that hand as well, then I pulled with all my might, but Penn must've had other plans because I heard his feet digging into the dirt.

He was using his feet to walk his way up the wall while holding onto my hands as leverage. I dug my own feet into the dirt, straining with my entire body to stay in place.

"Almost there," he said, and within seconds I felt the heat of his breath on my face. He let go of my hands one at a time as he gripped the edge of the sand pit and hopped out.

The firelight, now joined by four other lights, was getting closer. Penn and I ran to Shadow's pit as other prisoners started catching wind of what was happening, shouting for us to release them as well.

We got Shadow out in seconds.

"Fuck, fuck, fuck," Penn said in the dark beside me. "I have no idea how we're going to escape. My plan didn't include the entire guard knowing we'd gotten out."

That part might have been my fault.

"Let me out," a prisoner shouted from the pit next to us. "I'm ready to gut those guards for what they've done to me. Twenty years here for a crime I didn't even commit."

"That's it," I said and turned to Penn. "We have to let the other prisoners out. Create a distraction."

"That might actually work," Shadow said.

We wasted no time, all of us springing into action. We let out a prisoner just as the guards got closer, their fire magic illuminating the dingy space. I didn't have time to look at Penn, to notice my surroundings. We needed to release more prisoners. Shadow and the prisoner faced off against the guards as Penn and I worked to move more grates, pull out more prisoners from the pits, who joined in fighting the guards. Soon, more guards arrived, more prisoners released. The cavern erupted into chaos, blood spilling and spattering, screams wrenching the air, fire flying everywhere. Shadow slipped from the amassing crowd.

"This is our chance to escape," she said to me and Penn, who stood by my side.

"But how?" I asked. "We can't exactly just waltz out the front door."

"There's another way," Penn said, nodding toward a darkened corner, a big grate placed into the wall.

I didn't like the looks of that, but we also didn't have a choice, all thanks to me and my terrible planning.

I nodded. "Then let's get the fiery hells out of here."

Chapter Thirty

We ran toward the grate, all of us pulling on it until it came free. An awful stench floated from it, and I nearly gagged, bile rising up in my stomach.

"Oh, spirits below. What is in here?"

"Sewage," Penn said, once again in the dark as we got further away from all the fire magic.

My slippers splashed in what I assumed was waste water. "Oh, my dress." I groaned. It really had been so pretty.

"That's the least of your concerns right now," Penn said. "Rumor has it, fire lizards frequent these sewers."

Right. Because no part of this could be easy.

"So keep an eye out," Penn said.

We fell into silence as we made our way through the sewers, Penn scouting up ahead.

"Thanks for coming for us," Shadow said. "Penn didn't think you would."

That stung, though it shouldn't have. I shouldn't care what the thief thought of me.

"Well, Penn thinks a lot of terrible things about me."

"He doesn't, you know." She let out a soft laugh. "You bring out a side of him none of us have seen before, a playful side."

My eyes bugged out of my head. "Playful?" I pointed ahead of us, even though Shadow couldn't see me in the dark. "You call that playful?"

"You should've seen him before you arrived in Mosswood Forest," Shadow said. "Wayfinder almost fainted on the spot when Penn asked you to dance at the festival."

"Whatever the reason for the change in Penn, I can assure you, it had nothing to do with me."

I felt Shadow's hand on my shoulder, and she squeezed it. "You saved our lives. I owe you one."

"Hurry up!" Penn shouted from far ahead, and we quickened our pace.

I wondered how long it would take the guards to sort out the mess we'd caused.

My insides twisted at what I'd done, setting all those criminals free, and once again, I wondered if this was another reason why I didn't deserve to be queen.

I hit a hard wall of muscle and realized I'd run into Penn's back.

"Why are we stopping?" I whispered, then felt something slither against my foot.

Oh, blood and earth. It never ended. Ever since I'd gotten kidnapped by the king of thieves, my life was one chaotic event after another.

"Did you feel that?" Penn asked over his shoulder.

I nodded, then remembered he couldn't see me. "Yes."

Shadow sighed. "I don't know if I can summon any more magic. I had a hard enough time fighting those guards. We're tired. We've had no food and very little water, and Penn is still injured."

A bright light filled the sewer, and I looked down to see brown water floating around my feet. Bile once again rose to my throat. My gaze trailed to the light in front of us, fire blazing from a lizard the size of my hand.

"It's doesn't look so bad," I said.

Jasper had always warned me about fire lizards and how dangerous they were, but it actually looked kind of cute.

It hissed, and a fireball flew from its mouth toward my skirt, setting it ablaze. I shrieked and Penn used his hands to snuff it out before it could spread.

Never mind. Definitely not cute.

One by one, bright balls of light flickered on, little fires everywhere, until I realized we were surrounded by the creatures.

"You didn't say the sewers were infested with these things," I whispered behind me to Penn.

Shadow stepped forward, her knees bent as if she were ready for a fight. But I didn't even know how you began to fight these things. Their flames flickered bright over their bodies despite the fact that they stood in water.

"How do you defeat a fire lizard?" I asked, dreading the answer.

Penn stroked his jaw, no hint of panic on his face. I'd never understand how this man remained so calm in the worst of situations. "Arrows, swords, knives, heavy boulders that can squash them."

"So everything we don't have," I said.

"That would be correct," Shadow replied.

I glanced behind me, the fire lizards everywhere I looked. We couldn't even run without risking being set on fire.

"Well?" I asked Penn. "What's the plan?"

The lizards let out strings of hisses, a few stray fireballs whizzing past us.

"You do have a plan?" I asked.

Penn stayed silent.

"But you always have a plan."

Those forest-green eyes turned on me. "Yes, I do. But someone decided to break into the prison and rescue me when I didn't want to be rescued."

I crossed my arms. "Hmm, that sounds familiar."

"Not now, you two," Shadow said, her gold hoop earrings glimmering in the light.

We all crowded together, our backs to each other as the fire lizards closed in on us. I looked up, cocking my head at the loose stone in the ceiling.

"What are you doing?" Penn asked as I reached up and touched little roots that hung over our heads.

I looked at him and Shadow. "Do you two think you have enough magic left for one final push?"

Fire scorched at our feet, and we pressed closer together.

"What are you thinking?" Penn asked.

"Use your magic and pull those roots down as hard as you can. Whatever plants they're connected to above will create pressure on the soil, on the sewer." At least, I hoped they would.

Penn and Shadow looked at each other, then above.

"We'll bring the sewer down," Penn said.

"Exactly."

He paused, then gave a sharp nod as sparks flew at us. We stomped our feet, putting out the fires as quickly as possible.

"On the count of three," Penn said over his shoulder.

Shadow tensed.

"One."

Fire flew at my head, and I ducked.

"Two. Get ready to run."

A stray blaze caught my arm, scorching me, and I cried out.

"Three!"

Shadow and Penn lifted their arms, both of them crying out as they pulled the roots down, down, down. Cracks webbed across the stone overhead, and the ground and walls trembled around us. Chunks of the ceiling began to fall.

We wasted no time, all of us sprinting through the sewers as the lizards scurried from the carnage. I looked behind me to see the sewer collapsing down, dust rising and rushing forward like a flood.

Penn and Shadow ran ahead of me, faster and stronger despite how weak they must be right now. Shadow had talked a lot about endurance, and now I knew why that was so important. Why Arrow had made me continue to train even after I'd thrown up repeatedly. I gritted my teeth and pumped my arms but still couldn't keep up.

Penn glanced behind him. "Lilypad, I need you to move!"

"What . . . does it . . . look like I'm doing!"

I clutched my side, which felt like it had been stabbed with a knife.

A rock fell in front of me, and I had to jump to my left to avoid it. Penn stopped suddenly, and I almost ran into him as Shadow continued her sprint. He grabbed me by the waist and hoisted me over his shoulder, continuing to run.

"What are you doing?" I yelled over the sound of rock and debris crashing to the ground. "Put me down, Penn!"

He didn't listen, continuing to race through the sewers, splashing up muck and water that splattered my face. There would not be enough baths in this world to get me clean.

"Surely it would be faster if you just let me run!"

"I won't leave you behind," he growled, determination filling every word.

Of course not. Not when I was somehow the key to helping him destroy the mirror.

At this point, I couldn't see anything but dust and smoke, couldn't hear anything but the thunder of stone hitting the ground. One minute I was sucking in lungfuls of dust, the next, I was flying from Penn's shoulder and onto soft sand. I raised my head to see rock piling up in the exit of the sewer, the courtyard overhead crumbling and collapsing down.

Penn grabbed my arm and pulled me to my feet. "We have to find shelter," he said, out of breath. "I don't think anyone will be coming after us any time soon, but we can't take a chance of being spotted."

I thought my legs might give out from underneath me, but Penn's and Shadow's determined looks made me straighten and nod.

"Let's get out of here," I said as we ran from Jasper's destroyed home.

Chapter Thirty-One

W e eventually slowed to a walk once we were far enough away from Jasper's home to be spotted. Rock formations jutted up, tall rocky cliffs, arches, pillars to hide us, so many shades of brown and orange I never knew existed. Bright yellow and pink flowers sprouted from the ground, cacti littering the landscape. Penn and Shadow led me to a little cave tucked into a tall and thick rock wall. Their satchels already lay here, against the wall. This must be where they stayed before coming to rescue me.

Exhausted, we all lay down and passed out.

When I awoke, Shadow was gone, and only Penn remained, sitting by a crackling fire with rabbit roasting. He was also clean, all the sand and muck gone from his pale skin, his blond hair tied back at the nape of his neck, as usual. Handsome as hell. And far too close for comfort.

"As much as I love that gown on you, it's probably best if you burn it." He gestured to the clean trousers and tunic that sat nearby. Shadow must've left them for me.

"Where is Shadow?"

"She's on her way back to Mosswood Forest. She and the others have a mission to complete."

"A mission? Now? When we're stuck here?"

He shot me a grin. "No rest for the wicked."

Great. So it was just me and the king of thieves. And his handsome face. And kissable lips. And shameless flirting. And smirk that somehow made my blood boil and my knees go weak at the same time. I didn't know when all those things had become truths, but somehow they had, and it made me want to chase after Shadow and demand she come back and be a buffer between us.

I glanced at his stomach. "Is your wound okay?"

"It's healing," he said but didn't elaborate any further. He cleared his throat. "There's a spring nearby. You can bathe, and then we can eat."

I just nodded and grabbed the clothes, listening to Penn's directions on how to get to the spring.

"Be quick about it," Penn warned as I walked toward the entrance to the cave. "We don't need you getting spotted by anyone."

Despite the hot desert air, the spring was cool. I wanted to spend hours scrubbing my skin, but I heeded Penn's words, and used some nearby brittle bush to wash away the dirt and grime. Agave plants sprouted up from the ground, surrounding the spring, and I broke a few off, splitting open the plant and using the juices to cleanse my skin and hair.

By the time I returned to the cave, Penn had the rabbit off the fire and cooling, ready to eat.

He offered me a few chunks of meat, which I greedily accepted, my stomach rumbling.

Finally, we'd finished eating, silent up to that point.

"I have something," I said and walked to my dress, reaching into the hidden pocket and pulling out the ring. I offered it to Penn. "For you."

He studied it for a moment before accepting the ring and slipping it on his finger, his thumb rubbing over it. "Thank you," he said quietly. "It belonged to my father, and after he was killed it was taken from him, given to the fire court. I stole it back, and, well, then you know what happened."

I nodded. "Jasper told me it was a gift from my father, spoils from war that he gave to all the courts. I put two and two together and realized if you were wearing it, it must have belonged to you, or your parents. The false king and queen."

He winced. "Are you upset?"

I peered at him. "Why didn't you tell me?"

"I didn't think it would matter, to be honest." He grimaced. "You hated me either way. It didn't matter if I was king of thieves or king of Mosswood Forest. I was still your enemy. And then it seemed like you'd just started accepting me. I didn't know how to tell you about my true identity."

I stared at him, working through what he'd told me, but in the end, it didn't matter, didn't change anything. "I'm sorry about your parents," I said. "I'm sorry they died in such a horrific way."

His eyes grew hard. "Thank you."

"I want our people to live in harmony. I want the border between our two realms to be opened. I want us to coexist."

He nodded. "I want that too."

He studied the ring, tilting his hand this way and that as light caught on it. "How did you steal it?"

I shrugged. "Just a little trick Shadow taught me."

I thought about when I'd offered to shake Jasper's hand, how I told him it would be a truce, how I'd slipped the ring off his finger in the process, and he hadn't even noticed.

"This means a lot, Lilypad." He swallowed. "Why did you come after me?" He stared at me in a way he hadn't before, like he was seeing me for the first time.

"I know you think it was stupid—" I started.

"It was brave," he interrupted. "I meant what I said up on that mountaintop, about your nickname."

So he remembered. I certainly did—hadn't been able to stop thinking about what he'd said, why he'd chosen that name for me.

"Oh. Well, thank you." I fidgeted with my hands. "I . . . I'm so tired of my future being decided for me. Jasper was never going to rescue me. You were right. The minute I wasn't useful to him anymore, he broke off our betrothal and found someone new. All he wanted was a crown." I met Penn's gaze over the firelight. "He was going to marry me off, you know. Sell me like livestock. And you know what I realized?"

Penn stayed silent, still, hands resting in his lap, long legs stretched out in front of him.

"I realized that I never loved him. I was betrothed to him since I was three years old. My father decided I would marry him, and I never had a choice, so I accepted it like the good daughter I was." I paused, recognizing the lie in my words. "Not the good daughter. My father probably never would've labeled me as that. The good queen. I saw Jasper as something that would benefit my people, a way to forge an alliance with the fire court, something that would bolster trade and a new path forward. So I put my all into our relationship, determined that I would honor it no matter what. But the truth was I never had a choice. I had to accept him."

Penn still didn't move, didn't speak, just continued to stare at me, assessing as always.

"I'm tired of not having a choice. I rescued you because that's what I want moving forward."

"Okay," Penn said.

I nearly fell forward into the fire. "You're not going to argue with me?"

He shook his head. "We'll be partners moving forward into this mission to destroy the mirror. I'll ask your input, consult with you, and you'll always have a choice."

I sat in a stunned silence. Finally, my future could be in my own hands. The words broke the invisible chains that tethered me, and the first real smile I'd had in what felt like ages came to my face. "Thank you."

Penn spread out his arms. "Welcome to the academy, Lilypad."

I couldn't believe the next words that were about to come out of my mouth. "I'm not in the academy. Not yet."

Penn leaned back onto his hands. "And why is that?"

"I have to spar with you. Shadow told me on our first day of training that that was the final task everyone had to complete. A sparring session."

Penn quirked an eyebrow, shifting his big body. "You want to spar with me?"

"I want to be like everyone else. I want to earn my place."

And to kick his ass. His nice ass. Which I was not thinking about, to be clear.

Penn cocked his head, that same look—like he was seeing me in a new light—passing over his face. "Then we'll spar. But you need to rest first."

I shook my head. "There's no time for that. Every second we waste my people suffer. My best friends are still imprisoned." I took a deep breath. "Tell me about this mission. I want to know everything."

Penn let out a sigh. "Okay, we'll start with this: the mirror? I assume you know it came from Sorrengard."

The shadow court.

"Obviously. There's nowhere else dark magic can come from." I shook my head. "It doesn't make sense, though. How could she have gotten the mirror? She's never been to Sorrengard."

Penn's jaw ticked. "There are people who sail to the island, specifically to steal its magical items and bring them back to Arathia to sell on the black market. Have you ever heard of the pirate lord of the Dark Seas?"

I blinked a few times. "Are you telling me he's real? Not just a silly story made up to scare children?"

Parents often warned their misbehaving children that if they didn't listen, the pirate lord would come to steal them away when they were sleeping, forcing them onto his boat and into a life of piracy.

"No," Penn said, "he's very much real, and he's one of the few who's made it out alive from Sorrengard multiple times. He's infamous for the powerful items he brings back, selling them to the highest bidder. But there are also ways to get into Sorrengard. He sails people there, to the island—for a high fee, of course."

So that was how my stepmother did it? She bought the mirror off the pirate lord? I didn't even know how she got in contact with him, arranged something like that.

Penn leaned forward, a strand of blond hair falling over his forehead. "Do you know much about the dark magic of Sorrengard? How their magical items are made?"

I only knew what we'd learned in school. That those in the shadow court had the ability to steal a person's shadows. "I know that sixty years ago Sorrengard waged war on the rest of Arathia, targeting Shiraeth first. They decimated the star people, wiped the star court off the continent, and it became the Deadlands. That the other courts banded together to banish the shadow people back to their island, and they haven't been heard from since."

"That's not quite true," Penn said. "They haven't attempted to wage war on Arathia, but that doesn't mean they've disappeared. I think they've sent spies over the years, that they've been working to infiltrate the courts." He gestured outside the cave, to the desert. "Look at Gilraeth, the sorceress who's cursed Princess Seraphina. Something is stirring. Something dark, and I think it's all connected to Sorrengard."

I sat back, mind reeling with this information. This was all so much bigger than just my stepmother or the mirror or this sorceress.

"I have good news, though," Penn said. "Rumor has it Seraphina has awoken from her curse."

"What?" I said. "How? When? Where is she?"

Penn waved away my questions. "She's in good hands. She can handle herself."

Oh, I knew that. Seraphina was smart and brave, and I always knew she'd make an amazing leader to the fire court. I hoped she kicked Jasper's ass. After she killed the sorceress and foiled whatever plan Sorrengard had to infiltrate Gilraeth.

"We have to do our part," Penn said. "Destroy that mirror and unseat your stepmother. Right now, if Sorrengard were to attack, the earth court would be useless in the fight. No one has magic, the entire court is practically destroyed. We can't have that. Arathia has to be at its full strength for whatever Sorrengard has planned."

"So how does it work?" I twirled my hand in the air. "These magical items? How does Sorrengard have them? I know they have the ability to steal people's shadows, that when they do take the shadows, the people are then trapped on the island, never able to leave, never able to age."

My father had told me horror stories about people who were stuck in Sorrengard, puppets for the shadow people to use. Once they captured your shadow, your shadow was under their control and your body unable to leave their island, unable to age. It was like time had no meaning on that island. I shuddered at the thought.

"There's another piece to their magic," Penn said. "For every shadow they steal, a magical item is made, appearing on the island. It's full of them from the shadows they've taken. Dark magic, powerful items. That's what people go to the island for, and most end up getting their shadows taken, never to be seen again. Only the most desperate attempt it."

My lungs squeezed tight, and I felt like I couldn't breathe. Sorrengard was more dangerous than I realized. It wasn't just shadows they stole, but they also had powerful items at their disposal?

"So that's how the mirror got made?" I asked. "From someone's shadow being stolen."

Penn nodded. "But rumor has it that once a shadow is restored to the person it was stolen from, the item disappears, the magic holding it to Sorrengard no longer effective."

"That's what you want to do?" I leaned forward. "You want to restore a shadow to break the mirror?"

"We don't have that kind of time," Penn said. "I have no idea whose shadow produced that mirror. And I have no interest in traveling to the shadow court to find it."

My stomach twisted. "Then what *is* the plan?"

"We're going to Apolis."

"The water court?" I asked, unsure what Apolis could possibly have to do with destroying the mirror.

"They have a weapon, a powerful one, with the ability to break these magical items. If I can steal this weapon, I can use it to break the mirror and destroy it so no one else can ever get their hands on it. Once it's destroyed, then we can go after your stepmother."

I didn't like where this was going. "And what does that have to do with me?"

Penn sighed. "Apolis closed their borders over a year ago. No one has been allowed in . . . or out. It's almost impossible to get inside, and even if I did, I'd be recognized as a foreigner immediately. Word is you and Princess Gabrielle were friends, and if you show up at her border, asking for asylum, I'd bet she would let you, and anyone in your company, inside."

I didn't think I could be any more shocked, but here I was, once again hardly able to believe what I'd just heard. Gabrielle and I had been friends as long as I could remember. She and her parents visited our court, and me and my father visited hers on several occasions. We'd also met at various summits and conclaves over the years. We'd always gotten along, had a lot in common since we were close to the same age, but what Penn was asking . . .

"You don't want to steal the weapon. You want me to." My tone was accusing. "This was why you didn't tell me. You knew I'd never approve."

"Well, do you?" Penn crossed his muscled arms over his broad chest.

"Of course not!" I snapped. "She's a princess, a friend. I can't steal from her. It's wrong."

"Even if it's the only way to break that mirror? To ensure no one else can ever use its power?"

Damn it. He was right.

"I'll be there by your side, guiding you every step of the way," Penn said, as if that was what I was worried about.

His words were oddly comforting, though.

"I wonder why they closed their borders," I murmured to myself.

"No one knows." Penn held his hands out to the fire. "And it doesn't concern us. We'll get in, complete our mission, and get out."

"Easy peasy," I said, the sarcasm dripping from my words.

"If you know what you're doing, it is," Penn shot back.

I was starting to regret rescuing him.

"So what do you say?" Now Penn reached out his hand, across the fire, holding it in front of me. "Do we have a deal?"

"What are you doing?" I asked, looking at his outstretched hand.

"You said you wanted to be partners. You wanted to have a choice. Are you in or out?"

I paused for a moment. "Where is the mirror?"

Penn patted the satchel at his side, the one he always had with him. So I'd been right. "I never let it leave my sight. When we got to Gilraeth, I hid it here in the event that we'd be captured."

He truly always had a plan. I supposed that's what made him so great. "Can I see it?" I asked. "The mirror?"

"I don't ever take it out. It's covered, and I keep it that way. I don't know what kind of power it might hold over us if we lay our eyes upon it, and I don't want anyone tempted to use it. Magic always has a price."

I nodded, though disappointment filled me.

His hand stayed outstretched. "Well?" he asked.

I grasped Penn's hand, his enveloping mine, warm and rough, as we shook.

"Get some sleep, Lilypad." Penn let go of me and stalked toward the opening of the cave. "We have a sparring match you need to rest up for."

Chapter Thirty-Two

We stood outside the cave, feet planted in the sand, Penn across from me, gripping a long stick with a sharpened point. I held one in my hand too. It was the best we could do without our weapons, and Penn wouldn't use earth magic against me when I had none to fight back with. His sword had been confiscated when he was arrested.

"Are you sure you're ready?" Penn tossed his spear to his other hand.

"Yes." I bent my knees, holding up my own spear as if it were a sword.

Penn's blond hair glinted under the sun, and I noticed the way some of his strands shimmered gold.

Penn frowned. "You're positive you want to do this?"

My gaze met his. "Yes. How many times do I have to tell you that I want to do this?"

"Well, you were just staring at my hair, so I could only assume that meant you weren't ready."

Right. Eyes on his weapon. My gaze involuntarily dipped to the bulge in his pants. Not *that* weapon, which I had a feeling was equally as dangerous as the one he held.

I cleared my throat while Penn just stood there, looking bored with this entire thing, like it was an inconvenience to him.

I charged, and he easily sidestepped me, then swatted me on the butt with his stick, which sent me stumbling a few steps forward. I whirled, stick raised in front of me to find Penn right there, his weapon meeting mine. In a battle of strength, Penn would win every time. But Shadow had taught me ways to outmaneuver an opponent who was stronger.

I dropped to the ground, kicking my leg out and swiping it at Penn's calves. He fell to the ground with an oomph, which gave me immense satisfaction . . . until he rolled over, jumping and whirling to face me, sharp end of his stick pointed right at my neck.

"You have to always be five steps ahead," he said.

Well, damnit.

Then I noticed he wasn't guarding his stomach. I lifted my stick to point right at it.

"The fight was over," Penn said. "I won. You can't gut me when I've already sliced your neck open."

"Maybe you didn't hit an important artery," I said, jabbing my stick into his stomach. Just enough to make him scowl.

"So I just ran a sword across your throat, and you're telling me that while you're bleeding out, you have enough energy to stick your sword through my stomach? Mother fucking earth, I clearly needed to be sitting in on more of your training sessions."

I gritted my teeth and jabbed harder, though his stupid stomach was already so hard, the movement didn't seem to have a lot of impact.

Penn's scowl deepened. "Do that one more time, and you're going to regret it."

I held his stare from my place on the ground and slowly pushed the stick into his stomach again. It happened in a flash. Penn stepped back and brought his boot down on my stick, snapping it in half. Then he spun around me, dropped to his knees and crushed my back to his chest, arms around my neck, limiting my breathing.

"Now, come on, Lilypad," he purred into my ear. "You know I'm not one to make empty threats."

"Oh, I know," I rasped. "I also don't care. I'm not . . . scared . . . of you."

He chuckled darkly, and in that moment, it occurred to me that maybe I ought to be. Then I remembered Hammer putting me in this exact type of hold—and what he'd instructed me to do to get out of it.

I brought my elbow back and rammed it into Penn's stomach. He groaned, but his hold on me didn't loosen.

"Nice try," he said into my ear.

I thrashed. "Let . . . me . . . go."

"No," he said simply.

No? What in the good green earth did that mean? He was just going to hold me here forever? Well, not forever. I'd run out of air eventually and pass out.

"You wanted to do this," he said. "You wanted to spar, wanted to earn your place in my academy. I tried to end the fight, but you refused. So fight. Fight me."

His words lit a fire in me. Fight. Fight for my people. Fight for my friends. Fight for myself.

I let out a scream and brought the jagged end of my stick right down into his arm. He swore and his grip loosened enough for me to duck out of it. I hopped to my feet and kicked his stick out of his hands, bringing up a swath of dust that flew into his eyes. It was just the distraction I needed to push my boot into his back. I jumped on top of him, straddling him, weapon now pointed right at his throat.

My breathing was heavy, and sweat dripped down my head, but I felt . . . amazing. I'd just done that. I'd out-maneuvered the king of thieves.

"Well done," Penn said from beneath me, and an image flashed before my mind.

One of Penn underneath me in a very different situation. I imagined his broad, muscled chest, running my hands over it, imagined what it might feel like to have him inside me as I rocked on top. No, not going there.

"You're looking very pleased with yourself," Penn said, voice low and eyes glittering as if he knew exactly what I was thinking about.

I tightened my grip on the stick. "Careful, you're in a very compromising situation."

"Ah, but you're forgetting something." Penn's head tipped slightly in the direction of his hand.

He gripped a sharp rock, holding it up. One good thwack would be all it took to knock me out. I hadn't even seen him grab it when I'd tackled him. I'd been too busy living out some absurd fantasy in my mind.

Disappointment replaced my glee, and I stood, dropping the stick. "So what now? I fail?" I spread out my arms. "I don't get to join your academy?"

I leaned back against the outside of the cave wall. Suddenly everything felt so impossible. I couldn't even defeat Penn in a fight. How was I going to steal something from Princess Gabrielle? Defeat my stepmother?

"You wanna talk about it?" Penn leaned against the cave wall next to me.

I shrugged, playing with the frayed end of my tunic. "When I was young, I grew up thinking my father knew everything, that he was this amazing, strong man. Then I got older and started realizing all his faults, the ways I wanted to be better than him. I wanted to be the kind of queen my people deserved. I'm not an idiot. I saw the flaws of our court, that we didn't feel like a cohesive unit, everyone out for themselves. And it started at the top, with my father being so closed off. I wanted to create a sense of community." I shook my head. "I was always so sure about the kind of queen I could be. But ever since you took me from that prison, I feel like I've gotten further from that goal. If my people could see me now . . ." I gestured to Penn. "Working with the king of thieves, resorting to stealing in order to save the earth court—I don't know if they'd think I was any different, any better, than my father. I'm doing all these things that I'm not proud of, and I can't even do them right. I've been so focused on saving the earth court, but what if I doom them anyway because I don't know how to be what they need?"

"Lilypad," Penn said. "Look at me."

I raised my eyes to meet his.

"You're not your father, and that's okay. Because you're you. Have you ever considered that might be so much better?"

A gust of wind blew past us, the warm breeze filled with gritty sand. We both shielded our eyes from the onslaught until it had passed.

"What are you talking about, Penn? You don't know what kind of queen I'll be."

"Yes, I do. I've seen the way you take charge. You're not afraid of anything, You meet every challenge thrown at you, even if it's not something you're skilled at. You successfully planned your escape from both me and Jasper. It was impressive, by the way. The way you rescued Shadow and me from those sand pits."

"And I botched the rescue."

"No, you didn't." Penn took hold of my shoulders, giving them a light shake. "You don't have to be a great warrior or a great thief. Yes, I need you on this mission, but I don't need you to be something you're not." Penn swiped a hand over his head and blew out a frustrated breath. "Why can't you see how amazing you are? You don't have to be perfect. You don't have to prove anything. Just be you. You make your own magic."

His gaze bore into me, his hands so firm and steady on my shoulders. A warmth spread through my belly.

"Do you really believe that?" I asked, working hard to keep my voice from shaking.

"Yeah, I do." He let go of me, and I swayed on my feet, woozy from our interaction.

"We better pack up and get going. It's at least a week's trek to the border of Apolis from here." He marched into the cave, like he hadn't just said those words, told me he thought I'd make a good queen, that I . . . what was it? Made my own magic? I wasn't even sure what that meant, but it had felt like a compliment. Like maybe Penn didn't hate me at all.

I wasn't sure I hated him anymore either.

Chapter Thirty-Three

Penn and I huddled together over a small fire, the night sky spread out above us, stars strewn about like tinsel. It would've been a spectacular sight to behold if I wasn't so damn cold. We had to keep the fires small so as not to attract any kind of attention. We'd been traveling for a week, now, and I swore I'd spend the rest of my life getting sand out from every crack and crevice in my body. Places I didn't even know sand could be. Penn and I had fashioned scarves to go over our faces and protect us from windstorms, but the sand still managed to infiltrate every barrier, cutting like glass when the wind was particularly strong. I was truly starting to hate this place.

We'd had a few close calls, having to change routes often to drop anyone who appeared on our tail. We also came face-to-face with a dragon, but luckily it had gotten distracted by a group of camels wandering the desert and had decided they'd be a much tastier meal. I didn't blame the dragon. I doubted we looked particularly appetizing after surviving on little food and water. Finding either in the desert was a challenge, but Penn had been to Gilraeth several times and knew how to find water sources, thank the blood and earth.

Tonight, all we had was cactus. My stomach curled just looking at it. I was so sick of cactus, its slimy texture, its plant-like flavor, the way I had to chew and chew and chew before being able to swallow it down.

"You need to eat," Penn said from across the fire.

I knew he was going to say that. He reminded me every single night when I looked upon the cactus with a wrinkled nose. But we simply didn't have the time or energy to catch anything more.

He reached out his hand, giving me a strip, and I snatched it from him, shoving it into my mouth and choking while trying to force it down.

I gagged, and Penn had the water skin waiting. I took it from him and swallowed a mouthful of water, then handed it back.

"How did you become the king of thieves?" I asked. "Did you just wake up one day and decide I want to be the best criminal on the continent of Arathia?"

Penn snorted, and I could see the slight curve to his lips, lips that I'd found myself staring at more and more as we journeyed together.

"Most people don't become criminals out of boredom; they become criminals out of necessity."

I opened my mouth to argue, and he held up a hand.

"And before you tell me that there is always another way, think about what options I had. I was an orphan, had no one but myself. I was trapped in a forest with Elwen bordering one side and the Deadlands bordering the other. Everyone was afraid, desperate, but worst of all, they'd lost hope. I could see the cracks forming."

The firelight illuminated his face, shadows darkening his eyes as he spoke, memories lingering in those shadows.

Penn grabbed his rucksack, stuffing it behind his head as he leaned back. "When people get desperate, they do stupid things. Start turning on one another, start picking fights, start creating enemies. I didn't want that to happen. I felt an obligation to my people, an obligation to be the leader they needed now that my parents had died." He paused, hesitation flitting across his face. "I don't know what you know of the border . . ."

"I know it was my father who used his magic to erect it," I said. "Another secret he kept from me, but he must've had his reasons."

Penn looked away for a moment, jaw clenching. This must be a sore subject for him. And I understood.

"So what did you do, then?" I asked, wanting to get his story back on track. "How did that lead you to becoming a thief?"

That ghost of a smile reappeared on Penn's lips. "I'm getting there, Lilypad. One day, I decided to visit the border. I don't know what I was thinking. Hoping. Maybe that I could do something, find a way to destroy it? I went again, and again, and again. Every day I studied it. I studied the vines, the way they reacted if you came too close. I threw rocks in the air to see how they might attack, what direction they'd shoot out to defend. I learned. And finally, the day came I was brave enough to get to the other side."

I held my breath, mesmerized by his story. I'd never even thought about what it might take to cross the border between Elwen and Mosswood Forest.

"I got my ass kicked." Penn's lips quirked. "Got thrown into a tree by one of the vines. Another day, I almost got eaten by the border. Then I almost got crushed." He started ticking off his fingers. "Bit, scratched, bloodied, battered. My magic was ineffective against it, everything I threw at it destroyed. Until one day, when I finally made it over to the other side."

I realized my mouth was hanging open and snapped it shut.

"I'd lived in Elwen when I was young, before the war, but didn't remember much. I figured it couldn't hurt to explore a little. I stumbled upon a farm, and the people were kind to me. They bought my story about how I was traveling back home after seeking out a healer for my mother. They invited me to dinner with them, let me stay for the night at their house." He paused. "That was the first time I stole."

My brows shot up. "You stole from them? From these people who showed you kindness?"

"They also had far more than we did in Mosswood Forest. I saw an opportunity." His voice had a hard edge, held no remorse over his actions.

Curiosity overtook my urge to reproach him. "So what did you steal?"

A breeze blew through the air, and I shivered, frisking my arms and scooting closer to the fire. Sand scattered around us, rustling, creating a lulling harmony with the crackle of the fire.

"As they gave me a tour of their farm, their house, fed me dinner, I marveled at everything they had. Tools like knives, knife sharpeners, axes. They had seeds, they had livestock—things that didn't exist in

Mosswood Forest. So I pretended to go to bed, waited until I knew they were asleep, and I took as many of those tools, those seeds, as I could." He leaned forward, holding his hands out over the fire. "I took everything back to Mosswood Forest, and it was like a new life had been breathed into the community. No one asked where I'd gotten these things. I don't even think it occurred to them to. But as I took more trips, brought more back, they knew what was happening. They also knew it was our only way to survive."

I took a deep breath. "I understand why you stole from Elwen. My father never would've traded with you after the war, but why not trade with other courts? Why steal from everyone else too?"

"The other courts were banned from trading with us."

"What? But who . . ." I trailed off, realizing I knew who must've enacted the ban. "Why would my father do that?"

"To make us suffer," Penn said. "Politics can be nasty, Lilypad. The other courts knew if they traded with us, it would earn them the wrath of Elwen, and you know how desperate the courts are to keep peace at all costs."

Of course. No one wanted to earn the wrath of the Seven Spirits like the Old World had. No one wanted to risk getting our magic taken away, or worse, the Seven Spirits visiting and obliterating us from the continent.

"Is that what you would have done?" Penn asked, but his tone wasn't judgmental or condescending. He asked the question in a way that made me think he actually cared about my answer.

"I don't know," I said slowly. "I don't have all the information my father had."

I looked down at my hands. It hurt that my father had lied to me. I understood why he might lie to our people, but to me? I was his daughter, the future queen of the earth court. I wished he were here so I could confront him, ask him why he kept all these secrets from me. Then again, our arguments over how he ruled never led to common ground. They just divided us further.

"Whatever is going on in your head, stop it, Lilypad." Penn's voice was soft.

"What are you talking about?"

"I can see that little crinkle, the one you get in your forehead when you're overthinking something."

"I don't overthink," I said.

He just raised a brow in that infuriating way that he did.

"Sometimes I overthink," I admitted. "You don't understand, Penn."

"Why?" His voice was fierce, a rare defensiveness in his tone. "Why wouldn't I understand?"

I threw out my arms. "Because it's true." I paused. "My father and I had a lot of disagreements over how he ruled, yes. But outside of politics, I have good memories of him. He could be absorbed with his work, locked away in his office for hours at a time. But when he was just my father and not a king? We had fun together. He loved me, and I loved him, despite our differences. He would take me on strolls through the markets, he'd make me laugh by doing silly things like trying to juggle apples. He'd take me on adventures, and we'd talk about life in general, about gossip in the castle, the drama between the servants." A soft laugh escaped my lips. "It's hard having these conflicting memories of him, having these secrets about him come out, because at the end of the day, I still love him, even if I didn't like him sometimes. But I do want to be better, to ensure nothing like the Great War ever happens again."

Penn stayed silent, his gaze resting on my face as he listened. "And you don't think you can do that?" he finally asked.

"How could I?" Penn flinched at my raised voice. "Sorry." I looked around, but we were isolated, the nearest town miles back. "I've resorted to stealing. To working with the most infamous thief on the continent. And it does make me wonder if I'll ever be the leader I want to be. If I'm willing to compromise on my morals to get what I want, then do I even deserve to be queen?"

"You do," Penn said. "I just wish you could see what I see."

"And what's that?" I asked.

Penn just smirked. "Well, you're not ready to hear that."

I snorted. Another one of his little games. "So you stole a few items, and what? You became the king of thieves?"

Penn laughed and shook his head. "No, that took years, Lilypad. I started going on more missions, going further, stealing more items of value and bringing them back to Mosswood Forest. My people were thriving and that gave me a purpose, a drive. Soon enough, I began to earn a reputation, and I worried I'd be recognized. So the academy was born. I found other orphans like myself, ones who were lost or not on the greatest path, and I brought them into my academy to train." He spread out his hands. "The rest is history."

I thought about what Shadow had told me, about how Penn had saved them all. She'd never elaborated on that. They must have all had sordid pasts and hard lives.

"That was brave of you," I said finally.

An amused look crossed Penn's face. "Brave? Surely you're not calling a thief like myself brave."

I narrowed my eyes. "You're right. I take it back."

"Too late for that. I already heard the words, straight from your mouth."

"You're about to hear a few more words from my mouth if you don't drop it." I glared at him, regretting ever giving him a compliment. This man was insufferable.

"I can think of a lot of things I'd like to see that mouth do," Penn said, voice low.

I smiled sweetly, playing his game. "Come close and you'll see exactly what I'm capable of."

"That sounds tempting."

I realized my words sounded more like an invitation than a threat. Blood and earth, this man had a way of drawing out a side of me that even Jasper never saw.

Another strong breeze pushed through the air, and this time, my teeth actually chattered. The fire flickered, the heat unable to fight back against the chill of the night.

"You're cold," Penn said.

"Aren't you?"

"We need to sleep together tonight."

An image flashed in my mind: me, naked and writhing underneath him. "Absolutely not," I said, but just the thought of my body burrowed against his was enough to warm me.

"Then you'll freeze," he said, no emotion on his face. Clearly this was just a transaction to him, like everything with the king of thieves.

"The temperature has been dropping every night, and we can't build up a big fire that would draw attention to us."

Damnit, he was right. "Fine," I grumbled. "Get over here."

I spread out my bedroll and lay down, staring out into the darkness. I felt Penn's body behind mine, his arms coming over me, and suddenly, I was finding it very hard to breathe. My senses were on fire, the smell of earth and musk enveloping me, his heat seeping into me, the feel of his hands resting on my stomach, setting my skin alight. I hated that he made me feel this way when I clearly meant nothing to him. He'd used me over and over, was continuing to use me, even if he'd given me a choice. I was nothing but a tool to him, something to wield to help him get what he wanted. I had to remember that, to continually fight against whatever feelings were rising up in me the more I got to know him.

"Sleep, Lilypad," Penn said into my ear. "Tomorrow we arrive in Apolis."

Chapter Thirty-Four

We'd been walking for hours. My throat was dry, my legs aching from the effort of trudging through sand. I was so sick of sand. The grit, the way it cut against my face, got into my eyes, coated my tongue. I felt it everywhere, and it made me want to scream. I had no idea how people lived in this place. I'd once thought it beautiful. But that was when I'd been a guest. When I could come and go as I pleased. Now, I never wanted to see this place again.

"We're close now," Penn said from beside me, pointing. The landscape was slowly changing around us, the sand dunes spreading out, flattening, the sand growing thinner, and in the distance I could see the rocky terrain of the water court, the brilliant white houses with the terra cotta roofs, the sea spreading out over the horizon like a sparkling sapphire under the sun.

I almost cried in relief. Not only because I'd no longer have to deal with this terrible sand but because, soon enough, I'd get to see my friend, the first familiar person I'd seen in so long. Other than Jasper, but that clearly hadn't been a pleasant reunion.

I chanced a glance at Penn, arching my neck to look at him. He stared ahead, resolute, his skin coated in a light layer of sand, his hair glossy and shining under the sun. He looked at me, and I quickly looked away.

We'd woken up that morning, snuggled together. His arms had been wound tight around me, his cheek pressed against mine. Our legs were twined together like twisted vines, where you couldn't even see where one began and the other ended. Penn had still been asleep, his chest rising and falling with a slow motion, and I'd been frozen in his arms, unable to move. It had felt so good.

Why had it felt so good?

Maybe I'd just been imprisoned for so long, desperate for any kind of contact, that I'd have been thrilled to be snuggled by anyone. Except Jasper. I'd stab him in the eye if he tried to cuddle with me.

Plus, I'd just found out my betrothed wanted nothing to do with me, had never really loved me. My heart was aching. It didn't feel particularly achey, but maybe I was just numb to the feeling.

I certainly hadn't been numb this morning, heat spreading to my belly, my thighs shaking, my core damp with need.

It was a natural bodily reaction. Penn was handsome. Gorgeous, if I wanted to get specific. Which I didn't.

Any woman in my position would be feeling the things I was feeling. Spirits below, I didn't need to be thinking about this right now. We had a mission to complete—

"Are you sure you're going to be able to do this?" Penn asked, interrupting my spiral.

"Yes," I snapped, more irritated with myself than with him. "I already told you I would. Why are you asking me this now? When we're so close to Apolis?"

"Well, you've been worrying at your bottom lip all morning and spent the last half hour picking at your nails so much they're bleeding."

I looked down. Oh. So I had been.

"You look pale. Paler than usual."

I scowled at that.

His lips quirked. "And you haven't said more than two words to me today."

If he only knew what I really was worried about.

I cleared my throat. "I'm fine, Penn."

"Lilypad . . ."

"Are you ever going to call me by my real name?"

The truth was, I'd softened to the nickname ever since he admitted what it really meant to him.

He rubbed his stubbled jaw, and I wanted to feel that stubble against my cheek again, feel the gentle rasp of it as it scraped my skin. Blood and earth. I needed to get a hold of myself. Go throw myself into the cold ocean when we arrived in Apolis.

"You can do this, Lilypad. But I need you to believe that too."

He was being kind, and it unnerved me. He'd been kind a lot lately. Playful. Tempting. An unbidden image flashed in my mind of Arrow pressing herself into him at the tavern that night that felt so long ago. My mood darkened. Even if the king of thieves showed any interest in me, it didn't matter. He was taken.

"Arrow must be missing you," I said, changing the subject.

His brows bunched together. "Why would Arrow be missing me?"

I shrugged, trying to be careful with my next words. "I just noticed you two were together quite a lot. Specifically, she was in your lap several times. That doesn't seem casual to me."

Penn was smiling now, staring down at me, those mischievous green eyes twinkling, like he knew something I didn't.

"Why are you looking at me like that?" I glared at him.

"Are you jealous, Lilypad?"

"No," I said, keeping my tone even.

A gust of wind blew sand up in our faces, and we both pulled our scarves up at the same time, covering our noses and mouths.

"I'm making conversation, Penn. The walk is long. I'm bored. And you just complained that I've been rather quiet this morning."

Lies. All lies.

"So are you . . .?" I asked, keeping my tone light.

"Am I what?" I couldn't see his mouth but could hear the smile in his voice.

He was really going to make me say it. "Are you and Arrow together? A couple?"

"No" was all he said, not elaborating.

I whirled on him, and he stopped.

"No? But all those times she was all over you. If she was near you, she couldn't stop touching you."

"Did you notice she was all over everyone else too? That's what

Arrow does. She's handsy. Especially when she's been drinking. Also, she's been in love with Charming for years. She often tries to make him jealous by throwing herself at others."

I hadn't noticed her all over anyone else. I'd never paid attention to anyone else when Penn was around . . .

Oh, bloody fucking earth.

I didn't—I couldn't . . . have feelings for Penn. I hated him. He was the king of thieves. A criminal. He stood for everything that was wrong on this continent. But he was also brave and confident and determined. He was a leader, and people clearly respected him. He cared about the thieves in his academy, cared about everyone in Mosswood Forest. He sacrificed himself to help his people.

Okay, I might possibly have caught some feelings. I yanked my scarf down.

"There you go, chewing on that bottom lip again," Penn said, continuing to walk.

"I'm fine," I squeaked, horrified at my revelation as I trailed after him.

I couldn't have feelings for the king of thieves. Once I took back my court, I'd need to marry, find a good, respectable king to rule by my side. But rulers rarely had the luxury of marrying for love. My own parents loved each other, but my mother had told me that their love had grown over time, after they'd married.

It didn't matter. I'd complete this mission, and then Penn and I would go our separate ways, and my feelings would fade. I took a deep breath to steady my racing heart.

"Hey." Penn stopped, taking hold of my shoulders, staring into my eyes. "It's going to be okay. I will be by your side every step of the way. We're in this together now, okay?"

I laughed, but it came out all breathy and wrong.

Penn stepped closer. "Or is it something else that's bothering you?" His voice was low now, and it sent shudders down my spine.

I needed him to let go of me, to stop looking at me like he wanted to . . . to devour me. I couldn't play his games. Not now. Not when they might actually break me.

He lifted a hand and thumbed away some sand on my cheek. "You had a little something," he said.

I snorted, knowing that sand coated every inch of my body, just as it did his. The place where his thumb had been burned hot, and I wanted him to do it again.

"You know, you make some interesting sounds when you're sleeping."

"I—what?" I asked.

"Last night, I woke up several times to you moaning."

My mouth dropped open. "No, you most certainly did not."

He stepped closer, his hands moving up and down my arms in gentle motions. "What could have made you moan like that?" His eyes glittered.

I donned a confident smile. "Maybe I was dreaming of those delicious spiced pear tarts from Mosswood Village."

He lowered his head, his lips inches from mine now. So close that I could tip my chin and close the distance between us. He'd never been so bold before, and spirits help me, I liked it. I could just imagine myself rising up on my tiptoes and pressing my mouth to his, like I did that night that he rescued me. It felt so long ago now, but blood and earth, I wanted his mouth on mine.

"I wonder what I could do to get you to make a sound like that again. Because I have to admit, Lilypad, I kind of liked it." He pressed his lips to my jawline, and my knees went weak. "No? Maybe this." He pressed his lips to my neck, and his arms tightened when I swayed. "Still not good enough? Then maybe this will do it."

His lips trailed up my neck, hovering over my mouth, and heat flooded every inch of me. I wanted this. I wanted his lips against mine, his arms around me. I didn't care if he was playing games, if he enjoyed watching me squirm. I didn't care about the future or the fact that we could never be together. I didn't care about anything but him and me in this moment.

"Halt!" a voice yelled, and I jumped from Penn, all the warmth in my body replaced by a cold dread.

He straightened, a feral look spreading across his face like he wanted to gut the woman who'd interrupted us. Like he hadn't been playing a game at all.

The woman held out a spear made of shimmering water, and other women gathered behind her, all of them holding weapons pointed directly at us. Their white tunics wrapped around their bodies, flowing down to their sandaled feet. All of them had golden hair to match their golden skin, and from here, I could see the muscles in their exposed shoulders and arms.

My mouth went dry.

The woman glared at us. "You are attempting to the enter the water court, which is illegal, punishable by death. Take one more step, and you'll find this spear in your gut."

That didn't sound particularly pleasant.

Penn stepped forward, and they all lunged their spears at us. The woman in the front held out her hand, and out of the corner of my eye I saw a wave rise in the air, hanging in place, ready to crash down and sweep us away.

I grabbed for Penn's arm. "Did you not hear her?" I looked at the woman and called out, "He won't come any closer. I swear it."

"Relax, Lilypad," he whispered, no panic in his voice.

He gently shook me off of him and held up his hands. "I am here with Princess Liliath of the earth court, heir to the Elwen throne, rightful ruler. She's escaped her stepmother's prison and seeks asylum in the water court."

The guards faltered with their weapons, sending doubtful expressions at each other. A few whispered to the woman in front, but she held up her hand, the wave still towering over us. "Silence." She studied me, eyes narrowed. "You don't look like the princess."

"Because I've spent weeks traveling, hiding, being under constant threat, to get here. Please, just let me have an audience with Princess Gabrielle, and I'll explain everything."

The woman's eyes narrowed, spear still pointed at us. "And who are you?" She moved the spear toward Penn.

Penn stepped back, threading my fingers with his in one smooth move. "I'm her betrothed."

Chapter Thirty-Five

Penn's words rang in my ears, and I yanked my hand from his. "Your what?" I whisper-yelled.

His face remained bored, but his eyes flickered. "We have an audience, dear."

I looked back at the guards, all of them staring at us with confused looks. I smiled. "Will you just excuse us for a moment?" I glanced up at the wave still lingering in the air. "And please don't drown us. We just need to have a quick chat."

I grabbed Penn's arm and pulled him back a few paces. "Betrothed?" I said.

This was too far. I knew he liked to play his games, to make me feel uncomfortable. For whatever sick, twisted reason, he enjoyed it, and for whatever even sicker reason, I did too. But this? I couldn't be betrothed to him. Even if it was fake. That would take things between us too far, be too much of a risk, especially if anyone found out his true identity.

"How else am I supposed to get into the water court?" Penn asked.

I hadn't actually thought about it.

"Their borders have been closed for a year. No one knows why. They're not going to let just anyone in. But if I'm your betrothed, that shows you trust me."

"Not as far as I can throw you," I mumbled.

"You can't throw me at all," Penn said.

"Exactly," I snapped.

I looked back at the guards, the one in front now tapping her foot impatiently. I smiled again and waved. "Just a moment," I called out, then glared at Penn. "What happened to us being partners? To making all our decisions together?"

"I told you about this," he said.

"No you didn't!"

"In my head," he added.

I groaned out in frustration.

He flicked my arm. "You're cute when you're annoyed, Lilypad."

"Stop that." I pushed away his finger.

"It's just pretend," he said. "And you know I'm right. This will be the quickest way to get us both in and to find that weapon."

So this wasn't another one of his games to fluster me. It was his plan. That's why he had just been kissing my jaw like that. He was putting on a show before we'd even arrived, and I'd been a fool, thinking he actually wanted me. Yet again, I was just a tool to him. A means to an end. Exactly like I'd been for Jasper. It stung more than I wanted to admit. I hated myself for what I was about to do.

I grabbed his hand, and together, we walked toward the guards. "Sorry about that. I just needed to speak with my . . . betrothed for a moment. Please, I'm not lying, and if you'll just let me see Princess Gabrielle, I'll prove I am who I say I am."

The guards once again looked unsure, but finally, the lead one nodded, the tight bun on her head bobbing with the movement. "Fine. But you'll be entering the water court on our terms."

She flicked her hand and the wave crashed down, water splashing up and flying to wrap around our wrists like handcuffs. The guards turned. "Come," the lead one said. "And if you try anything at all, you'll get thrown straight into the sea."

"Welcome to Apolis," Penn muttered.

WE STUMBLED BEHIND THE GUARDS, over the sharp rocks that jutted out, slick with sea water. The rocks led upward in an incline. At one point my feet slipped, but I fell backward into Penn's hard chest.

A flowing river circled the water court, fed by the ocean and cutting through the rocks. We crossed a glass bridge, see-through, giving a view of the fish and other sea creatures that waded through the river.

Despite being handcuffed with the water links, Penn steadied me. "Careful, Lilypad," he said, no doubt playing up his role as the concerned fiancé.

I muttered a "thank you" and we continued on, climbing the rocks until we crested the top, and I sucked in a sharp breath. Apolis had always been the most stunning of the courts, in my opinion. Besides Elwen, of course. White houses with orange terra cotta roofs spread out among the cliffside, dotting the stone terrain, with a market and small village on a flat terrace that overlooked the ocean. On the far side of the cliff stood the brilliant castle, white and gleaming, perched right on the edge of the rock. It rose so tall it looked like it touched the sun.

I'd had a chance to visit Apolis just a year before my stepmother murdered my father and forever changed the course of my life. I'd been here under different circumstances then, as an honored guest. I'd spent my days walking along the shoreline, visiting the market with Gabrielle, and partaking in wine while we sat around a fire at night, gossiping. The trip was supposed to be a chance for me to make alliances as the heir to Elwen, but it had mostly been a chance for me to have fun and explore.

We descended the rocks, slipping, sliding, and stumbling until we finally landed on a dirt road that wound along the bottom of the cliffside and up toward the castle.

It looked like a long walk, and my muscles were already feeling the ache from the trek ahead of us.

"Can we take a moment to rest?" Penn asked. "My betrothed needs a break."

It would've been sweet if it hadn't all been an act.

The guards turned to glare at us.

"Will you shut up?" I hissed. "No need to anger them."

He smiled at them. "Surely you can understand. We've had a very long journey from Elwen, and we have quite a tale to tell Princess

Gabrielle about our travels. I don't think she'll be pleased to hear that her friend was mistreated."

I eyed him, then glanced back at the guards, my stomach twisting at the thought of one of their water spears slicing open my belly. But instead the lead guard nodded, curt.

"You have five minutes," she said, then stalked away with her guards.

I sighed in relief and collapsed down onto the road, Penn settling next to me.

"Okay," he said, voice low. "Do you remember what we discussed? Our story?"

"Do you ever stop working?" I asked, looking at him. "Yes, Penn. I remember. We talked about it in length, and you made me repeat it over and over. Of course, you left out the betrothal part, but believe me, I won't forget that any time soon."

His lips quirked. "That eager to marry me, huh?"

I glared at him. "On second thought, maybe I will forget and have you thrown into the sea."

"You'd miss me too much," he said.

I looked out over the ocean, letting the gentle crash of the waves calm my frazzled nerves.

"And I like to work," he said. "Working helps keep me focused on my goals, on making Mosswood Forest a better place."

I tore my gaze from the beautiful scenery and studied Penn for a moment. That hard jawline, blond hair, tied at his neck, his strong, straight nose, the planes of his cheekbone, all lined with the weight of the world. "You can do something for yourself sometimes, just because you need it." I spread my arms out. "We can sit and rest just to rest, not because you need to plan and connive and micromanage me."

His jaw ticked, and I knew I'd struck a nerve. "I do not micromanage."

"That's all you do, Penn. You got angry when I rescued you in the sand pits because I didn't follow the plan you apparently had."

"I apologized for that."

"It doesn't change that you were still angry." I put a hand on his arm, and his gaze snapped to me. "I'm just saying that when this mission is over, when you're back in Mosswood Forest, maybe you should take some time to figure out what you're running from."

"I'm not running from anything." His voice had a hard edge that told me the opposite.

"Then why don't you do anything for fun? For the few weeks I was in Mosswood Forest, I never saw you do anything that wasn't also aimed at working."

"I was at the tavern," he said.

"Where you tried to bring work."

"I went to the festival."

"So you could stock up on some materials for your upcoming mission."

He laughed. "You surprise me at every turn, Lilypad." He lifted his head and those green eyes bore into me—no mischief, no teasing, just a vulnerability I wasn't used to seeing in him.

"Enough!" a guard yelled. "Break's over. It's time to face Princess Gabrielle, and we'll see if she believes your little story about being princess of Elwen."

Penn and I continued to stare at each other until the guards yanked us to our feet and forced us back onto the path toward the castle.

Chapter Thirty-Six

Thirty minutes later, we made it to the castle, and my legs felt like they might collapse underneath me. I stumbled several times on our journey, so weak I didn't know if I could go on, but every time Penn was there, his hands steady as he grabbed me and told me I could do this, that I could make it to the castle, making me constantly question what was real, if he was being nice because he cared or because he wanted to sell our relationship to everyone.

Now here we were as the castle towered over us, a drawbridge stretching out that the guards led us across. The white alabaster walls glittered, and I ran my hand over the rough exterior. The castle rose into high peaks and towers, and statues of sirens were carved into the tower walls. I'd always loved looking at the statues, mesmerized by the detailed mermaid tails and flowing hair. Two big wooden doors opened up to the inside. As we walked across the white-marbled floor, dust smudged the ground, and I winced. I'd have hated it if someone came to my castle, leaving trails of filth everywhere. Two staircases wound up on either side of the room, the railings golden and gleaming as the sun streamed through the big windows that lined the walls. Paintings of what I assumed were former rulers hung in between the windows.

"Come," the guard said and led us in between the staircases and through another set of double doors, these ones golden and carved with tentacles, like an octopus had been plastered against the door and covered in gold. The doors opened and there sat a throne, Gabrielle occupying it, a crown resting on her head, auburn hair cascading down her shoulders in spiraled curls, not like the flaming red of Arrow's or Jillian's hair. Hers was a softer hue that reminded me of leaves turning colors in the fall. She'd always been beautiful, this glorious light that shined bright, but something immediately felt off. Her skin was paler, not like its normal golden hue, and she looked thin, too thin, like she hadn't been eating. I wondered if this had to do with the reason the border to Apolis had been closed.

"What's the meaning of this?" Her voice echoed around the room, which was lined with tall white pillars on either side.

The guards bowed, and the one who'd trapped us with the water cuffs stepped forward. "I'm sorry to disturb you like this, Your Majesty, but—"

"Gabrielle!" I lurched forward, unable to help myself. "It's me. Liliath. Princess Liliath."

Her eyes widened, and she slowly stood, her head tilting as she studied me. She didn't silence me, didn't protest my words, so I continued on.

"I'm sure you know that I've spent that last two years imprisoned by my stepmother." I swallowed. "She killed my father and took the throne." I gestured to Penn, who stood right behind me, a solid wall to remind me I wasn't alone. "This is Penn. He rescued me, and we fell in love." I thought about the rest of our story, what we'd discussed. "We tried to go to the fire court for help, but Jasper trapped me and wanted to sell me off to be married. I once again escaped with Penn's help, and we came here, hoping for asylum. We need to get back to Elwen so I can fight my stepmother and take back my throne, but right now, we need food, rest, and . . ." My voice broke. I was tired. So, so tired of running. "I could use a friend."

That part we hadn't rehearsed.

Penn stiffened behind me.

Gabrielle stared at me for a moment, her mouth hanging open. Maybe she wouldn't recognize me. Maybe Penn had made a grave error in believing she'd grant us asylum. Maybe we were about to get thrown off the cliff and into the sea like the guard had promised.

All of a sudden, Gabrielle was rushing forward and throwing her arms around me, hugging me tight. Her salty sea scent enveloped me, and she squeezed me even tighter.

"Liliath, my friend."

I choked out a sob of relief, and the tears started flowing.

"I'm so glad you're safe," Gabrielle said into my hair. "When we'd heard what happened—it's awful. I can't believe you were betrayed like that, and I'm so sorry you lost your father in such a horrible way."

She stepped back, and Penn took his place next to me, grabbing my hand and squeezing it. No doubt putting on a show for everyone.

"And you," Gabrielle said to Penn. "Thank you for rescuing her. You must be incredibly brave to do such a thing. Of course we'll grant you asylum. You can stay however long you need before you're ready to return to Elwen." A smile came to her face, lighting it up in that familiar way I was used to. "I never liked Jasper, by the way."

I snorted a laugh, wiping at my tears. "Apparently you're not the only one."

Her gaze caught on the water still looped around our wrists and binding our hands. She twirled her hand and the water splattered to the floor, splashing at our feet and dissipating. "I'm sorry about all this. We're just being extra cautious lately." She sent a sideways glance at her guards.

Before I could ask what had happened here, she clapped her hands together.

"You two must be exhausted and hungry. Let me show you to your rooms, and I'll have food sent up."

"Gabrielle," I started, but she held up a hand.

"Rest, eat, and then we'll talk." She nodded toward the guard that had interacted the most with us, a short woman who only came up to my shoulders, stout, plump, with a serious face and her blonde hair in a tight bun. "Leoni, show them to their rooms, please, and make sure they get plenty of food." She looked at me. "I'll also have some fresh clothes sent up while we launder yours. We should be about the same size, and . . ." She studied Penn for a moment, who didn't flinch under her hard gaze. "You're slightly bigger than my two brothers, but my father might have some clothes that would fit you."

She walked past us and out of the room without another word. Penn and I exchanged puzzled glances at the abrupt way she'd left, almost like she was afraid to stay any longer. Gabrielle was hiding something—I just didn't know what.

Chapter Thirty-Seven

One room. As in singular. Gabrielle had said rooms, but it was clear Penn and I were going to be shoved into the same space together.

Leoni frowned from next to me. "Is this room not to your satisfaction? Because I'm not carting you around the castle like some tour guide, Princess."

Well, she was pleasant.

"It's fine," Penn said, stepping forward. "Thank you for your time."

Leoni looked between us, then bowed and left the room, closing the door behind her.

I glared at Penn. "Fine? This is not fine." I gestured to the bed. "There's only one bed."

"I noticed, Lilypad."

Windows lined the wall, giving unobstructed views of the shimmering blue ocean. At least we had a balcony so I could escape from Penn when I needed to. When whatever this was between us became too much.

"Relax, Lilypad. I can sleep on the couch." He gestured to the white sofa that sat in the middle of the huge room. I looked up at the gold ceiling, embossed with waves and sea foam. Everything was so bright and airy, and the briny air breezed through the open windows, the white curtains fluttering.

"This is all your fault," I said. "If you hadn't told them we were betrothed, we wouldn't be sharing a room."

He crossed his arms. "It's better this way. We can be in constant communication, make sure we're on the same page about our plan."

A knock interrupted us, and a lady's maid slipped in, carrying clothes, just like Gabrielle had promised. She sat them down on the end of the bed and excused herself.

I lifted one of the garments, a beige chiffon that would drape across one shoulder and hang to the floor. Not exactly what I was expecting. Penn lifted his own dark green chiffon, about three times the size of mine, and snorted.

"Perfect," he muttered.

I wouldn't mind seeing Penn in one of these, seeing his muscled shoulder on display, along with his thick calves, bare arms.

I hadn't realized I was staring until Penn stood in front of me, gazing down at me, eyes twinkling. "There you go staring again," he murmured.

"No one's here," I said, pushing him. "You don't have to put on a show."

Blood and earth, this fake betrothal might be my end. I needed to remind myself all the reasons we couldn't be together.

1) This was pretend
2) Penn was using me
3) Penn was a criminal
4) This. Was. Pretend.

I couldn't get distracted just because Penn was good-looking and had some (okay, many) muscles and was brave and strong and looked at me like he'd destroy the entire world just to make me happy. Jasper had once looked at me that way, too, and see how that turned out? I swallowed. He was a good actor, I'd give him that. A little too good. He must have perfected his skills over the years as king of thieves.

I turned abruptly, grabbing my toga and marching toward an adjacent room that I assumed was the bathing chamber. I stopped inside and gasped at the grotto-like room, made of natural stone, with a pool laid in the floor and oils that lined wooden shelves hanging on the wall.

"What's wrong?" Penn rushed inside behind me. "Ah. Get yourself cleaned up, and then we have some work to do."

"No." I turned to him.

"No?"

"We're going to eat. We're going to rest. Then we're going to let Gabrielle take us on a tour of the water court."

Penn raised a questioning brow. "You've been here many times."

"But you haven't, at least not for a while, and it will give us a chance to speak with Gabrielle in a casual way."

I actually didn't know how many times Penn had been here, if he'd stolen from them or sent his thieves to do it for him.

"We have just been on a long journey," I said. "I've been kidnapped, imprisoned, threatened, terrorized, almost died from some fire lizards and a dragon. I can't just dive into our next mission without a break first."

He frowned down at me. "I thought you wanted to destroy that mirror as much as I did."

"I do. More than you could ever know. Believe me. But I also know my limits." I swallowed and walked over to the small pool, staring at its shallow depths. "My father wasn't great at taking time for himself. Watching him overextend himself made me realize you can't be at your best if you're constantly going. In a backward kind of way, he taught me the value of taking time for myself, of spending time in nature, spending time with friends, doing things I enjoyed, so that when it came time to do my job, I could be what everyone else needed. I told him he needed to relax more, but he rarely listened. On the days he did, it was like some special treat. He'd take me on adventures, exploring new and beautiful places. Those are my favorite memories with him."

"He did that for you?" Penn's voice was hard.

I turned to face him. "Yes. And right now, I know that what I need is a break. Can you handle that?"

Penn nodded. "You win, Lilypad. But we do have to get to work eventually."

I rolled my eyes. "I know that. Trust me." I stood and pushed him toward the door. "Now out. I'm not letting you watch me bathe."

"I thought you said we got to do things we enjoy. What if that's what I want to do to unwind?"

There he went again, playing his games.

"Then I'd say I remember there being a brothel somewhere around here."

I shoved him again, then slammed the door behind me before he could see the effect his words had on me. I was going to be naked in this room with only a door separating me and the king of thieves. Good green earth. I hoped when I stepped into the water, it was ice cold.

I walked through the forest, a small one near my castle. It was a sunny day, warm and beautiful out. The trees rustled in the breeze, birds and insects flitting through the sky. I let my hand trail over all the plants, bushes, flowers, leaves, then I held out my hand and a flower rose up in my palm. I twisted my wrist, the flower sinking down to the ground and planting itself in the soil.

My magic filled me, and I tugged at that spark inside of me, feeling my earth magic flood my veins. I breathed it in and pushed out both hands. The trees around me answered, dipping their branches as if to say hello.

I stopped suddenly when I saw a man standing in front of me. Not just any man. My father.

My feet stood frozen to their spot, my body unable to move.

"Father," I breathed out, wanting to run to him, to make sure he was real.

He held his arms open, and I struggled, but no matter how hard I tried I couldn't move.

"No," I yelled, fighting harder. The more I fought, the more my slippers sunk into the ground. "No!"

A dark shadow loomed over my father as the Huntsman stepped out behind him. He reached out his branches, curling them around my father's throat.

Tears spilled down my cheeks as I screamed at my father to run, but he just stood there, gesturing for me to come to him while his face turned from red to purple, while the Huntsman squeezed the life from him.

"Lilypad," a voice said. "Lilypad."

My eyes fluttered open to complete dark, save for the big round moon hanging in the sky outside our windows. Tears soaked my face, and it took me a minute to remember where I was, who I was with.

"Hey, shhh . . ." that voice said again.

Penn sat next to me on the bed, stroking my hair, so gentle with his touch. "I'm here. It was just a dream."

"My father," I got out before I burst into tears.

Penn gathered me up in his arms. "It's okay. Everything is going to be okay."

I didn't know why, but in this moment, I believed him.

He held me like that until my tears subsided. He made to move, but I caught his arm.

"Stay with me. Please." I didn't even care that I was whining. I couldn't handle another nightmare like that. "I can't be alone right now."

I scooted over on the bed and lay down. Penn didn't say a word, and I heard rustling as he slipped under the covers, his big body warm next to mine.

I was just drifting off to sleep when I could've sworn I heard him whisper, "Just so you know, you're not alone."

Chapter Thirty-Eight

After I fell asleep next to him, I'd had no more nightmares to terrorize me. We awoke the next morning curled into each other, neither of us acknowledging the previous night as we got out of bed.

"We can be adults about this," I told him. "We have one bed, and it's big enough that we can both use it."

"Whatever you say, Lilypad," he'd said, a gleam in his eyes that once again made me think he was toying with me—and enjoying it. I rushed into the bathing chambers to get dressed and away from Penn.

Shortly after, we met Gabrielle and Leoni outside the castle and walked the stone streets of Apolis together. The sun shined bright overhead, not a cloud in the sky, and the ocean stretched out as far as the eye could see.

"I don't know how much of this you remember," Gabrielle said, gesturing to Apolis.

The water court was much smaller than Elwen, everyone living in the seaside town surrounding the castle, the glittering river circling the entire court, whereas the earth court was made of many villages and small towns. I always liked the quaintness of Apolis. Everyone knew each other, and it had felt like one big family—similar to Mosswood Forest, now that I thought about it.

I looked around the stone street at the little white stores, all of them with the same terra cotta roofs and windows that gave view to bakeries, a seafood market, a butcher, a blacksmith, multiple restaurants.

I remembered running these streets with Gabrielle when we were younger, trying to lose her guards as we crisscrossed through the narrow alleyways and ducked under clotheslines. We'd run all the way to the cliffs, then dive down into the water to swim. We also got a stern talking-to by both my father and Gabrielle's parents about the dangers of doing such things.

But we were wild, young, and free. We didn't know mortality back then, how precious life was, how easily it could be taken away.

"I remember everything," I said and peered at her. "Does that little bakery still exist, the one with those filo-dough pies? A man ran it with his wife. He was so kind, always sneaking us extras when our parents weren't looking."

I expected Gabrielle to laugh, but her face darkened. "He died, unfortunately, and his wife couldn't run the bakery without him."

I exchanged a look with Penn, and he nodded. He'd noticed it, too—that strange tone to Gabrielle's voice.

"We have other bakeries," Leoni said quickly. "None can rival that of Master Theo, but they're still very good."

"Of course," I responded, careful to keep my tone light. "Are we going to dine with your mother and father tonight?"

"They're indisposed right now, I'm afraid," Gabrielle said. "Both came down with some kind of sickness, and I don't want either of you to be exposed."

"That's thoughtful of you," I said. "Still, I'd like to see them at some point."

Gabrielle stared out at the horizon, her eyes distant, like her mind was somewhere else. "Perhaps they'll feel better before it's your time to leave."

A hard edge lined her words, and I didn't want to push, to ruin what had been a pleasant morning so far.

We continued to walk down the stone streets, passing people by. Women and young children. I had to keep my gaze straight ahead and make an effort not to keep glancing at Penn in that damn outfit Gabrielle had left for him.

Just like I'd predicted, he looked far too good in the toga. It slashed down across his chest, revealing one shoulder thick with muscle, then dropped down just above his calves, strong and cut, covered by thick blonde hair. I wanted to unpin that toga and let it drop to the ground, see what else it might reveal.

Which was exactly why I wasn't looking at him. All he needed was to catch me staring again. His head would probably explode from how big it was at this point. Hopefully he thought I was playing games as much as he was. At least I had an excuse now. We had to act betrothed.

"My father loved it here, you know," I said, trying to break whatever tension had developed after I'd mentioned Gabrielle's parents. "He always talked about the eel your father served at feasts. He loved it."

My voice wavered, and I squeezed my eyes closed for just a moment. Penn's hand closed around mine, warm and comforting, as he played the perfect fiancé. He never forgot his role.

"The town feels so empty today," I commented. "I've seen a few people, but I remember it being so lively and active when I was last here."

Gabrielle shot us a smile that looked more like a grimace. "Yes, well, that same sickness that's affected my parents seems to have spread to others here as well. That happens when you live in such a small town. Illness tends to spread quickly and hit us all at the same time."

"I'm glad it hasn't affected you," I said.

"Me too." A guard came rushing up and whispered something in Gabrielle's ear. "If you'll excuse me, I must get back to the castle. Official business. Leoni will stay with you."

Leoni frowned like that was the last thing she wanted to do.

"We can walk around on our own." I gestured to the street. "It's really no problem."

"No," Gabrielle said quickly. "That's not necessary. Better to have an escort so you don't get lost."

I thought it was very unlikely we'd get lost but held my tongue.

Gabrielle walked away with the guard, leaving Penn and me with our chaperone for the day.

Leoni faced us. "I don't trust you. I don't like you. I think you're manipulating Gabrielle to get something that you want." She stepped close to me and Penn, and I tensed. "And if I catch so much as a whiff of misconduct, you'll be thrown off the cliffs and into the sea faster than you can blink. Are we clear on that?"

"You have nothing to worry about," I said, hoping it sounded convincing. I wasn't as accustomed to lying as Penn was.

"Are we clear?" she asked again, ignoring what I'd said.

I swallowed and nodded, and she spun on her heel and stalked ahead. "Good. Gabrielle wanted me to show you the fish market and beach where you can go to swim. Let's get this over with."

Penn looked at me. "What was that about enjoying ourselves and having fun?"

I pulled my hand from his and elbowed him. "Shut up."

But despite the guard's warning, the ominous meaning behind her words, I couldn't help the smile that came to my face as Penn once again reached for my hand.

Chapter Thirty-Nine

Rough hands on my mouth jolted me awake in the middle of the night. I let out a muffled scream as my eyes popped open. The hand pressed down firmly, and my instinct was to call for my guards. It took me a minute to realize I'd been trained for this sort of situation. I brought my knee up, right toward the groin of my assailant, but they caught my leg before I could make contact. Their grip was surprisingly gentle, thumb brushing against my bare skin. I blinked a few times, eyes adjusting to the dark room, and realized Penn stood over me. He released my leg from his hold and pressed a finger to his lips.

"What is wrong with you?" I sat up, covers falling off me as Penn lit a candle, illuminating his face.

His gaze froze on my chest, and my face flushed when I realized what he was staring at.

Gabrielle had told me she'd send nightgowns to my room, a special surprise for me and Penn to enjoy—and she had. Slinky black nightgowns made of lace and silk that hung just above my thigh. The neckline dipped low, revealing my breasts, my shoulders bare with only the thin straps of the dress hanging over them.

I quickly grabbed the covers, pulling them up to my chin and clearing my throat. "Gabrielle had them delivered today, and the maid took my other nightgown so I had nothing else to wear."

When I'd seen them, I hid them in the armoire, then waited until it was completely dark and Penn was already asleep to sneak into the bath chambers and change.

Penn didn't say anything, his eyes consuming me.

I cleared my throat. "She must have sent these because of your ridiculous betrothal scheme. She probably thought after everything we've been through we deserved a nice, romantic night together." I was rambling now. I knew it, but somehow I couldn't get the message from my brain to my mouth to just shut up. "Because if you saw me in this, there would be no resisting me." I laughed. "Too bad she doesn't know you. All work. No play."

"I think I might be persuaded to play a little." His eyes dipped back down to the blanket, like he was remembering what he'd seen just moments ago, what it now covered.

I hated how much this man flustered me. I'd rarely let anyone get under my skin as princess of the earth court, yet Penn seemed to be able to do it all the time.

"Is there a reason you woke me with your hand over my mouth?"

"You always have to be prepared, Lilypad."

"Seriously?" I should have known. "It's the middle of the night. I was sleeping. Very peacefully."

"I know," he said. "Your snoring woke me."

I grabbed a pillow and swung it at him, but before it landed in his face, he caught it and dropped it to the floor. His gaze trailed up my arm, and he reached out, lifting the strap that had fallen over my shoulder and putting it back in its place. His fingers grazed my skin, and I shuddered at his touch, so gentle and soft, so unlike him and the hard edges I was used to.

I shifted in bed. "Is there anything else? Unlike you, I need my rest."

I hated that the lines between us seemed to be constantly blurred these days. That I couldn't trust anything he said or did, always wondering what the motivation behind his actions were. It was exhausting and exhilarating all at the same time.

He was already walking toward the door and said over his shoulder, "Get dressed. We're going on a mission."

I TRAILED after Penn down the dark corridors, lit by streaks of moonlight that shined through the windows. Shadows crept over the walls and floor, and I hurried to keep up with Penn's long strides.

"Are you sure this is a good idea?" I whispered. "We've only been here for a day. Shouldn't we learn the guards' schedules? Map out the castle? Talk about a plan?"

"What do you think I was doing last night?" Penn asked. "While you were asleep?"

Unbelievable. I stopped, and Penn kept walking until he must've realized I was no longer with him. He turned, holding up the candle as wax dripped down into the candle holder in his hand. "Let's go," he said.

"No." I crossed my arms. "You didn't mean any of it, did you? About me being your partner, having a choice in all this? You've done nothing but determine every move we've made since we got here."

Boot heels clicked on the marble floor, and Penn rushed toward me, grabbing me and spinning both of us behind a large statue that lined the hallway. We ducked down and Penn quickly doused the flame. Guards rounded into the hallway, marching past us, thankfully unaware of our presence.

He removed his arms from me, and we sat there facing each other, centimeters apart. "Why don't you trust me?"

"I do, Lilypad," he said, his tone sincere.

He licked his lips and pushed a hand over his hair. "I'm used to being in charge, to making the plans, making the decisions. I've never had a partner before, so this is new to me."

"Your thieves aren't your partners?"

"They work for me. There's a difference."

We slowly crept out from behind the statue just as more guards rounded the corner. Penn snatched me again and reeled me into his body as we spun behind the statue.

Once the guards passed, I sighed and arched my neck to look up. "I thought you learned their schedule?"

"I did," he said. "But someone decided to change the plan by being stubborn."

"I could argue you're the one who ruined the plan by not letting me in on it," I whispered back.

He let out a soft chuckle. It rumbled through his chest, vibrating against my breastbone.

"I'm sorry," he said to me. "I've spent my entire life alone. I'm not always the best at working with others, but I'll do better."

"Then let's start now. Where are we going?" I followed him as he crept out into the hallway.

"To see the king and queen."

Chapter Forty

"That seems like a really bad idea." I scurried after Penn, and we turned a corner, then immediately ducked into an alcove as guards passed by.

"Only if we die," Penn said over his shoulder.

Truly helpful. "Thank you for that," I mumbled.

We continued on our way, all the hallways lined with windows—these ones not facing the ocean, which meant we had to be on the western side of the castle. I'd never been to the king and queen's chambers, but I knew they were on the upper floor.

We came upon a steep staircase that spiraled upward, and Penn held out his hand, keeping me in place as he scoped out the area. He motioned for me to follow, and I could barely see him without the candle, but he'd already doused the flame and there would be no getting it back now.

"Why are we seeing the king and queen?" I asked.

"Gabrielle is lying," Penn said from in front of me.

He stepped on a stair and it let out a loud creak. Both of us froze in place, but when nothing happened, we continued our ascent.

"Yes, obviously, but why does that matter? What does that have to do with this weapon we need to steal?"

"Can we have this conversation later, Lilypad? I'm not used to all these questions in the middle of a mission."

I poked him in the back. "That's what happens when you have a partner. Get used to it."

He grumbled what I thought was "pain in my ass," and this time, I flicked his head. He just shook it as we got to the top of the staircase, arriving at another hallway. Sconces lined these walls, candles flickering from them. Maybe Penn thought that whatever Gabrielle was lying about connected to this weapon, that if we found the king and queen, we could figure out what was really going on with them. I hadn't seen Gabrielle's brothers either, which wasn't exactly suspicious. They were often gone, going on diplomatic trips to other courts, sailing the seas and having adventures. Gabrielle had always been jealous that they got to gallivant around the continent while she'd been stuck here, learning how to be a queen.

We rounded a corner lined with doors, and Penn slowed to a stop, pulling me against the wall. "Around that next corner are their chambers. Two guards are posted there at all times."

I nodded. "So how are we going to get inside?"

"We're not getting inside." Penn opened a door next to us and led me into the room. All kinds of artifacts filled the space, covered by white sheets and dust.

"I don't like the sound of that," I said. "Please tell me we're not . . ." I pointed to the window.

"That's exactly what we're doing."

"How high up is this?"

Penn strode to the window and unlatched it. "No idea."

"So helpful," I mumbled.

He turned. "You trained with Shadow for this very thing."

"Yes, trained. As in practiced. I was always safe."

Penn pushed the window open and climbed outside.

"Penn," I whisper-shouted. "Penn, get back here! We are not finished discussing—"

Before I could complete that sentence, Penn reached back inside and yanked me out. I yelped as he pulled me to a ledge. A very narrow edge.

"Don't look down," he warned.

Too late. I gulped as a briny gust of wind pushed past us, making me sway as I caught sight of the sharp rocks far below. I glared at him. "You are telling me every detail of every plan in the future so that I can tell you how stupid it is."

He flashed me a grin that was far too charming for the situation we were in. "Now where's the fun in that?"

"Fun?" I asked, flattening myself against the outer wall of the castle. "This is your idea of fun?"

He winked, which sent a thrill through me, then turned and made his way across the ledge and toward the window next to the room we'd just been in.

Bright purple wisteria slithered from his fingers, along the ledge and toward the window. I glanced at Penn, a question in my gaze, then back at his magic as it twisted up and clicked open the window.

I held my breath, sure they'd notice the now-open window. But it had been so quiet, so imperceptible, the window only open an inch, if even that.

The wisteria shrank back and disappeared.

Penn motioned for me to follow. I took a deep breath, said a short prayer to Spirit Earth that I didn't die on this stupid mission, and then inched my way over the ledge, doing my best to not look down to the rocky cliff below.

Penn crouched outside the window, and I crouched next to him, hearing voices float out into the night air.

"Oh, spirits below. I'm so sorry." It was Gabrielle. She should have been sleeping right now, not visiting her mother in the middle of the night.

"She was here last night too," Penn whispered. "I have a hunch she comes every night."

Why on the good green earth would she visit her mother every night?

As if he could read my mind, Penn whispered, "Rumor has it the queen suffers from terrible night terrors, and her daughter is the only one who can soothe them away."

"This is all my fault." Gabrielle's voice wavered. "It's my fault they're all gone."

Penn and I looked at each other, both of us trying to decipher what that meant.

"It's my fault you're like this, that you've been so completely debilitated." Gabrielle broke into sobs. "I wasn't supposed to inherit the crown like this, Mother. And now we have visitors, and they're not stupid. They're going to figure it out."

Gabrielle was speaking in riddles, all of her statements vague and not connecting to anything I understood. Clearly, whatever she was referencing was why they'd closed down their border. She was only speaking to her mother, which meant the king had . . . what? Died? Disappeared? Something had happened to him for Gabrielle to assume the crown, and that meant she was no longer a princess. She was queen of Apolis. I'd always thought Gabrielle would make an amazing queen. She was fierce, confident, loyal, and she'd do anything for those she loved. I admired that about her.

But right now, she sounded so broken and lost and . . . alone. I knew what that felt like. So did Penn.

Gabrielle started singing, then, a soft melody.

Penn looked at me and gestured for me to go back to the room we'd been in. I nodded and once again flattened myself to the wall, creeping across the ledge and back to the room. Once I was inside, I could breathe again.

Penn hopped in behind me and quietly latched the window.

I turned. "Time for me to assign a mission."

Penn just leaned against the wall, waiting for me to continue.

"I'm going to take the princess—queen—out for a walk tomorrow and get information from her. Use my friendship to get her to divulge what's happening in Apolis. The more I get her to trust me, the more she'll open up, and maybe we can even get her to tell us the location of this weapon we need to destroy the mirror."

I swallowed, guilt rising up in my throat like bile. It felt wrong. I didn't want to use Gabrielle's pain against her, use it to steal from her.

Penn clapped, slowly approaching me. "I'm impressed, and I like that plan."

Just then, the door burst open, and without any hesitation, Penn dipped his head down and pressed his lips to mine.

Heat exploded in my stomach. I curled my fingers into the hair on the nape of his neck as he tightened his hold on me. I let out a soft moan, his lips coaxing mine open.

"What is going on here?"

We jumped apart. For a split second, I'd forgotten there'd even been someone standing there.

A guilty look crossed Penn's face, so unfamiliar, and I realized what he was doing. He scratched the back of his head. "Well, this is embarrassing."

Unlike the king of thieves, I didn't have to act embarrassed. I touched my lips, still dazed over that kiss. It had been so short, too short, but it still blazed through every inch of my body. My heart thundered as Leoni glared at us.

"What are you two doing in this part of the castle?"

Penn cleared his throat and stepped next to me, roping his arm behind my back. "We like to keep things fresh, if you know what I mean."

Leoni crossed her arms. "I'm afraid I don't."

Oh, blood and earth.

"Lilypad," Penn said, "maybe you could explain, woman to woman."

I was going to murder him. "Um, well, just, our bedroom gets a little boring sometimes." I could not believe these words were coming out of my mouth. "So we like to explore, and—"

Leoni held up her hand. "Oh, stop talking. I don't want to know anymore. This is already far too much information." She gestured out to the hallway. "I'm escorting you back to your room, where you are expected to stay. No more nightly walks through the castle."

I followed Penn out of the room, and Leoni walked us back to our chamber, slamming the door behind us and letting us know we'd have a guard posted outside from here on out.

Once the door closed, Penn burst out laughing, shoulders shaking. I glared at him but couldn't help the laughter that bubbled out of me.

"You should've seen the look on your face," he said.

"Well, I wasn't expecting you to kiss me!"

"It was the only thing I could think of in that moment. The only explanation for why we'd be wandering the castle in the middle of the night."

"I sleepwalk." I ticked off my fingers. "We got lost looking for the kitchens. You're very bad with directions."

He stepped closer, his voice lowering. "I liked my idea far better than any of those." His eyes dipped to my lips, and warmth pooled between my legs. I clenched my thighs together.

It's just a game.

It's just a game.

It's just a game.

I stepped back, cool air rushing between us. "We better get some sleep. Big day tomorrow with Princess Gabrielle."

Penn nodded and watched me as I nestled under my blanket, eyes wide open as I faced the window. The mattress dipped as he lay down next to me, and soon I heard his breathing grow heavy.

I lay awake for a long time, tossing and turning, replaying that kiss over and over. His lips prying mine open. His kiss so firm and probing, like he couldn't get enough of me, like he'd wanted more as much as I did. When I finally did fall into a fitful sleep, my dreams were taken over by the king of thieves and all the ways he could break my heart if I wasn't careful.

Chapter Forty-One

The next day, bleary-eyed and exhausted, I met Gabrielle by the shore. Her sapphire blue chiffon whipped in the wind, her auburn hair pulled back in a simple ponytail. Clouds gathered in the sky above, the day dreary and dull. Waves crashed and washed up over our feet as we walked.

"So." Gabrielle nudged me. "I heard from a certain guard that you and your betrothed had quite an interesting night."

I flushed. "Oh, Gabrielle, I'm so sorry." I turned to her to see her shoulders shaking, laughter spilling from her.

"Don't apologize." She winked. "I'm glad someone is having fun."

I smiled, realizing this was my opening. "Do you not have any suitors of your own?"

She snorted. "No. It's hard to have suitors when no one is allowed in or out of my court."

"Right."

The cool sand felt good against my bare feet, so different from the hot, gritty sand in Gilraeth. This was softer, squishier, and it was nice to walk with no shoes. I'd often loved walking through the fields near our home with bare feet, able to just feel the earth, connect with it.

She didn't supply any more information, both of us falling into silence. I had to get her to open up, but I didn't think I'd be able to do that without sharing some of my own secrets.

"I understand, you know. Penn and I, we didn't fall in love instantly. He rescued me, hoping that by doing so, I'd be able to take back my crown and save the earth court, but my first request after he got me out of that prison cell was to go find Jasper."

Gabrielle looked at me with wide eyes. "Really?"

I nodded. "I thought Jasper and I were still betrothed. I thought Jasper was going to rescue me and he just hadn't figured out how."

"Oh, Liliath." Gabrielle placed her hand on my shoulder.

A seagull flew in front of us, dipping down over the water and catching a fish in its mouth. The fish flopped wildly as the seagull flew away with it.

"What happened with Jasper?" she asked.

"Well, we got to the fire court, he had Penn imprisoned, and then he revealed that he had no intention of coming to save me."

It felt good to talk about this, even if I was leaving out a few key details. It was nice to share my pain with a friend, to let out all these feelings of anger.

Gabrielle stayed silent, so I continued, "He betrayed me. He didn't even care about me anymore." I hadn't realized how much it actually hurt until now, when I was speaking to Gabrielle about it. "I was just a tool for him to use. Our betrothal had been all about him becoming king. That's what he wanted. A crown. He never wanted me. And I'd been so blind. I knew our arrangement would benefit both our courts, make a strong alliance between the earth court and the fire court, but I thought we'd bonded over the years, had come to care for each other." I snorted. "I thought I loved him. But I never had."

"So how did you realize you loved Penn instead?" Gabrielle asked.

The question sent a shock through me. I swallowed, tripping over my words. "W-when Jasper had him imprisoned. I saw it all happen from my window. I was terrified watching Penn get taken away, knowing he was going to be thrown in the sand pits. I realized I couldn't imagine a life without him."

A little crab skittered in front of us, dragging a trail behind it in the sand before digging down and burrowing away, exactly how I wanted to burrow away from the feelings surfacing in me right now. *No*, I reminded myself. This betrothal, this story, it wasn't real.

"You lost love to find something new, something better. Plus, Penn has some very nice . . . assets," she said, which made me burst out laughing. "I hope you enjoyed those nightgowns I sent over."

I swore my face was on fire.

"Oh," Gabrielle said, "with that reaction, I'm guessing Penn enjoyed them much more than you."

"Enough about me." I gave her a light shove. "Now we just need to find you someone."

The smile disappeared from her face, and I worried I'd said the wrong thing. "No, I'm done with love." Bitterness filled her voice.

Yes, I'd definitely said the wrong thing. "Do you want to . . . talk about it?"

She was silent for moment, and I thought she was going to shut me out, that I'd somehow botched this mission already.

"Yes, please." Her voice was quiet, vulnerable, not at all like the fierce Gabrielle I was so used to.

"What happened?"

Gabrielle gestured to some rocks behind us and we sat. The clouds grew darker overhead, but I wasn't ready to go back to the castle, not when Gabrielle was just about to open up.

"Have you heard of the pirate lord of the Dark Seas?" she asked.

My brows crinkled. "Yes, he steals magical items from the shadow court and sells them on the black market." I paused, thinking about what Penn had told me. "He sold a powerful mirror to my stepmother. It's how she planned her entire coup that killed my father and imprisoned me."

Gabrielle's eyes hardened, and I leaned forward, gathering her hands in mine and squeezing them.

"What happened with the pirate lord?"

"I fell in love with him," she said simply, and I couldn't help the gasp that escaped my mouth, even though it shouldn't have been all that shocking. Gabrielle had always been the wildest of the princesses on Arathia. Fierce, adventurous, carefree. Since I'd gotten here, she'd been a shadow of her former self. Maybe what happened with this pirate lord was why.

"It was so stupid, Liliath." She shook her head. "It was a year ago. My brothers were off on yet another adventure at sea while I was stuck here, learning how to be queen of a court that I didn't even want to rule. I'd begged my parents to let one of my brothers rule, and of course, they told me I was the heir, the oldest, and that it was my duty to my people."

I kept a tight hold on her hands as she continued.

"I never wanted to be chained to a crown, and I grew resentful. One day, I was out walking along the shore in a secluded part of our court, on the northern side. No one ventures out there because it's where the sea is at its wildest. Even with our water magic, many don't want to risk getting swept away by the volatile waves. But I love it there, where everything is untethered and free."

She looked up at the sky, still dark, but no rain fell yet. I hoped it would stay that way, give us more time to talk. We were getting somewhere, but I hadn't gotten all the information I needed from her yet.

"I saw a ship docking near the rocky cliffs," Gabrielle said. "A dangerous place to dock any ship, and I realized what I was seeing. The infamous pirate lord. Here in Apolis. I should've reported him. Told my guards immediately and had him arrested. Instead, I let him charm me. I visited him in secret every time he came. I opened myself up to him, told him about my dreams and my hopes. I believed him when he told me I could have the future I wanted. And then he betrayed me. He's the reason my brothers are gone, my father is gone."

I stilled, heart beating so hard I could hear it in my ears. "What do you mean?"

"They took their shadows, Liliath. Because of him. He helped them. He's in league with them."

"Who?" But I knew. The only people with the ability to steal shadows.

"Sorrengard," Gabrielle said. "There's some mysterious king that's risen up on the island, and he took my brothers' shadows. Now he has them, on the island. He's taken all the boys' shadows. The pirate lord helped them come and steal our boys away. All in one night. Vanished."

My eyes widened. That's why I'd mostly only seen woman and girls. Why Gabrielle's guards were all female. I wondered why he took only the boys, but now didn't seem like the right time to ask.

"I'm so, so sorry," I said, not knowing what else I could say.

Then I realized she'd said boys. They took the boys' shadows. "What happened to your father? To all the men?"

"My father organized many of the men to go with him to Sorrengard and get back our boys. We haven't seen him since. That was three months ago."

Horror washed over me. "Have you seen the pirate lord since?"

Gabrielle looked out over the sea, like his ship might appear at any moment. "I told him if I ever saw him again I'd kill him. He hasn't been back since. It's another one of my failures. I should've driven a sword through him, but I couldn't, not when I loved him. I did, at least, manage to steal something from him. A weapon that was important to him, a powerful weapon."

I sucked in a breath at the mention of it. That had to be the weapon Penn was after. The one that could destroy my stepmother's mirror.

"I also destroyed his ship, let it crash right into the jagged rocks of the northern cliffs. His pride and joy. It's still there today. He had to flee Apolis on a rowboat. I thought destroying something he loved would make me feel better, but somehow, I just felt worse afterward." She shrugged. "I was an idiot. I was weak."

"No." My voice was firm and hard. "None of this is your fault."

She turned her brown eyes on me. "It is my fault. I didn't see the warning signs. I told him too much, gave him more information than I should have. All because he was vulnerable with me. Told me a stupid secret about his fear of the water. What kind of pirate lord is afraid of the ocean?" She shook her head. "I thought he loved me. I was . . . I was planning on running away with him."

"Oh, Gabrielle," I said.

"My mother has been so heartbroken over losing her sons and her husband that she hasn't been able to leave her chambers. My people are scared and confused. They want their boys back, their husbands back. And I can't do anything about it." Her voice shook.

That didn't sound like the Gabrielle I knew, the woman who never backed down to an injustice. She sounded so broken.

"Do you know what Sorrengard wants? Why they're doing this?"

She shook her head. "I have no idea. We're closest to them, of all the courts, and they have the easiest access to us, but . . . I don't know how or why they're choosing to attack now after all these years. We all assumed we'd defeated them so badly after they wiped out Shiraeth that they couldn't recover. But somehow they've risen, and we should all be afraid."

"They've been wreaking havoc in the fire court as well," I said. "They planted a sorceress who's cursed Princess Seraphina and taken over. And they have a hand in what happened in Elwen. The magic my stepmother used to usurp my father came from the shadow court." My stomach clenched. "None of this can be a coincidence. They're planning something. Something big."

Gabrielle's eyes widened. "And now they have an army of boys at their command. Strong boys who are young and can fight."

And with the boys' shadows in their possession, they had full control over them. Could use them in any way they wanted. The thought was terrifying.

A wave crashed against the shore, washing up and taking all the seaweed and algae with it. I stared at it until the water receded. "We have to reach out to Valoris and Fyriad." The sky and frost courts. "Find out if Sorrengard has struck against them in any way."

Gabrielle let out a shaky breath. "Thank you for listening to me, for not judging me. I closed down our borders because I was afraid of showing any weakness, afraid the other courts might turn on us if they found out what happened. I don't know if I'm ready to tell them the truth yet."

I nodded. "I understand. I promise you I won't reveal your secret to anyone, not until you're ready. But we do have to face this, Gabrielle. Sorrengard is planning something, and we have to be ready. After I've taken back the earth court and restored some order, I promise I'll do anything I can to help you find your brothers and your father."

She shook her head sadly. "It's hopeless. All I can do is move forward at this point."

I sputtered. "You're just giving up?"

That didn't sound anything like the Gabrielle I knew.

Rain started to patter down around us.

"I'm doing what a good queen does," she snapped. "I'm protecting the people I have left. I can't send out more victims to Sorrengard so they can disappear and never be seen again." She massaged her temples. "I'm sorry. I need to get back and check on my mother."

"Of course," I said.

She stood as rain drizzled around us. "Are you coming?"

My gaze strayed out to the distance, where I saw a figure swimming in the ocean. A muscled figure with blond hair that, at this point, I'd recognize anywhere.

"I'll be back shortly. I just need some time to think."

Gabrielle bit her lip as if trying to decide if it was a good idea to leave me here. Then she nodded. "Okay. I'll see you later for dinner."

I waited until she disappeared into the fog rolling in from the coastline, then turned and walked toward Penn.

Chapter Forty-Two

I stopped at the edge of an outcropping of rocks, looking down into the swell of waves as Penn moved his body. His back muscles rippled with each stroke, and he kept his head down, periodically raising it to get a breath of air. I stood mesmerized, unable to take my eyes from his magnificent form. The clouds darkened above, and rain pounded down harder, the rocks slick under my feet.

Penn lifted his head and his gaze caught on me. He swam closer until he faced me, droplets of water trailing down his face, hair slicked back.

"There you go, staring again," he said.

He wasn't wrong, but I was not about to admit that to him. "I just thought you'd like an update on my conversation with Gabrielle."

"How about a swim first?"

I raised my eyebrows. "A swim in this weather?"

He lifted a shoulder. "We're already wet. Afraid of a little more water?"

I narrowed my eyes at his stupid taunt, knowing it was working. "Not at all."

In one fluid motion, I dove in next to him, not even caring that I was fully clothed. The cool water enveloped me. I emerged and splashed Penn in the face.

He nodded his head. "C'mon. There's something I want to show you."

He turned in the water and swam, and I followed him, loving the feel of the sea water gliding against my skin. I used to swim in the ocean with my father. We'd travel hours to the Elwen coast. The water was cooler, the temperatures that far south not ideal for swimming, but I never cared. Whenever we visited the coast, I'd beg my father for a chance to swim.

Eventually we came upon a little cove, smooth rocks spread out around it. The water became shallower as we got closer, and I no longer had to swim. I stood and splashed through the ocean until my feet hit the rocks. My chiffon stuck to my skin, sticky and thoroughly soaked. I took a step forward and slipped, falling backward and right against Penn's very hard, very bare, chest. My fingers curled into his skin, and for a moment, I just stared at the soft blond curls on his chest, the ridges and defined muscles of his abdomen, that stark V that dipped down below his trousers. The contact left me breathless until I realized what I was doing and quickly jumped away.

Penn's gaze bore into me.

"Thank you," I said, looking to the sea and cursing myself for once again acting like a lovesick fool around him.

We walked into the cove, and my breath caught in my throat at the sight. Crystals shined on the walls, glowing purple, blue, yellow, and pink.

"It's beautiful." I stood in the middle, taking it all in.

Rain pounded down outside, the crash of waves accompanying the sound. But in here it felt safe, cozy, and beautiful.

I sat on the sand before laying down and looking up. Penn lay next to me, resting his hands on his stomach.

"I didn't know you liked to swim," I said.

"My parents used to take me to the southern coast in Elwen, and we'd swim together in the ocean."

I let out a soft laugh. I never thought I'd have anything in common with the king of thieves.

"I haven't been able to swim in the ocean for a long, long time. So I decided since you were busy with Gabrielle, I'd do something I enjoyed."

I turned my head. "The king of thieves? Doing something for fun? Surely I couldn't have heard that right."

"Well, someone told me I'm too obsessed with work."

"She sounds wise," I said.

"She's a smart-ass," he replied. "But she might also have been right."

"I'm going to need you to say that more often."

He brought his hands up behind his head. "The smart-ass part?"

I shoved him, and he laughed.

"I discovered this place and thought you might like it," he said. "You told me you and your father loved to explore new places together, discover the beauty in nature."

I had told him that. I was surprised he remembered. And . . . touched. "I love it," I said softly. "And I think he would've loved it too."

Penn sat up, leaning back on his hands in a way that showed the bulge of his muscles. I sat up and crossed my legs in front of me.

"So what did you find out from Gabrielle?"

I told him everything she'd said about Sorrengard, the missing boys, the king and his mission, the pirate lord, and his weapon. Gabrielle had trusted me with so much information, and relaying it all to Penn felt like a betrayal.

When I finished, he stroked his jaw.

"Sorrengard is up to something." He shook his head. "But we can't focus on them."

I couldn't believe what I was hearing. "How could we not? We need to organize a summit with all the leaders on the continent. When Gabrielle is ready, of course."

"Gabrielle is focusing on her court, her people. We need to be doing the same."

I leaned forward. "This is bigger than all of us."

Penn's jaw locked. "What do you think will happen if you take back the earth court? That will hurt Sorrengard's plan, whatever it is. It'll disrupt their attempt to sow the seeds of discord before they strike."

It made sense, but I still didn't like it.

"We need to focus on getting that weapon and getting the fiery hells out of here," Penn said.

I hesitated. "I've been thinking . . . maybe I could just talk to Gabrielle about it. Tell her why we need the weapon."

"No." Penn shook his head. "That's too risky. If she says no, then what? Our chance at stealing it will be blown, and she'll likely ask us to leave once you reveal why we're here."

I bit my lip. "But she revealed so much today, was so open with me. I think she'd be reasonable about this."

"Lilypad," Penn said. "I know you don't want to steal from your friend. But leaders have to make hard choices sometimes. This is one of those choices."

Penn was right. Though I still couldn't shake that niggling feeling that I could find another solution, one that didn't compromise the kind of queen I wanted to be.

Penn's finger hooked under my chin. "What's wrong?"

Thunder rumbled through the sky above, and I drew my knees to my chest.

"The more I try to save my court, the more I feel like I'm not worthy of it. I'm a criminal. A thief. The type of person who betrays a friend. What kind of leader will that make me? How will I enforce the laws of Elwen when I, myself, haven't even followed them?"

Penn opened his mouth to speak, but I cut him off. "I know. I know what you're going to say. That I'm a leader, not a follower. That you know I'll make a good queen. I just wish I could believe it as fiercely as you seem to."

The thought of stealing from Gabrielle made my stomach tighten into knots. She'd welcomed us into her home, told me painful secrets, and I was going to turn around and take something valuable from her.

"Then I won't tell you you'll make a good queen." Penn's finger dropped from my chin. "I'll just tell you that you are fierce. You are brave. You are wise. You are loyal. You will do anything for your people, even if it's meant becoming the very person you abhor. I'd follow that kind of leader into the depths of the Spirit World."

We locked eyes, and I could've sworn something like need flashed in his. Lightning struck, lighting up the cave, and I looked away, once again reminding myself that I was just a tool to him, nothing more. "We should get back," I said. "Gabrielle's going to be wondering where I am, and we don't need to raise any suspicions right now."

I stood, clothes still sticking to me, hair plastered to my head.

"Lilypad, wait."

I turned to see Penn still sitting on the ground, brows furrowed and fists curled.

"Yes?" I asked.

He shook his head. "I'm going to stay here awhile. Be careful walking back in the rain."

"Sure," I said and turned, walking out of the cave and wondering what in the hell that was all about.

Chapter Forty-Three

Gabrielle and I walked through a bustling market that lined the cobblestone streets of the water court. Penn stayed behind at the castle, hoping to do some reconnaissance since the queen's guards would be out on our walk with us. We'd stayed up late into the night, looking at the map Penn had sketched of the castle and brainstorming a list of places the weapon could be. Penn was going to try and sneak into as many of those places as possible while I kept Gabrielle occupied. I was supposed to get more information out of her, but I just wanted to enjoy the beautiful day. Penn would not be pleased if I returned with nothing, though. I could tell he was eager to return to Mosswood Forest, and I was just as eager to get back to Elwen and face my stepmother.

Little wooden stands lined the street, which overlooked the shimmering ocean. Clouds gone, the sun once again shined bright today. I noticed the majority of stands were run by women, with the odd man here or there.

Gabrielle's inner circle flanked us, Leoni close behind.

As if she could read my mind, Gabrielle said, "Many of the women have taken over running businesses, caring for their daughters, and grieving the loss of their sons and husbands. It's been so hard."

I gave her arm a squeeze as we stopped at a stand with fresh fish and eel splayed out across the counter.

Gabrielle held her hand out, and Leoni placed a few gold coins in her palm. She smiled at the woman behind the counter, whose eyes had purple smudges underneath, her hair unkempt in its bun like she didn't have it in her to run a brush through it. I understood. Grief could be debilitating.

"Hi, Mara." Gabrielle dropped coins into the woman's palms.

She smiled and curtsied, thanking Her Grace.

We kept on walking. I looked back, confused. "But you didn't buy anything."

"I try to support different businesses every day. It's not much, but it's all I can do. We just need to keep surviving."

We continued walking, stopping at various stands: one that sold flowers, one with dried seaweed and kelp, one with herbal tonics, one with oysters and clams. Everyone smiled politely, but there was no warmth behind their eyes, no life.

"I should've said something," Gabrielle said as we munched on spicy fish pies that were as small as the palm of my hand.

I wrinkled my nose. "About what?"

She'd stopped walking and was staring off into the distance, watching the rolling waves. "To my father, about his plan. I should've told him it was a bad one. I should've been brave enough to speak up." She huffed. "I didn't ever want to be queen, to rule this place, but I still knew attacking Sorrengard head-on was a bad idea, and I said nothing. Just stood by and watched him sail to his death."

"You don't know that he's dead," I said quickly. "Don't give up, Gabrielle."

She tore her gaze away from the ocean and back toward me. "What else am I supposed to do?"

I finished my last bite of fish pie, brushing the crumbs from my chiffon.

"I know what it's like to feel guilt over your actions." I frisked my arms despite the warm sea air brushing down the street.

We continued our stroll, everyone bowing at Gabrielle as we passed their little stands.

"My stepmother," I said. "It's my fault she killed my father, my fault she imprisoned me. Everything that's happened to the earth court is my fault."

"That can't be true." Gabrielle shook her head slowly. "Your stepmother conspired with the pirate lord, just like you said. She chose to use dark magic."

"Because of me," I said. "She hated me because of my actions." I took a steadying breath. "When my father first married her, I instantly disliked her. I never had a lot of time with my father since he was always busy doing his duty as king. She was a threat to the little time I did have. I believed she only wanted to be queen, didn't love my father, was using him so she could rule Elwen. I had no basis for these accusations. She wasn't my mother, though. That was the true crime she'd committed."

Gabrielle listened as we walked, head down, hands twined behind her back.

"I watched her constantly, always looking for evidence she was guilty of something, anything, that would force my father to banish her, strip her of her crown. My friends warned me I was going too far, that I needed to just accept her as my father had. But I refused. I was so stupid, Gabrielle. I was fifteen years old at the time, but I was old enough to know better, to know that what I was doing was wrong."

Jillian and Driscoll had begged me to stop following her everywhere. They'd even threatened to tell my father if I wouldn't let it go, but I'd refused, and it had cost me everything in the end.

"I lied to my friends, told them I'd stop, but I just became better at hiding my obsession with her. One day, I followed her to the border between Mosswood Forest and Elwen, and I couldn't believe what I saw. She was meeting someone, someone from Mosswood Forest."

Gabrielle sucked in a sharp breath. Everyone on the continent knew of the war between Elwen and Mosswood Forest, that there was no communication between the two realms.

"I hid behind a tree and watched her use magic to help someone over to the other side. They developed a whole system for it, one that must've taken a long time. They embraced, crying and laughing, chatting. All I saw was betrayal. I immediately ran to my father, telling him of what my stepmother had done. I thought that would be it. He'd banish her and she'd be out of our lives forever. I didn't know the consequences would be so much worse." I swallowed. "A few days later, I awoke to screams in the courtyard, Elwenians gathered as the guards brought out someone to hang. It was the woman my stepmother had let through the border. Her friend, as it turned out. They'd been best friends, separated by the war, but they'd been meeting in secret, my stepmother letting her through the border." Tears slipped down my cheeks. "I caused that innocent woman's death. I'd been so sure my stepmother was conspiring with the people of Mosswood Forest, spying for them, and that I'd found proof."

Gabrielle put a hand on my shoulder.

"That's why she imprisoned me, you know," I said. "She told me that I ruined her life. That she could have been happy with my father if I hadn't constantly pitted him against her. She said I made her into the villain she was, and that she would spend the rest of her life making me as miserable as I'd made her."

I was so ashamed of my actions, I hadn't told anyone that, not even Jillian and Driscoll. Truthfully, I was worried they wouldn't forgive me or that they'd look at me differently.

I didn't realize I'd stopped walking, that my shoulders were shaking, tears now flowing freely, until I felt Gabrielle's arms come around me.

"It's my fault," I said between sobs.

Women and their daughters passed us, shooting glances my way.

"I'm sorry. This is completely inappropriate." I wiped at the tears, sniffling.

Gabrielle pushed me to arm's length, her hands still on my shoulders. "So it seems we both carry guilt for things that aren't our fault."

"How can you say that?" I asked. "Did you just hear anything I said?"

Gabrielle gave me a soft smile. "What I heard was a story about a girl who missed her mother and was afraid she was being replaced. You acted like a bratty fifteen-year-old, and yes, your actions were wrong. But your stepmother cannot blame you for her choices. Those were all her own."

I wasn't sure I believed Gabrielle, but nonetheless, her words made me feel better, lightened a burden I hadn't known I was carrying.

"What are those?" I pointed to blue ribbons tied around wooden posts. Now that I'd noticed them, I realized the blue ribbons were everywhere.

"It's an homage to the water spirit. Normally, at this time of year, we'd be preparing for a grand ball at the castle, with everyone in Apolis invited. It was our most treasured tradition here."

My eyes widened. "Today? The ball is supposed to be today?"

Gabrielle nodded. "Another thing we've lost."

I stared at the ribbons. "No."

Gabrielle flipped her auburn braid over her shoulder. "No what?"

"No, you haven't lost your traditions. You haven't lost your ability to celebrate the water spirit."

"What are you saying? That we should throw a ball with half our citizens missing?"

"That's exactly what I'm saying."

The guards shot looks at each other, Leoni scowling, which I was starting to think was the only expression she knew how to make.

Gabrielle looked at me like I was crazy. "We can't throw a ball."

"Why not?" I threw out my arms. "Your people need hope, Gabrielle. But more than that, they need something to celebrate. Just because you're grieving doesn't mean you can't find moments of happiness. I think now more than ever you need a reason to look for the joy in life." I grabbed her hands. "What better way to find that joy than with dancing and music and food?"

A slow smile came to Gabrielle's face. "A ball."

"You can't be serious," Leoni said, but the other guards were smiling too.

Gabrielle gave a nod. "Spread the word. I want everyone in attendance tonight, wearing their finest dresses and tunics. Apolis is going to celebrate."

Leoni snorted. "A ball? We're just going to ignore what's happening and . . . dance?"

Gabrielle looked at me. "We're going to find the joy."

Chapter Forty-Four

Gabrielle insisted that we get ready together. We spent all afternoon trying on dresses, her tailors coming to cinch our waists, to ensure that the dresses fit perfectly. We got our hair and makeup done, and I had to admit, I loved it. I loved feeling like a princess again after so long feeling like anything but.

I couldn't help my envy over Gabrielle's long waves that hung down past her shoulders, her red strands shining and voluminous. With my shoulder-length black hair, I had little to work with, but the lady's maid curled my strands into soft waves and tied green ribbons in that matched my green dress Gabrielle loaned me.

When I stood in front of the mirror staring at myself, I realized I liked what I saw. No, I no longer had my beautiful long hair, but I could get used to this new look.

The sleeves of my dress hung off my shoulders, exposing my collarbone. The bodice clung tight to my mid-section, and the skirt hung loose down to my golden-slippered feet. It was gorgeous. Fit for a princess. A queen.

"Are you ready?" I turned to see Gabrielle, stunning in a form-fitting golden dress that clung to every inch of her curvy body.

She lifted up the skirt to reveal daggers strapped to her calves. She was always ready for a fight.

I just laughed and shook my head at the gleaming weapons as she dropped the skirt of her dress. It trailed behind her on the floor like a shimmering pool of molten lava.

"I'm ready." We linked arms and left her chambers, walking through the hallways and down the grand spiral staircase until we came to the double doors that led to her throne room.

Two servants stood on either side of the doors and threw them open.

I gasped at the room, which had been completely transformed from the last time I'd seen it.

Long tables stretched between the columns, filled with roasted fish, oysters, mussels, salmon, crab, and lobster. Bread, cheese wedges, pastries, cakes. My mouth watered at the sight.

Blue streamers wrapped around the columns, twinkling in the light.

A huge waterfall fell from the ceiling, right in the middle of the room. I studied it as people walked through, not getting wet. It was some kind of illusion, the water shimmering, almost translucent.

"How did you put this together so fast?" I asked, taking it all in.

"We do this every year. Not to say it was easy, but I think everyone was excited to do this. To have this distraction . . ."

Her words trailed off as she stared at something, and my gaze followed hers. I let out a soft gasp. There stood her mother, surrounded by people, talking, laughing, wearing a gorgeous blue gown, her gray hair piled on top of her head.

Gabrielle's mouth hung open. "I told her about it, but I never expected she'd come. She hasn't been out of her chambers in months."

I placed a hand on her shoulder. "Go to her. Find the joy."

Gabrielle lifted her skirts and strode toward her mother, the two of them embracing.

I walked over to one of the tables and grabbed a goblet of wine, sipping and observing. In the corner of the room a band played music, and people started dancing, laughing, conversation bubbling over. At least I'd been right about one thing: Apolis had needed this. I was glad I could contribute something.

My gaze strayed back to Gabrielle, now surrounded by a group of people who chattered away. It all felt so informal, so personal.

I doubted my father knew the names of any of the townspeople in

Elwen. The earth court might have been much, much bigger, but I wanted this kind of relationship with my subjects. My father told me it was important for leaders to separate themselves from their people, that getting too close made it harder to remain objective when faced with hard decisions. But Gabrielle was close with her people, and she'd still made hard decisions. And it was clear everyone still loved her, smiling at her, ooh-ing and ahh-ing over her dress. They respected her. Her relationship with her subjects wasn't a liability. It was a strength.

I took another sip of my drink and turned to find Penn staring at me from across the room. His hair hung above his shoulders, golden and gleaming. He was freshly shaven, showing off that strong jaw. He wore a white chiffon with gold trimmings and an emerald green sash that was draped over his shoulder and came down across his body. He looked . . . magnificent. Like a king.

He strode toward where I stood, never taking his eyes off of me until he was right in front of me, and his gaze dripped down over my body, slow and languid.

"You look . . ." he started, at a loss for words possibly for the first time in his life, or at least since I'd met him. "You look stunning."

I set down my goblet and gave him my own assessing gaze. We were supposed to be betrothed, so we needed to act like it, and like I'd told Gabrielle, tonight was about finding joy. I couldn't think of any better way to do that than dance with Penn.

Like he'd read my thoughts, he placed his hand in the small of my back and led me to the dance floor.

The music, the people, the weapon, everything faded away as I pressed myself against Penn's body and felt every inch of him against every inch of me. My hands rested around his neck, while his gathered around my back.

"Careful, Lilypad. Looking like this people might start to mistake you for a queen."

We whirled around, never taking our eyes off each other.

"I can't be a queen without a court, without people willing to bow down to me."

"There's not a single person in the earth court who wouldn't kneel in front of you and vow their allegiance."

I tilted my head further up. "And would you be one of them?"

His voice dropped low. "There are many reasons I'd get on my knees for you. And I'd enjoy every one of them."

My breath caught in my chest, and Penn dipped me low, then lifted me back up, but the heat spreading through me was quickly doused by that little voice questioning if this was once again just for show.

"You're looking a little flushed," he noted, grinning.

"Well, with all the dancing, I think I need some air."

What I needed was space from this man before I combusted. The song ended, everyone bursting into applause. Penn bowed, and I curtsied, then spun on my heel without another word and marched toward the balcony.

I PRESSED myself against the white banister, looking up at the star-strewn sky above and taking deep breaths of the cool night air.

"Lilypad," Penn said from behind me.

I turned to see him click the door closed, cutting us off from everyone else. Just me and him. Alone.

"Why did you run from me?" He prowled toward me like a predator about to catch its prey.

"It was hot, like I said." I backed further into the banister as Penn approached, inches from me.

He looked down, studying me. "I meant what I said inside." His eyes blazed. "I'd get on my knees, and I'd show you just how much I want to worship you."

I couldn't breathe, couldn't think. My body thrummed with those words, with the images those words conjured. Before I knew it, I was reaching for him, pulling him toward me, and his lips crashed against mine, my body slamming into his.

His hands wove around my back, roaming up and down as if he wanted to touch all of me and couldn't decide where to start. I ran my fingers through his soft hair, relishing in the earthy scent of him, the feel of him all over me.

Blood and earth. This was my joy. This was it. Penn Vanderbilt. The king of thieves.

He probed my mouth open further, his tongue slipping inside. Our teeth scraped together, but our mouths never stopped touching, tasting, teasing. We kissed and kissed, and I didn't know that I'd ever be able to stop.

"It's a good show we're putting on," he murmured against my mouth.

I stiffened in his arms. The words jolted me back to reality.

Penn slowly straightened, confusion flashing across his face.

That was why I couldn't do this. I'd reminded myself again and again that this was a game to him. Always a game. And soon, I was going to lose.

"Lilypad," he started, but I held up my hand.

"I'm going to retire to my rooms now that we've given a sufficient *show* for the people of the water court. I've played my part, and based on your reaction, I think I played it rather well."

A muscle feathered in Penn's jaw, and he looked away, planting his hands on his hips.

"Good night, Penn." I pushed past him and didn't look back.

Chapter Forty-Five

I woke up to see Penn already dressed, ready for the day. He looked like he'd slept just fine, while I'd tossed and turned all night, dreaming of his lips turning into razor-sharp thorns about to cut me, replaying his words in my mind over and over.

It's a good show we're putting on.

It hadn't mattered how many times I reminded myself this was all a game to him, I still let myself feel things, want things, that weren't possible. Penn clearly didn't return my feelings. We might have been treading a friendship lately, sharing more with each other, working well together, but that didn't mean any kind of romance was blooming between us, at least not on his side. I was going to get hurt.

Before he could bring up the kiss last night, the awkwardness that had followed it, I dove right into his favorite topic: work.

"Tell me what you found yesterday," I said from the bathing chamber, relief flooding me when I spotted my tunic and pants, clean and folded. Blood and earth, I'd missed these.

"A whole lot of nothing," Penn replied from our room.

He went into more detail, but the gist was clear: the weapon hadn't been anywhere.

I came out of the chamber, dressed and feeling more defeated than ever.

Penn sat on the couch and patted the spot next to him. "Tell me about your conversation with Gabrielle yesterday, and then let's go over your first conversation with her again."

I joined him and recounted both conversations down to the very last detail: everything she'd told me, everything I'd told her, including how I'd betrayed my stepmother.

Penn's eyes widened at the revelation, and he rubbed the back of his neck. "That's why you said she wouldn't invade Mosswood Forest. Because it's where her best friend was from, a friend her husband had executed."

I nodded. "She wouldn't want to see it destroyed, not like Elwen."

Penn just looked at me for a moment. "She's right, you know. Gabrielle. You can't shoulder that guilt forever. Just like she can't shoulder hers." He smirked. "I can't believe she wrecked his ship. That takes some guts to destroy the pirate lord's most prized possession."

I sat up straighter. His most prized possession.

"We have to go." I jumped up and ran across the room, not waiting for Penn or answering as he called after me. I raced past the sleeping guard sitting outside our room and out into the cool morning air. I clambered across the rocky cliff, over the glass bridge, and to the sandy shores down below. Penn swore behind me, running to catch up.

"Are you going to tell me where we're headed?" he asked as he finally jogged up beside me. "What in the bloody earth is going on?"

"There was no time," I said between heavy breaths. "We need to get there before our sleeping guard wakes up and realizes we're missing."

The poor guard outside our room was probably still sleeping off the wine she'd drunk the night before. But it wouldn't be long before she awoke, along with everyone else, and wanted to know where we'd snuck off to.

"Gabrielle mentioned the pirate lord's ship, that she'd stolen the weapon from him and then damaged it beyond repair. She said she'd wrecked the ship in the place where the pirate lord always docked. So what better place to hide the weapon than the most obvious one?"

Penn jogged to keep up with me. "You think she hid the weapon in his ship?"

"He wouldn't dare come back there, not after he betrayed her like that, betrayed her entire court. It would be far too risky."

Penn stroked his chin. I could still feel that smooth skin pressing against my own last night. "Hiding the weapon in the most obvious place, which might make it the least obvious. That's not a bad idea, Lilypad."

"I know."

We quickened our pace, the excitement growing between us. This could be it. We could have that weapon in our hands today. I could be back in Elwen, ready to face my stepmother. I glanced at Penn. Without the king of thieves.

Suddenly my excitement faded, turning to something like . . . what? Dread? Sadness? It was like I was already mourning the loss of him. Blood and earth. I needed to focus on this mission and nothing else. My people were what was most important right now.

It took another hour of walking, but soon we came upon the northern shores. Penn and I both looked at each other, then broke into a run toward the shipwreck in the distance. Waves crashed against the rocks with a promise of violence. The wind blew, letting out a harsh whistle. Gabrielle was right, it was dangerous here, and I couldn't believe this was where the pirate lord chose to dock his ship. He must've been a talented captain to be able to navigate these rough waters.

We stopped at the edge of an outcropping of sharp rocks. "How are we going to get onto that ship?" I gestured to it, parts of it decimated, the hull sticking straight up into the air, a huge crack in the middle that caused both sides to bow.

"I think using earth magic would be too unpredictable here." Penn scratched his jaw, then pointed to a rope dangling down the side, the wind whipping it wildly. Of course.

He looked at me. "How are your climbing skills?"

I heaved a huge breath, remembering the countless vines Hammer had made me climb. Over and over and over. And I'd never reached the top.

He chuckled before I even had a chance to respond. "Let's go."

He leapt from rock to rock with expert precision while I stumbled behind him, feet slipping on the slick stones, water misting my face from the crash of waves below.

Penn stopped and turned, seeing me far behind him. No annoyance flashed across his face like I expected. Instead, he jumped back, landing right in front of me, balancing on the rock. A question in his eyes, he held his hand out.

I swallowed and grabbed it, remembering that hand pushing up through my hair last night. Penn turned and slowly led me to the ship, no snarky comments about how slow we were going, no snippy remarks about how I could've trained harder to prepare for something like this. He went at my pace, and I realized I wanted to trust him. So badly. But something was holding me back.

We reached the last rock, the rope swaying a few feet in front of us.

Penn faced me, my hand still in his. "I'm going to have to jump to the rope. Once I'm up on the ship, I'll swing it back to you. Unless you want to wait here?"

"No," I said. "I'm coming."

Something like pride flashed in his eyes. "Okay, then." He dropped my hand and leapt, grasping onto the rope with his strong hands. He pulled himself up, and now I realized how he must've scaled my castle walls so quickly. He did this sort of thing all the time, like it was no effort, even with the wind beating at him, the waves threatening to swallow him whole.

He climbed over the edge of the ship, the railing gone, blasted away by the ocean.

"Okay, Lilypad." He lifted the rope. "I'm going to throw this to you. You'll need to catch it and swing to me."

I swallowed a few times, then nodded.

He swung the rope to me, and the wind blew it sideways. I reached for it, but it was just out of my grasp. Then another blast of wind hit, pushing me backward. The rope swung by my head, and I took the opportunity to snatch it.

"There you go," Penn said. "Now you're going to push off the rock using as much force as you can to swing to me, okay?"

I really didn't want to do this, but no way in hell was I going to miss finding that weapon.

"You can do this," Penn said, and he meant it. He really believed in me.

My heart thudded as I basked in his praise, then remembered it was all fake.

I gripped the rope tight and used my feet to push myself from the rock. I instantly regretted my decision. The strong winds whipped me this way and that, in every direction except the one I wanted to go. Penn reached his hands out, trying to grab the rope, but he was too far away. I was going to drop straight into the sea—and straight to my death.

I held onto that rope, remembering Hammer's words.

Keep yer core tight and lock those hands together.

At this point, there was nothing I could do but hold on. I heard Penn shouting over the roar of the ocean but couldn't hear the words coming from his mouth.

I gritted my teeth as the rope swung me back toward the rock, sticking out my feet and pushing with all my might in the opposite direction. It didn't do much, but it was enough. My body flew toward the ship, close enough that Penn could grab it and pull it toward him. I fell into his arms, and he cradled me to his chest, both of us breathing heavily.

"Are you alright?" he whispered into my hair.

"Yes." I pushed myself out of his arms. "Now let's find that weapon."

Hours later, we sat back in our room in silence, both of us tired, hungry, wet—and weaponless. We'd searched every part of that ship, the weapon nowhere in sight. Then we'd taken the long walk back to the castle in complete silence.

I took off my boots, massaging my sore feet.

"Listen, Lilypad," Penn started, but I held up my hand.

"It's fine. I had one job to do. Get information from Gabrielle, and I failed at it."

Anger rose to the surface, and my hands curled into tight fists, nails digging into my palms. I jumped to my feet, pacing as Penn watched me from his seat on the couch.

"If we don't get that weapon, we don't destroy the mirror. If we don't destroy the mirror, we can't ensure my stepmother won't stop searching for it, that she won't get it back and continue her reign of terror. I'm so tired, Penn."

He slowly stood. "I know, but we're going to find it."

"How do you know?"

"Because I always get what I want." His eyes blazed, and heat rippled through my body.

"Stop it," I said quietly, anger once again flashing, but this time for a different reason.

"Stop what?" Penn took another step closer, his voice low.

I gestured to him. "That. Whatever you're doing. The games you're playing. I'm sick of it, so just stop. Please."

The words had flown out of my mouth before I could stop them, but regret instantly surfaced. Penn's entire posture changed, the playful predatoriness disappearing, replaced by confusion.

"Games?" he said.

"The flirting," I said, exasperated. "The suggestive comments, the looks, the touches. I can't do it anymore. I don't want to play. I understand we have to put on a show, like you so aptly reminded me last night after our kiss on the balcony. But in private, when we're alone, just stop."

"That's what you want?" he asked, voice curious now.

"Yes." I crossed my arms, forcing myself to meet his gaze. "That's what I want."

He prowled toward me now, a gleam in his eyes. "I don't think that's what you want at all."

"You're doing it again. I'm not your entertainment, Penn. I'm not here just so you can laugh at poor Liliath who gets flustered and bumbling under your piercing—"

"Piercing?" He now stood before me.

"You know what I meant," I growled.

Penn swept me into his arms, and my head tipped back as I looked up at him, all the breath gone from my lungs.

"It's not a game," he said.

I stilled. "What?"

"When I was on that mountaintop, nearly unconscious, and I had to hear you talk about making love to Jasper, hear the nickname he wanted you to call him, I wanted to rip his head from his shoulders."

He'd heard all that? Spirits below, I wanted the ground to open up and swallow me whole.

He drew me to him. "I don't make suggestive comments or flirt or touch you because it's a game." His voice was so steady, so firm yet gentle.

"Then why do you do all that?" I asked, not sure I could handle the answer.

"Because I like it."

"Oh." My voice came out breathy, quiet.

Penn tightened his hold on me, and I felt just how much he liked it, his hard length pressed against me.

"I like the way your cheeks go pink when I flirt with you." He brushed a strand of hair out of my face, then let his thumb trail down my cheek. "I like the way your eyes go dark when you're looking at me. I like the way your mouth feels against mine." He brushed his thumb over my bottom lip. "The way your body fits perfectly into mine when we fall asleep together."

At this point, I didn't know if I'd ever be able to breathe again, to feel anything other than his words rumbling in my mind, in my entire body.

"How could you not see it?" he murmured, head dipping lower, lips closer to mine so that I could feel his warm breath on my face. "How much I want you?"

A hunger filled me. I reached my hands up, placing them on either side of his face. "Then prove it."

He smiled that feral smile of his, and then his lips crashed against mine.

Chapter Forty-Six

Our kiss was a meeting of teeth and tongue and lips. Penn pushed me back toward the bed, keeping his arms hooked around me as his mouth probed my own.

"Good enough for you?" he said.

"Mm . . . I don't think so."

He pressed me down on the bed, hovering his big body over mine. I grabbed at the front of his shirt and pulled him down to me, loving the way his heavy body felt on top of mine. His mouth trailed kisses to my cheek, to my chin, then down to my neck. I bucked under him, and he ground into my raised hips in a way that made me moan. Heat seared every place he touched with his lips, and I wanted him everywhere. His hands roamed down my sides, sneaking up under my tunic and caressing my bare skin. For how rough his hands were, his touch was so gentle, feather-light, as his fingers danced up my abdomen.

"Off," I said. "Get your clothes off."

My hands fumbled at the ties on his trousers, and I felt him smile into my neck. "Patience, Lilypad. I can do a lot of things with my clothes on."

A growl escaped my lips, and he chuckled into me, his mouth coming back up to meet mine.

His hair had escaped out of its tie and curtained his face like a damn halo. He was so fucking handsome.

His tongue pushed into my mouth right when I threaded my fingers through his hair, and we both let out moans that only seemed to fuel our desire.

We kissed like that for what felt like hours, or maybe it was minutes. Time had no meaning right now. Nothing had meaning but him and me and our bodies pressed together. We touched and explored and tasted until my lips were swollen, and I thought my body might explode from need.

"Penn," I murmured against his lips, unentangling my fingers from his hair. "Please."

It was all I could manage right now, but he understood.

He sat up, and I sat up with him, tugging my tunic over my head. He helped me when it got stuck, and we both laughed until the top half of my body was fully exposed. The laughter died on Penn's lips as he drank me in, and his eyes darkened.

"You're so fucking beautiful, my Lilypad."

His. I was his. I touched my hair self-consciously.

"Don't." He caught my hand before I could tug on the short strands.

"It's not . . ." I paused. "I used to be—" I shook my head. "Or *have* longer hair."

He let out a laugh. "You're sitting half-naked in front of me, and your hair is what you're self-conscious about?"

I gave him a look. "Should I be self-conscious about something else?"

He grabbed me, and in one movement had me pinned against the bed. "No," he said, voice rough. "I meant what I said. You're so fucking beautiful." He reached down and pinched a strand between his fingers, letting the hair run through them. "I don't know what you looked like with longer hair. I'd only ever seen you from afar."

I tucked that piece of information away. We'd talk about that another day.

"But I can tell you that it doesn't matter what hair you have. When I first laid eyes on you in that prison cell, your hair a rat's nest"—I shoved him, and he shot me a wicked grin and kissed my nose—"I still thought you were the most beautiful godsdamned woman I'd ever seen."

I swatted at him. "No you did not."

"Are you calling me a liar?" he asked, trailing a finger down my collarbone, eliciting a shudder from me.

"What if I am?"

"Then I'm just going to have to work hard to convince you."

I raised my chin. "I told you that you were going to have to prove yourself."

He dipped his head down, lips hovering over my breasts. "Well, then I better get to it."

He took a nipple in his mouth, and I let out a gasp. His tongue circled it, the rasp of it against my skin making me arch.

"Enough proof?" he whispered into me.

"I think I'm going to need more," I said, breathless.

"I was hoping you'd say that." His mouth continued down my stomach, pressing featherlight kisses until he came to my trousers. His deft fingers worked them open and he tugged them down, my undergarments along with them, his lips touching every inch of my skin as he went torturously slow. I squirmed under him, but he never increased his speed, and finally, he pulled my trousers and undergarments over my feet and threw them to the floor.

"Is that enough proof?" He smiled up at me from the end of the bed.

"Not even close."

He straightened, his hard length showing through his pants. I stared and swallowed.

He tsked. "Just what am I going to do to show you how serious I am?"

"I can think of a few more things."

He cocked an eyebrow. "Oh?"

I sat up, now fully naked before him, and his eyes raked over me. He drank me in like I, indeed, was the most beautiful thing he'd ever seen.

I got onto my knees and straightened, keeping eye contact with the king of thieves, then reached down and grabbed the hem of his shirt, lifting it. Wordless, he raised his arms and let me stretch it over his head. Now it was my turn to drink him in. I ran my fingers over every muscle, every defined edge of his arms, chest, and abdomen. Every pebbled scar. He watched me, watching him.

"Tell me," he said.

"Tell you what?"

"What you want me to do."

My fingers itched to pull down those trousers, but I hesitated for a split second, and it was enough.

He brushed his knuckles against my cheek. "If you don't want this . . ."

I looked away. "No, it's just that—" My cheeks flushed. "I've only ever been with . . ."

"Jasper," he finished for me, saying my former betrothed's name like it tasted foul on his tongue.

"Yes. And you're probably very experienced compared to me. I don't have a lot of moves, exactly." I stared at his sculpted abs, unable to meet his eyes.

He cupped my cheeks, forcing me to meet his gaze. Then he grabbed my hand and slowly placed it on his hard length.

I sucked in a breath.

"This is what you do to me, Lilypad. This is how much I want you. How much I need you. You're perfect, and if that's all that's bothering you—" He pushed a hand through his hair. "Trust me when I say you have nothing to worry about."

I massaged his length through his pants, and he let out a deep groan. Blood and earth, I didn't think I'd ever be able to get enough of that sound. I relented, lifting my hand with a teasing smile.

"Now tell me more about these moves," he said. "You've piqued my curiosity."

"Shut up." I grabbed his head and pulled his mouth toward mine.

Our lips met in a hungered frenzy, and I fell back onto the bed as he hovered over me, letting me undo the laces of his trousers. He shed the rest of his clothes, kicking them to the floor, and his cock sprang free, long and thick, a bead of moisture at the tip that made my core throb.

"Do we have to worry about . . . ?"

I shook my head, immediately understanding his question. "I'm not fertile right now."

"Good, because it might kill me if I can't have you this very second."

"Finally ready to prove yourself?" I teased.

In one swift move, he thrust into me, and I let out a cry. His entire length filled me, stretched me open. This, him, felt better than I ever could have imagined. He captured my mouth with his, drowning out my cries as he moved inside me. Our bodies rocked together, matching each other's rhythms. He ground his pelvis against mine as he gained speed, both of us almost frantic in our movements.

"Come for me, Liliath."

Hearing my name on his lips while he was buried inside of me sent tendrils of pleasure ebbing through me, that pleasure cresting into a bigger and bigger wave. I wanted him to say my name again and again and again.

I dug my nails into the hard contours of his back, and he growled, making that wave grow until I couldn't take it anymore. It crashed, and I let out a final cry as I felt Penn spill himself inside me.

He collapsed over me, his body coated in a light sheen of sweat. I held him tight and burrowed my nose into his neck. He gave my forehead a light kiss, then rolled off of me onto his back. We both lay there for a moment, breathing, letting our bodies come down from the high we'd just felt. He reached out an arm, and I nuzzled into his side.

"Do you believe me now?" he asked.

I lay my hand on his chest, my head in the crook of his shoulder. "Mmm, I don't think so. I'm going to need more proof, I'm afraid."

He let out a low laugh. "Give me a few minutes, Lilypad. I'll spend the rest of the day proving myself to you."

His fingers dipped low and in between my thighs, where he started rubbing in slow circles.

And as I found out, the king of thieves was a man of his word.

Chapter Forty-Seven

We lay cuddled together in bed, Penn's fingers trailing up and down my arm as I lay draped over his chest. The sun sank in the sky outside, and empty silver trays lay on the floor, the food consumed earlier when we'd finally taken a break to eat something. We'd stayed in our room all day, exploring each other's bodies in so many different ways every part of me now ached. No one bothered us, the guard posted outside our door probably hearing enough to know we didn't want to be interrupted. It had been the perfect day, and I didn't want it to end.

"I think I could sleep for three days straight," I said into Penn's chest. "But we do have a weapon to find."

He chuckled, chest rumbling underneath me, a sound I was coming to love.

I propped myself up on my elbow and looked down on that handsome face. "I can't believe I got you to spend a whole day in bed." I tsked. "You're getting lazy."

A smile tugged at his lips. "Nothing about what we did today was lazy, Lilypad."

My finger moved in slow circles over his chest.

"You know what I mean. No work for the king of thieves. That's surely against a rule."

"What rules? I'm a thief. We're not exactly known for following a code."

"Still. You love your work." My tone was light, teasing.

Penn leaned up to nip at my arm. "Work is overrated."

I laughed. "If only your thieves could hear you right now. They might just pass out in shock."

He huffed. "They'd probably break out in applause, cheer you on for finally getting me to do something other than obsess over our latest mission."

"First swimming in the sea, then spending a whole day in bed with me." I pressed my lips to his for a brief kiss. "What's next for the king of thieves? Morning tea? A trip out to the tavern without mentioning work?" I snapped my fingers. "Or maybe a picnic in Mosswood Forest? Complete with wine and cheese. That would be a sight to see."

I laughed just imagining Penn sitting on a checkered blanket, a grumpy look on his face while I lay next to him, indulging in wine and food.

He smirked. "A picnic? Is that what you like?"

"Yes, as a matter of fact it is. My mother and I used to go for picnics all the time, and my father carried on the tradition after she was gone. He'd bring dried meats, cheeses, bread, tarts, sparkling wine. Jasper came with us when he visited, but most of the time it was just me and Father. Something we did on special occasions: name days, holidays, anniversaries."

His green eyes were bright and clear as he watched me. "Why do you love the picnics so much? The memories?"

I tipped my head in consideration. "That . . . and the specialness of it. It made me feel loved and cared for. Both my mother and father would pack my favorite foods, jams, wines. They'd pick places they knew I loved."

He leaned over and kissed my arm. "Then we'll go on a picnic."

I raised my brows in shock. "Really?"

He bristled at my tone. "Yes, really. I am capable of doing more than work, you know."

I ran my hand along his chest. "So I've learned today."

"You know," he said, "once upon a time, my parents liked to take me exploring too. We'd travel all over Elwen, visiting different villages, my mother using her special herbs and powders to heal."

"Your mother was a healer?" It was odd to think about the false queen as anything other than a rebel.

He nodded.

"My father was a carpenter. They didn't like to stay in one place. They liked to constantly be on the move. We'd travel outside Elwen, to the farthest corners of Fyriad, to the isles of the sky court, and down to the coast of Apolis. I don't remember a lot of that time. But I know that I loved to explore. I loved laying out under the stars at night. I loved feeling so connected to the land."

I'd felt the same. We were more alike than I ever thought.

I adjusted my hand, propping it further under my head. "And you've gotten to do all that as an adult. Live out the life your parents gave you."

"Not exactly. They were merchants. They traded their goods, their services, for coin." He swallowed. "They weren't dishonest in how they earned a living. Not like me."

I hesitated, not wanting my next words to sound judgmental or harsh. "Do you think they'd be proud of you?"

It was a question I often asked myself, not about my parents. I already assumed my father wouldn't approve of my methods. He already hadn't approved of me when he was alive. But I did think about my people, what they would think of all this. Especially lately, after everything I'd done. After what I was about to do to Gabrielle. I shoved that out of my mind. Today was not the day to think about our mission.

"I don't know," he said honestly. "I've done what I could, the only thing I knew how to do, to help my people survive after the Great War, after the border closed. Would my parents agree with my methods? It's hard to say. They were honest people. Good people."

My finger stopped circling. "You don't think you're good?"

He rolled on his side to face me. "I don't know. You've made me wonder more than once over our time together. I've told you that I believe you'd make a good queen, and I'm not lying. You're a born leader, Lilypad. You light up every space you're in."

I winced. "Penn, I'm sorry. I—I shouldn't have judged you so harshly. I thought I was better than you, that I knew better. Jasper wanted to sell me off in marriage to some man. That's allowed in his land by law. But does it make it right? I think maybe the laws in Elwen need to be re-evaluated, and not just by one person, but a council, maybe like the one you have in Mosswood Forest." I took a deep breath. "You've helped so many in Mosswood Forest. You saved them, Penn. If that isn't good, then I don't know what is."

"Does that mean when you take back your crown you're not going to arrest me?" He smirked.

I kissed the corners of his mouth. "I'll think about it." I moved my lips down his chest. "If you can convince me?"

"Another test?" I looked up to see his eyes darkening again. His hands came to my ass. He gripped it and rolled me on top of him. I let out a playful shriek, but warmth gathered between my legs. "Careful, Lilypad," he crooned. "Or I'm going to have to show you just how convincing I can be."

THE NEXT MORNING, I woke up with Penn's muscled arms cradling me into him. I wanted to wake up like this every single morning. I'd slept with Jasper many times but had never felt this safe in his arms. Not like I did wrapped in Penn's.

He shifted behind me, and I felt his hard length pressing into me. "Good morning," he murmured into my ear, bringing a smile to my face.

I turned to him, and he reached a hand up and gently caressed my face.

"What's the plan for today?" I asked, not ready to face reality but knowing we needed to.

He leaned forward and kissed my lips. "Let's stay in bed all day. There are still so many things I want to do to you." He nuzzled my neck, and I laughed.

"Who are you and what have you done with the king of thieves?"

He rolled on top of me, and I pushed my hips into him. "I've been bewitched by a most beautiful princess."

I let out a moan as he ground against me. "Penn!" I swatted his shoulder. "We have to find that weapon."

His face sobered, and he sat up, pushing a hand through his wavy blond hair. I gathered the sheets around me and sat up next to him.

"There is nothing I would love more than to spend today, every day, like this." I gestured between our naked bodies. "But my court needs me. Jillian and Driscoll need me. Plus, Gabrielle might be getting worried about us at this point."

He opened his mouth like he wanted to say something but closed it. Finally, he said, "I know. I think you have to speak with Gabrielle again, try and get more out of her about this weapon, about the pirate lord. And I'll keep searching. It was a good idea yesterday, the pirate ship."

My shoulders sank. "We have no leads, nothing to go on. This is a disaster."

"We'll find it, Lilypad."

I met his gaze, the sun brightening his green eyes. "How do you know?"

He trailed a finger down my arm. "Because I always find my mark."

"Mm," I said in agreement. He'd proven that yesterday. Over and over and over and over again.

"Do you have any weaknesses?" I asked in a teasing tone. "Or are you really as invincible as you seem?"

He held my gaze. "I used to think I didn't have any weaknesses, but I'm starting to realize that's not true."

My heart squeezed at the words.

"There's something I want to tell you."

"Okay." I tucked a strand of hair behind my ear.

"Um." He scratched at the back of his head.

My stomach dropped. I'd never seen him hesitate like this. Maybe he was about to tell me there could never be anything between us, that it was just sex.

Oh, blood and earth. I'd actually fantasized about him and me having a future together. How stupid of me. I'd been a fool to think we could be together. Of course we couldn't. Penn knew that, and he was about to bring my fantasies crashing back down to reality.

"It's fine," I said airily. "I understand. You have needs as a man, and I fulfilled those needs, and now it's time to get back to work. You don't have to say anything else."

"Lilypad—" he started.

"No, really." I couldn't bear to hear him say the words, so I kept talking. Well, rambling. "It was stupid of me to think there could be anything more between us. That you would ever want to explore more with me. You're the king of thieves and I'm the princess of Elwen—"

I stopped when I noticed that huge smile on Penn's face. "You are not and will never be someone who just fulfills my needs." He pressed his forehead to mine.

I huffed out a laugh. "Well, that's good."

I couldn't believe this was happening. I couldn't believe I was so happy, that I could be so happy with so much going wrong. But with Penn by my side, I felt like everything was possible. If I was Penn's weakness, then he was mine.

I threw my arms around him, and he tightened his around me. "So about what I wanted to tell you—"

I gasped, not even hearing him, thoughts stuck on that word. "Weakness . . ." My mind raced, the word playing over and over. "Gabrielle said the pirate lord's weakness was water, the ocean. She said it was his greatest fear."

He frowned. "The pirate lord of the Dark Seas is afraid of the ocean?"

"That's what she said. What better place to hide his most treasured weapon than where he most fears?"

"What are you thinking?" Penn asked slowly.

"I think we went to the right location. We just weren't looking the right spot. It's not on his ship. It's in the ocean."

Chapter Forty-Eight

We wasted no time getting dressed and sneaking out of the castle, both of us careful to make sure the guard posted outside our door didn't see us. We'd had to use the window to get outside, which was only slightly terrifying, but now our boots pounded the sand as we raced back to the place we'd gone yesterday.

Today, clouds gathered in the sky above, threatening rain. We needed to beat the storm, which would only make the sea wilder.

"Gabrielle told me about a spot," I said, "the most dangerous place on the entire coast. Where the sea is at its most vicious."

Penn nodded, and I could see the excitement lighting his eyes. I couldn't believe this might be it. That we might find the weapon today.

We reached the rocky shores and picked our way over the slick rocks, just like yesterday, Penn holding my hand every step of the way.

We reached the edge of the rocks, ocean waves rolling big, the skies puckering above. Wind roared around us, and both of us were already soaked by the spray of the sea.

"Where is it?" Penn yelled. "Where's the spot?"

I looked around. "Gabrielle said it was in a place where the ocean is at its full strength."

We both turned and, unlike yesterday, continued along the rocks and around the shipwreck. Once we got to the other side, I gasped.

Bones and skeletons scattered along a sandy beach, and soon I saw why. A wave three times my height crashed down with a thundering sound that shook the ground. It was unrelenting, wave after wave after wave pounding the little shore. And there right out in the open sat a treasure chest.

"Huh. She really is taunting the pirate lord." Penn wiped the spray of water from his face. "Now how are we going to get it?"

"I think it's time to use your earth magic," I said.

He stroked his chin, then nodded. "It'll be the least risky way to do it."

I arched my neck, looking at the cliff that towered over the shore. "What if we come from above? You can create a vine to wrap around me and drop me down. I'll get it, and then you can reel me back up."

"I'm not going to put you in that kind of danger," Penn said.

I faced him. "Then why do all of this? Why train me? Why initiate me into your academy? You have to believe in me, Penn. Someone has to."

He studied me for a long moment. "Okay. Let's do this."

We stood on the cliff, the vine that Penn had produced with his magic now secured around my waist. Penn held the other end, tying it around his own waist, my anchor.

"Are you sure about this?" he asked.

"Yes," I said. "The treasure chest is right there, Penn. We're so close to getting it."

Something like guilt flashed across his face, gone so quickly I thought I must've imagined it.

"Okay." He pointed to the cliffside. "Make sure to always keep both hands on the vine as you climb down. Use your foot and find the ridges. When you get down there, you run as fast as your legs will carry you and open the chest to get the weapon, then I'll pull you up."

I nodded, heart hammering in my chest. "I'm ready."

I made my descent, going slow and steady as Penn coached me

through it. I held onto the vine with my hands while I used my feet to walk myself down the side of the cliff.

"How are you doing?" Penn yelled.

"I'm good," I said, even though my muscles were beginning to shake from the effort.

A blast of sea water sprayed the cliff, and the rock shook under my feet. I swallowed at the thought of being down on the sand in just moments, of the waves crashing over me and threatening to sweep me under.

Finally, my feet touched the sand. I spun and sprinted toward the chest. A wave plowed into the shore and the water slammed me back against the cliff, my head ramming into the rock. The vine tightened around my waist.

"Liliath!" Penn yelled. "Are you okay? Talk to me!"

I touched the back of my head, and my fingers came away with sticky blood. My temples throbbed, and I coughed out seawater, but then the wave receded.

This was my moment.

I raced back toward the chest and clicked it open. I blinked a few times. It was filled with gold, rubies, sapphires, all kinds of valuable trinkets. How was I supposed to know what the weapon was? I dug through it frantically, throwing out gold coin after gold coin.

"You need to hurry!" Penn yelled.

"I don't know what the weapon is!" I plunged my hand deeper, feeling for anything that might be it.

"I'm pulling you up. This is too dangerous."

The vine tugged at my waist, and I resisted, digging my feet into the sand. "No!"

A wave crashed over my head, and the vine snapped as the ocean yanked me away. A storm of water pushed me this way and that, everything going dark as I sunk deeper, deeper. My lungs burned, and I kicked and thrashed wildly, but it didn't help. The sea had me in its grasp now, and it wasn't letting go.

A rush of water pushed me further down. I wheeled my arms, trying to get any traction I could, but it was no use. My entire body grew cold, and my vision blurred. I wouldn't be able to last much longer.

Then I felt it. Two vines wrapping around both my arms, another around my waist, and they lifted me up, up, up, until I could see a light. I surfaced from the water and took a gasp of air.

Penn stood at the edge of the cliff, hands out, commanding the vines that stretched from his palms. "You're coming back up. I'm not risking your life like this. We'll find another way!"

I gritted my teeth as I landed with a plunk on the shore and looked behind me, the vicious wave receding.

"I can do this," I shouted and raced toward the opened chest. Using all my strength, I dumped it over, watching as gold and gems spilled out. And then I saw it, a glimmering vial, full of what looked like dust.

"Lilypad." Penn's tone held a note of warning, but I held up my hand.

"This is it," I said. "It must be."

I snatched the vial just as the vines lifted me to the cliff.

A power thrummed through me with that vial in my hand, and it felt good after not being able to access my magic for so long. A shadow loomed overhead, and I glanced up to see a wave about to pummel me.

"Lilypad, hold tight!" Penn yelled, yanking me up.

The water battered me, and my entire body clenched, my hands locking around the bottle, all while its power threaded through my veins.

The water pulled me in one direction while Penn tugged me in the other. All the while, I didn't let go of the dust, knowing if it slipped through my grasp, the ocean would claim it and we'd never see it again.

I sucked in a breath and inhaled a lungful of water, which made me sputter and cough, burning my lungs and throat. Finally, Penn yanked me out of the vicious wave.

"Are you okay?" Penn yelled down to me.

"Yes," I managed.

He continued to pull me at a steady pace, and I stared at the dust in awe. I couldn't believe we'd actually done it. We'd gotten the weapon.

Suddenly, Penn stopped pulling me up, and I hung there, suspended on the side of the cliff.

"Penn?" I asked, panic twisting my gut. "Penn!"

I looked up and gritted my teeth. I had to get to the top. Now. Something was wrong.

Suddenly, I was being lifted again, and my panic subsided. He must've just needed a break.

"Penn, we did it!" I shouted.

But he didn't respond.

Finally, I crested the top, and my mouth dropped open in horror.

Penn was on the ground, the guards pinning him, his mouth gagged. He looked at me, eyes wild, and Leoni stood over him, a smile spreading across her face. "Yes, we did it, indeed."

Chapter Forty-Nine

"Leoni, please," I said as I walked behind her, my hands now tied together in those water cuffs, the dust in her possession. "You don't understand."

"Shut up," she said, yanking the rope and causing me to stumble.

The sky above rumbled, and rain began to fall as we trekked back toward the castle.

"I knew you were up to something," she said. "I told Gabrielle you couldn't be trusted, that your intentions weren't pure. And I was right. You were after the pirate lord's pixie dust."

Pixie dust. I stared at the vial now clutched in Leoni's hand. I'd heard of pixie dust, dust that had magical powers, and the only way to procure it was from a pixie. They lived in Sorrengard, in the jungle. But how was this dust going to help us with the mirror?

I glanced at Penn, his jaw locked.

Guilt stabbed at me. Not only were we going to lose the weapon, but Gabrielle was about to find out how badly I'd betrayed her. That I'd lied to her.

Penn walked in front of me, his shoulders stiff, his entire body tense. It took three guards to wrangle him and get his hands tied, and he'd fought them the entire way. Now he walked with no fight left in him. I could talk to Gabrielle. Speak reason to her. She'd understand why I wanted this weapon. I'd make her understand.

Our journey to that shore had felt like an eternity this morning, but this walk back to the castle was far too short. We arrived in front of the shining white palace, and Leoni pushed us across the drawbridge and through the front doors. Our boots squeaked against the floor, and water dripped from all of us into puddles.

"Let's go." Leoni yanked me again, and we walked through the double doors to the throne room.

Gabrielle sat on the throne, speaking with some of her advisors. When she saw us, she straightened in her chair.

"What is the meaning of this? Leoni, explain yourself."

Her advisors scurried away as Leoni pulled me forward, and this time I fell to my knees in front of Gabrielle. Penn kneeled down beside me.

Leoni shoved my back. "I'll let her do the explaining." She held the pixie dust out, and Gabrielle gasped. Her brown eyes filled with that sorrow I'd been so afraid to see.

"I'm sorry," I said.

"Why do you have the pixie dust?" Gabrielle asked, voice shaky. "What is going on here?"

I swallowed. "Do you know what this dust has the power to do?"

"I know it's from the pirate lord," Gabrielle snapped. "I know that it's magic. I know that magic always has a price."

"But sometimes that price is worth paying," I said.

Gabrielle's face paled, and she blinked like she couldn't believe what she was hearing. "You don't even know what the price will be. It could be your life. Mine."

"It will be worth it," I ground out. "Because this pixie dust will destroy the mirror my stepmother has been using. It will destroy her power and weaken her. It will allow me to take back my court."

Gabrielle shook her head. "No. No, Liliath. Listen to yourself. You can't be serious. There has to be another way. Look what's happened to the earth court because of that mirror. Your stepmother has used its power and destroyed your entire court. She thought she could steal magic from your people, from you, but the magic is corrupted. You told me so yourself. Why would you want to risk that?"

"It's the only way," I pleaded.

Gabrielle stood and took the vial from Leoni. "No. I won't let you use this. I won't let you put me or my people at risk. I hid this weapon for a reason, and you—you manipulated me." She glared at me. "Is that why you told me all those sad stories about your stepmother, about your court? So you could get information out of me?"

Shame filled me.

"It's not her fault," Penn said, voice firm.

"Stay out of this," Gabrielle said, voice sharp.

Penn struggled against his restraints. "She wanted to tell you the truth. I wouldn't let her. This was all my plan. We're not betrothed."

"Penn!" I didn't want Gabrielle to know I'd lied about even more.

Gabrielle's eyebrows drew together. "What?"

"I didn't rescue her," Penn said. "I kidnapped her, forced her to come here because I wanted that weapon. She tells the truth. I wanted it to destroy the mirror." He looked up at the vines that crept over the walls. Vines. Everywhere. He was using his magic, an immense amount of magic, and they didn't even realize it.

My heart stopped in my chest as he wiggled his fingers, still tied behind his back, and the vines dipped down, slithering like snakes.

Leoni looked out of the corner of her eye. "He's going to attack us!" She and the other guards immediately summoned their water magic, water whooshing around us as the vines snaked out around their ankles and pulled them to the floor.

"Penn, no!" I yelled. "We don't have to do this!"

He looked at me but said nothing.

I studied that look in his eyes. The one I'd seen time and time again that I couldn't quite place, but in this moment, I recognized it: guilt. He felt guilty about something, but what?

"Penn?" My voice shook as water wrapped around my body, and I fell to the floor. The vines snaked up and under the water cuffs, snapping the water around his wrists. He jumped to his feet, commanding the vines to tighten around the guards.

Gabrielle looked at us with wide eyes, fury lining the features of her face. She drew her sword and jumped down in front of Penn just as he swiped his arm, and a vine knocked the sword from her hand. A sword, made from wood, thick vine, and other plants grew from his hand, while one made from water grew from Gabrielle's. Their weapons clashed, their bodies meeting before Penn spun around Gabrielle, kicking his boot into her back.

"Penn, stop it!" I screamed, still restrained by the water, unable to move on the floor. "You have to stop this!"

Gabrielle fell down next to me, her guards now throwing out discs of water that Penn dodged. Leoni slid across the floor, sending out water ropes that tied Penn's feet together. He wouldn't be able to beat them— not in their territory, where their magic was at its strongest.

Penn crashed to the floor.

I swallowed, still unable to move.

Penn locked eyes with me as the guards shook off his vines and stalked toward him. He held out his hand, a vine curling from it and shooting straight into his satchel. It pulled the mirror out, and I sucked in a breath at the tarnished gold object. Rust and grime covered the glass, and moss flecked the handle. It didn't look like anything spectacular, just an old mirror. Maybe that was the point, so no one would suspect its power.

He lifted his other hand, revealing the pixie dust. He'd swiped it off Gabrielle when they were fighting. The guards shot more water out at him, but it was too late.

"I'm sorry, Lilypad. I need you to remember that I meant every word I said."

"What are you about to do?" My stomach dropped to the floor.

"No!" Gabrielle screamed from next to me, getting to her feet.

Penn dumped some of the dust into his hand, then dropped it onto the mirror. Glass shattered into thousands of pieces, a bright light flashing. I covered my eyes from the blinding glow.

He'd done it. He destroyed it. But why had he been sorry?

"Liliath?" I heard, and I stopped breathing.

I'd dreamt of that voice night after night for the past two years. I'd have given anything to hear it again. It couldn't be real.

I removed my hand, and my father stood there, staring down at me, tears shining in his eyes.

My gaze flicked to Penn, who now stood and held Gabrielle's sword in his hand, pointing it directly at my father's throat.

Part Three

"*She made a poisoned poisoned apple . . . but anyone who might eat a little piece of it would die.*"

Chapter Fifty

The water's hold on me weakened, and I rushed forward, pushing myself in between the sword and my father.

"What are you doing?" I hissed at Penn. "This is my father. He is not your enemy. I know there's a lot of complicated history between Elwen and Mosswood Forest—"

Penn didn't move his sword.

I sent a pleading look toward Gabrielle as her guards surrounded us, water spears out. "Please just give us a moment," I said. "I will accept whatever punishment you deem fit, but please, Gabrielle. It's my father. He's here."

Her gaze was hard, and she stared at me for a long minute before giving a firm nod. Her guards lowered their weapons. I turned back to Penn, his sword still pointed at my father's neck.

"What has gotten into you?" I asked. "I know you have no love for my father, but this is extreme."

"You knew," my father said slowly, his voice hoarse, his dark brown eyes focused on Penn. "You knew this entire time, didn't you?"

I looked between them. "Knew what? What is going on?"

But neither man looked at me, their gazes locked on each other.

"He knew I was trapped in this mirror," my father said, "imprisoned by your stepmother to be her eyes and ears in my own court."

"No." I shook my head. "No, Penn wouldn't lie about that . . ."

I trailed off, recognizing all the things I'd missed. The holes in those conversations I'd overheard between him and Wayfinder, how Penn wouldn't let me look at the mirror, how he'd kept trying to tell me the truth in different ways.

Except he didn't tell me.

I was furious.

"You," I snarled at him. "How could you?"

Penn's face remained a stone mask, the man I'd spent all day in bed with yesterday no longer standing in front of me. "I know he's your father, but he doesn't deserve to live, Lilypad."

"Don't call me that. Don't you dare." My voice shook.

"He killed my parents." Penn's grip on the sword tightened.

"Because they betrayed Elwen!" I said. "I know the false king and queen were your parents, and I'm sorry for their deaths, but they started a war."

"No, they didn't." Penn shot an accusing gaze at my father.

I turned. "Father, tell him. This is all a huge misunderstanding."

But my father didn't deny Penn's accusations.

"You freed me just to kill me?" my father asked, ignoring me. "That seems like an awful lot of effort when death would be welcome compared to what I've been through these last two years."

"I freed you so I could finally have my revenge," Penn said. "You betrayed your court, you started a war to cover up your secrets, and you killed my parents and lied to everyone about why."

None of this made sense. There had to be something missing, here. "That's what this was all about?" I asked Penn. "You didn't want to break the mirror to save the earth court. You wanted to break it so you could have your vengeance?"

Penn didn't move a muscle. "I didn't lie. I wanted to help you win back your court. I truly believe you'll be an amazing queen. But I have to do this. I promised my parents I would avenge their deaths."

Horror washed over me as this new reality sank in. I'd been so foolish, actually believed Penn and I might have something between us. But he'd lied to me, used me, to get this mirror and kill my own father.

"Please step out of the way," Penn said.

"No." My fists curled. "I won't let you hurt him. No matter what he's done, he doesn't deserve to die."

"Then you leave me no choice." He brought up a hand, and a vine slithered around my ankle and yanked my feet out from under me.

I watched as Penn pressed the sword firmer into my father's neck, drawing blood.

"Penn." My voice broke. "Please."

He hesitated. For a split second, he paused, and my father slashed his hand forward, unwinding the vine from my legs and directing it straight into Penn's chest. Penn flew backward with the impact as I screamed out, "No!"

Chaos broke loose. Vines and water shot through the air, bodies tangling, falling. Penn and my father now fought with a mixture of earth magic and weapons. My father had found one of the guards' daggers and slashed it at Penn while directing another vine to slink from his hand and jab at Penn. The king of thieves jumped over it, just as the guards started shooting streams of water at them, trying to capture both my father and Penn. This was a disaster. I moved to stop the madness when I felt water slinking around my arms, holding them to my body.

I turned to see Gabrielle standing there, directing her water magic at me.

"I told you I'd give you a minute," she said. "I kept my word."

I darted a glance at Penn and my father, who were now back-to-back, surrounded by the guards, water swirling around them so they couldn't move.

"Gabrielle, let me fix this."

"You don't deserve any more chances. All of you need to be thrown into our dungeons until I can meet with the other leaders of the courts and figure out what to do with you."

"I know you're angry with me," I said as the water tightened, making me wince. "You have every right to be. But my stepmother is somehow connected to Sorrengard. It is in everyone's best interest if I can defeat her and restore the earth court to its former glory."

"Is it?" Gabrielle asked, hands still out, still directing the circle of water to constrict tighter around me. I squirmed. "You didn't even know your own father was harboring all these secrets. He lied to you, just like you lied to me. You're not the person I thought you were, and you're certainly not someone I'd want to see on the throne."

Tears sprang to my eyes because she was right. I'd lied. I'd stolen. I'd fallen for a criminal who betrayed me. All this time I'd questioned if I deserved to be queen, and now I knew the answer.

"No!" a voice yelled.

Gabrielle's eyes darted behind me, but I couldn't twist enough to see what she was looking at her. Her hands faltered, and the magic around me loosened enough that I could turn.

Just in time to see Penn swinging across the room on a vine, my father unconscious in his arms. He landed on a ledge.

"Get him!" Gabrielle yelled as the guards shot water magic up at Penn, water swirling through the air toward them like a mini hurricane. But it was too late. Penn gave me one last look before he ducked out of the window with my father.

I FELT NUMB INSIDE. This should have been one of the happiest moments of my life. I'd been reunited with my father. He wasn't dead, after all, but trapped all this time. Instead, grief swallowed me whole.

I sat on the steps leading up to Gabrielle's throne while she sat next to me, both of us silent, neither knowing what to say after everything that had transpired.

The guards returned an hour later, without Penn or my father. They'd scoured the land but had found no trace of the king of thieves or the king of the earth court.

I sank my head into my hands as Gabrielle dismissed her guards.

"Your Majesty," Leoni said, a hard edge to her voice.

Gabrielle only held up her hand. "I will be fine. I need a moment alone with the princess."

Leoni looked between us, distrust flashing in her eyes. I didn't blame her. I wouldn't trust me either. Finally, the guard nodded and strode from the room, closing the doors behind her.

For the first time, I noticed the wreckage our actions had left behind. Water lay in puddles everywhere, torn vines scattered across the floor. It was a mess.

"I'm sorry," I said, voice quiet, and I wrapped my arms around my waist. "I'm so sorry. You let us in, gave us a safe place to stay, opened up to me, and I betrayed you."

Gabrielle's jaw clenched.

"I just wanted to save the earth court, and Penn convinced me this was the only way. I didn't know what else to do, Gabrielle." I swallowed. "I made bad choices, and in the end, that is my fault. You're right. I don't know that I deserve to be queen, either. I've been questioning that very thing ever since I escaped from my stepmother. I've wondered if my people would approve of anything I've done over the last few months."

I looked at her, and she still stared straight ahead, giving no reaction to what I'd said.

"You're an amazing queen," I said. "I see you with your people. They admire you, respect you. You know them by name. You support their businesses, even in a time like this. You're so strong. You rose to the occasion when your court needed you most." I turned to her. "Let me go after my father and Penn. I don't know where they've gone, but I have to find them before Penn kills my father. You have no reason to trust me, but I will return, and I meant what I said before: I will accept the consequences of my actions."

"Go," Gabrielle said, voice monotone. "And don't come back."

She stood and walked out of the throne room, leaving me alone.

Chapter Fifty-One

I fled from the castle and out onto the rocky cliffs where it sat. I had no idea where Penn had gone. If the guards couldn't find them, then how would I expect to?

I worried my father was already dead, that I'd be too late to save him. I couldn't lose him, not after I'd just found him. Penn wouldn't want to stay in the water court. But he'd also been injured after that fight with my father and the guards, and he wouldn't be able to travel to Mosswood Forest right away, especially not with my father in tow. He'd want to wait until he was closer to full strength. He'd want to hide.

I thought about that cove he'd shown me with all the crystals. It was the only place I could think to go, the only place I knew of that might be secluded enough for Penn. It wasn't too far, and it was relatively easy to get to. I took a deep breath and went in the direction of the cove, ready to save my father—at any cost.

I ARRIVED outside the little cove and slowed, creeping over the rocks and across the sand until I was just outside. I flattened myself against the rocky wall of the crystal cave and peeked my head in. I gasped. There lay my father, unconscious, Penn nowhere in sight.

"Father!" I ran inside and sank down next to him, gently shaking him.

He didn't stir, so I did the only thing I could think of: I scooped water that washed up near us and splashed it on his face.

His eyes fluttered open.

"Father!" I threw my arms around his neck and helped him up to a seated position as he groaned.

I finally had a moment to take him in: his black hair had turned silver, his beard overgrown and unkempt, something I was sure he hated. Wrinkles lined his face that hadn't been there just two years ago. But still, he was here. I hugged him again.

"What happened? Where is Penn?" I looked around. "Are you okay?"

I ran my hands over him, checking for injuries.

He gently grabbed my hands and pushed me away. "I'm okay, sweetheart. I'm here."

A sob escaped my mouth. "I can't believe this whole time you were trapped in that mirror. I don't understand. I thought the Huntsman killed you. That's what she said . . ." I trailed off, realizing it had all been a lie. "Why did she do that to you? Why did she do any of this?"

My father took a deep breath. "I think there are some things we need to talk about."

My entire body tensed at the words. "Like what?"

"I . . . I haven't been honest with you. There are things that you don't know, that no one knew, not even your mother."

I thought about the accusations Penn had hurled at my father. "Was Penn telling the truth? About the Great War?"

My father clasped his hands together. He looked so small, so frail, sitting here in front of me, wearing the same torn and tattered clothes he'd been wearing the night my stepmother betrayed us.

"Liliath, I—I was in alliance with Sorrengard."

I went completely still at that.

"Twenty-three years ago, I started hearing whispers, rumors that some weren't happy with the way I was ruling the earth court. I feared a coup. I didn't know what else to do."

"So you turned to the shadow court?" I asked, horrified.

"I had no one else," my father said. "All the damn courts of Arathia are so terrified by conflict of any kind, I knew if I came to them with this, they'd intervene—and not in a helpful way."

I threw out my arms. "What would they do?"

"Insist on shadowing me, studying my court, searching for any failing on my part. They might've even insisted on putting a new ruler on the throne. It would've been insulting."

I sat back on my heels. "How did you even get in touch with the shadow court?"

"There are ways." He pushed a hand through his hair. "Smugglers who get people in and out. I asked the pirate lord to take me to the shadow court, and I met with their king."

My hand floated up to my mouth. This was beyond what I ever could've imagined my father doing.

"I didn't like their terms, and I realized I didn't want to deal with them, didn't want anything to do with them, but their island—Liliath, it was full of magical items, items with power. Rings with the ability to make you invisible. Cups that will poison any who drink from them. Bracelets that can burn skin."

The hunger in his eyes as he spoke of these items made my insides shrivel.

"What did you do?" I asked with a shaky voice.

"Nothing. I swear it. I left the island and came home to you and your mother, but the damage had already been done. Two travelers from the earth court had found out about my dealings."

Penn's mother and father.

"I don't know if they saw me boarding the ship or just heard about it somehow through their travels. I thought I'd been so careful. So I had them arrested, but they escaped, and that's when they began spreading the rumors, the lies."

Blood and earth, I'd been so stupid. "But they weren't lies," I said and stood, pacing. I needed distance from my father right now. "They weren't lies at all."

"They were!" my father snapped. "They said I was in league with the shadow court."

I whirled around. "You might as well have been!"

He stared out at the rolling waves like he hadn't even heard me. "They were gaining popularity, on the run, gathering followers who wanted to see them on the throne. If the information got out, especially to the other courts, I'd be done for. Removed from the throne, killed even. So I did the only thing I could. I started a war."

"You made us all believe they started the Great War."

His eyes darkened. "I staged a fake attack on our castle, blamed it on them, and just like that, the Great War began. I backed them into Mosswood Forest, finally caught the false king and queen and had them killed, and then I erected the border to keep their people, and my secrets, trapped away."

"How could you do that?"

His shoulders hunched.

"Mother's death—"

"Is on my hands," he said. "Something I'll always regret. I didn't know she'd get so sick, that the only plants that could save her would be in that damned forest. But they would've taken my crown, Liliath. They would've taken the earth court from us."

It was like I was listening to the ramblings of a mad king. I always knew my father had his faults, his failings, but this went beyond anything I could ever have imagined.

"I needed to marry again," he said. "Improve my image. I found your stepmother. She was bright-eyed and naive. She worshipped me. Exactly the kind of queen I needed."

That's why he had chosen my stepmother? Here I'd thought she was using my father, but really, he was using her for his own ego. He just wanted someone to make him feel like he deserved the crown on his head. I felt sick, and I stared at my father, unable to do anything but listen as he uncovered one horrible truth after another.

"Things were good for a while. You were growing up before my eyes, and we might have disagreed about the way I ruled, but we were happy. Elwen was doing well. Then I started hearing about this king of thieves. From Mosswood Forest. How he was traipsing all over the continent, stealing from other courts, stealing from our court. I suspected he might be the false king and queen's son. I'd thought the prince dead, but my sources confirmed he was alive, and he was causing trouble.

"The other courts had already been displeased over our war with

Mosswood Forest, unhappy with the border that had trapped those mountain dwellers. I feared that if I didn't get a handle on the king of thieves, they'd blame me, that they'd step in and intervene like I'd feared so many years ago. I tried to catch the thief, sent my best men out to find him, but no matter what I did, I couldn't capture him. Once again, I turned to the shadow court."

He'd been after Penn, not because Penn was breaking the law, but because Penn threatened his power.

"I found the mirror on the island and realized it would be perfect. I could use it to track the king of thieves and capture him. Not only would that take care of my problem, but everyone would see me as a hero."

I thought back to my conversation with Penn about the mirror and realized he never told me who took it or how it arrived in Elwen. I assumed it had been my stepmother, but I'd been wrong—and Penn hadn't corrected me. I wasn't sure I could hear anymore. I wanted to run from this cove and forget everything my father was telling me.

"How did you just waltz into the shadow court and steal those items?"

He sighed heavily. "I think that's exactly what they wanted me to do. All the items on their island have a darker purpose; all require a price to be paid." He sucked in a shuddering breath. "They knew these items would sow the seeds of discord, that by using them I'd ruin us so they didn't have to."

So I was right. We all were. Sorrengard was yet again at play.

"I returned to our castle with the mirror, but in order for it to work, someone had to pay the price, give up their freedom and be the eyes and ears of the mirror. I decided your stepmother would be perfect."

"You were going to trap her?" I asked, yet again horrified.

My father nodded, no regret, no shame, no emotion coming from him. "But she was more cunning than I'd given her credit for, was no longer the naive girl I'd married. She stole the mirror."

"That still doesn't explain how she's taken our magic."

My father pursed his lips. "I wasn't the only one in league with Sorrengard. She also got something from them, something that helped her steal our earth magic, but that's all I know." His head hung. "She betrayed me on your wedding day, trapping me in that mirror. I had to watch as she destroyed my court, threw my daughter in prison, stole magic from my people, turned that magic into something twisted and dark. I've watched it all for the last two years." Finally, his calm voice broke. "And I've realized how stupid I was. I thought your stepmother nothing more than some idiot girl who thought herself in love. But she'd been watching, paying more attention than anyone else."

"She protected herself. Like you, she went about it in the wrong way. But this is your fault, Father. Not hers."

"I know that." His voice was quiet. "Believe me, I know."

I sat back down next to him. "As I got older, I knew I wanted to do things differently than you. I had ideas, and you shut them down at every turn. When I was supposed to ascend to the throne, you told me I wasn't ready. It hurt at the time, but then I grew up and realized it wasn't about my failings, but yours. That maybe you wanted more time to right your wrongs, to do better. That wasn't it at all. You just wanted to hold onto power. Were you ever going to let me be queen?"

His shoulders hunched at my words, my confident, assured father gone, a broken man in his place.

"Of course I was, but you have to understand, it was hard . . . I . . . I'd ruled for so long, and—"

I straightened, no longer needing to hear any more. I knew what needed to be done. "You're going to stay here, and I'm going to ask Gabrielle to keep you locked in her dungeons. Once I've taken back the earth court, then I'll deal with you."

My father reached out to me, but I flinched away, and he withdrew his hand. "Let me help. Let me come with you."

"No," I said. "After everything you've just told me, I don't know if I can even trust you right now. You caused so much pain, so much death, with your selfish actions."

"Liliath, what was I supposed to do?" His tone was pleading. "I had to protect the crown!"

"You wanted to protect yourself!" My chest rose and fell, my pulse hammering. I thought of Penn, how he'd shouldered the burdens of everyone in Mosswood Forest. How he did everything for his people, sacrificing his own happiness. I thought of Gabrielle, how much she cared about her court, how she knew everyone by name. "You want to know what you could've done?" I asked. "You could've listened. You could've taken the time to hear your people and their concerns. You could've addressed the issues they had. Not ignored them."

His eyes welled with tears. "Liliath, please—"

His voice caught in his throat, and he made a gurgling sound, clawing at his stomach. His face turned red, then purple.

"Father!" I rushed to him, grabbing him and laying him down as blood dribbled out of his mouth. "Father!" I shook his shoulders. "What's happening? Did Penn do this?"

He rasped out a "no," and whispered, "All magic has a price." He grasped my shoulders tight, eyes widening as he rasped out, "Fight the dark with light, Liliath. Fight with the light." Then his eyes fluttered closed, and he was gone.

I pounded his chest. "No, no. You can't just leave me again." I grabbed his shoulders and shook him. "No, please. Wake up. You have to wake up."

His words echoed in my mind. *All magic has a price.* But the price for the mirror had already been paid. We hadn't used any other magic, except . . . the pixie dust. Penn used the pixie dust to destroy the mirror, and my father had paid the price.

I squeezed my eyes shut, numbness once again overtaking me.

Then I lay beside my father's dead body, and I let the tears come.

Chapter Fifty-Two

I didn't know how long I lay there like that, tears falling, eyes swollen, but I couldn't manage to tear myself away from my father. I'd lost him twice now, and this second time almost seemed worse than the first.

I was angry with him for the things he'd admitted to me, for the lies and the greed and the selfishness, but he was still my father. He was still the man who'd sung me to sleep at night when I was little, who'd been there when I woke screaming from nightmares, who took me on adventures in every corner of our court. I couldn't quite reconcile the two men: the father I'd known and the power-hungry king he'd revealed himself to be, but I also hadn't been ready to say goodbye. Not again.

I dragged myself to a stand and promised my father I would be back for him. For now, I had to go to Gabrielle. She'd told me to leave and never come back, but I needed to speak with her. Needed her help.

One final time.

I HEARD the clang of swords before I saw her. Outside her castle, in a circle dug into the rocks and filled with sand, Gabrielle whirled and jumped, jabbing her sword at Leoni, blocking her guard's attack. Leoni forced out her hand, balls of water flying toward Gabrielle like rocks. She ducked, the water missing her head by inches.

Leoni saw me and stopped, right as Gabrielle elbowed her in the jaw and flipped her onto her back. Gabrielle had her sword pointed at Leoni's throat when she laid her eyes on me and stood, sword dropping to the ground.

"I thought I told you to leave."

"My father is dead," I said. "Again."

Gabrielle swallowed but didn't speak.

"Your Majesty." Leoni came to stand beside her. "She disobeyed your orders. She needs to be taught a lesson."

"No." My fists curled at my sides.

"No?" Gabrielle asked.

"You cannot throw me into your dungeons. My court needs me. You were wrong, Gabrielle."

Gabrielle crossed her arms. "About what?"

"You said I wouldn't make a good queen, that I wouldn't be a good leader for the earth court, but that's not true. When you said those words, it struck a chord because I'd been questioning the same thing about myself for so long." I stepped forward. "What I did was wrong. I should never have lied to you, never should have stolen that weapon. And my father paid the price for my actions. I made a mistake, but that does not define who I am, who I would be as queen."

A gust of briny wind pushed past us, blowing strands of my hair into my face. I brushed them aside. Gabrielle still didn't speak.

"My father did a lot of bad things. Things that I don't have time to get into right now. He started a war, he lied to the other courts, he put his needs first, and that's how I know I'll be a good queen. Because I've done the opposite ever since I escaped that prison. All I've thought about was my court, my people. I did things I didn't want to do, things that made me uncomfortable, things that pushed me and challenged me. And I do believe I'm a better person for it, even if the methods weren't the best." I took a step forward, and Leoni's hand tensed over her sword.

"I watched you, you know. I watched how you were with your people. You love them. You know them. You know their needs, you know their worries, their fears, and you do everything you can for them. You didn't want to throw that ball, but you did, and you did it for them." I spread my hand out to her court, scattered down below along the sea. "You're a good queen, and I will be too. But you have to let me go so I can fight my stepmother and take back what's mine. So I can rectify the mistakes my father made and build a better future for my people." I took another step forward. "I don't want to be your enemy," I said. "I understand if you want nothing to do with me or my court moving forward, but I want to work together. Once I've set things right, I want to find your brothers and get their shadows back. I want to figure out what Sorrengard is planning and stop them. But mostly, I want my friend back. When you're ready. If you think you can."

Gabrielle stared at me for a full minute, not saying a single word. I was about to turn and leave when she said, "I'm not a good queen."

Leoni's head snapped to her.

"What do you mean?" I asked.

"You were willing to go to the ends of the earth for your people, and what have I done for mine? I've sat here, hiding away, keeping anyone from coming or going. I never should've said what I did to you. You shouldn't have lied to me, but . . . but I understand. You did what you had to for your people, and that is admirable, Liliath. I'm sorry about your father. We'll ensure his body is brought back to the earth court."

"Thank you," I whispered, tears filling my eyes.

"Go save your people," she said. "I'll be here waiting when you're done."

Relief flooded me, then I straightened. "Um, Penn? Has he . . .?"

Gabrielle looked at Leoni, who shook her head.

"He stole one of our ships and fled."

Right. So he was gone. I didn't know how to feel about that, but I didn't have time to think on it. It would be a long journey back to the earth court, and I'd have to go through Gilraeth to get there, then somehow get to my castle without being detected.

Gabrielle stepped forward. "Before you go, I have something you might want to see."

She started walking out of the circle, Leoni following her. I trailed after them, over the rocky terrain and down some stone stairs that went underneath the castle to their prison cells. Cells faced each other, iron bars keeping various prisoners locked away.

"Liliath!"

I stiffened at the voice.

That couldn't be right. I was hearing things, hallucinating, maybe? Dreaming all of this up? But I walked a few feet further, and I saw their faces behind bars: Jillian, Driscoll, and Shadow.

Gabrielle turned to me. "They showed up at our border, said they were your friends. I didn't believe them, especially since you'd just left. So I had them thrown in prison, but because you're here now, I figured I'd give you a chance to tell me if they're speaking the truth."

I let out a sob and reached out a shaky hand, grasping Jillian's through the bars. "You're here. You're actually here." Jillian, with her wild red hair, and Driscoll with his tall, lanky form and those tight black curls. And Shadow, so lithe, standing in the corner like at any moment she might melt into the darkness and disappear.

I had so many questions.

Gabrielle nodded to Leoni, who unlocked the cell.

Driscoll gave the guard a smug smile. "Told you."

Jillian flicked him. "Maybe now isn't the right time to goad the guard."

I barreled into them. "I missed you two so much. How are you here?" I looked at Shadow. "What happened?"

Jillian grabbed my hands. "They rescued us. From the castle."

"They?"

Driscoll waved his hand in the air. "The thieves. You know, Sleepy and Goofy and Happy and all those other weird nicknames they have."

Jillian rolled her eyes, and despite everything that had happened, I let out a laugh. It felt so good. I hugged them again.

"Why would you come here? Why not go into hiding in Mosswood Forest?"

Shadow stepped forward. "We tried, and they insisted on coming to see you."

"I think my exact words were 'Go fuck yourself' when Shadow told us we had to stay in Mosswood Forest," Driscoll said.

"Of course we were going to come wherever you were," Jillian said.

I stared at them in disbelief. "Well, now we have to leave."

Driscoll and Jillian looked at each other.

"Do we want to know?" Driscoll asked.

"Probably not, but I'm going to tell you anyway, and we'll have time." I nodded my head toward the exit. "On our journey back to the earth court."

Driscoll groaned. "I knew it. I knew she was going to want to go back there."

Jillian smiled, pride shining in her eyes. "Of course she does. She's going to save us."

Gabrielle cleared her throat. "We can lend you horses."

I nodded. "Thank you." I turned to my friends again. "We must leave immediately."

Jillian roped an arm around my shoulder. "We're with you 'til the end."

Driscoll made a face. "Well, 'end' is a little dramatic, don't you think? We're with you on the journey. I don't want there to be an end."

"I'm already sick of you," I said teasingly.

"You love me." He blew me a kiss.

Shadow pushed past us. "Oh, this is going to be a long trip."

"Hey," Gabrielle said, grabbing my arm and stopping me. "Do me a favor?"

I sent her a questioning look.

"Go kick your stepmother's ass."

Chapter Fifty-Three

We rode the horses until they needed a break. My thighs and butt ached, my shoulders and neck sore from the long journey. The sky above darkened, sand spreading out in rolling waves as long as the eye could see. I already missed Apolis and the view of that sparkling sapphire ocean. Pink and purple muddled across the sky as the sun sank lower, and I could already feel the night chill of the desert sneaking in. I frisked my arms.

"We should stop for the night," Shadow said from behind me. She and I shared a horse, while Driscoll and Jillian shared their own.

She tugged on the reins and pulled the horse to a slow trot as it kicked up sand behind us.

"Oh, thank the blood and earth," Driscoll said. "I feel like my ass might fall right off my body."

"Well, there's an image," Jillian said.

We stopped at the base of a huge stone arch, the giant round stones stacked on top of each other to create a sort of shelter. Rock formations surrounded us here, providing good coverage from any enemy that may find us.

"I hope Jasper isn't still looking for me," I said.

Shadow hopped off the horse. "Jasper has problems of his own."

"What does that mean?" She held out her hand and helped me off.

"Princess Seraphina has broken her curse and returned to Gilraeth to defeat the sorceress."

I gasped. "That's amazing."

Shadow tied the reins to the arch while Jillian did the same with her horse. "Don't get too excited. She still has a shadow court sorceress to defeat."

Hope swelled in me. If Seraphina defeated the sorceress, and I, in turn, defeated my stepmother, the fire and earth courts could be back to their full powers soon. But I couldn't get ahead of myself. Seraphina had her own battle to fight, and I had mine. I needed to focus.

Soon enough, we had a fire going, Shadow had caught some small rodents for us to eat, and we huddled around the warmth, holding out our hands, the cold nipping and biting. Shadow dug into her satchel and pulled out a cloak, then threw it to me.

"Here," she said. "I have an extra."

"Thank you." I wrapped it around myself, then looked at my two best friends, who both were shivering. "And thank you for coming for me. I didn't know just how much I needed you until you appeared. Now I don't know how I'd be able to make this journey without you, face my stepmother without you."

Driscoll finished his last bite of the rat Shadow had caught, then licked his fingers. "Who said anything about facing your stepmother? We are gonna let you handle that."

Jillian elbowed with him. "Of course we're with you," she said. "Always."

"I'll escort you as far as the border," Shadow said, "and then I have to get back to Mosswood Forest."

"I can't believe you rescued them," I said to her. "I'll never be able to repay you for ensuring their safety."

"Well, when Penn gives orders, we follow. We had another mission we were supposed to complete up in Valoris, but Penn told me to cancel all upcoming missions, to make this our new priority and nothing else until we accomplished it." She took a deep breath. "It was not easy, especially not after Penn had already rescued you. It took all of us and many days to figure out a way in."

I stopped at that, realizing what she'd said. Penn had ordered this.

"But why would Penn want you to rescue them? How does it benefit all of you?" I asked.

"It doesn't," Shadow said like I was an idiot, like I was missing something obvious. "In fact, some of us, whom I won't name, were adamant that this was a fool's errand."

"When did Penn give these orders?" I asked. "We've been in Apolis for over a week."

"At the fire court, after you rescued us. He told me to get back to Mosswood Forest and do whatever it took to get these two"—she jerked her head—"out."

I sat back in a stunned silence.

"Okay," Driscoll said. "So let me get this straight. You got rescued—"

"Kidnapped," I corrected.

"By some hunk of a guy who turns out to be the king of thieves. You escape from him, and he chases you across the continent, then he has your two best friends rescued, even though it doesn't benefit him in the slightest. You two have spent over a month together now." Driscoll looked around. "Yet he's nowhere in sight. I need some explanations here. Specifically about why you're not currently sticking your tongue down his throat and getting some because, hot damn, he is one fine specimen."

My mouth hung open while Jillian smirked and Shadow hid a smile behind her hand. "You don't even know what he looks like."

"We saw him the night he rescued you. His hood fell down when he grabbed you from your cell and swung with you like a freaking man-ape out of the prison cell."

My shoulders slumped. "Oh. I thought maybe you'd seen him recently, somehow saw him on his way back to Mosswood Forest."

Which obviously wouldn't have been possible, given that he'd stolen a ship.

Driscoll and Jillian shared a look.

"What?" I asked, drawing the cloak closer around my body.

Jillian squinted at me. "You care for him."

"I did care for him," I said. "Until I found out he was a lying bastard."

My heart betrayed me in that moment, squeezing at the thought of him, at the thought of how much I wished he were here right now. But he wasn't. He'd run away and left me now that he no longer needed me.

Jillian leaned forward. "What happened in Apolis? Shadow was able to catch us up on everything that happened up until she left you and Penn to complete the mission to destroy the mirror. Did you destroy it?"

I huffed, not wanting to relive the last nightmarish twenty-four hours but knowing I had to open up to someone before my bottled-up emotions destroyed me.

I started talking, the words pouring out of me until I'd told them everything that had happened in the last two weeks.

WELL, not everything. I left out the lingering glances, the make-out sessions, the earth-shattering sex. They didn't need to know all that.

Everyone sat in a stunned silence, staring at me.

"Your father was in the mirror?" Jillian asked.

"And now he's dead again?" Driscoll asked.

"That's why Penn wanted that mirror so badly," Shadow said. "We all knew it must have been about more than just destroying it to hurt your stepmother."

That took me aback. "You mean to tell me you didn't know the true reason he wanted the mirror?"

Shadow shook her head, those gold hoops of hers swaying with the movement. "Penn found out your stepmother had that mirror years ago, and he'd been working on a plan to retrieve it. None of us understood why it was so important to him to find it. He claimed it had a dark power, that in the wrong hands it would be dangerous, as we later saw happen with your stepmother. But there were many dangerous objects scattered around the continent, and Penn didn't care about any of those, just the mirror. He'd send us on missions to retrieve items for the people of Mosswood Forest, but his sole focus these last few years has been on finding a way to destroy that mirror."

Now all the conversations I'd overhead between him and Wayfinder made sense, why Penn was so obsessed with work, why he had no time for fun and games. His vengeance drove him, gave him purpose.

It made me feel sad for him.

"We all told him there were more important things to worry about," Shadow said. "Like his people, like freeing Mosswood Forest so we didn't have to be thieves anymore. But he was single-minded in his focus and wouldn't listen to any of us." Shadow sighed. "Fuck. Your father. Your father was trapped in that mirror. The man who killed Penn's parents, who waged a war on us to hide his secrets." She looked at me over the firelight. "I'm sorry you had to find out that way, about your father. That's not how it was supposed to happen."

Jillian's eyes shone with tears. "I'm so sorry, Lil. I never suspected . . . never even thought your father was capable of that kind of evil."

Driscoll shrugged. "He was a little shady—" Jillian cut him a glare. "But I'm sorry, too," Driscoll amended quickly.

"Wait a minute." Jillian straightened, tugging at her red curls. "You said that your father died because Penn used the pixie dust. That your father's death was the price paid for the magic used."

I nodded.

"But Penn couldn't have known that was going to be the price. You can't control what the magic demands as payment."

"Okay . . ." I said.

"So Penn didn't kill your father," Jillian said.

"He might as well have!" I said, a defensiveness rising up in me. "He lied to me, Jil. Used me and didn't even tell me the full truth about why."

He'd kissed me, made love to me, made me feel things I'd never felt before—all while he knew my father was still alive and trapped in that mirror. It was unforgiveable.

"I know," Jillian said quickly. "I'm not excusing the behavior. It wasn't right, but can any part of you understand his perspective? Your father murdered his parents to cover up his own evil dealings. He waged a war to get rid of the people who knew his secrets. He manipulated your entire court—"

Driscoll cut her off. "Maybe now's not the right time to remind Liliath about her father's shortcomings as king."

"No," I said, tears welling in my eyes. "She's right. My father did awful things that cannot be undone. I understood why Penn wanted his revenge. I understand the lengths he went to get them. But I don't think I can forgive the way he used me."

Sorrow shone in Shadow's eyes.

"But that's what I'm saying," Jillian said. "He didn't kill your father, Lil. He'd spent his entire life wanting to avenge his parents' deaths, and then he let your father go."

"You don't know that," I said. "Maybe my father escaped."

"Really? From Penn?" Jillian arched an eyebrow.

Driscoll nodded. "Yeah, I have to agree that doesn't check out."

My heart hammered in my chest. "What are you getting at?"

"Well, from everything Shadow told us, from everything you've told us, I think it's pretty obvious. The king of thieves is in love with you."

The words shook me to my core. "No, no, that's not—" I started, but Jillian cut me off.

"So he never showed any kind of interest in you?"

Penn's lips on mine.

"You two didn't bond while spending weeks alone together?"

Penn whispering all the ways he wanted to worship me.

"You're telling me there was nothing between you two at all?"

Penn hovering over my naked body.

I swallowed.

"Oh my good green earth," Driscoll said. "Something happened between you two."

"That's another hundred gold coins Hammer is going to owe me," Shadow said, studying her nails.

I glared at her.

"We might've made bets about you two getting together."

"What?" I screeched.

"Oh, come on. I told you in the sewers that you brought out a side of Penn we hadn't seen for a long, long time. He came to the tavern. He never came to the tavern."

"He brought work with him!" I said.

"Baby steps," Shadow replied with a smirk. "Then he came out to the festival. He danced. He actually moved his feet to the rhythm of a song."

I shook my head.

"He was playful with you, teasing. He actually flirted," Shadow said. "I didn't think the man had a flirtatious bone in his body."

"He's got many fine bones in that body," Driscoll commented.

Shadow tugged at an earring. "And when you left with Jasper, I'd never seen a man so frantic in his life."

I tucked a strand of hair behind my ear. "What do you mean?"

"He was desperate to get you back, and not because of the mission. He was sick with worry. He lost his mind, doing such stupid things. Why do you think we got caught? The king of thieves never gets caught."

I stared at the fire, so many emotions rolling through me.

"So now, the only question is," Driscoll drawled, "do you love him back?"

"No," I burst out. "Absolutely not. He's arrogant and stubborn and a liar and .. and . . ." I swallowed.

Jillian gasped. "You do love him."

"I knew it," Driscoll replied.

"It doesn't matter," I said. "I'm to be queen of the earth court, and I can't have a thief as my king."

"Why?" Jillian asked. "Everything Penn did was for his people. Except the mirror thing, that was more for him. But everything else. He sacrificed so much."

The opposite of my father.

"Who wouldn't want a man like that as their king?"

"As their husband?" Driscoll said with a wink.

"I can't think about this right now," I said. "I have to focus on defeating my stepmother. Penn left. He didn't stay to fight for us. Love is not always enough. So, please, just leave it alone. You said you're here for me, so be here for me and help me defeat my stepmother. That's what I need right now."

Jillian, Shadow, and Driscoll shot each other looks before giving reluctant nods.

"Thank you," I said, laying down and rolling over, not letting them see the tears forming in my eyes and slipping down my cheeks.

Chapter Fifty-Four

The border between Elwen and Mosswood Forest stood before us. Luckily, Shadow had been right. Everyone in Gilraeth was so preoccupied with the return of their princess, they barely took notice of the four strangers making their way through the fire court.

Shadow gave us each a hug as we entered the blackened, gray land of Elwen. "This is where I leave you," she said. "I have to return home."

I nodded. "I understand. Thank you for all of your help."

Shadow hesitated.

"It's okay," I said. "This is a battle I have to fight on my own. You can't help me. Not with this."

She grasped my hands. "We will meet again." She kissed my cheek, and then she was off, running toward the long tree line in the distance.

"Well, this is going to be fun," Driscoll said. "Can't wait for our reunion with your psycho stepmother."

"Do we have a plan?" Jillian asked.

"Defeat her?" I said with a shrug.

"Okay, so we don't," Jillian said. "Just wanted to be clear on that."

I let out a groan as we trekked across the land, the grass crunchy like it had been burned to a crisp. "I don't know how to form a plan. I don't know what's going to happen. She doesn't have her mirror anymore, and that's going to be a blow to her, especially when she realizes I was the one who helped destroy it. She doesn't even know I'm coming for her. But . . . as to how I'm actually going to kill her? I haven't figured that out yet."

"We're going to die," Driscoll said. "At least it'll be on our terms."

Jillian linked arms with both of us. "That's the positivity I like to see."

The ground trembled under our feet.

"Huh." Driscoll looked down.

The ground shook again, with more force this time.

"I don't like that," Driscoll said.

"Uh, Liliath?" Jillian asked.

"Yes?" I looked at her, her finger pointing straight ahead.

"Remember when you said our visit would be a surprise to your stepmother?"

I followed the direction of her finger, pointed at the Huntsman, who was currently walking straight toward us.

Oh, fuck.

"Spread out!" I instructed.

Behind us, I heard the whinnies of our horses as they ran from the Huntsman.

"Oh, not the horses!" Driscoll yelled, but they were already too far away.

"Let them go," Jillian said. "We can walk from here."

"If we survive," Driscoll mumbled.

We had nowhere to run, nowhere to hide. The land was flat and barren for miles, nothing but cracked earth and broken trees. And the Huntsman was relentless. He'd find us anywhere in Elwen.

His tree-trunk legs pounded the dirt as he walked, every step he took eliciting a shudder from the ground. Shadow had left us with a few weapons: a dagger for Driscoll, a sword for me, and a few throwing stars for Jillian. None of that was going to be very effective against the Huntsman.

I braced myself as he came closer, holding up my sword, remembering the footwork Wayfinder had taught me during our lessons.

"This really isn't how I wanted to die," Driscoll said, his dagger clutched tight in his hand.

"There's a way you preferred to die?" Jillian asked, eyes darting from the Huntsman to Driscoll.

"Do you have to always be such a smart-ass?" Driscoll asked.

"Can we focus on the problem at hand?" Panic tinged my voice as the Huntsman neared.

He opened his mouth, revealing the sharp thorns that lined it. His beady black eyes stared at us, the vines and branches making up his face twisting and writhing.

"Attack!" I yelled, surging forward and slashing at the Huntsman.

Driscoll let out a war cry and flung his dagger at the creature, missing. "Oh, shit," he said.

Jillian let her flying stars go. They swiped the Huntsman's face, then circled back to her, and she caught them.

"Wow, that was impressive," I said as I dodged a swipe from the Huntsman's arm.

"I got it!" Driscoll yelled from behind us. "I found my dagger."

"Great!" I jabbed my sword at the Huntsman's leg to no effect. "Can you use it?"

"I could really do without your snark right now." Driscoll drove the dagger into the Huntsman's calve, where it got stuck. He yanked and grunted, but the dagger wouldn't budge.

This was a disaster. The Huntsman reached out a hand, and before I could jump away, it snatched me in its grip. I wriggled and pushed at the wooden fingers curled around me, but it was no use. I'd been caught.

"Let her go!" Jillian yelled, launching her throwing stars, but they glanced off the Huntsman's chest and fell to the ground.

"No, you are not taking her from us!" Driscoll latched onto the Huntsman's leg, getting dragged as the Huntsman took a step.

"Just leave me," I said, the Huntsman raising me higher and higher until I was eye-level with it.

I glared at the creature. "My father created you, used his magic to make you, and this is how you repay him? By working for his killer?"

The Huntsman grunted, then sat me on his shoulder. I stilled, looking down at Jillian and Driscoll.

"What is happening?" Driscoll asked, hands now on his hips.

The Huntsman reached down and grabbed Jillian, who gave a shriek as he sat her on his other shoulder.

"I am so confused," Jillian said.

The Huntsman reached behind him and plucked Driscoll from the ground, setting my friend next to me.

Then he turned and began stomping toward the castle.

We all looked at each other, bewildered.

"Okay, crazy theory, but I think the Huntsman is helping us?" Driscoll said.

"I can't believe I'm saying this, but I agree." Jillian leaned over. "He didn't hurt us."

"Maybe my stepmother ordered him not to," I countered.

The Huntsman stopped and kneeled. We all screamed as we clutched tight to him.

He reached his hand back and yanked the dagger from his calf, then handed it up to Driscoll.

Driscoll blinked a few more times as the Huntsman stood and continued on his way toward the dark castle that loomed in the distance.

I stared ahead. We would find out soon enough if the Huntsman was friend or foe.

<h1 style="text-align:center">Chapter Fifty-Five</h1>

We arrived at my stepmother's castle, the iron gates surrounding the courtyard rising high over our heads. The Huntsman punched the gate door and it swung open.

Driscoll gulped from beside me as the hedge maze loomed in front of us. We knew all too well how deadly that maze was. We'd watched person after person get crushed, eaten, impaled by it over the years—until Penn, the only one I'd ever seen successfully get through it.

I wouldn't think of the king of thieves, not right now. He was back in Mosswood Forest, probably planning his next mission. Maybe this time he'd pick a new princess to betray. Maybe Seraphina, now that she was no longer cursed. I thought of him gazing at Seraphina the way he had me, of him kissing her like he had kissed me, him naked over her. My fists curled at my sides, and I suddenly wanted to punch something. Good thing I'd be seeing my stepmother soon.

Jillian let out a shriek as the first hedge rose up, twisting and curling its thin branches, its black leaves rustling as it formed into a giant snake.

"Oh, good, a new one," Driscoll said. "So glad we're getting to see the snake for the first time before it eats us."

The hedge snake opened its mouth and lunged. I held up my sword, readying myself for a fight, but the Huntsman punched out his fist right in the throat of the hedge snake. Branches and twigs snapped, and the leaves scattered, flying away on the breeze.

"Maybe he is on our side after all," I said, looking at Jillian and Driscoll, who both stared with wide eyes.

The Huntsman continued to tromp through the maze, stomping, punching, and barreling his way through. I couldn't believe what I was seeing. Maybe the Huntsman never meant to kill me. Maybe when he came to find me in Mosswood Forest, he was trying to save me from what he perceived as a threat. This whole time I'd thought of him as the enemy, but maybe he was loyal to my father after all and was doing what he could to protect me now.

The crows cawed overhead, diving at the Huntsman as he swatted them away. The dark sky rumbled overhead like it knew something ominous was about to happen.

Driscoll looked down at me. "Are you sure you're ready for this?"

"A little late to ask her now," Jillian said. "We need to hype her up."

"Oh, right. You got this," Driscoll said in a monotone voice, pumping his fist in the air weakly.

I groaned. "You guys are not helping right now."

The Huntsman continued on his way toward the castle, to the green moat surrounding it, smoke rising from it and curling in the air. He sloshed through it, the water sizzling around his legs but seeming to have no effect. I'd seen more than one animal disintegrate in this moat.

The Huntsman kicked in the tall wooden doors, which were now riddled with holes. The doors creaked as they opened. My breath caught in my throat. I hadn't seen this room in over two years.

Dust covered the windows above us, and cobwebs spread across the corners. Cracks webbed across the wooden floors, and dirt and grime crusted them. Dim light flickered from the sconces on the wall. This once had been a beautiful room, filled with light and beautiful vases full of flowers and plants. It had breathed life. Now it reeked of death.

Trees, vines, and invasive plants had taken over the room. Moss crept over the walls, everything black and gray and sick.

"I knew you were useless," a voice said from above, and I stiffened. I looked up to see my stepmother standing on the upper floor above us, looking down her nose with disdain over the broken railing. "I gave you one job," she said to the Huntsman. "Bring me her heart. And instead, you bring her into my home, heart still beating in that chest."

The Huntsman let out a growl and gently placed me, Jillian, and Driscoll on the floor, one by one. He stepped in front of us, a slight bend in his knees. He was readying for a fight.

My stepmother just laughed and flicked her wrist.

"Watch out!" I yelled as thick black vines punched up through the floor and wrapped around the Huntsman. He snapped them in half, but more threaded through the floor, until there were so many he couldn't fight. They constricted around him like the legs of an octopus, tearing off his arms first, then his legs, and finally crushing his neck until he was nothing but mangled wood and plants. I covered my mouth in horror, then glared up at my stepmother.

She walked down the stairs slowly, her black dress trailing behind her, her gray eyes blazing. "You were stupid to come back here." She flicked her wrist again, and a tree branch dipped down, caressing my back. I jumped from it. "I'd hoped to keep you imprisoned, to make you suffer like you made me suffer all those years ago. But I see now that it's too much of a risk. While you're still alive, there's hope, and that I cannot have." She smiled as she continued down the stairs, almost to the bottom now. Jillian and Driscoll joined me, standing on either side.

"So, unfortunately for you, now it's time to die."

The doors creaked closed behind us, and a stone settled in my stomach like a weight of heavy dread.

Chapter Fifty-Six

"It doesn't matter if you kill me," I said. "The mirror is gone."

She stilled at that, considering my words. "Well, I'll just have to find another way to ensure no one in Elwen has earth magic. After all, Sorrengard is just full of little gems they're more than willing to loan us. I'm sure you've heard all about the island by now."

I swallowed. "I know everything. My father told me the truth. Right before he died."

"So he's finally gone as well?"

There was a sadness to her voice that surprised me.

She smacked her red lips, that sadness gone in an instant. "It's for the best. He died knowing I destroyed everything he loved."

"No, you didn't." I stared at her, a challenge in my eyes.

"I'm looking forward to breaking you." She walked toward me, her gown rustling against the floor. "Piece by piece by piece."

"And for what?" I gestured around the room. "For this? For magic that's corrupted and sick? So you can rule over a land of death?"

Her hands curled into fists.

"Was this what you dreamt of when you became queen?" My own anger flared. She'd never once visited me in the prison cells. I hadn't laid eyes on her since that fateful night she killed my father and ruined my wedding, and it turned out I had a lot to say.

"Quiet," she said with a deadly calm.

Everything about her was sleek, regal, her black hair slicked back into a bun, her pale skin hugged by a tight black dress that flowed to the ground, the black crown atop her head glinting in the dim light. But for all that, there was a sadness in her eyes, a sadness I knew too well.

"You don't know what to do now, do you?" I asked, taking a step forward. "Now that you've gotten your revenge, there's nothing left for you."

"What are you talking about?" she snapped.

"Yes, Liliath, what are you talking about?" Driscoll asked between gritted teeth, both he and Jillian frozen, watching the exchange between me and my stepmother.

"You loved him," I said softly. "My father. When he chose you to be his queen, you thought you were getting some fairy tale, a happily ever after."

"Shut up," my stepmother said, a warning in her voice.

I stepped closer. "But instead, you got a husband who just wanted someone to worship him, and eventually, someone he could use. Someone who was expendable."

"Yes, and how did that work out for him?" She gave me a wicked smile. "He brought that mirror home with him, the idiot, thinking I was that naive, that stupid, that I wouldn't know what he planned to do. I'd had spies tailing him for years. After he killed my best friend." She took a stuttering breath. "After you ratted us out and had her killed."

I swallowed. "I'm so sorry, Elayna."

Her eyes flashed at my use of her name.

"I know it will never be enough. I don't expect your forgiveness. I don't deserve it. It was an awful thing of me to do, and I have no excuses. All I can do is learn from my actions and grow, to do better, to be better."

"She was all I had. We got separated during the Great War, but we found our way back to each other. We'd meet at the border, would talk for hours. She was the first person I told when your father picked me to be his queen. She trusted me, and she died thinking I had betrayed her, that I'd given her up to my husband to win his favor. I'll never forgive you for that. But you both paid, in the end. Instead of your father trapping me in that mirror, I trapped him."

"And our magic?" I asked. "The magic you've stolen from the people of Elwen? The magic that you've corrupted?"

"Ah, yes." She held up what looked like a vial hanging on the end of her necklace. It swirled with green, blue, and yellow smoke. She pinched it between her fingers, her long manicured nails clacking against the glass. "After your father's visit to Sorrengard, I knew I had to do something. Trapping him in that mirror wouldn't be enough, not when the guards could simply detain me and free him. I had to take away everyone's power, to ensure no one could fight against me." She tapped the vial. "This did the trick. It sucks away anyone's magic who's in its vicinity. I paid the pirate lord a hefty price for it."

"And you used the mirror to seek out any new baby born, so you could take their magic."

"Yes, among other things. The mirror was very helpful in finding information, shutting down attempted coups, ferreting out those who wanted to rise up against me."

I shook my head, looking around at the gray, lifeless plants that surrounded us. "All of that effort, for this?" I laughed.

Anger flashed across my stepmother's face.

"All magic comes with a price, so yes, you took something from us, but you turned it ugly. You rule over a dying court. What do you think is going to happen if Sorrengard attacks? Who do you think they'll wipe off the map first? You're doing their work for them, killing us so they don't have to."

"You don't know what you're talking about," my stepmother said. "I won. I made your father pay for the way he used me. I made you pay for the way you treated me, always so high and mighty, always leaving me out, looking down on me, never accepting me no matter how hard I tried."

A lump grew in my throat at her words. "I know. I was a brat. I'll admit it. I missed my mother, and I wasn't ready for my father to find someone new. I treated you horribly, but you can't blame your actions on me. You did this all on your own, and now you have nothing left to achieve. My father is dead. The mirror is broken. Our land is ruined."

My stepmother's jaw locked. "Enough of this. You're not going to be able to distract me, if that's what you're trying to do. To weaken my resolve." She snapped her fingers and the trees dipped down and lifted Jillian and Driscoll into the air.

"No," I yelled, running at her with my sword. I slashed it in the air, and the tip of it caught onto her necklace, the vial crashing to the ground. I held my breath, but the glass didn't shatter. The drop didn't impact it at all.

My stepmother smiled. "Dark magic. Really hard to break," she said.

Then she swiped her hand over and a flurry of black leaves flew toward us and whipped the sword out of my hand. "I'll make you a deal," she said as a vine wrapped around my waist and slithered up my body.

A tree bent down in front of me, and hanging from it was an apple, covered in dripping, black sludge. "One bite. One bite of this apple, and I'll set your friends free and stop stealing magic from your people."

"You're lying," I said.

"I'm not. Unlike your father, I don't lie. Now that your father and the mirror are gone, you're right. I don't need any of this." She pointed a red nail at me. "You're the last annoying weed that needs to be pulled from my life. Your death will finally bring me peace."

It wouldn't, but there was no point in arguing.

"Don't you dare, Lil," Jillian yelled before a leaf flattened over her mouth and silenced her.

"That is most definitely going to give you food poisoning," Driscoll added.

"You'll let them go?" I asked. "You won't imprison them or kill them? You'll stop terrorizing my people?"

"I swear it. Are you a woman of the people, or are you like your father, a ruler who only cares about herself?"

I bit the inside of my cheek, eyes darting to the apple. This would be the end for me. I wouldn't survive it. But maybe that's what I needed to do. I couldn't let Jillian and Driscoll die. Couldn't let my people suffer anymore. I had to believe Elwen would one day rise again. I just wouldn't be here to see it.

"What's it going to be?" She tapped her foot on the ground.

"Okay," I said.

"No," Driscoll shouted, and Jillian struggled against her constraints, her muffled yells echoing through the room. "She's manipulating you!"

The vines loosened, and I reached out for the apple with a shaky hand. It was sticky and mushy, not at all like the firm, ripe apples my stepmother always grew on her prized trees.

She watched me with dark eyes that gleamed as I brought the apple to my mouth and took a bite of the rotten fruit.

"No," a voice that I recognized yelled out.

I swallowed the bite just as Penn and the seven thieves burst through the doors.

"What have you done?" Penn asked, but it was too late.

I fell to the ground, hearing muffled voices all around me. My gaze focused on an object lying near me. The vial. Arms weak, vision going fuzzy, I reached for it, rolling it between my fingers. I couldn't break it. Couldn't. Break.

My last thought was that maybe I couldn't break the magic; maybe I could set it free, and then I fell into darkness.

Chapter Fifty-Seven

I saw myself. It was like I was there, but I wasn't. I hung overhead, watching my lifeless body on the ground. Penn screamed, a gut-wrenching scream that seemed to come from the deepest depths of him. He ran to me and fell to his knees, all while my stepmother stood there and laughed, and for once he didn't look like his stoic self. He looked panicked, all sense of calm gone from his wild eyes.

Penn shook my shoulders. "Liliath, wake up. Please, wake up." He snarled up at my stepmother. "What did you do to her?"

"I didn't do anything. She's the one who ate the apple."

Penn stroked my cheek. "Liliath, you have to come back to me." His voice broke, and that broke something in me. "I love you, Lilypad. I'm sorry I never told you, but I need you to hear me now. I love you. I know you're angry with me. I know I did terrible things, but I never meant to hurt you. And now I need you to wake up so you can kick her ass—and then you can kick mine."

I didn't move. I didn't know how to.

Penn looked up at my stepmother again. "What was in that apple? What did you do to it?"

"It's just your standard dark magic. You know, magic that's been corrupted," she said. "She ingested it, which I generally don't recommend."

"I'm going to kill you," Penn said. "I'm going to make it slow, to make sure you feel every bit of pain and suffering you inflicted on her."

"Ah, ah, ah." She wagged a finger, and that's when Penn stiffened.

I watched as a green smoke seeped from him, from all the thieves, traveling straight into the vial pinched between my fingers.

She was stealing their magic, and there was nothing they could do about it. She'd slaughter them, kill them all.

She'd won. It truly was over.

"You swore you wouldn't steal any more magic," Driscoll shouted, still clutched in the grip of a tree. He struggled against it.

My stepmother studied her nails like she was bored. "I believe I said I wouldn't steal any of her people's magic. Correct me if I'm mistaken, but these are not her people."

Penn watched as his magic flowed into the vial in my hand. He didn't fight it, didn't do anything except lean over and press his lips to mine.

The kiss, like a force of the purest magic, jolted something in me, a power I didn't recognize. Like it was lighting my path out of the darkness.

Fight the dark with light.

My father's words right before he died echoed in my head.

A determination settled in me. That vial. Everyone's magic was trapped inside, and opening it would be the key to truly saving my court. My people. I felt Penn's lips against mine, felt that force of light flowing through me, and I summoned every bit of strength I possessed, then watched as my fingers twitched, just the smallest amount, to open the vial of magic.

The top popped off, and smoke poured out of it, filling the room with all the colors of the rainbow. I didn't need to break the magic, I just needed to set it free.

"How is this happening?" Jillian asked.

All the thieves raised their weapons, suspicion on their faces. Penn just held me in his arms, stroking my cheek.

"No." My stepmother scrambled toward the vial, but it was too late.

Penn's magic zapped back into him, and he jumped over my body and barreled into my stepmother as the other thieves gained their magic back, fighting against the sudden onslaught of tree branches and roots, flying leaves, slithering vines, and falling moss. My stepmother frantically flung out her hands, commanding her earth magic, but it was weakening as the vial emptied. The thieves were easily fighting back—and the trees, the leaves, everything was gaining its color again.

"What's happening?" My stepmother looked around wildly. "What did you do?" she snarled at me while I still lay unconscious on the ground.

"She saved us," Penn said, and then he drove his sword straight through my stepmother's stomach. She gasped, slowly looking down as if she couldn't believe it. Blood bloomed between her fingers, and she choked out a surprised sob. Her gaze wandered around the room, and she watched as the magic she'd kept trapped for so long slowly returned.

"I don't understand," she said between grunts.

Then she fell to her knees, her hands now completely painted by the blood.

She let out a harsh laugh. "You . . . didn't win. They're coming . . . for you."

She collapsed to the ground, then, body still, resting in a pool of crimson.

I mourned for her, just like I'd mourned for my father.

She hadn't deserved what happened to her. Hadn't deserved my betrayal, hadn't deserved my father's. She made her choice in the end, cemented her fate, but this wasn't the victory I thought it would be. It was just a sad end to a sad woman's life.

I wanted to stay and watch, but I could feel myself fading, feel it getting harder to focus. They were going to be okay. My work here was done. I'd saved Elwen, and in doing so, I'd doomed myself.

Part Four

"You, my queen, are fair: it is true. But the young queen is a thousand times fairer than you."

Chapter Fifty-Eight

I heard his voice.

Come back.

Don't leave me.

Fight.

I love you.

I wanted to stay in the dark, to burrow in and never leave, but that voice, that light, it drew me to it. I retreated back into the comfort of darkness over and over, yet the voice wouldn't stop.

Come back.

Don't leave me.

Fight.

I love you.

My eyes opened to bright light, buttery and warm on my face. I blinked a few times, trying to figure out what I was seeing above me. A canopy, pink and delicate. *My* canopy. I shot up in bed and immediately regretted it as pain lanced through my head.

"She's awake," a voice called. "She's awake!" Jillian threw her arms around me, and I winced.

She reeled back into her chair, sitting by my bedside. "Sorry," she said, then her eyes welled with tears. "I just can't believe you're awake."

I looked around my room in disbelief. The floors were cracked, and

dust and grime covered the walls and furniture, but it was my room, and
—I looked outside to see the blue sky, the bright sun full and round and
shining down. I got out of bed, bare feet pressing against the cold floor
as I ran to the window and gasped.

Green. The grass was green. The trees had leaves again. Flower beds
spread across the courtyard, fountains bubbling.

"You did it," Jillian said. "You saved us all."

I turned. "How?"

Her eyes crinkled right as Driscoll burst through the doorway.
"You're awake." He shot a glare at Jillian. "Why didn't you call for me?"

"I did, but I suspect you were too busy making out with a certain
thief to hear me."

"Excuse me?" I sank onto the bed, clutching at my chest.

"We're supposed to be keeping her calm." Driscoll swept into the
room.

Jillian stuck out her tongue at him.

"How long have I been sleeping?" I asked, rubbing my throbbing
temples.

"Three weeks," Jillian said.

My eyes widened.

"You were really sick after eating that apple," she said.

"What were you thinking?" Driscoll asked. "That was so incredibly
stupid."

"And brave," Jillian added. "But stupid."

My brain was foggy as I tried to remember everything that had
happened. "Is she dead?"

Jillian nodded. "She's gone."

"Is our magic . . .?"

Jillian wiggled her fingers, then pointed to the corner of the room as
a flower sprouted from the little pot that sat there. A sunflower
unfurled, bright and yellow.

My hand floated to my chest. "I can't believe it. So all our magic has
returned? And it's not corrupt anymore?"

I shuffled back and rested against the headboard while Driscoll came
to sit on the end of my bed. "Your stepmother's death and releasing all
that magic she'd stolen returned everything to normal." He tipped his
head. "Well, maybe not normal. But better than before."

I stared at the sunflower in wonder. "Who's been in charge? What's been happening with our people? Are they okay?" I attempted to sit up, but Jillian gently pushed me back down.

"We assembled a team, inviting well-respected leaders from each village to represent their people, just until you woke up and could assume your place on the throne."

"It was Penn's idea." Driscoll crossed his legs and Jillian shot him a glare. "Well, your idea, according to Penn, but he's the one who suggested it."

I wrinkled my nose. "Penn? Has he been here . . . to visit me?"

Driscoll gave me an odd look. "How much do you remember about what happened with your stepmother?"

"I remember lunging at her with that sword. The apple, taking a bite, and then . . ."

And then his voice. I remembered his voice, so strong and sure and comforting. I remembered him drawing me back from the darkness.

I shook my head. "That's it," I said, sure I would sound crazy if I revealed the rest. "What happened? How did I save you all? I was unconscious."

My stomach gurgled, and I placed a hand to it.

"Maybe we should wait until you're feeling a little better to dive into all that." Driscoll waved his hand in the air. "You should rest now."

My entire body ached, muscles fatigued like I'd spent the last three weeks running nonstop instead of here, in bed. "I can't rest. My people need me. There's so much to do, so much to figure out. I have ideas," I said weakly.

Jillian once again pushed me back down, this time with a little more force. "And you can implement all those wonderful ideas when you're better. Your people will wait for you. You saved them. You saved us all, Lil. There's no rush, I promise. The earth court is in good hands right now."

I grumbled but, despite my protests, felt my eyes growing heavy with sleep. Jillian started humming a familiar song, one that my mother used to hum to me, and I fell into a restful sleep.

IT WAS HIS VOICE AGAIN. It was always his voice these days.

Come back.

Don't leave me.

Fight.

I love you.

I jolted awake, and both Driscoll and Jillian straightened. Jillian still sat in her chair beside me, this time with some knitting, and Driscoll sat on the couch by the window, writing something in a journal.

"Hey." Jillian grabbed my hand. "Are you hungry?"

I clutched my stomach, which still roiled, and shook my head. The apple had done a number on me.

"Well, you need to drink something."

Driscoll lifted his head. "We've been forcing water down your throat, but it'll be much easier now that you're awake and can do it yourself."

I rubbed my eyes. "How long was I asleep this time?"

"Just a day," Jillian said. "The healer came by to check on you and said everything is looking good. You can be back on your feet soon, when you're ready."

"Good." I swept the covers aside and stood on shaky legs. "I'm ready now."

Jillian's eyes widened, and she opened her mouth to speak, but I held up my hand.

"We can either do this the easy way or the hard way. If you want to fight me and further weaken me and possibly injure your queen, then that's what we'll do. Or you can help me get dressed and finally tell me what in the bloody earth happened."

"She's definitely back," Driscoll muttered, swinging his legs over the side of the couch and closing his journal.

Jillian looked at me with a knowing smile. "She's back, and she's ready to be queen."

Chapter Fifty-Nine

We met with the council first, and I thanked them all for their service and also told them I hoped they planned on keeping their positions, because I was in need of a council. They'd stood in stunned silence as I dismissed them.

Now we rode to the border. I breathed in the fresh air, marveling at the little sprouts of green grass poking up through the dark soil. We'd have to come up with a plan for rebuilding, but I could just imagine the flowers, the trees, the plants that would once again fill the earth court.

The people of Mosswood Forest would be free to come and go as they pleased, no longer trapped inside, and in turn, my people would be able to use the forest and its resources. I'd have to talk to Penn about it, of course. He might have different feelings on the matter, but despite our past dealings, I was sure we could come to an understanding.

He wanted the best for his people, just like I wanted the best for mine.

Jillian rode behind me, and Driscoll sat atop his horse, which trotted next to ours. At Jillian's insistence, we went at a slower pace, and I didn't argue, afraid she and Driscoll would chain me to my bed if I pushed too much.

I glanced at Driscoll, who was humming, smiling.

"What's got you in such a good mood?"

"Just a handsome fellow named Kohl." He shot me a look. "You might know him as Wayfinder."

"But he has a boyfriend!"

"Not anymore." Driscoll winked, and I gasped.

"Well, that's scandalous, you rogue."

He and Jillian just laughed.

"Thank you two, for everything," I said. "For standing by my side throughout all of this. Without you, I'd be completely alone."

Driscoll gave me a pointed look. "I think we all know that's not true."

My stomach fluttered. "What is that supposed to mean?"

"He came everyday you were sick," Driscoll said. "He held your hand and talked to you. He wouldn't let anyone near you, insisted on bathing you and dressing you and feeding you. He slept in the chair next to your bed. He only finally left when his thieves came and told him he needed to eat and drink and preferably bathe because he was beginning to smell like a sewer rat. You woke up a few hours after he finally left your side."

Jillian stiffened behind me, and my heart hammered in my chest. Penn had come for me?

Driscoll threw out his hands. "Oh, come on. We can't keep dancing around the subject. He's in love with you. You're in love with him. Your love literally saved our court."

I stilled at that. "What are you talking about, Driscoll? Our love? What does that even mean?" I narrowed my eyes at him. "Did you hit your head or something?"

"No, I didn't. I'm just the only one willing to tell you the truth."

"She just woke up," Jillian said. "I figured we'd give her at least twenty-four hours before dropping huge, life-shattering truths on her."

Our horses arrived at the border, and Jillian and Driscoll hopped off, then helped me down.

The border stood tall, vines writhing and jabbing out at us, branches rustling at our movement. I couldn't believe my father had created this, and I wasn't sure exactly how to destroy something so huge and monstrous. I'd have to consult with the council now. My council. It felt good knowing I'd have people to rely on.

I turned to Jillian and Driscoll and motioned for them to sit beside me, far enough away from the wall that it couldn't eat us.

"It's time to tell me what happened." I looked at Jillian before she could protest. "Driscoll's right. I can't be coddled right now. I need the truth so I can move forward."

"Penn kissed you, and it was the most romantic thing I've seen in my life," Driscoll burst out, words running together so I almost didn't understand him. "You held that vial of dark magic in your hand, and you were unconscious, but then Penn kissed you, and some light burst from you both and your hand twitched and you somehow popped the top off that vial."

My mouth had dropped open. "What?" I shook my head. "Okay, you definitely hit your head on something."

"He's telling the truth," Jillian said. "We all saw it. It was so weird, but somehow Penn kissing you triggered something that broke open the vial and set all our stolen magic free."

My chest tightened. "Then what happened?"

Driscoll jumped to his feet, jabbing out his hand. "Penn leapt over your body and drove his sword through your stepmother, killing her." He twirled around, wielding an imaginary sword. "Then the magic started spreading, color returning to everything, leaves perking back up, the moss and inky vines disappearing." He kneeled down. "And Penn dropped down and scooped you up, then cradled you into his big, strong chest." Driscoll wrapped his arms around himself. "What I wouldn't give to be held like that."

"Focus," Jillian said.

"Right, and then we took you to your room, and Penn brought healer after healer to look after you."

I stared at Driscoll, unable to speak, rooted to my spot by his words. "Are you telling me Penn's kiss healed me? That's the stupidest thing I've ever heard."

Driscoll waggled his eyebrows. "Those are some magic lips."

Jillian rolled her eyes. "Technically the kiss didn't save Liliath. It's what broke the dark magic, allowed all of our magic to return." She looked at me. "You got a bad case of food poisoning from that apple, and it took time for you to heal."

Driscoll made a disgusted face. "I still can't believe you took a bite of that thing. It was covered in sludge, Liliath. Sludge."

I looked between them like they'd both grown two heads. "How did our kiss break the dark magic?"

Jillian bit her lip. "We're still working on that. Well, Brains is."

"Brains, from the Academy of Thieves?" I asked.

Jillian nodded. "She's been working with other scholars in Elwen, scouring the library for any information, but so far our best guess is, uh, something called true love's kiss."

I blinked a few times.

Driscoll cleared his throat. "True love. When two people are meant to be together, that love between them is more powerful than any kind of dark magic. Basically, the pureness of your love broke the dark magic."

Fight the dark with light. That's what my father had said. Is that what he'd meant? But how would he even know about something like that? I sat there in shock, hardly able to believe what my two best friends were telling me.

"Lilypad," a voice said. I whipped around, and there stood Penn, looking straight at me.

Chapter Sixty

Driscoll and Jillian scrambled to their feet. "Well, we should probably . . ." Driscoll scratched the back of his head.

"We have laundry to do," Jillian said quickly.

"Laundry?" I quirked a brow.

Her face flushed. Driscoll grabbed her and led her to the horse. "So much laundry. We need to get started on it."

"Did our laundress quit?" I asked, crossing my arms as they hopped up on the horses.

"Need to find a new one, it turns out," Driscoll said as he turned his horse around. "So, in the meantime, Jillian and I have taken up that mantle. We'll see you later!"

They galloped away, and I glared after them. Traitors. My gaze turned to Penn, who took a few tentative steps toward me. I got to my feet.

He looked wonderful in those brown pants and beige tunic that hugged all his muscles, those wisps of blond hair falling over his face. I wanted to reach up and brush that hair away.

"I'm sorry," Penn said. "I'm sorry I lied to you. I'm sorry that I acted like an idiot." He took another step forward while I stayed frozen to my spot. "I'm sorry that I left you. I'm sorry about your father."

"Why did you run away?" I asked, voice shaking. "Why did you leave like that?"

"Because that's what I've always done." Penn swallowed, Adam's apple bobbing. "Instead of staying and leading my people, I let a council run Mosswood Forest while I spent all my time going on missions, looking for revenge. It was easier to run than stay and face reality. It was easier to run than to depend on others. It was easier to throw myself into these missions and let them consume me so I didn't have to feel anything else."

I swallowed, tears welling.

"And then I met you." He took another step forward. "A princess who was born to be a queen. Someone who made me want to stop running."

Another step.

I could barely breathe, just standing there, staring, unable to look away from him.

"I watched you throw yourself into something so foreign, so hard, and put your all into it. I watched you fight and fight and fight to get back to your people, and I knew you were the kind of leader I wanted to be, the kind I didn't think I could ever be. But more than that, I wanted to know you. I wanted to hear your ideas, to learn of your past, to know what you wanted for your future. I wanted everything from you, and I wanted to give you everything in return."

"Why didn't you tell me about my father and the mirror?" I asked.

"At first, I never planned to because I was afraid you'd stop me, would ruin my chance at avenging my parents' deaths. Then I started falling for you, and I wanted to tell you, but I was afraid."

"Of what?"

Another step.

"Of losing you. Then I thought if I could just get you back to Mosswood Forest, if I could delay, maybe I'd have more time to tell you the truth, do it in the right way, but"—he heaved a breath—"that all went to shit in Apolis."

"You didn't kill my father, though. Why?"

Another step, and now he was within arm's reach. "Because my love for you is greater than my need for revenge."

A quiet gasp escaped my lips, and Penn closed the distance between

us. He didn't touch me, didn't reach for me despite being so dangerously close.

"I want you, if you'll have me," he whispered, voice low. "Say the
word, Lilypad."

I thought about everything that had happened between us. The lies,
the betrayal, but also the love. Penn believed in me, encouraged me to be
the kind of queen I wanted to be. Penn didn't kill my father. He could
have, but he didn't. Penn had my two best friends rescued. Penn came
for me, to fight with me against my stepmother. Penn stayed by my side
when I was sick. He never actually used me at all.

Penn loved me.

"Yes," I said without hesitation.

He reeled me to him and pressed his lips to mine. I brought my
hands up behind his neck, kissing him back, needing him.

"I love you," he said.

"I love you too," I murmured into his lips.

He deepened the kiss, his lips probing mine open as his tongue
slipped into my mouth. I let out a groan, and he stiffened, moving back.

"Are you okay?"

"No, no, I'm okay. Just kiss me again." I motioned for him, but he
narrowed his gaze.

"You need rest."

"No." I heard the whine in my voice and didn't even care. "I need
your mouth on mine."

"I'm taking you back to the castle. I'm tucking you into bed."

I trailed a finger down his arm. "I like where this is going."

"And then I'm leaving you alone to sleep."

"You're a real buzzkill," I mumbled, and he laughed, the sound
lighting up my soul.

He gathered my hands in his and pressed gentle kisses into them.
"Patience, Lilypad. We have plenty of time." He glanced down at my
hands. "Have you used it yet . . . your magic?"

My chest tightened, and I studied my palms. I'd wanted to the
minute I learned our magic had been returned. A small part of me was
afraid mine still wouldn't work, that something had broken inside
of me.

I knew what Penn wanted from the curious way he stared at my hands. I wanted it too, and there was no person I'd rather have by my side as I accessed my magic for the first time since it got taken.

I took a deep breath and tugged at that thread of magic inside of me, and suddenly, my magic filled me, rushing through my veins, the feeling like nothing else. It felt like a delicious surge flowing within me. Powerful and pure. A flower grew from my hand, purple petals, splashed with yellow.

I almost collapsed to my knees in relief.

"It's perfect," Penn said, but he was staring at me.

I tipped my hand over and the flower floated into the ground, planting itself. Spirits below, I'd missed this.

"When you're better, we'll make a whole field of them." Penn bent down and ran a finger along the petal. "It's my new favorite flower, I think."

I laughed and looked up at him as he stood. "We have a lot to talk about, you know. A lot of decisions to make."

He nodded. "We do. But we'll make them together." He led me away from the border wall. "Come, let's return to the castle."

I liked the sound of that. So I let Penn lead me toward the horse, toward our future. Together.

Epilogue

I stood before a full-length mirror, periwinkle gown falling to the floor, the skirt like a waterfall.

"You look amazing," Jillian said behind me, and Driscoll wiped at the tears in his eyes.

"You look like a queen," Penn said, leaning against the doorway to my chambers, arms crossed.

Jillian and Driscoll both whirled around while I smiled at Penn in the mirror. He looked magnificent in his black dress pants and royal blue tunic with gold buttons.

"We'll leave you two alone." Driscoll winked as Jillian dragged him past Penn and out of the room.

The king of Mosswood Forest strode in, coming up behind me and pressing a kiss to my neck. "The way I wish I could bend you over that desk and do a lot of very bad things," he murmured into my ear.

I turned, arching my neck to look up at him. "Who says you can't?"

"Your damn head of council is standing right outside the door to make sure I behave." His voice dropped low as he nipped my ear, and a shudder ran through me.

"Careful," I teased, "Shadow takes her role very seriously."

He nuzzled my neck. "I still haven't forgiven you for poaching her from me."

"It was your idea that she be my head of council."

"Yes, one I'm very much regretting at this moment." He pressed kisses up my jawline.

"I can hear every word you're saying, and I'm about to haul you out of the room," Shadow yelled.

Penn's face darkened, and I burst out laughing. I pressed a quick kiss to his mouth. "All in good time."

He took a few steps back, and I twirled for him, my gown fanning out around me.

"You look stunning," he said. "Are you ready for today?"

I took a deep breath. "I think so. We have a long road ahead of us to rebuild Elwen, but a new era starts today." I held out my hand, and he took hold of it. "One where Elwen and Mosswood Forest are united."

"I'm proud of you, Lilypad."

"Do you think we'll be ready?" I asked. "For whatever Sorrengard has planned? They managed to curse Seraphina, to steal away all the boys from Apolis, to plant dark magic here that ruined the land. They must have a bigger motive, something we're missing."

"We'll figure it out," Penn said. "We'll speak with the other leaders of the courts. We'll work together to ensure that Sorrengard does not pose a threat to us."

"They already have," I said. "They've gotten to us, formed cracks in our courts. We're weak, Penn."

"No." He kissed my forehead. "Not with you as our queen. Not ever again."

"Do you think everyone in Mosswood Forest will accept me as their queen?"

"I know they will." His voice was fierce. "They respect you because you told them the truth; you told everyone about your father, how you intend to be different. That took courage to expose his lies and deception. They're wary, but you'll earn their trust."

I bit my lip as he tucked a curled strand behind my ear. "What else is worrying you?"

"I feel bad about leaving Gabrielle like I did. She's in such a bad place. The pirate lord broke her heart. Her brothers are missing. Sorrengard has their shadows. Her father and most of the men are gone. Her mother has been driven mad with grief. She's all alone."

Penn frowned.

"What?" I narrowed my gaze at him. "What aren't you telling me?"

He sighed, rubbing the back of his neck. "Rumor has it that the pirate lord washed up on the shores of Apolis just days ago, sick with a mysterious illness."

"I have to go to her—" I started, but Penn cut me off.

"Gabrielle is stronger than you think," he said. "She's going to figure it out. She'll make her own way, and I have a feeling she won't take any prisoners while doing it."

Blood and earth. The pirate lord. Back in Apolis. I hoped Gabrielle ran a sword through him after what he'd done to her.

"Do you think she'll find her brothers?" I asked.

Penn's brows furrowed. "That I don't know. But I do think she'll restore Apolis to its former glory. I also think right now our focus needs to be here. Let's rebuild Elwen first. Then we can worry about the other courts."

I nodded, taking a deep breath. "You're right."

He shot me a mischievous smile. "I like your mouth saying those words." His voice dropped low. "I like your mouth for a lot of reasons."

"Seriously, Penn?" Shadow yelled. "She has to be in the throne room in exactly five minutes."

"I can do a lot of things in five minutes," Penn called back, and we both heard Shadow's groan.

I shoved him but couldn't help the smile that came to my face.

He looked at the golden crown sitting in a glass case by the window. He strode over and opened it. "May I?" he asked.

I nodded, my throat growing thick. "I always thought my father would be here for this."

"I know." Penn picked up the crown and walked it over to me. Flowers and vines were engraved around it, diamonds studding the points. It was beautiful. "He'd be proud of you, proud of the way you saved Elwen."

I straightened my shoulders. "Okay, it has to go back in the case now. For the coronation."

He studied it, then gently put it back and held out his arm. "Are you ready to be crowned queen of Elwen?"

I looped my arm through his. "As ready as I'll ever be."

We walked out the door, arm-in-arm.
I was walking toward my duty.
I was walking toward my future.
I was walking toward my destiny.

WANT MORE of Penn and Lilith? Click here to get this spicy bonus chapter from his point of view.

TO FIND out if Gabrielle ever finds her brothers—and gets her revenge on the pirate lord, start reading Ship of Shadows now!

Ship of Shadows: A Sneak Peek

I'd never seriously considered the merits of flinging myself off a cliff until today.

Now I was walking toward said cliff, stars twinkling above, sand squishing under my bare feet. A warm breeze flowed through the air, and my white chiffon fluttered, brushing against my skin.

It would be quite the scandal if anyone knew the princess of the water court was currently slinking around outside, alone and unprotected.

But that was the point. I wanted to be alone. This would likely be the last night I would ever be able to do something like this, and I was going to take advantage of it. A final reckless act before everything changed.

I could just imagine my mother's voice in my head. *You've really let me down this time, Gabrielle.*

If she only knew the ways I'd actually let her down, but I was not thinking about that tonight. Not when I had more important things to do. Things like freediving off cliffs.

The ocean waves rushed up over my feet, the water warm and inviting. I looked out over the inky black of the sea, a sheath of heavy fog hanging above it, the view murky.

High and jagged cliffs rose up in the distance. In the night, they looked like monsters, snaggletoothed and ready to devour anyone who attempted to climb them. I remembered the stories I'd tell my brothers about them when we used to sneak out, the three of us, adventurous and carefree. But my brothers never cowed like I expected them to as I'd described the stony jaws of death that would snatch them up should they come too close. They were as fearless as me.

Now I was alone. Carrying on the torch of stupidity for all three of us. If they were here, they'd no doubt be by my side, likely the only ones encouraging this foolish mission.

"Have you lost your ever-loving mind?" a voice said from behind me.

I jumped, turning to see Leoni standing there. Okay, so apparently I wasn't as alone as I thought.

A scowl lined her face, her red-gold hair in a tight bun atop her head. I looked down at her as she planted her hands on her wide hips, adorned by a golden belt that cinched her chiffon to her waist, a sword hanging at her side. "I knew you were careless, but attempting this, on the eve of the most important day of your life? You're being an idiot."

I crossed my arms. My captain of the guard wasn't known for having any kind of filter, especially not when speaking to me. "You realize you're talking to your future queen?" I asked.

She cocked a brow. "Apologies. You're being an idiot, Your Majesty."

I gave her a look and spun on my heel. "Well, this was a nice chat. Let's just pretend you didn't see me. None of this happened," I called behind me, continuing on my way down the shoreline.

"I know what you're doing," she shouted, "and I'm not going to let you."

The point of something sharp poked into my back. Spirits below. I sighed. "Is this really necessary?"

"Yes, because if anything happens to you, it will be my fault, and I will lose my job, and probably my fucking head along with it."

"Wow, that's so sweet." I put a hand to my chest. "Glad to know you care so much about me."

That wasn't fair. Leoni had been my best friend since we were children. I knew she cared, and I also knew this job meant the world to her. She loved what she did—was my fiercest protector. That's why I'd recommended her for the position. But tonight, I didn't want her to be my captain of the guard; I just wanted her to be my friend.

I slowly turned. "Put down the sword, Oni. I'm not going to fight you."

As many times as we'd sparred and trained together, I wasn't in the mood for it tonight.

She eyed me warily and slowly lowered her weapon. The gold cuffs around her arms glinted in the moonlight as she relaxed her shoulders. "There's a reason you and your brothers never actually attempted this. Because it's stupid. It's dangerous. And it might get you killed."

I eyed the tall cliffs in the distance, and my heart squeezed. Yes, it was all of those things, but I had to do this. Leoni didn't get it. After tomorrow, everything would change. I wouldn't have the freedom I had now, wouldn't just have Leoni watching me. It would be everyone, all the time. This was truly the last day of my life I'd be able to do something so reckless, and I wanted to. Not just for myself, but for Mal and Lochlan.

Leoni's face softened. "Fine," she said.

I narrowed my eyes. "You're not going to stop me?"

"Would I actually be able to?"

I smiled. "Not likely."

She heaved a big breath. "Then let's get this over with. But if you die, I will find a way to bring you back just so I can wring your neck."

I believed it. She might have been half a foot shorter than me, but she'd bested me enough times in the sparring ring that I knew she could injure me if she really wanted to. I blew her a kiss and continued on my trek along the beach as Leoni grumbled something about me being a "pain in her ass" while she followed, her sandals squishing in the sand.

"I never got why you and your brothers wanted to do this, anyway," she said. "It's the Cliffs of Death. The name has death in it. Why would you want to jump from them into the Dark Seas?"

I laughed. "Because it's fun?"

"Fun?" Leoni echoed. "Blood and water, your idea of fun is so twisted."

I threw out my arms. "I don't know how to explain it, Oni. It's the thrill of it. The danger, the adventure."

The feeling of freedom, something I sorely lacked as princess of the water court.

"If you want danger, then go try Mistress Tessa's fish rolls." She shook her head, then mumbled, "Trust me, that's about as dangerous as it gets."

A smile quirked my lips. The fish rolls supposedly tasted amazing but also came with a great risk of food poisoning.

Leoni jabbed a finger at me. "You know, being captain of your guard has aged me at least ten years." She pointed to her hair. "I found a gray hair this morning. I'm twenty-eight, and I have gray hair. Yet look at you: thirty years old and hair as auburn as those pretty leaves in the earth court."

I ignored the comment about my hair. "And you're attributing that to me?" I asked. "It could just be bad genes, you know."

"No, it's definitely the stubborn princess whose ass I'm always saving."

"You know, at some point you need to learn to filter yourself. You're going to be the captain of the queen's guard now. That mouth will get you in trouble."

She'd always had the mouth of a sailor.

"Oh, fuck off."

Worse than a sailor.

I wondered how tomorrow might change our relationship. I'd never censored Leoni, never had to, but now we'd be front and center, all eyes on me, us, all the time. I couldn't imagine reprimanding her, what that might even be like. I wasn't the only one losing a part of myself tomorrow. Leoni was, too, in a way, and I wondered if she'd even thought about it.

She huffed. "Just worry about yourself, okay? If your mother knew you were here, she'd have a heart attack. She'd kick my ass. Then she'd kick yours."

I lifted my chin. "If you're going to be negative about this, then I'd rather you go back to the castle."

We neared the cliffs, their sharp edges and ridges outlined under the bright moon.

"I'm not letting you do this alone."

I nudged her. "Thanks, Oni."

"Don't thank me." She nudged me back. "I still think this is stupid, but I also know you're as stubborn as the Seven Spirits and won't listen to reason."

"You know me well."

I flipped my braid over my shoulder as we came upon the curve of the shoreline that rounded the tall cliffs. Vicious waves rose high and then crashed down with a thundering force. Leoni winced.

No one ventured to this part of the water court, the wildest part, where the waves rolled untethered. That's why I loved it so much, why Mal and Lochlan had loved it. It had been a respite from everyone, everything, we constantly had to deal with. My father's stern, watching eye, my mother's badgering. Out here, we could just be us, talk about our hopes and dreams. Pretend we could actually have things like hopes and dreams.

I swallowed. But that had been a different life.

My gaze trailed to a ship jutting out of the water near the shore. Well, ship was a generous term. It was bent in half over the rocks, planks askew and splintered, the sails torn to shreds. A shipwreck. Which was what generally happened to any vessels that came near this part of the water court.

"Well, are you just going to stand here all night? I'd like to get some sleep, so let's hurry this idiotic scheme along please." Leoni shooed me forward.

I gave a stiff nod, then began my climb, fingers and feet digging into the crevices and cracks. I'd climbed these cliffs so many times I could probably do it with my eyes closed.

But then Leoni might actually kill me.

I looked down as she stared up at me, sea water spraying us from the unrelenting waves crashing at the little cove.

"Are you coming?" I called.

"No I'd like to not break all the bones in my body, thank you," she said.

I snorted a laugh and continued my climb, muscles stretching, hard rock cool and firm under my hands and feet. My breaths grew labored as I ascended, and sweat formed on my brow, trickling down the sides of my face. Finally, I made it to the top and pulled myself up, walking along the edge and to the point that jutted out over the sea.

"Took you long enough," Leoni called up.

I just shook my head, taking a moment to look out over the shimmering dark waves. Leoni was right. This was stupid. But I was going to do it anyway.

I inhaled a deep breath, bracing my legs and readying myself to jump, when my gaze caught on something in the distance. A ship. I could just see its outline through the fog.

"Oh, don't tell me you changed your mind," Leoni said. "It's all good and fine if you don't want to jump, but I'd have appreciated this revelation much more if you'd had it before we made the trek out here."

I squinted at the dark form, sails billowing, ship gliding through the waters. No ships came to the Cliffs of Death. It was too violent, too dangerous to even attempt to dock a boat here. No one came here, except . . . *him.*

I stilled. But no. I'd told him to never return, that I never wanted to see his face again. Besides, he didn't have a ship anymore. My gaze flicked to the wrecked vessel below, its remains scattered among the jagged rocks of the shore. I'd made sure of that.

I looked closer, recognizing the blue and green flag flapping in the wind. The colors of Apolis. I'd know that flag anywhere.

My father's ship—which hadn't been seen for eight months. Eight long months since he'd left to find my brothers. Eight long months of guilt weighing on my shoulders for the role I'd played in their disappearance. My heart hammered hard in my chest. Had he found them? Was he back with all of them safe and sound? But why would he sail here? It didn't make sense.

"Hello?" Leoni asked. "What has gotten into you?"

My eyes snapped to her round face, dotted by freckles, and I pointed. "There's something out there."

She spun, facing the water, rising on her tiptoes and arching her neck. "I don't see anything," she said.

I looked back up. Nothing but fog rolled across the ocean.

I'd just seen it. It was there. It had to be. Unless I was imagining things, wishing it into existence. Because if my father had returned with my brothers, then everything would be alright. My life wouldn't have to so drastically change tomorrow.

I shook my head, still searching. Leoni was right. There was nothing, just the dark expanse of the sea and the thick gray mist.

Leoni turned back to me. "What did you think you saw?"

"I—my father's ship—I swear it was there."

Leoni's eyes softened. "Your father is gone. He's not coming back. I know you miss him. I know you miss Mal and Lochlan, and I know you feel guilty over what happened to them—"

"Don't," I snapped, and suddenly the weight of everything crashed over me.

"Is that what all of this is about?" Leoni asked.

I sighed and sunk down on the edge the cliff, legs hanging over the side.

Leoni stepped toward the cliff. "I know you think it's your fault—"

"It is my fault." I massaged my temples.

"This"—Leoni gestured to the cliff right as another wave crashed, shaking the rock underneath me—"isn't going to bring your brothers back."

I squeezed my eyes shut. She was right. What was I doing out here? What was I thinking? That I'd jump off the cliff and somehow feel closer to my brothers, feel like I was honoring them in some way? That I'd do this ridiculous stunt we always said we'd do and my life would magically be okay? Maybe part of me thought the sea would swallow me up—and my guilt along with it.

But none of those things would happen. Blood and water. I'd been so stupid.

I started climbing down, Leoni silent until I hopped into the soft sand, facing her. Disappointment welled in me. This entire trip had been a waste of time. A silly fantasy that I'd actually thought was a good idea. This grief, this guilt, was twisting my mind.

She put a hand on my shoulder. "You can't keep blaming yourself for what happened to them—or to your father." I'd never stop, but she didn't understand. She couldn't understand. "C'mon, let's get back to the castle. Hopefully you can at least get a few hours' sleep."

Right. I'd need it.

Tomorrow I would be crowned queen of Apolis, and my life, as I officially knew it, would be over.

Continue reading . . .

About the Author

Tee Harlowe writes fantasy romance focused on strong and determined women. After years spent traveling, Tee settled down to start writing her own adventures and is now living out her dream. When not writing, Tee can be found wrangling her children, attempting to bake, and losing to her husband at pretty much every game they play.

www.ingramcontent.com/pod-product-compliance
Lightning Source LLC
Chambersburg PA
CBHW051301130726
47987CB00004B/1615